MONSTER HUNTER
BLOODLINES

To purchase any of these titles in e-book form,
please go to www.baen.com.

MONSTER HUNTER
BLOODLINES

Larry Correia

Copyright © 2021 by Larry Correia

A Baen Books Original

Baen Publishing Enterprises
P.O. Box 1403
Riverdale, NY 10471
www.baen.com

ISBN: 978-1-9821-2549-3

Cover art by Alan Pollack

First printing, August 2021

Distributed by Simon & Schuster
1230 Avenue of the Americas
New York, NY 10020

Library of Congress Cataloging-in-Publication Data

Names: Correia, Larry, author.
Title: Monster hunter bloodlines / Larry Correia.
Description: Riverdale, NY : Baen, [2021] | Series: The Monster Hunter
    International series
Identifiers: LCCN 2021021982 | ISBN 9781982125493 (hardcover)
Subjects: GSAFD: Fantasy fiction.
Classification: LCC PS3603.O7723 M56 2021 | DDC 813/.6—dc23
LC record available at https://lccn.loc.gov/2021021982æ

Pages by Joy Freeman (www.pagesbyjoy.com)
Printed in the United States of America
10 9 8 7 6 5 4 3 2 1

MONSTER HUNTER BLOODLINES

CHAPTER 1

A couple years ago my company picked a fight with an ancient chaos demon. The last round had ended in a bloody draw. Nobody knew when our battle would kick off again, but when it did, we had a new strategy to put that immortal bastard down once and for all. My idea was to harness the power of Isaac Newton's crazy space magic in order to kick some monster ass.

The only problem was alchemical superweapons don't exactly grow on trees. We'd had one once but used it up obliterating a Great Old One. There were only a handful of Ward Stones left on Earth, and mankind had lost the secret of how to make new ones. Except we had just gotten word that one of the rare treasures was up for grabs. Which was why two teams from Monster Hunter International were currently staked out around an office park in Atlanta, waiting for a supernatural arms deal to go down, in the hope that we would be able to steal the arcane equivalent of a suitcase nuke from the forces of evil.

My name is Owen Zastava Pitt and I have the coolest job in the world.

"Z, anything on your side?" my boss asked over the radio. Earl was in a car parked at the end of the block.

I was sitting in the back of a nondescript work van parked down the street, watching the front of the building through a pair of binoculars.

1

"Nothing new, Earl. Just the same bunch of security guards standing around looking bored." The muscle had been hired by the shady legal firm which had arranged this transaction, but as far as we knew the guards were regular human beings, who probably had no clue what they'd gotten involved in, which meant us hurting them would be illegal.

"Alright, keep your head on a swivel."

Trip was sitting in the back of the van with me and checked his watch for the tenth time in as many minutes. "We've still got a little time before the mystery buyer is supposed to show."

"And lunch hour traffic is terrible around here, especially with the convention in town, so don't be surprised if he's late," said our driver. He was a new guy on Boone's team named Hertzfeldt. "Who do you think the buyer is going to be anyway?"

"No idea."

"If this deal's even real," Hertzfeldt muttered. "We're putting in a lot of effort over an anonymous tip."

It had been Management who had notified us about this sale on the Dark Market. The billionaire dragon had tried to bid for the item himself, but apparently he didn't have enough baby souls or whatever horrible thing it was these particular scumbag monsters had wanted in trade. But since most of the rank and file of MHI didn't know of Management's existence, we had to keep our tipster's identity secret.

"Trust me, man. The info will be good," I assured the Newbie. "And with the sellers being PUFF-applicable, we'll still get a payday out of this no matter what."

That didn't seem to placate him much. Hertzfeldt had come out of the company's last training class, so I barely knew him. He was still pretty new to all this weird stuff, but he knew his way around Atlanta, so he had been assigned to drive me and Trip around in the surveillance van. The local team had been divided up so that each of us out-of-towners had a guide who actually knew the area. Which was good, considering half the streets here seemed to be named Peachtree something for some baffling reason.

While we waited, Hertzfeldt tried to make small talk. "Hey, Pitt, if you don't mind me asking, there's this rumor going around about when you all went to that Russian island, that... well..."

"Yeah?" But I already knew where this was going.

"It sounds nuts, but they told us in training that you got trapped on the other side for *six months*. But there's no way that's true, right?"

Get stuck in a dimension made out of hunger and nightmares for half a year *one* time, and everybody has to freak out about it. It had been hard, but the guys I had rescued from the Fey had been there way longer than I had. I'd gotten off relatively easy compared to them.

"Yeah. It's true."

I could see him looking at me in the rearview mirror. I didn't know what Julie had told the last Newbie class about that place, probably about how the whole warped dimension could twist reality on a whim, and it had been a dumping ground for banished and lost monsters, but whatever my wife had said, the idea of me spending that much time there seemed to unnerve the Newbie. He was probably thinking *what the hell did I sign up for?*

"What was that like?"

I'd fought mutants, Fey knights, and faced off against the immortal embodiment of Disorder. I'd barely survived by sheer stubbornness and a desire to see my family again, but that was none of his business, so I just waved it off by saying, "Time flies when you're having fun."

Luckily, Earl Harbinger got back on our radio net and saved me from having to talk about that miserable suck fest further. *"Holly, how's it going in there?"*

Holly Newcastle and a couple other Hunters were seated at the outdoor patio tables of the little restaurant next to the target location. *"All clear here. Just businessmen having lunch. I don't see anyone who looks particularly culty. The lobster bisque is excellent though. Over."*

I keyed my radio. "Save your receipts. The company will reimburse for that."

"In that case, I'm ordering the bottomless mimosas."

"Don't lie, Holly. We all know you already did."

"Guilty as charged." But Holly was professional enough she'd keep the day drinking to a minimum. Probably. There were still death cultists to tail back to their secret lair. Plus we would have to deal with the mystery buyer, who we could totally shoot if it turned out to be something PUFF-applicable. Perpetual Unearthly Forces Fund bounties were our bread and butter.

The intel Management had given us was limited because the Dark Market had really beefed up their information security after my wife had killed a bunch of their regular clientele in Europe. We didn't know the buyer's identity at all, except they were from out of town. The sellers were local, and we were pretty sure we knew what they were because the Atlanta team had been hunting them for months. Management had confirmed that the place we were watching was the neutral location they'd agreed upon to make the exchange, and when our dragon was certain of something, it usually panned out. He had sources everywhere.

The area seemed remarkably normal. Our target was just a regular business, next to an architectural drafting company, a brew pub, a graphic design shop, and a little plaza with benches and a fountain. It was broad daylight, on a nice afternoon, with dozens of witnesses wandering around. You'd think monsters would prefer someplace more ... gothy. Or at least shadowy and menacing or something. Hell, there was a food truck selling tacos. Tacos are the antithesis of evil.

The building we were watching was one of those bland, featureless, two-story brick places. With a nebulous, forgettable name on the little sign like INSERT STRONG WORD HERE CONSULTING, or NOBODY, NOBODY, AND DOUCHEBAG LLC, where you could never guess what they actually did inside. Such businesses were common and unnoticeable, which I guess made them perfect for monsters to secretly conduct their affairs.

"Milo, Skippy, how's the view from up there?" Earl asked.

"Nothing suspicious yet, Earl," Milo answered cheerfully. "These drones are really neat though."

The two of them were on the roof of one of the nearby high-rises so they could have an unimpeded radio signal. Earl had wanted some eyes in the sky for this operation, but our giant noisy helicopter would have been super obvious. Luckily our supremely skilled orc could fly just about anything, even by remote control.

In the background of Milo's radio could be heard a deep voice grumbling, "Skippy make tiny thing do the tricks! Whee. Barrels roll!"

"Stop that," Milo insisted. "It's not a toy!"

He wasn't kidding. The invoice for the drones was still on my desk. Milo had taken Earl's instruction to *get something nice* to mean *max out the company card on high tech surveillance gizmos.* Between the actual flying machines, and the really expensive software package they used, it probably would have been cheaper to buy Skippy another Russian attack helicopter. If our orc crashed one of those drones, Earl was going to be severely annoyed.

"I've got some activity at the back." That voice belonged to Boone, the experienced Hunter who had been the Atlanta team lead since I'd started with the company. *"There's a black SUV coming up on the parking garage. I bet this is our seller. Hold on. Make that two, no, three SUVs. We've got us a convoy."*

"So much for just having to handle one delivery minion," I said to the other guys in the van. "Our tip told us that the seller was supposed to come alone."

"Think it's a setup and they're just going to rob the buyer?" Hertzfeldt asked.

"No way," Trip answered. "A rip-off would bring the Dark Market down on their heads, and even dumb monsters aren't that stupid. As valuable as this thing is, it's no surprise they're rolling heavy. From what Julie said about their rules, the seller is responsible until the buyer takes physical possession. If it gets lost before that, they're still on the hook, and these things do not like to mess around when it comes to contract enforcement."

From what Julie had learned in Europe, that was the understatement of the year there. The Dark Market was an illicit underground organization that horrible creatures used to make deals. My wife had told me a really unnerving story about watching some poor German kid get sucked down to hell or someplace equally awful for not reading the fine print on one of their contracts. Sad part was the only reason we knew anything about that organization at all was because my kidnapped son had been the prize in one of their auctions. Except thankfully Julie had ruined that deal, and by ruined, I mean she shot a lot of scumbags in the face and got our boy back.

One of the security guards in front of the building got a message on his radio, probably to notify him about the VIP's arrival, because he snapped at the others to look sharp. Cigarettes were stubbed out and cell phones were put away.

I scanned the street through the binoculars, but still no sign of the buyer. The taco truck was busy and had a decent crowd waiting in line. It was Labor Day weekend, but it wasn't as hot as usual, so people were sitting around the plaza, eating and having a nice time. There were other people walking by, but nobody was heading toward the unremarkable building of boredom.

A bullet bike drove past our van. The rider was obviously female. Though she was wearing a helmet, the riding outfit was so formfitting it didn't leave a lot to the imagination. Hertzfeldt whistled appreciatively. Even Trip, who tried ever so hard to always be the gentleman, obviously noticed her, though unlike the Newbie, he at least tried not to stare. Plus, Trip was currently in a serious relationship and if there was ever anybody who took the concept of loyalty seriously, it was Trip.

The rider slowed down enough that I thought for a second she might be our mystery buyer, but then the bike passed by the front of the building and kept going.

Boone got back on the radio. *"They're getting out of their vehicles and heading inside. I'm guessing snake cultists from the sleeve tats, but there's one larger figure wearing a hood and a mask and carrying a big red backpack. That's got to be our seller. Way he's dressed, he's gotta be the real thing."*

"Nasty-ass reptoids." Hertzfeldt shuddered.

So only one of the sellers had come. By their standards they were still within the terms of the auction contract, because from what I'd heard, the lizard monsters thought of their human cultists more like pets than equals.

"Alright, everybody," Boone said. *"The stone is probably in the backpack. We let the deal go down, let them part ways, then Team Harbinger nails the buyer, and my boys will tail the snake morons back to wherever they've been hiding so we can clean out their nest."*

"We can't make that call until we see who the buyer is," Earl cautioned. *"I know these scaly assholes have been a thorn in your side, Boone, but if we have to choose between letting them get away, or grabbing the package, the package comes first. That's the big picture. Keep your eye on the prize."*

"Roger that." Boone obviously didn't like it much, because when a tribe of reptoids moves into your city, starts eating people, and idiots start worshipping them and doing human sacrifices in exchange for dark magic blessings, that gets super annoying. However, Boone had been at Severny Island and seen the world-ending magnitude of the threat gathering there. He knew what was

at stake. It wasn't every day MHI could score an Isaac Newton original capable of smoke-checking a chaos god.

"No matter what we'll stick at least one car and one of Milo's drones on the lizard lovers' convoy," Earl said. *"Things that mostly eat the homeless really piss me off too. It's not like those folks don't already have it hard enough already without being terrorized by reptoids."*

"Thanks, Earl."

I noticed a car approaching from the opposite direction. The blinker came on as it slowed to enter the parking lot. "This is Pitt. I've got something in front. A silver BMW sedan is pulling up to the front entrance now."

The car stopped. Two security guards moved to get the rear door. Oddly enough, I noticed that one of the men was carrying an umbrella. He popped it open to protect the new arrival from the sun.

"Curious." Trip raised his new camera with the giant telephoto lens and took a picture. Milo hadn't been the only one to go nuts putting new equipment on the company card once given the surveillance excuse. "Somebody must have requested shade."

"Maybe it's a vampire," Hertzfeldt suggested.

What a Newbie thing to say. I started to correct him, because it would take way more than an umbrella to protect a vampire from bursting into flames beneath the sun, but then I watched a very tall, very thin, very pale man unfold himself out of the back seat. Once safely under the umbrella's shade, he checked out the street, his eyes hidden behind odd persimmon-colored sunglasses.

"This is way worse than a vampire."

Trip, who almost *never* used profanity, simply said, "Aw, shit," when he recognized the buyer.

"You know that albino guy?" Hertzfeldt asked, worried.

"Unfortunately, yes." I got on the radio. "We have eyes on the buyer. And, uh... Earl?"

"Go ahead, Z."

"Promise not to hulk out."

"Spit it out already."

I looked over at Trip, grimaced, then reluctantly pushed the transmit button. "It's Stricken."

The radio was silent for a long time. Trip and I exchanged a very nervous glance, because Earl *hated* Stricken probably more than anyone or anything on this plane of existence. To be fair, we all hated the former head of Special Task Force Unicorn, but for Earl, it was *really* personal.

"Are you sure?"

Holly got on the radio. *"I can see him too. I can confirm it is Stricken. If I can get a clean shot, want me to blast him?"*

"Naw. I'll handle that son of a bitch," Earl snapped.

On the bright side, Stricken no longer worked for the government, so murdering him was no longer off the table. The word was that the Feds had busted him for committing hundreds of felonies, up to and including treason. Last I heard, he was a fugitive being hunted by the MCB. So if Earl lost his shit, went all werewolf, ripped Stricken's head off and kicked a field goal with it, it wouldn't be *that* illegal. Heck, there might even be a reward.

It was Boone who had the guts to point out the obvious. *"Hey, Earl, good buddy, what was that thing you were just telling me about big picture keeping our eye on the prize?"*

The reply came a moment later, because no matter how angry he might be—and enslaving his girlfriend into a secret government monster death squad tended to make a man righteously angry—Earl was still a professional. *"Alright. That's fair. Priority is grabbing that package. But once we have that in hand, Stricken's mine."*

I looked at Trip again and shrugged. I could almost pity anybody who ended up on the receiving end of Earl Harbinger's wrath. To his people, Earl was a good friend and great leader, but to his enemies, Earl was a terrifying force of unrelenting murder. But this was Stricken...who frankly deserved it, so *good*. I went back to watching.

Flanked by umbrella guard, Stricken walked up to the entrance. Another guard held the door open for him but the former head of Special Task Force Unicorn stopped and scanned the street again. I swear his eyes lingered on our van just a bit too long, but that was probably just my imagination. He had been some kind of secret agent superspy, and we knew he routinely used dark magic artifacts that regular sane people would be terrified to mess with, but he wasn't omnipotent. Though he sure liked to act like he was.

"Oh, man. Earl is gonna wipe the smug off his face," Trip said.

"More like Earl is going to eat his face."

"What?" Hertzfeldt asked.

Newbies weren't in on the secret. Earl Harbinger being a werewolf was kept on a need-to-know basis. "Nothing." I keyed my radio. "Stricken has entered the building."

"*The reptoid and six cultists have gone inside,*" Boone said. "*There's at least four more I can see staying with their vehicles.*"

"It's showtime." We had the place totally surrounded but knowing Stricken was the buyer changed things. He was a slippery bastard who always had a trick up his sleeve. A cold lump slowly formed in the pit of my stomach. I'd gone from wary but professionally confident to having a vague sense of unease. Stricken had that effect on people.

Trip asked, "What does Stricken want with a Ward Stone anyway? He claims to be trying to defend Earth from Asag too. You think he wants it for the same reason we do?"

"Maybe. With that slimeball, who knows? I wouldn't trust him as far as I could throw him, and as skinny as he is, I bet I could get some serious air on the toss."

"So . . ." Hertzfeldt interjected. "I take it you guys got some history?"

"We do. Stricken used to be in charge of . . . well, let's just call it a federal agency. He's lied to us, used MHI, risked all our lives for his personal gain, and is basically the poster child for that saying about absolute power corrupting absolutely."

"Luckily for us, he got fired," Trip said. "So now it's game on."

I ran the binoculars across the plaza, looking for anything out of the ordinary. Stricken didn't have the full might of a secret government black ops unit at his fingertips anymore, but he still struck me as the sort who'd want lots and lots of backup, especially when dealing with a bunch of backstabbing lizard people and the morons gullible enough to worship them as deities. Except everything seemed really normal. Maybe too normal. Which was when I noticed something that felt a little off.

"Trip, check out the taco truck. Notice anything weird?"

It was one of those hippy-dippy, brightly colored, urban-trendy kind of things. Where the food was usually overpriced, used the word "fusion" a lot in its menu, but tended to be really tasty. Trip watched it for a few seconds. "Well, I guess the dude taking orders in the window is white. I don't think I've ever seen a white dude work in a taco truck before."

"Stop being racist. Tacos are for everyone."

Trip snorted.

"I mean watch him. He's busy, but since Stricken's arrived he keeps glancing toward the target. Gut feeling. I think he's watching the place, same as us."

"Maybe..." Trip snapped a picture, then blew it up on the camera's screen. "Hey now. Look at that."

"What?"

"Imagine taco guy without the beard, glasses, or hairnet and tell me who that looks like."

Skinny beard, blocky hipster glasses. It was a decent disguise, but... I started to laugh. "Oh, man! It's Grant!"

"Who?" our poor Newbie asked, perplexed as usual.

But I got the radio instead. "This is Z. Attention everybody, the Feds are here. MCB is staking the place out too."

"Are you absolutely sure?" Earl asked.

"Either that or Grant Jefferson's twin brother is slinging artisanal tacos for a living." Of all the Monster Control Bureau agents I'd met, I knew Grant the best. Hell, I'd broken his nose once, so I was pretty sure that was him. Having the Feds here was bad, but worse, last I'd heard, Grant had been partnered with the single scariest thing in the federal government's arsenal, and that's saying something about people who have intercontinental ballistic missiles and the IRS. "If Grant's here, Agent Franks is probably nearby too."

Earl didn't say anything over the radio, but I knew from experience right now he would be using a whole lot of profanity, because the MCB's presence ruined everything.

We were private contractors. We had an excuse to be working here because reptoids are PUFF-applicable monsters. Boone had a great working relationship with the Atlanta PD: so long as we were discreet, the locals stayed happy. But the Federal Monster Control Bureau were the supreme law of the land when it came to anything related to keeping monsters secret from the public, and they had the authority to tell us to go pound sand. Since they had jurisdiction over all things magical, they would also seize the Ward, and we'd be shit out of luck.

I searched for other cars that might be doing the same surveillance thing as us. There were a bunch that had been parked here the whole time, and several of those had windows tinted enough that I couldn't see if there was anyone sitting inside. There could be a tac team waiting across the street for all I knew. Hell, with the MCB's insane budget and how much they wanted to catch Stricken, they probably had a spy satellite overhead.

"How do you want to proceed, Earl?"

"I'm thinking."

"Better think fast," Trip said, though he certainly didn't say that over the radio.

I heard the motorcycle engine before I saw it. The same bike that had passed by a minute ago had turned around and was coming back, only much faster this time. She zipped between a few slowly moving cars, turned into the parking lot, and stopped right next to Stricken's BMW.

I hit transmit. "A white and red bullet bike just arrived at the target. Female rider, dressed all in black. Can't see her face with the helmet. I don't think security was expecting her though. They're headed her way aggressively." Of course we couldn't hear anything from way over here, but it was obvious the guards were telling her to move along. Nobody, Nobody, & Douchebag was currently closed to the public. She ignored them, put down the kickstand and took off her helmet. Trip snapped some pictures.

"The rider is an Asian female, late teens or early twenties. Maybe five foot five or so." It was hard to estimate from this distance, but she appeared really young and relatively petite compared to the beefy security thugs who were telling her to hit the road. She shook out her long black hair, smiled at the nearest guard, and then whacked him upside the head with her helmet.

Before I could key my radio she'd sprung off the bike, spin-kicked another man in the neck, and judo-tossed the next guy across the trunk of Stricken's BMW. "We've got some action here." I tried to provide a play-by-play. "The girl's jumping on the car. And she just leapt on a security dude's head! She's monkey-crawling onto his back. He's flailing! Oh shit, she's got the choke. That girl's riding him like a pony!"

"Slow down." Apparently, Earl didn't appreciate my color commentary. *"What's happening?"*

"The rider is beating the hell out of the guards. Really well too!"

"Everybody hold your positions," Earl ordered. *"Do you recognize her, Z?"*

"Never seen her before." The last two security guards charged, but she rolled off the one she'd been strangling, ducked beneath a clumsy swing, and palm-struck that poor fool in the nuts so hard that all three of us in the van winced in sympathy as he collapsed. Then somehow, she pulled off a leg sweep like something out of Mortal Kombat, which put the supervisor flat on his back on the cement. She ran for the door, having plowed through a wall of meat in just a few seconds. "And she's inside. Okay, that was really impressive."

"Like human impressive, or supernatural impressive?"

"Hard to say." I'd better get this one right, because there was a vast gulf between how we were allowed to deal with human beings versus how we dealt with monsters. She'd had surprise on her side, but physics were unforgiving and weight classes existed for a reason. That waif-fu stuff where tiny ballerina-looking women routinely beat the hell out of guys my size only happened in the movies. "Probably not *all* human." But as soon as I said that, umbrella guard was hurled through the front window and landed in the bushes about ten feet away. I couldn't have thrown him that far, and I was built like a model for protein shakes. "Amend that. Definitely supernatural."

With nothing to see at the building besides some dazed and battered security guards, I turned the binos back toward the food truck. Sure enough the taco vendor was headed toward the door, ditching his hairnet and pulling off his apron. From how fast he was sprinting, yeah...that was Grant. He'd always been a motivated sort. Several of the people eating lunch around the plaza must have also been MCB, because they jumped up, pulled the handguns they'd been concealing, and rushed toward the building too. I reported that to the others.

"This is Holly. A table full of people just bolted from the res-taurant without paying their bill. I'm guessing undercover Feds."

"Damn it." A whole lot of our effort and scheming had just been flushed down the toilet. Apparently, we'd not been the only party tipped off about this deal.

"I see Feds swarming toward the back too," Boone confirmed. *"Bad guys are busting out guns. Looks like they aren't going down without a fight."*

The MCB were always gung-ho, so Earl was probably going to order us to retreat to keep us from getting shot or arrested. Whenever the MCB decided that MHI had been meddling in their business, it turned into a legal nightmare. But Earl surprised me. *"Everybody hold your position. We're just watching. If MCB sees us, we've got a valid excuse for being here."* He must have really wanted that Ward Stone...Or more likely, he was hoping to see Stricken get shot while running from the law. If that jerk tried to resist arrest with Agent Franks around, Franks would probably handcuff Stricken, then pull his arms off to use them like nunchuks to beat Stricken to death. That would be hilarious.

Several unmarked cars along the street were suddenly moving to block off the parking lot. Red and blue lights started flashing. This was a pretty big show of force for the MCB to use in public, but Monster Control Bureau was really good at pretending to be other mundane federal agencies when they needed to. The running MCB agents reached the front of the building. Most of them went through the door, guns drawn. The rest started handcuffing the downed security guards. Stricken's driver got yanked out of the car and thrown down on the pavement to get cuffed. Nobody was dumb enough to resist.

But who was the biker girl? Was she with the MCB? Only that didn't feel right. They'd held their position when Stricken had arrived. They hadn't freaked out and revealed themselves until she'd rushed in, like her sudden and violent arrival had forced their hand.

The building was three stories tall. And long before the Feds had a chance to make it up the stairs, one of the big windows on the top floor shattered. That must have been where the meeting was being held, because a man—probably one of the snake cultists from the tats—crashed through the window. A second later the biker girl *leapt* through the window after him.

Somehow, she hit the parking lot feet first, rolled, and popped right back up, seemingly unharmed. I couldn't say the same for the snake cultist, who'd landed flat on his back. Her sudden arrival surprised the MCB agents, and I got my answer as to whether they were on the same team when she throat-punched one, kicked another in the knee, and ran. Trip took pictures.

She now had a big red backpack.

A female agent tried to shoot her, but the rider slid toward her like she was stealing home plate. There was a *pop pop* as the MCB agent launched a couple of desperate rounds—too high— before the girl hit her in the legs. The agent did a flip. The girl hopped back up and onto her motorcycle. She'd even picked up her helmet during the slide. Not only had that been damn near Earl Harbinger speed, it had been *smooth*.

As much fun as it was watching the MCB get their asses kicked, I wasn't even going to try and narrate what I'd just seen to the others, so I just told everyone, "I think the rider's got the Ward Stone. She's making a break for it."

Tires squealed, and then the bike took off, crazy fast. The girl popped a wheelie through the parking lot. Feds had to leap out of the way to not get run over. She hit the street on both wheels and accelerated, zipping between cars.

"Follow that bike!"

CHAPTER 2

The Newbie punched the gas. Except there was no way this lumbering tub was going to keep up with her, let alone with her being able to weave through traffic. "Milo, Skippy, there's a motorcycle heading south. She's got the Ward. You got eyes on her?"

"Got her, Z. Skippy's following."

There was a bunch of noise, followed by lots and lots of gunshots. I couldn't tell if it was from inside the building, the parking garage, or both.

Boone got on the radio. *"Cultists are shooting at the Feds. We've got us a gunfight back here."*

"Get the hell out of there, Boone," Earl commanded. The MCB wouldn't want our help anyway and the last thing we needed was for one of us to catch a stray round. Knowing the MCB, they'd probably bill us for the bullet.

"Already moving. So much for quietly following these assholes home so we could pop them all at once. Stupid Feds."

The MCB would be focused on their rapidly unfolding gun battle with the reptoid and friends. They were probably here for Stricken, not the Ward Stone. We could still salvage this. Earl must have seen the opportunity too, and immediately started giving a series of rapid-fire orders. The bike was moving fast, but we had an aerial view, and four vehicles in motion. Five, if Holly and the Atlanta Hunters she was with could get to their car before the Feds locked the plaza down. We just needed to stick with the thief long enough to find a place to corner her.

The biker kept accelerating. Hertzfeldt drove like a maniac. Which I guess was the default for Atlanta anyway. Angry drivers honked at us. We made several hard turns. I got tossed off my perch and ended up sliding around on the open floor of the surveillance van. If I'd known we were going to get into a car chase today, I wouldn't have volunteered to ride in the vehicle that didn't have any real seats in back. Trip was smart enough to climb forward and get in the passenger seat to buckle himself in.

"She's trying to shake us," Hertzfeldt warned as we careened wildly around a corner. Cars honked as we zipped through a red light.

"I doubt she knows we're behind her," Trip said. "She's just trying to get some distance between her and that office before a hundred cops show up."

"I'm going to lose her."

"That's fine. That's what Skippy's for. Everybody's got their job. Yours is to not crash." Trip keyed his radio. "This is the van. She's too fast. We can't maintain visual."

All I could see was sticky van floor. Luckily Milo had the rider on camera and kept giving everyone directions. *"She's southbound on West Peachtree, passing Ponce De Leon."*

"What is up with you people and all the friggin' peach trees?" I asked no one in particular. But this was where having the local team driving really came in handy. Boone's team lived here. This was home turf for them. All Milo had to do was read street names off a computer screen and our locals would know how to box her in. I could hear sirens closing fast. The MCB's antics had attracted the regular police. I struggled upright so I could see out the window. "I bet she slows down to avoid attracting attention now."

Sure enough, once we were several blocks from the altercation, Milo told us that the rider had stopped zipping between cars and was now blending in and not breaking any traffic laws. That meant lights and congestion were going to slow her down, but it was better than drawing the attention of a cop. We'd mounted a police scanner in the van, and from the sounds of it, the local cops were pretty agitated because some unexpected downtown bust by Immigration and Customs Enforcement had turned into a gunfight. Good old MCB and their fake credentials.

"Okay, Hunters. Try to get close as you can without being seen and get ready for her to bail," Earl warned. "We're dealing with a pro. I bet you she's got another vehicle stashed, or she's got some other escape route planned."

Trip told Hertzfeldt, "Keep gaining but try not to look like you're chasing her."

She went several more blocks and crossed over the freeway. I was glad she didn't get on it. If she decided to open that bike up on there, I really didn't know if our little drone could keep up.

"Oh, hell I forgot," Boone said. "It's Labor Day weekend. Can you guys grab her now?"

"Negative," Trip responded. "She's too far ahead."

"Get closer or you'll lose her in the crowds."

But before I could ask what crowds, Trip pointed through the windshield. "I see her again."

I was holding onto the back of his seat so Hertzfeldt wouldn't break my neck. I spotted her too, a couple hundred yards ahead, and she was still wearing that big red backpack. If it was empty, and the Ward Stone was back with Stricken getting busted by the MCB, I was going to feel really stupid. "This is Z, we've got visual on the bike. She's half a block ahead. Looks like she's got the Ward."

She was checking her mirrors, but we were driving normal now, and there were lots of unremarkable work vans like this in the city. But I was still getting a bad vibe. This was a busy part of town with a bunch of gigantic hotels. Which meant lots of parking garages and big crowded buildings to duck into. "What if she bails and goes into something Skippy can't follow?"

"Grab that bag if you can but be extremely careful. Whatever she is, she's dangerous."

She was fast enough to beat up a bunch of goons and Feds and jump out a third-story window after brazenly robbing a former spy and some underground lizard monsters, so yeah, my money would be on very dangerous. I had Abomination in my gear bag, but a full-auto shotgun and grenade launcher might stick out a bit if I needed to hop out and follow her on foot. Abomination wasn't exactly low key.

"She's heading south again," Trip said.

Milo confirmed that a moment later with some more street names, one of which, I kid you not, was Peachtree Center Avenue Northeast. But I was zoomed in, focused like a laser beam, watching that bike, because my gut was telling me something was about to go down. We were in the shade of a bunch of tall buildings. Traffic had gotten really snarled up. We were barely moving at all now. The sidewalks were absolutely packed with pedestrians.

"Crap. I know where we are," Trip said.

"What?" As we crept closer, I realized there was a *ton* of people here. I'm talking thousands upon thousands of people packing the sidewalks. And most of them were in costume. Superheroes, GI Joes, anime characters, etc. "What the hell is this?"

"I was so focused on catching the reptoids I forgot to warn you guys about Dragon Con," Boone said.

"I should have thought of it myself," Trip said apologetically. "I went last year. I took Polyphemus to thank him for helping us with the siege. I was kind of hoping we'd wrap this mission up fast enough I could go again since we're in town anyway."

"Is that the big party thing where you played dress-up?"

"It's not dress up. It's *cosplay,*" Trip corrected. "Poly needed a disguise to go out in public and you've got to admit my Witcher was amazing."

The glamor shots he'd taken had been pretty badass. That's what happens when an extremely physically fit geek also has crazy amounts of disposable income. Only, Trip's fake yet high quality movie poster he'd framed and put up in the office didn't change the fact we were now screwed. If we tried anything here, there would be a thousand eyeballs on us, and unlike the MCB, we couldn't just flash fake badges and talk our way out of anything.

"Never been myself, but Dragon Con is nerd Mardi Gras," said Hertzfeldt. "It's a hundred thousand people packed into a few blocks. If she disappears into that mob we'll never find her."

Sure enough, the rider pulled her bike over to the curb, in a place where parking clearly wasn't allowed, and put the kickstand down.

"She's bailing," I transmitted. "Trip and I will follow on foot."

"What do you want me to do?" our driver asked.

"Follow as best as you can, I guess." But it was already obvious that it would be totally impossible for him to keep up.

Hertzfeldt hadn't actually stopped, but the flow of traffic had slowed to such a crawl that it didn't matter. I left my shotgun behind and made sure my pistol was concealed beneath my untucked shirt. I slid the door open, hopped out, and then closed it behind me. Trip got out the front. We both started walking fast. The rider was about a hundred yards ahead of us.

And when she took off her helmet, she wasn't a dark-haired Asian, but rather a white girl with short, brightly dyed, pink hair.

"We've been had!" Trip keyed his radio. "It's a different rider. We were following a decoy."

"This is Milo. No way, I could see you and her both the whole time. That's the same bike; it had this neat little white box around it on the computer and everything. It never left my sight, I swear."

I looked to Trip. "You got a better idea?" He shrugged. We were committed now either way, so we kept walking fast, trying to get closer. It was hard because the sidewalk and several feet of road were filled with bodies, and they were going both directions. I bumped into a shirtless man in a loincloth who I think was supposed to be Conan the Barbarian. "Excuse me." Then I collided with a fat dude who made a very disturbing Sailor Moon. "Sorry."

The decoy got off the bike and started walking with the general flow toward the nearest hotel.

Thankfully, our target was on the small side, so couldn't exactly bull her way through the crowd like me and Trip. I'm six foot five and three hundred pounds of impolite muscle. Trip was several inches shorter and a whole lot lighter, but our company nerd had also played college football, so shoving people came naturally to him. We were gaining on her. We just needed to be chill enough doing it to not cause a commotion. If she spotted us and ran, this was going to get really complicated. Thankfully, it was extremely loud. Groups of friends were talking, music was playing, horns were honking, and there were guys with coolers hawking bottled water for five bucks a pop. Which they were probably getting, because standing in the middle of thousands of people meant that it had gotten a whole lot hotter real fast. I felt bad for the people in the really big costumes. Who in their right mind wears fur in Atlanta in summer?

"You know this place better than I do, so you'd better handle giving everybody else directions," I told Trip.

"Sure. But I've only been here once, and if she goes inside the hotels, it's a maze." Our radio setup consisted of an earpiece and a microphone that hung around our necks, which was about as discreet as you could get. So Trip vectoring the rest of the

Hunters in on us would just look like he was having a conversation with me, or maybe just talking to himself. Which, all things considered, wasn't even sort of close to the weirdest thing on the street right now.

I had to put my hand over my ear to block the crowd noise. *"This is Earl and Gregorius, coming in from the Hyatt side on foot. Boone's trying to go around and will be waiting in a car on the south side. Holly is coming up behind Z and Trip."*

We closed to within fifty yards and our target still hadn't seen us. She kept looking around too, seeming calm but alert. But there were so many people that even as big and ugly as I was, we didn't stand out that much in jeans and T-shirts. Losing her in the crowd was our biggest danger, but simultaneously our biggest asset because it was slowing her down. The mob had to stop at an intersection, waiting for the light to change before they could cross. And that was a huge mess because cars were trying to make it across the intersection but getting stuck and blocking traffic from the other direction when those lights changed. Which led to a lot of distracting angry honking from drivers who had unwittingly blundered into this.

Our target was short enough I lost her in the clump at the crosswalk, hidden behind five Deadpools. When the light changed again and the crowd started across the street, I couldn't find her.

"Where'd she go?" Trip asked. Had she ducked into a business? Turned down the other street? "Milo?"

"Uhh...I can't see the pink hair anymore, but the white box thingy is still going in the same direction."

Ain't technology grand? I was walking and pushing about as fast as I could without knocking anybody over, but I still couldn't spot the decoy. Then I saw the big red backpack, and the woman who had it over her shoulder was still in the same black riding clothes, and still about the same age, height, and build...Only now she was black with braids. There hadn't been a handoff either. This wasn't somebody else carrying the same bag. I was about ninety percent sure I was looking at the same girl, just wearing an entirely different face.

Trip spotted her about the same time I did and came to the same conclusion. The key to being a successful Monster Hunter is having a flexible mind, so neither of us got rattled too much by this new development.

"We've got a shapeshifter. I repeat, she's some kind of shape-shifter." He hadn't said that into his microphone very loudly at all, so either she had supernatural hearing or the timing of her glance back was just really unfortunate, because she turned her head and caught the two of us gawking at her. There was only a split second of hesitation, the slightest bit of a grin…and then she ran.

And the girl was *quick*.

We went after her. It was on now.

Trip was a far smoother runner than I was, and he darted between the brightly costumed people, then found an open patch of flowerbed to sprint down. When that ran out, he jumped a little metal fence into the street and started dodging between slowly moving cars.

I, on the other hand, wasn't that graceful, but I was really big and really loud. "Make a hole!" Subtlety went right out the window as I plowed my way through the con goers. "Emergency!" I, of course, did not specify the nature of said emergency, because the MCB had zero sense of humor when it came to monster business in public. "Coming through!"

The girl darted back and forth, swiftly making her way through the crowd. Miraculously, Trip was keeping up. They were both starting to leave me behind. And that was before I tripped over Batman's cape and ate pavement. I jumped right back up and kept going, ignoring the people yelling and calling me all sorts of names, many of which I deserved because I was being very rude. But if I didn't get that Ward Stone, then an ancient chaos demon was probably going to destroy the world and consume all their souls anyway, so they could suck it up.

Trip was still shouting directions into his radio. *"She took a left and is heading for the Marriot,"* he said. Which wasn't helpful for me at all. But thankfully people were starting to get out of the large maniac's way, so I had that going for me. One angry little buffed dude, who was either supposed to be casual Wolverine, or who wasn't in costume at all but just really liked tank tops, threw his soda in my face while calling me a dick, which was super helpful.

There were security people or volunteers checking badges at the hotel entrance, but apparently our little shape-shifting thief hadn't bought a ticket, or didn't slow down enough to show it, because by the time I got there, the poor fellow was lying on the sidewalk, holding his bloody nose.

Trip was just inside. "I didn't hit him!"

"I know. Which way did she go?"

"This way." He'd already started running again. "Now she's a white chick with red hair and freckles."

"Crap." She could change faces so fast, if she ditched the distinctive clothing, or had a chance to transfer the Ward to a different bag, we would never catch her.

Apparently, the actual convention itself was inside the hotels, and the mob in the street was just the people moving from event to event, because the interior was even *more* crowded than the street. Plus, there were lots of volunteers in matching shirts talking excitedly into their radios, probably about the badge checker who had just gotten sucker-punched, which meant we'd have cops on hand shortly. And since we were having to sprint to keep up with her, who were the cops going to notice first? The tiny inoffensive girl? Or the gigantic scary thug looking guy and his dreadlocked and nearly as scary-looking companion, chasing her?

Yeah... We were probably going to get shot.

I spotted the now redhead, booking it across the room, and chased after her. The interior was one of those gigantic spaces where you could look up and see the landings wrapping around all the way to the top. It made me kind of dizzy. It was either the vertigo, or I just really hate running. She slid under a railing, leapt onto a bar, ran down it, and did an actual fucking *back flip* over some Power Rangers waiting to have their picture taken. She landed smoothly, ducked behind a bunch of people waiting to catch an elevator, and when she ran out the other side, she was deeply tanned with dark brown hair.

"Are you kidding me?" I shouted.

"Trip, Owen, come in." It was Earl. *"We've got a complication."*

"Like this isn't complicated enough!"

"We ran into some snake cultists and whooped on them. They had some kind of tracking thing on their phones." Earl probably meant an app, but give the guy a break, he was born in 1900. *"They must have planted a bug on the Ward. They're following her too."*

"Can you track her position?" Because, frankly, that sounded a lot better than running after an acrobat until I had a heart attack.

"No. His phone got broke when I threw him down the stairs. But there's more of them here, so be on the lookout."

She turned down a hall and we sprinted after her. A security volunteer tried to grab Trip, but he ducked under the arm. He watched Trip go, like *shoot, missed him*, then turned and saw me coming. When he saw how big I was and how fast I was moving, he thought about it, but wisely decided to get out of the way.

"Really sorry about this!"

The girl was insanely athletic, but Trip was keeping up. I'd been pretty religious about my cardio since training up for the siege, but I was getting winded. Worse. I looked back and saw the volunteer pointing us out to a cop, who immediately started talking into his radio. There had to be a ton of uniforms here and they would all be descending on us in short order.

"Boone, come in." Wow. I was really getting out of breath. "APD is after us. Can you call your contacts and tell them we're the good guys?"

"*I'll try. We've got a pretty good working relationship on the downlow. This city is lousy with monsters.*"

"Great." When I looked back there were two cops running after me. "Hurry."

The next minute was a blur of me crashing into people while Trip kept getting farther ahead. My concerns, in order, were get the Ward, don't get shot by the cops, don't get shot by the attendees, because this was the South after all, which meant at least a quarter of them were probably packing heat. Thankfully, I temporarily lost my police pursuit, because the cops violently collided with a bunch of stormtroopers. It was like two bowling balls hitting a bunch of pins. Strike! And they all went down in a tangled mess.

I didn't know where the hell we were. Trip hadn't been exaggerating when he called this place a maze. There were crowded halls, lots of turns, and now we were chasing her across a glass sky bridge with a busy street below us.

For the first time since the chase had begun, she stopped running.

Oh, thank goodness. I needed some air.

At first I thought that maybe she'd froze because some of the other Hunters had gotten to the other end of the sky bridge to block her. Trip had been giving directions the whole time after all.

Only it wasn't our guys waiting at the other end of the bridge. It was more snake cultists. They were all in leather vests that showed off green scaly tats. And I didn't know if one of them was actually some sort of reptoid-human hybrid, or he was just that friggin' ugly and had gotten fang dental implants and was wearing yellow contacts. But there were five of them plugging the exit.

So the girl turned back, saw that there were only two of us, did the math and started toward Trip. Except he shook his head in that assertive manner which was sort of like the universal signal for *fuck around and find out*. The girl paused, realizing that we were far more ready for her kung-fu antics than the unsuspecting security goons and MCB agents had been.

Since this was about to turn ugly I roughly stopped the people coming up behind me, while still letting the people who were already crossing off. "Sky bridge is closed for maintenance. Sorry. Go around."

"Aw, come on," said a very round, very red, Kool-Aid Man. "The food court's right over there."

"Trust me, pal. You don't want to crash through this wall." I really wasn't in the mood. "Seriously, we're about to have a rumble here."

"Ooh, a flash mob." He took out his phone to take video.

For a very tense moment, the regular, unwitting people kept getting off the sky bridge, as an increasingly annoyed crowd backed up behind me, until it was just us, the girl, and the snake people, one of whom was staring at his phone, then at the red backpack, and then back at his phone. "That'ss her." He hissed, and by hissed, I mean he really put the accent on the *s* sounds. "Sseize the ssstone."

That was a very obnoxious affectation. I'd long thought the Church of the Temporary Mortal Condition held the title for most annoying death cult, but that fake lisp nonsense sure bumped these guys up the rankings. "Shove it up your asssss," I said. "Just talk normal, doofus."

From the way they all pulled out knives, I think my words actually hurt the snake cultists' feelings. They had been trying extra hard to be frightening.

The girl looked between us and the cultists, then grinned and said, "Ooh, MCB dorks versus snake pricks. Nice."

"We're not MCB, and we don't want to hurt you." Trip was ever the diplomat, as he appealed earnestly to the possibly psychotic shapeshifter. "I can't say that for these other guys. We just want the Ward. We can protect you from them."

She actually laughed. "Aw, that's cute." The girl had a very normal, vanilla, middle-American accent, and sounded about as old as all her faces looked. "But I don't need protecting."

Then she punched the wall, cracking the thick glass with one tiny fist, and then threw her shoulder against it. The glass shattered as she crashed through.

It was a pretty good drop to the street. Easily far enough to break a bunch of bones, but she didn't actually hit the street. She fell in a shower of broken glass, landed on the roof of a moving car, rolled, slid down the trunk, and somehow hit feetfirst, as we all stared in shocked disbelief. She saw me watching, then put her hand to her forehead, pointer finger and thumb extended to make an L, calling us losers. Then she started running again.

The witnesses loved that stunt and started clapping for her.

Trip immediately transmitted. "She's jumped off the sky bridge and is on the street level...heading...I have no idea at this point. I'm lost."

"Oh, screw that. I am not jumping out the window after her."

Even if I had been tempted to break my legs, I wouldn't have had the opportunity anyway, because that's when the cultists decided to try and murder us.

The five of them rushed Trip. I thought about just pulling my .45 and dropping them all, but overpenetration is a bitch, and there were about a hundred innocent bystanders just behind them whom I really didn't want to put holes into by accident. So we'd do this the old-fashioned way. Hopefully Trip wouldn't get stabbed before I got there.

Except Trip surprised me by pulling out a canister of pepper spray and hosing them all down with it. The cultists screamed and clutched at their eyes. One still managed to slash at him, but Trip leapt back before he could get clipped. I passed Trip by and threw a hook to the cultist's midsection hard enough to pancake his liver. He bounced off the glass.

Even partially blind and gasping, a moron with a knife is still extremely dangerous. I caught an incoming stab and twisted the wrist hard. He squealed when the bones broke, and I slung him around into one of his buddies. Their heads hit so hard that I knew they were on a one-way trip to concussion town. Trip kicked the next one in the leg, and when that dirtbag dropped to one knee, Trip slugged him right in his stupid fake fangs. Or at least I was assuming they were fake the way they snapped off and went flying. Trip managed to hit him three more times before the silly-looking weirdo flopped to the carpet.

The last snake man still standing was orange dye-faced, crying, wheezing, coughing, and had dropped his goofy butterfly knife, but in his other hand was his phone. Since he'd been looking at it earlier, it must have had the tracking app on it. "Give me that." I snatched the phone from him. Then I kicked him in the balls really hard, just on general principle.

It had only taken a few seconds to leave them all unconscious or weeping on the floor.

"That was awesome!" shouted Kool-Aid Man, because apparently the observers thought that had been some sort of elaborate staged event. "I'm posting this on Instagram!" Thankfully for us the crowd's density and enthusiasm were the only thing keeping the cops from getting through. Except then the cloud of pepper spray wafted over and people started to freak out when it got in their eyes. They thought they had it bad? I'd been closer and it was really irritating my asthma.

"We've got to go." I did glance briefly out the hole the shapeshifter had made, calculated the drop, and decided that I liked my ankles unshattered, thank you very much. We started toward what had been the snake end of the bridge. We were moving through the crowd again fast, but pretty much lost, and on the lookout for the cops. "I didn't know you carried pepper spray."

"I never leave home without my spicy treat dispenser." Trip shook his hand out. "Ouch. This is why right here. I think I broke my pinky on that guy's head."

"Yeah, that happens. You need stronger bones." Which was total BS, because I'd lost track of how many fingers I'd broken over the years against various skulls, human and other. "Drink more milk."

"Those poor saps will want some milk to wash out their eyes."

"That's actually a myth. You want to scrub your face with Dawn dish soap, and then rinse it off with water," I explained. Trip gave me a quizzical look, wondering how I knew about getting pepper sprayed. "I was a bouncer, remember? Hazard of the job."

"Oh yeah..." he said. "What do we do now?"

I handed him the cultist's phone. It was a map of the area with a blinking dot that was steadily moving away from us. "We can use this, but we need to find a way to disappear before we get busted." This place had to be covered in security cameras.

Trip immediately started relaying directions to Earl as we kept our heads down and kept walking, nice and calm, nothing to see here, officer. APD would certainly arrest us. By the time Boone got everything sorted out with his local contacts, our quarry would be long gone.

We'd wound up in some gigantic food court area. There were hundreds of people waiting in line at dozens of establishments, and every available table was taken. Unfortunately, a bunch of witnesses from the sky bridge were still pointing at us and talking about the fight. And of course, from the opposite direction, more cops were coming, but they hadn't seen us yet.

"This way," Trip said, and I followed him around a corner, and then another, where it was slightly quieter. There were still lots of people, but none of them were currently gesturing at us or taking our picture. Down some stairs, and then another turn—this place really was a maze—and now it was just people who looked really tired or hung over, sullenly eating their takeout in quiet.

"If we go after her, we're just going to get picked up. The cops will all have our descriptions by now."

"They will," Trip agreed. "Be on the lookout for a ruggedly handsome black man and the Rock's chubbier stunt double."

"Hey now. It's getting thinner up top but I've still got most of my hair. If we're going to get back in the chase, we're going to need to hide our faces." At least disguises couldn't be too hard around here.

Trip kept giving the others directions from the tracking device as we went down some more stairs and out an employee-only door that led into a narrow alley. A few people in costumes had snuck out here for a vape break. I could tell they were a group because of the matching costumes. One of them was close to my size, only he was dressed in a gigantic blue suit. A Cookie Monster helmet was sitting on a post next to him.

"Hey, man, how much for the costume?"

"What?" the guy asked, obviously confused. "It wasn't that much, I guess. I just got it off of Amazon."

"No." I took out my wallet. "How much to buy it from you *right now*?"

"Uh...what?"

I checked my wallet. I had eight hundreds, six fifties, a bunch of twenties, and no time to haggle. *Damn it.* Earl had better reimburse me for this. I pulled out all the cash and shoved it toward the perplexed cosplayer. "Here, take this, and give me your costume, right now. There's no time to explain."

He took the money, looked at it surprised, but then said, "But I can't take it off. I'm not wearing anything under here. It's really superhot in this thing." In fact, his face was really sweaty.

"Gross," Trip said.

"Okay, just the helmet thing then." Then I pointed at his buddy. "But you've got to throw in Elmo's head too, for my friend."

"Oh, come on," Trip said. "Can I at least have Oscar?"

"No!" It turned out the one wearing a garbage can was female, and she put her hands on her mask protectively. "Mine's custom. I put a lot of work into it!"

"Fine," Trip said as he begrudgingly took the Elmo helmet from the other guy.

Headless Elmo and Cookie Monster counted their money. "Whoa, thanks, dudes!"

It was costing me about thirteen hundred bucks to avoid getting arrested, but hopefully this would work. I put the helmet on. It smelled like someone had been eating goat cheese in there.

We hit the street, following the tracking app. She was way ahead of us, but it looked like the shapeshifter was moving at walking speeds, probably trying to avoid any further attention. Trip kept giving directions to the others. Hopefully one of them could get eyes on the Ward before she vanished.

Thankfully, Skippy's flying skills saved the day.

"This is Milo. The drone is over the location Trip gave. I do see one woman carrying a red backpack. She's no longer in the black jacket though. Looks like she had a white shirt under it."

Despite the giant googly eyes on my head, the vision on this thing was horrible because I had to look out a mesh-covered slit in the mouth. I kept bumping into a lot of people, but I tried to get into the spirit of it. "Me so sorry! Me clumsy!"

"You look like a ridiculous bobblehead," Trip muttered.

Doubtlessly true, because so did he, but sometimes you just

needed to embrace the absurdity. "Me want cookie! Me want catch shapeshifter to get arcane superweapon! Nom nom nom!"

"I refuse to do the voice. I've got too much dignity," Trip insisted.

"Elmo need tickles!"

"Don't make me shoot you."

I switched back to my real voice. "Well, someone's in a mood."

"I didn't realize I got pepper spray on my hand when I punched that cultist, until I touched my eye putting this stupid thing on my face."

Trip had a good excuse to be cranky. That shit burns.

The blip on the phone kept moving in the same direction, coinciding with the info Milo was feeding us. She must not have known about the cultist's bug or the drone. She could ninja leap and shape-shift all she wanted, but slow and steady was going to win this race...I hoped.

We were moving away from the main hotels, so the crowd was thinning out some. But there was still a lot of foot traffic, and every place that sold food or drinks was packed and had a line out the door.

"*The target is turning into a building on the west side of the street,*" Milo reported. He had a street address from the computer program, but no information as to what was located there. Holly checked in. She was close too. Earl and Gregorius were a minute behind her because they'd also had to dodge the law, only I couldn't imagine either of them wearing costumes. Gregorious because he was just so dour, and Earl on general principle...Though come to think of it, he could have turned into a werewolf and in this crowd people probably would have just complimented him on how realistic it looked and then tried to take their picture with him.

"*Sorry, guys, the drone has lost visual.*"

We got there a moment later and saw that it was an office building where a bunch of different kinds of firms rented the lower floors, but residential apartments above. There were a lot of people inside the lobby area, but none of them had a big red backpack. Trip and I got strange looks from the business-casual-dressed people, which meant it was time to ditch our silly disguises. I pulled Cookie Monster's head off and tucked it under my arm before approaching the receptionist.

"May I help you?" she asked suspiciously.

"Did a young woman come through here a minute ago?" Since I didn't know what face our shapeshifter was currently wearing, that was all the description I could give, but come to think of it, her being limited to young and female was just a guess on my part based on her behavior so far. "Or maybe somebody else with a big red backpack?"

We must have looked like shifty, sweaty, dangerous types, because she said, "I'm afraid that's none of your business, sir." Except as I had asked the question, her eyes had flicked unconsciously down the hall to the left.

"Thanks." The two of us started walking in that direction, but then I paused briefly when I saw the sign on the door. It was the lady's restroom. Trip checked the tracker, then nodded. I shrugged, dropped Cookie Monster's head, drew my handgun, and pushed the door open.

"You can't go in there!" the receptionist shouted after us. "Security!"

We swept in, guns up. It appeared to be empty. There was a red backpack sitting on the sink. I rushed to it, while Trip checked both of the stalls.

The bag was flat. Empty. No magic rock.

"The stone's gone."

"Clear," Trip said after shoving open the second door. "Where'd she go?"

About ten feet up, with no practical way for a regular person to reach it, was a window. From all her jumping and flipping, it wouldn't have been too hard for her. It was open. I keyed my radio. "The target has snuck out the back. She ditched the backpack with the tracker, but she's got the Ward."

"What's Skippy looking for then?"

"I have no idea."

"We'll do what we can. Milo out."

"Damn it!" I kicked the garbage can in frustration.

"Boost me up," Trip suggested.

"Good idea." We hadn't been that far behind her. He might be able to see something. So I holstered my gun, made a stirrup with my hands, Trip stepped on them, and I lifted. Hunters have to practice for weird crap like this, so hoisting Trip up there was a piece of cake.

I grunted. "See anything?"

He held onto the windowsill and peered out. "Just a parking lot. I think I can fit. I'm going after her."

Trip had far broader shoulders than the shapeshifter, so it took him a few seconds of precarious struggling, but then he made it and I could quit holding him up. He wiggled through. "I'll catch up," I shouted as Trip dropped into the parking lot on the other side.

As we were pulling off that clever maneuver, I could hear the receptionist screaming at somebody else they couldn't go back there, again. That was probably our friends.

Only the thing that came through the door was no Hunter. In fact, it was bigger than me, and clad entirely in dirty, tattered robes. My nostrils got hit with a smell like the reptile house at the zoo. Rags covered most of its face, but in the shadows beneath its hood could be seen two unblinking yellow eyes. Its green, scaly hands were visible, each finger ending in a long black talon. In those hands was an iPhone in a pink bejeweled case which was incongruously cheerful and really didn't match the rest of the creature's ensemble.

This was probably the one time of year a thing like this could walk around downtown Atlanta and not get shot on sight. This was no squishy human cultist. This was the real deal.

The reptoid glared at me, then it glanced down at the blinking light on the phone it had surely taken from one of its human cultists, then it looked over at the sink and the empty backpack. When it saw that the stone was gone, the monster let out a really perturbed hissing sound.

"Dude, I know how you feel."

I'd vented my anger by kicking the garbage can. Apparently, the creature decided it was going to take out its frustration over losing the Ward on me, because it came over and tried to swat my head off.

CHAPTER 3

It turns out reptoids are shockingly fast.

I managed to draw my pistol. There wasn't time to bring up the sights, but we were so close it didn't matter. I fired twice from the speed rock. The .45 was deafening in the small, tiled room. Both silver hollowpoints nailed it in the chest.

It slammed into me anyway.

My back hit the wall. I ducked as claws cut across the tile, shoved my pistol into its robed belly and pulled the trigger repeatedly. The monster grunted but didn't go down. That wasn't good. I'd never fought one before, but my Newbie classes had never mentioned reptoids being bulletproof.

I tried to angle the gun up toward its head, but claws flashed across my forearm and opened me up. Fat droplets of blood splattered on the wall. My STI went sliding across the floor.

"Shit!"

I narrowly dodged aside as the lightning-fast swipe of one hand ripped through my T-shirt and left four shallow lines across my chest. I thought I'd made it, but the reptoid kept spinning, and I'd forgotten they have tails.

Its tail swept my feet out from under me. I was briefly airborne. Then I hit the floor hard with my hip.

It was coming toward me, but I managed to get one boot up to kick it square in the face. There was a meaty crunch. It stumbled back into one of the stalls. The rags covering its face fell away, revealing a hideous lizard visage, bumpy skin, no nose, and an incredibly wide mouth filled with pointy teeth.

Reptoids are downright fugly.

It wiped its bloody nostril holes with the back of one hand, then swore at me in its weird hissing language. Or at least I was pretty sure it was swearing. I would be if I'd just gotten kicked in the mouth.

Milo was yelling in my ear, asking what was happening, but I was a little too busy to get on the radio. My STI was lying a few feet away. I rolled over and reached for it.

But the reptoid bent down and caught me by the ankle before I could grab my gun. It had a grip like a vise. My fingers were inches from the grip. Then the monster pulled, and it turned out that they weren't just crazy fast, but also extremely strong. My body made a squeaking noise against the tile as I was dragged. Then it slung me around and launched me into the mirror.

The glass shattered as I bounced off the wall. That *really* hurt. I rolled across the sink and snapped the faucet off with my back. Water sprayed. Somehow, I managed to land mostly upright. It probably thought that toss had broken me, because it charged, hands extended, claws spread wide.

Only I wasn't broken, I was just getting warmed up.

I stepped inside one of the arms, locked up on it, and then flipped the reptoid around hard. We both crashed into one of the stalls and the sheet metal walls collapsed around us. The other claw tried to disembowel me, but I struck that arm aside. We ended up sliding across the stall, me desperately holding onto each of its wrists. It had far more physical power than I did, but it had probably never fought a human being as strong as I was. It seemed a little taken aback that it hadn't killed me yet.

We ended up face to scaly face. Its breath was hot and stank like roadkill. A forked tongue flicked out and hit me in the eye. I twisted my head back as those nasty teeth snapped shut half an inch from my cheek. So then I head-butted the fucker right in the snout. The yellow eyes blinked in surprise.

Then I threw a knee into its side and shoved off far enough to give me time to go for the fixed blade on my belt. I let go of its wrist, yanked out the little knife and went to stabbing.

It swung its claws at me, but it hadn't seen the knife yet. I cut it across the bicep, through the robes, and deep into the muscle. Reptoid blood is so dark it's almost purple, and I proceeded to paint the walls with it. The other arm came around, nearly tagged me, but I pushed back in right behind the attack, went up and over its defenses, and stabbed it in the side of the neck. The reptoid's hands flew reflexively toward the wound, so I kicked it in the chest.

It flew back and cracked its head against the toilet, hard. That must have brained it, because it let go of its squirting neck, and sank slowly to the floor, bleeding out.

I stood there for a second, breathing heavily. I picked up my pistol and aimed it at the downed reptoid, but I was pretty sure it was done for. Then I realized my right arm was bleeding like crazy. Reptoids lived in sewers, so their claws had to be really unsanitary, so I went over and stuck my arm into the sink geyser. I winced as the spray turned pink. I could already tell that was going to need stitches.

I keyed my radio. "This is Pitt. I got attacked by a reptoid at the site where the tracker is. I'm injured but I don't think it's that bad." The cut hurt like a son of a bitch, but it hadn't hit any major veins or arteries. I'd get medical attention after we got that Ward Stone. Direct pressure would work for now. I looked around for paper towels to shove in the gash, but of course the bathroom only had one of those stupid air blowers. So I helped myself to a roll of toilet paper.

The bathroom door opened. I really hoped it was my fellow Hunters, and not more reptoids. A giant, hulking figure strolled into the room.

Only it was *worse* than reptoids.

"Franks," I muttered.

"Pitt." He didn't seem surprised to see me or the destruction. The legendary MCB agent was wearing his usual cheap suit and clip-on tie, so muscular and intimidating that he made me look downright cuddly in comparison.

It had been a while since I'd seen my favorite made-out-of-spare-parts federal problem solver and all-around killing machine. "Is that a new nose?"

"Yeah..." He took off his sunglasses, revealing his beady little eyes that had probably been scooped out of a death row inmate's head. "You like it?"

"Not really."

"Good." Then Franks looked down at the dead reptoid and frowned. "I was gonna take it prisoner."

"Then you should have got here sooner. It didn't give me a lot of choice in the matter. But on the bright side, PUFF on these assholes is like fifty grand a head." I discreetly keyed my radio so that everybody else would know who had shown up, and that I was probably going to be indisposed for the rest of the chase, because our working relationship with the MCB was contentious at best, and Franks was seldom what could be described as help-ful. "What are you doing here, Agent Franks?"

Earl's voice was in my ear. *"Z's out. Somebody call the lawyer."*

But Franks didn't respond to my question. He just went over to the downed monster and thumped it with his shoe. The robe fell open, revealing that the thing was wearing a bulletproof vest beneath. My bullets were mushroomed against it. No wonder it hadn't gone down when I'd shot it. I hated when monsters took advantage of modern technology.

Speaking of which... I went to retrieve the creature's phone, but Franks beat me to it. He snatched it up, glared at me suspiciously. Then he checked the blinking dot on the screen, then looked at the bag, which had ended up on the floor during the struggle. Franks went over, rifled through the pack, and then pulled a little electronic gizmo out of one of the pockets. That must have been the bug.

"Whoever stole this assaulted my men."

"I saw that. I don't know who she was."

"What was Stricken buying?" Franks demanded.

So the MCB hadn't known what the deal they'd been staking out had been for after all. Since MHI really wanted that device, I sure as hell wasn't going to tell the government so they could just seize it and stick it in some crate in a giant dusty warehouse next to the Ark of the Covenant.

"Did you catch Stricken?" Of course, he didn't give me an answer. That didn't even rate his usual cursory response of *classi-fied.* "Is this the part where you can't tell the difference between the good guys and the bad guys and waste a bunch of time messing with us instead of them?"

Franks just glared at me because he was the living embodi-ment of unhelpful grumpiness.

"Fine. We got a tip the auction was some dark magic cult stuff. You know, the usual."

Franks—who had always been supergood at telling when I was lying—cracked his knuckles.

"So this is where you say let's do this the hard way and beat it out of me? Just like old times…Just kidding!" I held up my hands in surrender. I'd just gotten my ass kicked by a lizard man. I really wasn't in the mood to catch a beating from Agent Franks, but who am I to spoil our traditions? "I'll cooperate. But before you arrest me, can I at least get some medical attention here?"

"No." Franks gestured for the door. "Let's go."

Some of Agent Franks' little Fed minions had arrived to clean up the dead reptoid and spin a cover story to the cops and news. Other agents had cuffed my hands behind my back, patted me down, taken my weapons, phone, radio, wallet, and keys and put them into a plastic Ziplock bag, poured some iodine and slapped a bandage on my arm. Then they'd locked me in the back of a black government SUV, where I'd waited, with the windows up and no air conditioning, for about twenty miserable, hot minutes until Franks had come back.

When he got into the SUV, he looked grumpy, but he always looked grumpy, so I couldn't really tell what was going on. "I haven't seen you in forever, and this is the greeting I get? Are these handcuffs really necessary?"

"Policy."

"Am I being detained?"

Franks didn't bother to state the obvious. He started the engine.

"What for? I haven't done anything wrong. We were just doing our jobs. Can I at least have the Cookie Monster head back as a souvenir? I paid an absurd amount of money for that."

"Shut up."

Franks seemed angrier than usual. We drove in silence for a while. Thankfully, Franks turned the air conditioner on but I was still pretty miserable. I think I might have pulled a muscle in my back when the reptoid had slammed me into the wall. But even in my discomfort, the longer we drove, the more sure of it I became: Franks really was seething about something. It said a lot about our relationship that I could tell the difference between regular angry Franks and extra-angry Franks. But what could be infuriating him this time? There was one thing sure to piss him off.

"Please tell me you guys didn't let Stricken get away?"

"Classified."

I laughed at him. "You dumbasses! Are you serious? There were like a hundred of you there. You're the friggin' MCB. You've got satellites and shit! How could you lose an albino scarecrow?"

Franks didn't say anything, but his meathook fists were squeezing the steering wheel so tight I could hear the plastic creak.

"Come on, Franks, after everything we've been through together you can level with me. I mean, seriously, we blew up a squid god together. That's pretty hard core for a team-building exercise. Way better than a ropes course. And remember that time you had a falling out with the government and they put the biggest PUFF bounty ever on your head, and I specifically said nope, MHI's not touching that."

"Because I would've killed you all."

"Maybe." He had done a real number on Grimm Berlin and Paranormal Tactical during his vigilante rampage though. "But *then* we stitched your happy ass back together after you got ripped to shreds. Hell, we're practically friends."

Franks grunted.

"You know how I can tell you like me? You haven't even punched me once yet today. Admit it, we're like BFFs."

Either that was way more persuasive than I thought, or Franks was just annoyed and needed to vent, because he relented and actually used his words. "Stricken's in custody but I'm not allowed to kill him."

"That's got to be really frustrating for you." If there was ever anyone in dire need of extrajudicial killing, it was Stricken. Word on the street was that he had caused the government so much consternation that if they had dropped a Hellfire missile on downtown Atlanta to pop the guy, none of us Hunters would have blinked an eye. "How come?"

"Orders."

"Orders for what? Why would the government possibly want that sneaky bastard taken alive?"

"Classified."

I groaned. Now he was just leaving me hanging out of spite. "Considering your history, I'm surprised you didn't just ignore orders and waste him anyway."

"Things have changed," Franks said.

"What? You're turning over a new leaf? This is a kinder, gentler MCB?"

But he didn't elaborate. Whatever had changed, it had to be one heck of a motivator to keep Franks from simply offing somebody he really didn't like.

The rest of the ride was done in silence, Franks feeling bitter that he couldn't just snap Stricken's scrawny neck, and me wondering why the federal agency that had zero compunction about killing uppity witnesses who talked too much about monsters existing, was keeping that two-timing scumbag alive. But knowing Stricken, he had dirt on everybody important. He was like a supernatural J. Edgar Hoover, only without the cross-dressing.

Our destination was a very unremarkable building. The Atlanta MCB office had no signs. There was nothing to indicate it was even a federal building except for the uniformed security guards manning the gate to the underground parking garage. But the MCB was so small that their local office wasn't even taking up the whole building, just the bottom floor. None of us Hunters actually knew how much staff the MCB had, but I bet the small army of MCB we'd seen earlier must have come in from other offices to help. We drove down a couple levels and parked by an elevator that had a few more guards posted. Amusingly enough, Grant's undercover taco truck was parked there too. I couldn't wait to ask Grant about his exciting new career path.

Franks got out, then opened my door and roughly dragged me out by the arm. Thankfully it was my uninjured one, not that Franks would've cared. One of the guards at the door immediately reported, "The others have already arrived, Agent Franks. They're waiting for you in the briefing room."

I didn't know who *others* entailed, but now I was curious. Franks hadn't harassed me further about what had been in the backpack, and I had no idea what he'd dragged me here for. That sort of confusion was normal when dealing with the notoriously taciturn agent.

From the reaction we got when we walked in, Franks was like a celebrity to these agents. It was Agent Franks the man, myth, and legend. The local Feds stared at Franks like he was some kind of rock star. A few even looked like they wanted to throw their panties on stage.

Despite being a field office of a top-secret government agency dedicated to keeping the existence of the supernatural secret from the world, the interior looked like any other generic law enforcement office, with cubicles, desks, computers, potted plants, and bulletin boards. The main difference was that most of the pics on their Most Wanted wall weren't human. Ten through six were an assortment of charming types I'd never had the pleasure of meeting: some kind of succubus demon woman who was strangely attractive even with the horns and fangs, a West Coast gnome who had to be pretty freaking hard core for a gnome to make the list, a necromancer, a mad scientist, and a scruffy-looking werewolf. Lucinda Hood would surely be disappointed to know she'd been bumped clear back to number five, but the Condition had been relatively quiet for the last year. Number four appeared to be a very surly-looking bullman. The vampire Susan Shackleford would probably be proud to know she'd made the list at number three. Second was some kind of translucent tentacle monster I'd never seen before. And of course, supernatural enemy number one with a bullet was Stricken.

In celebration, somebody had recently drawn a big X across Stricken's face with a Sharpie.

"You know Asag should be the top priority on that list. Right, Franks?"

"I don't set policy." I took that as a yes. Then he shoved me down a hallway.

I couldn't bag on the MCB's list too much since Asag was usually incorporeal, and I'd killed the last body he had been inhabiting. Nobody knew what poor sucker he was currently wearing as a meat suit, so what picture would they put up? A blank sheet of paper? A question mark? He was the immortal embodiment of chaos, dedicated to dismantling reality. It was kind of hard to sum that up on a bulletin board.

Grant Jefferson was waiting outside the door labeled CONFER-ENCE ROOM, still dressed as the tacomeister, though he'd ditched the hairnet, glasses, and apron. It turned out the beard was real. It actually looked good on him, not that I would tell him that. Dude already had a big enough ego as it was.

"Owen." He gave me a nod. I wouldn't go so far as to say it was a respectful one, more like, *ugh, this asshole again.*

"Hey, Grant." I resisted my reflexive knee-jerk desire to be insulting to him, because when I'd been stuck in the Nightmare Realm and my family had been in danger, he had tried to help

Julie get our son back. That sort of thing balanced a lot of scales. "Been a while."

"Yeah. How's the family?"

"Good. Julie's holding down the fort in Alabama. Ray's growing fast. He's a smart and healthy kid."

"Good for you, guys." He almost sounded sincere about that. "And the gang?"

"Milo just had twins."

"That's those Mormons for you." Grant laughed.

"How's Archer? Is he around?"

Franks grew impatient at the annoying humans talking about our annoying human relationships. "Nobody cares." He opened the conference room door and roughly pushed me through. Grant followed us in.

There were four people already seated around the long wooden table, three of whom I didn't know. I recognized the last one though. As an attractive, athletic redhead, she was hard to miss. I grinned when I saw my second favorite werewolf. "Heather!"

"Why the hell is he handcuffed, Franks?" Heather Kerkonen demanded. "This was supposed to be a voluntary invitation."

"Really?" I asked.

"This was easier." Franks shrugged, took out his keys, and unlocked my cuffs.

"And look at his arm!" Heather gestured angrily toward the sloppy bandage and the bloodstains all over my shirt. "He needs medical attention. Is the concept of civil liberties completely alien to you?"

I could answer that one for Franks. "I don't think he's familiar with those, no."

"I was there when they wrote the Bill of Rights," Franks muttered.

"But did you pay attention to what was in it?"

He shrugged.

I rubbed the circulation back into my wrists. It was weird seeing Heather here. She'd served her time, earned her PUFF exemption—which meant that she was one of the only werewolves in the country not legal to kill on sight—but then she'd surprised everybody by deciding to stay on with Special Task Force Unicorn voluntarily to help the other unfortunate monsters who were stuck there.

"Earl didn't mention you were in town."

"He doesn't know."

"Ah . . ." I avoided that minefield. Earl was not exactly enamored with his girlfriend's employers. "Are you here on *official* business?"

"I'm working." Heather left it at that. It wasn't good to talk about her ultra-top-secret job in polite company. Instead she introduced me to the other people around the table. "This is Owen from Monster Hunter International." Then she nodded at the suit sitting at the head of the table. "This is Director Cueto of the MCB."

He had a shaved head, a goatee, and looked a lot more like a trigger puller than the expected paper pusher. I remember hearing that he used to be the MCB's elite strike team commander, so that made sense. "Yeah, I've read up on this one. The name Owen Zastava Pitt seems to show up in a lot of the really annoying reports that land on my desk."

Even if it wasn't meant that way, I took that as a compliment. "Great."

Heather gestured toward the fifty-something woman seated next to her. She struck me as dignified and professional. "This is . . ."

"You can call me Beth." She gave me a wry smile. "Just Beth."

"So what secret government outfit are you with, just Beth?" I asked.

"Heather works for me. You're smart enough to figure out the rest."

Oh shit. This must be the woman who had replaced Stricken as the head of Special Task Force Unicorn. This was the leader of the organization who used Santa's naughty list as a recruitment tool. Monsters who served on her black ops kill squad could eventually become exempt from PUFF bounties and live like normal citizens, and she was the ultimate arbiter of whether those monsters earned that exemption or not. This was the lady who got shit done. The MCB sort of colored in the lines, but from what I'd seen, STFU did pretty much whatever it felt like, all while everybody else pretended they didn't exist.

I'll be honest. Knowing all that, Beth made me kind of nervous.

"Oh, relax, Mr. Pitt. I'm not my predecessor."

"Good."

"I don't play mind games like he did. If I want someone dead, they die." She snapped her fingers. "Just like that. No reason to drag it out." Beth gestured at an empty seat. "Now sit. There's matters of national security to discuss and we're on a timeline."

Well, that was one hell of an invitation. I pulled up a chair. Franks sat down too. Grant looked to his director, but Cueto just shook his head in the negative. Apparently, even though he was Franks' partner, Grant didn't have the rank, clout, or clearance for this particular discussion. Grant quickly left and closed the door behind him.

The last person at the table hadn't been named yet, and he didn't seem inclined to introduce himself either. He was a rather plain-looking, innocuous little bald man in a brown suit. He was old and really short in that hunched-over way. Heather looked at him like she was trying to think of what to say, but then she didn't say anything at all.

So I asked, "Who're you?"

"You may call me Mr. Coslow."

"And you are?"

"None of your concern."

Heather gave me a warning look and a little shake of her head. I trusted her and shut up.

"So why am I here? Because the sooner we get this all cleared up, the sooner I can get some stiches. I'm getting a little woozy here. I just killed a reptoid in hand-to-hand combat."

"Who hasn't? You'll be fine, you big baby." Director Cueto picked up a remote control, pressed a button, and a giant screen lit up on the wall behind him. It was a satellite image of the office park we had been staking out. "So we're all on the same page, approximately an hour ago, the MCB executed Operation Kill Stricken."

"That was the actual name of the operation?" I chuckled. "Who came up with that imaginative title?"

"We were going to use the official computer-generated random op name, which was Husky Duckling, but Franks insisted on this one and he's kinda hard to debate with," Cueto explained.

That was obviously true. It also illustrated why Franks was so bitter that the operation hadn't lived up to its name yet.

"This was the culmination of months of investigation and cooperation between the MCB and ... certain other government agencies, which led to the capture of this man." Cueto pushed another button, and the image changed to that of Stricken. It was the same picture as the one on the Most Wanted board. Gaunt and haunted, yet smug. "The dickbag in question you all have had personal dealings with, so I'll spare you his résumé, most of which is bullshit made up by the CIA from back when he was a spook, because at this point literally nobody knows what the hell this guy's actual deal is. It turns out all the official records on him were replaced with forgeries a long time ago, so nobody in the government even knows what his real name is or where he comes from, so we all call him by his obvious codename instead. The important thing to my bureau is that he's a treasonous piece of shit responsible for the death of my friend, Dwayne Myers, and a bunch of other good agents. Ergo, fuck him."

I was kind of liking Director Cueto's management style.

"Intel indicated that Stricken has been collecting various magical artifacts, for some as-of-yet undetermined, but certainly nefarious, purpose. We set up on this location where we had reason to believe he would be picking up one such item in person. Our raid was forced to launch early due to the arrival of this unknown subject—" Cueto changed the picture again, this time to a photo of the shapeshifter leaping out the window. It was a great action shot. "—who stole the item in question and fled the scene, only to be pursued by members of Monster Hunter International . . . who, I might add, failed to file the proper paperwork with this local MCB office notifying us of any operation in the area." He gave me a pointed look.

"Beats me. You're going to want to talk to our Atlanta team leader, Jay Boone. That's B-O-O-N-E. I'm just the finance guy. I don't do the liaison stuff."

Cueto snorted. "Uh-huh. Did you catch her though?"

I spread my hands apologetically. "How am I supposed to know? Franks took my radio and left me locked in the back of a hot car like an abused dog."

"If your tale of woe becomes any more tragic I fully expect to hear Sarah McLachlan start singing 'In the Arms of an Angel.' Regardless, MCB swept in and apprehended Stricken and his accomplices. Some dumbass cultists and one lizard man got thoroughly ventilated in the process. However, before Stricken could accidentally fall down the stairs repeatedly, we were interrupted by Mr. Coslow here, who informed the MCB that it is absolutely vital for national security interests that Mr. Stricken doesn't suicide himself while in MCB custody, for some inexplicable fucking reason."

All eyes turned to the mystery man, who remained as enigmatic as ever. "Ours not to reason why, ours is but to do and die." Then he tilted his head and acknowledged the director's complaint. "Current projections indicate Stricken is of far more value to mankind alive than dead. During the coming trials, the forbidden knowledge which he has gleaned will surely be of use to us. All must play their part."

"I'm not even going to pretend to wrap my little GS-15 brain around that mystical bullshit," Cueto said. "Beth?"

She obviously didn't like the state of things either, but she shrugged. "Orders are orders."

"So—" I interrupted. "I'm guessing this creepy, bossy guy outranks you seemingly more sane and pragmatic government employees."

"Something like that," Cueto said. "Mr. Coslow is outside the regular chain of command, but he was brought out of retirement, due to recent events, and is acting under the highest authority."

"Should've stayed retired," Franks muttered.

"That was not my decision, nor yours, Agent Franks. We each have our cross to bear." Coslow was tiny and fragile compared to Franks, and from the way these people were acting toward him, he had to have the clearance to know what Franks was. Except he didn't seem to give a shit. Coslow turned to me. "Which brings us to why Mr. Pitt's presence was requested. Before Stricken will cut a deal, he insists on speaking with one of the Chosen."

I blanched. I sure didn't like that term getting tossed around by a bunch of Feds who'd have no issue with dissecting my brain. "I don't know what you're talking about."

"Yes, you do. I am certain of that." Coslow reached beneath the table and pulled out a battered old leather briefcase. He popped it open and took out a handwritten journal. He immediately turned to a page near the middle and scanned down the list. "Yes. There you are. As you can see, you are not alone. You are one of many, for there are a multitude of competing factions. You are simply the one who is most conveniently placed for our needs at this time."

Beth gave me a curious look. Apparently, this was a new revelation to her. "Owen Zastava Pitt's been chosen in the eternal war? Really?"

"Hold on. For the record I am totally, one hundred percent human, so you can buzz off if you're thinking about drafting me into any Unicorn bullshit."

"I didn't say anything like that." Beth tried to appear innocent.

Coslow continued, like his little notebook was a pronouncement from on high. "Agent Franks has been chosen. As has your lovely bride, Mr. Pitt. Though they were both picked by drastically different factions, each has a part to play." He read for a moment. "There are a few others currently in the region... Ah, it appears that Heather Kerkonen also bears the mantle of a Chosen."

"I'm a what now?" Heather asked, obviously confused.

"Your destiny is intertwined with Earl Harbinger, my dear. I thought about calling upon him for this interview since he is in the area, except I fear his animosity toward Stricken would be too great for him to proceed rationally."

"So I take it you've met Earl then," Heather said.

"Yes," said Coslow. "A few times."

Director Cueto was obviously baffled. "Well, I ain't been chosen to do shit but protect the United States of America from the forces of evil so I'm feeling a little left out here, Mr. Coslow. Could you please bring this discussion back to planet Earth now, so I can figure out how to proceed with my prisoner?"

"Of course, Director. Before Mr. Stricken will agree to a deal, he insists on speaking with one of the Chosen. Of those currently available, I believe Mr. Pitt to be the best option."

"You're offering him a *deal*?" Cueto shouted. "Stricken orchestrated the cold-blooded murder of MCB agents!"

"I am sorry, Director. The needs of the many outweigh the needs of the few."

"That's fucking awesome, Mr. Spock, but that don't change the fact he turned monsters loose in MCB headquarters to slaughter my friends and gut-shoot my predecessor."

"Told you you should've let me kill him," Franks said.

"I understand your righteous anger, Director. Yet it is what it is. The Subcommittee agrees with my assessment. If you do not accept it, feel free to turn in your resignation in protest."

Cueto was red-faced, but he stopped yelling. "It'll be a cold day in hell before that happens."

"As Agent Franks can attest, every day in hell is a cold one, Director," Coslow said.

"Fine. Whatever. But let the record show that I think this is a terrible decision and am only doing this under direct orders from the Subcommittee on Unearthly Forces."

"Do not be silly," Coslow said. "There will never be any record of these proceedings. Do you also wish to voice your displeasure, Beth?"

"I think this is a mistake. Stricken turned my organization from a force for good into his personal mafia, and I've spent the last few years trying to repair the damage he did. Stricken doesn't deserve a deal. He deserves a bullet and a shallow grave in a landfill."

"Dissent noted—and immediately disregarded... Very well then. It is settled. We shall proceed. To the interrogation room then. We will listen in on the conversation between Mr. Pitt and Mr. Stricken. It should prove rather enlightening."

"Whoa, hang on." I held up one hand, like I was a schoolkid trying to get called on by the teacher. "My experience with Stricken isn't exactly sunshine and roses either."

"Yet, you remain the least likely of those present to immediately tear his head from his shoulders in a fit of monstrous rage," Coslow said as he stood up.

Heather shrugged. "That's accurate."

Franks grunted. "Eh."

"All of you are forgetting something else. I don't work for you."

"Then on behalf of a grateful nation, thank you for performing this voluntary service for your government, Mr. Pitt. That is the carrot. Or would you prefer I use the stick?"

Coslow wasn't even sort of threatening in how he said that, but I couldn't even imagine what a man who could boss around the MCB and STFU considered a *stick*. "Can I at least get my arm cleaned up first?"

"It is true the egg children of the Lacertus are unclean things." Coslow reached out and touched my shoulder as he passed by. His hand was abnormally cold. "That should handle it for now." Then he opened the door and walked out.

There was a sudden odd tingling in my arm. The best way to describe it was that it felt like there was static in my blood. Then there was an audible electric *snap* beneath my hastily applied bandage. I jumped. A little puff of smoke drifted out from beneath the gauze. I hurried and pulled it off, only to discover the gashes had been cauterized in angry, jagged, burnt lines. It smelled like somebody had just burned a piece of meat, and it hurt like a son of a bitch. *"What the shit, man?"*

But Coslow was already gone.

I'd experienced orc healing magic before, but this was like the microwave oven version to Gretchen's slow cooker. I glared at the others. "What the hell is he?"

"Don't look at me," Beth said. "It's compartmentalized. There's still some things that are classified above my pay grade."

"What he is, I don't know, but his official title is the PUFF Adjuster," Cueto said.

"Bullshit! I've dealt with those before," I said. "They're just the bureaucrats who make calls on one-of-a-kind bounties."

"You're missing the point. Those are PUFF adjusters. He's *the* PUFF Adjuster, like the original guy who started the program."

That didn't make any sense. The Perpetual Unearthly Forces Fund had started during Teddy Roosevelt's administration. I looked between the heads of the MCB and STFU, but Beth just gave Cueto an annoyed look and shook her head, like he needed to shut up.

"All that is an innocuous way of saying he's a mystical weirdo they brought out of cold storage to babysit the Subcommittee again after Stricken nearly tricked those idiots into building an army of monsters." Director Cueto stood up. "Now come on, kid. Let's find out how bad Stricken is about to screw us all over."

Seeing my tax dollars at work kind of sucked.

CHAPTER 4

Stricken was on the other side of the one-way glass, already seated inside the interrogation room. He was dressed the same as when I'd seen him earlier, though they'd taken his tie—probably so he couldn't hang himself with it—and at some point one lens of his funny-colored glasses had gotten cracked. He looked a little worse for wear but considering how badly all the super-dangerous people here wanted to beat him like a pinata until candy came out, Stricken appeared remarkably unharmed.

His hands were chained to a big steel ring on the big steel table and his ankles were chained to a big steel chair. There was an MCB agent standing quietly in each of the four corners of the room, and one more at the door. That seemed like overkill. Stricken wasn't dangerous because of any physical strength. He was dangerous because he was a really smart, connected asshole who had zero qualms about screwing around with evil shit that was better left alone.

I was in the observation room with Franks, Heather, and Beth. The director and the PUFF Adjuster were off printing up copies of Stricken's deal with the government. Once they had those ready to sign, they were going to let Stricken have his requested conversation with a Chosen. Lucky me.

"I'm actually kind of amazed you're going along with all this," I whispered to Franks.

"I don't like it."

"Then why not go on another vigilante rampage? You seem pretty good at those."

Franks just glared at me but didn't say anything. Probably because rampaging was tempting. Guards or not, Franks could have jumped through the window and squished Stricken before anybody here, other than maybe Heather, who wouldn't be that motivated to stop him, would be able to do much about it. I'd only been joking about the *kinder and gentler* MCB, but there was actually something up with Franks. Maybe they had amended his mysterious contract after the whole Nemesis debacle to keep their attack dog on a shorter leash? He was being remarkably restrained all things considered.

Grant came into the room and handed me a T-shirt. "I figured you would want to look more presentable."

My current attire was all torn up and bloody, so that was appreciated. "Thanks." I pulled off my shirt, threw it in the nearby trash can, and took the offered replacement. Which was when I saw it had TRAINEE printed on it and had the MCB's two-headed eagle seal on the back. "You asshole."

Grant laughed. "Deal with it."

I pulled the shirt on. Of course, it was way too small. Franks scowled at me. When we'd sewed him back together last time one of the arms had the MHI logo tattooed on it, so this wasn't nearly as permanent.

"By the way, Pitt," Beth said. "We've all been so distracted by the Stricken question, that you never said how MHI knew about the auction."

"Nope. I didn't."

"Nor did you say anything about what the item was that was so important that both MHI and the reptoids chased the thief across the city to get it."

"I already told Franks it was some dark magic stuff. I don't know the details. Not my department. I'm just the accountant."

"Uh-huh . . ." Beth obviously wasn't buying my BS. "Whatever the item is, it was important enough to Stricken to get him to risk showing his face in public. Having it in our possession might provide leverage. Heather, call your boyfriend."

Heather groaned. "Do I have to?" Except she didn't have to wait for her boss's orders to know that her protest was in vain.

"Fine. I know, I know. National security." She got out her phone. "Mind if I do this in private? You know how Earl feels about this organization."

"Put him on speaker," Beth said, with just a hint of malicious glee. "I can stand my ground."

Heather hit the call button. "This is a terrible idea."

Earl picked up on the third ring. *"Hey, Heather. What's going on?"*

"There's something I needed to talk to you about."

"Can I call you back?" From the background noise it sounded like he was in a moving car. *"I'm kind of busy on a case right now."*

"You're trying to find someone in Atlanta."

"How'd you know? Wait... This personal, or business?"

"Hello, Mr. Harbinger," said Beth. "You are on speaker."

Earl was quiet for a moment. *"Mrs. Flierl. To what do I owe this incredible annoyance? Let me guess, is this little thief I'm tracking one of your slaves?"*

"No. She's not one of mine, though I am very interested in speaking with her now. However, you need to get one thing straight. We're under new management. I'm not like Stricken. My people are *not* slaves. They're volunteers, willingly serving their country in exchange for the opportunity to earn their PUFF exemption."

"Sure they are. I'll be sure to pass that on to all my buddies who died in involuntary servitude while we were doing dirt for Uncle Sam... Dammit, Heather, it's one thing for you to be soft-hearted enough to try and help their captives, but do not drag me back into their foolishness. I tried to warn you that you can't trust these assholes. We can talk about this when you're in Alabama again. I'm hanging up."

"Wait, Earl, it's important."

Earl really must have loved Heather because he stuck around. *"Damn it. Fine. Talk."*

"We've got Owen here. He's safe."

"Hey, Earl," I said. "The government's about to cut a deal with Stricken."

"What?"

Heather covered her phone. "That's not helping!"

"Have you people lost your gawdamned minds?" Earl bellowed. *"That bastard let an entire hotel full of Hunters get sucked into*

nightmare world to justify a budget increase, and you're cutting him a deal? What's he get? Time served? Witness protection?"

"It's complicated," Heather said. "And it wasn't our call. Stricken's a bigger monster than any of the real monsters who worked for him, but there's a lot going on I can't tell you about yet. These are orders from on high. They think they need his expertise for something big. Just listen, please. It's important. Did you catch the thief?"

"I don't think I'd tell your boss even if I had."

"What was Stricken trying to buy?"

"Sorry, babe. I ain't saying nothing to Unicorn. So don't even push, because me not answering will just piss us both off. If your boss wants anything else, she can get a warrant."

Beth cut in. "There's no time for that. Since I'm here at the MCB regional office with their director, how about instead I pressure him into yanking MHI's charter, seizing your assets, and putting you out of business again?"

"Beth!" Heather exclaimed. "That's not right!"

"No, but it will be necessary if Mr. Harbinger continues to put his pride ahead of the safety of this planet."

"Oh, now you did it," Heather warned her.

It was obvious that particular threat had really set Earl off. *"Lady, who are you to judge the safety of jack shit? The guy who used to sit in your chair would've let loose a bunch of demons if it hadn't been for Agent Franks having the balls to go to war with the entire government."*

I looked over at Franks as Earl said that, and I swear, maybe, just maybe, for a moment, Franks showed some small bit of pride at being recognized for that by someone like Harbinger. But then it was gone, and it was back to his regular old face of stone. I'd probably imagined it.

"Do you think I care about your threats right now? My people spent a year freezing our asses off north of the Arctic Circle fighting a horde of underground cannibal mutants, and I didn't see shit for support from you people that whole time. Asag sent the thing that killed my son and kidnapped my blood, and I still don't know who I'm more afraid of, the lunatic chaos god, or the ineptitude of my own fucking government. I'll never understand why Heather decided to waste her time trying to save you fools from yourselves, but that's her decision, not mine. Unicorn can bite my hairy ass. I'm calling your bluff, lady. You saw the body count stats from the

last time MHI got shut down, and I don't think you're the kind
of monster who wants that on her hands. Goodbye."

That time he did hang up.

Well, that had certainly been uncomfortable for the rest of us.

Heather put her phone away. She was obviously not happy,
but also not at all surprised. "I tried to warn you. This is a
contentious subject for the two of us."

"It was maybe a little obvious," I said.

I'd also heard Earl vent about it several times. He thought
the world revolved around Heather, but he hated her job with a
passion and couldn't for the life of him understand why she'd
stick around and try to help the people who'd taken her away
from him and forced her to serve on a black ops monster death
squad. But then again, I'd also heard Heather lament about how
Earl just didn't understand that she wasn't doing this for STFU,
she was doing this because she saw herself in the other poor
monsters who were trapped there, who hadn't had someone like
Earl to teach them how to control themselves enough to coexist
with humanity. Basically, the whole situation sucked, and I didn't
have any answers, not that either of the stubborn werewolves
would have listened to my advice anyway.

Beth didn't care about any of that. She had a black ops monster
death squad to run after all. "Don't worry, Heather. Harbinger
was right. I was bluffing. Rocky relationship with the authorities aside, MHI makes a difference. If Harbinger doesn't want to
cooperate, I'll put my people on it. We'll find the shapeshifter
ourselves. Unless of course, you want to just make life easy for
everyone and spill the beans, Pitt?"

"Sorry. I trust Earl's judgment way more than you people."

I hadn't meant that reply as an insult to Heather. Honestly,
I'd not even thought of it that way, but when I saw the look on
her face, I could tell that she'd taken it personally, like I was
saying she liked Unicorn more than her partner.

Before I could say anything else, the door opened and Mr.
Coslow stuck his bald head in. "The paperwork is ready. This
is a reminder to everyone that Stricken is not to be harmed or
else there will be *severe* repercussions." He looked pointedly at
Franks, and then at Heather . . . and then back at Franks again
for good measure. "Come with me, Mr. Pitt."

❖   ❖   ❖

We entered the interrogation room and Stricken scoffed when he saw me.

"When I made my list of demands, this sure wasn't the Chosen I was expecting you to scrounge up, Harold."

Harold must have been Coslow's first name. "It meets the letter of the law," the PUFF Adjuster said.

"Technically correct is the best kind of correct," Stricken agreed. "Oh, well. A deal is a deal, but I was hoping for one of the smarter ones."

Ten seconds in and I already wanted to kill him. No wonder they hadn't sent Franks or one of the werewolves. "Oh, fuck off, Stricken. I forgot to bring my Mensa card to show you. I don't want to be here either."

He lifted his narrow hands and waved his spidery fingers so the chains would make a rattling noise. "I think I've got it worse."

"And deservedly so. I will admit seeing you as a prisoner makes me smile."

"If you're still capable of smiling, then I take it Harold hasn't told you what's in my deal. You are going to be so disappointed when I leave here a free man. It turns out I'm too pretty for jail."

"That's okay. I figure as many powerful things as you've pissed off, something is bound to pop you sooner or later. You're a dead man walking."

"Yet I'm still walking out of here. Like you've got room to talk about making powerful things angry though, Mr. I blew up the Dread Overlord and woke up Asag so he'll kill us all." Even in chains, Stricken was still acting like he was the one holding all the cards. "You know what? Never mind, Harold. I withdraw my objection. The living embodiment of Monster Hunter hubris will do *perfectly* for this. Welcome to the team, Pitt."

"I am not on your team."

"It's like they say, Pitt: There is no I in team. But in my experience there are often a bunch of suckers who get themselves drafted." Stricken nodded at Coslow. "He'll do."

"Good," Coslow snapped. "I find mortal attempts at witty banter tiresome."

Mortal? Stricken noticed my confusion and smirked, because as usual, he knew more about what was going on than I did. He didn't even need to say anything to rub it in.

Mr. Coslow glanced around. With so many guards in the

small room, it was really crowded. "All of you, wait outside."
Mortal, immortal, amortal, whatever he was, the MCB agents
were obviously scared of Coslow and happy to leave. Once the last
one closed the door behind him, Coslow said, "Let us proceed."

I pulled up one of chairs on the opposite side of the table.
Coslow took the other one. He moved with authority. It was all
business as he opened his briefcase and pulled out a fat stack of
papers. He dropped them in front of Stricken, and then placed
a plain disposable pen on top. "Sign here."

Stricken looked at the paperwork but didn't touch it. Then
he turned back to me. "Nice shirt."

"I always need more rags for cleaning guns. Why am I here?"

"You're here because I need someone to take care of something I probably won't be able to now because of my current
predicament. There aren't that many people in the world who
can actually make a difference at this point, and you're the one
Harold found, so now you're getting stuck with a new assignment. We need to get on the same page and fast. Speaking of
pages, seriously, nobody told you what's in this agreement at all,
did they? Because if they had, you'd probably be torqued. I've
seen your work. Men like you are the reason they invented anger
management classes."

"These government types never tell me anything."

"Well, I've certainly been guilty of that myself at times. At
STFU we used to call our assets mushrooms, because we kept
them in the dark and fed them shit." He looked past me to his
reflection in the mirror. "Hey, Red. If you're listening, screwing
you over was nothing personal."

"Time is of the essence, Mr. Stricken," Coslow said, annoyed.
"Read over it if you must, but your demands are all there. We
need to proceed."

"Hold your horses, Harold. I get to talk to Owen here in
private first."

"Very well." Despite his decrepit appearance, the PUFF Adjuster
didn't stand up like an old man. There were no arthritic winces
or creaking knees. "You have ten minutes." Coslow walked to the
door, knocked, and one of the MCB agents let him out.

Stricken watched him go. "Amazing. You don't even know
what our illustrious adjuster really is, do you?"

"I'm sure he's some malevolent or ambivalent supernatural

something or other, either working for or loosely allied with the stupid Feds."

"That's remarkably close actually. You want me to tell you the juicy details about old Coslow?"

"Is this the sort of thing that if I know, it'll probably put my life in danger because some other shadow government douchebag decides"—I made quote marks with my fingers—"*I know too much*?"

"Well, obviously. But learning the mysteries, how things really tick, what's really happening, that's half the fun of this life. Knowledge is power." Stricken reached out and tapped the signature sheet. "This agreement is a perfect example that if you know the right things, and you offer those things to the right people at the right time, you can literally get away with murder."

"Like how you murdered Myers?"

"Are you trying to get Franks to shoot me through the glass? I actually respected Dwayne a lot, but sometimes sacrifices have to be made."

"Gee whiz. I can't imagine why they sent me in here instead of Franks."

Stricken leaned back in his chair and grinned. "Yeah, that pile of parts can certainly hold a grudge. Now, onto business. I wasn't just blowing smoke about this agreement. I need you to know what's in it, what they're willing to offer, despite my multitude of crimes and my troubled past because it will demonstrate a few things." He began to tick them off on his long fingers. "One, just how desperate they really are. Two, that what I'm about to tell you is the real deal. And three, that as bad as you think I am, what I've done has actually been for the greater good."

"I seem to recall Martin Hood telling me something about the greater good once, and how his conquering mankind was really doing us a favor, because the Old Ones doing it would be so much worse."

"Marty was delusional, but he wasn't entirely wrong either. But no, this is different. I'm not trying to hand the Earth over on a silver platter to one cosmic tyrant or another in exchange for a more merciful brand of slavery. War's coming. You know it. I know it. Only, unlike Marty, I'm not big on surrender. I don't want man to just survive. I'm in it to fucking win it. I want to destroy these things so badly it sends a message across the galaxy that mankind is not to be trifled with ever again. I know you feel the same way. So while everybody else gets squeamish, it's time for men like us to rise to the occasion and do what's necessary."

I looked over the gaunt figure and scoffed. "We're nothing alike."

"You keep telling yourself that, Owen. But I know what you've done, the calls you've had to make, and the people you've left behind to do it." My face must have betrayed my reaction at that, because Stricken immediately followed with, "Oh, don't get mad at me. I say that as a compliment. When it really counts, you put the mission first. That's an admirable trait."

"If you're admiring me, I need to reexamine my life choices."

"It's one trait of many. Don't worry. I think the rest of you is garbage. Why one of the factions picked you as their champion, I'll never be able to fathom. You're too merciful. You're too forgiving. You're too soft. You've got the capacity to be effective, but you let human frailty hold you back."

He could spare me the moral sanctimony. "Says the asshole who has had a few of his insane plots spiral out of control, like those things you created trying to copy Franks. Get to the point, Whitey."

"That's hurtful." Stricken feigned being wounded. "You know how I wound up like this, Pitt? I used to be healthy, fit like you wouldn't believe. I waltzed through Ranger School. I could run a marathon every weekend after banging hot chicks all week. I was one good-looking dude. But you know what happened to me?"

"Whatever you tell me will probably be a lie anyway."

"That's fair. But cross my heart, hand on a Bible, this is the truth."

I had a sneaky suspicion that if Stricken actually touched a Bible, it would burn his hand. "I was guessing the whole sickly pallor thing, and your trying-too-hard codename, was because you sold your soul and now you're cursed for it."

"Actually, that's not too far off." Stricken paused. "Let's never mind the details then. The important thing isn't the how, or the who, it's the *why*. I did this to myself. I was willing to sacrifice my life, my health, some pussies would say my humanity, all that jazz, and I gave it up without hesitation in order to save the world."

"You saved the world?" I tried not to let my voice drip with incredulity. I probably failed.

"I did. What? You think you're the first or only person who's ever done that? Different type of threat than yours, but this shit happens all the time. Join the fucking club. We have a newsletter. Only when I did it, it left my body ruined. It turned me into this, a husk of the man I once was, while your lucky ass got a tune-up from the Old Ones, which is pretty unfair if you ask me. But that's neither here nor there. I got started down this path because there were things that needed doing, but far too often the men in charge have the spine of a pool noodle. If we wait around for the powers that be to solve the problem, we're all doomed. Asag might not be as big and flashy as what we've seen before, but he's far more clever, willing to play the long game, and that makes him far more of a threat."

I couldn't actually disagree with that take but agreeing with the likes of Stricken about anything made me feel icky, so I looked at the wall clock. "You've got a few minutes left. Get to the point."

"The point is, I never stopped doing what needed doing. Sometimes that means taking risks, which leads to unfortunate accidents like the aforementioned demonic super soldiers. Whoops. My bad. Can't make an omelet without breaking a few eggs."

He was so flippant about that incident, I was a little surprised Franks didn't walk in and strangle him to death. "That's one hell of an omelet."

"My action hero days are in the distant past, but I was smart. I could see things coming that nobody else could. Eventually I ended up in charge of the Task Force, which for someone like me, was Christmas morning. All those wonderful toys." For a moment, Stricken seemed positively gleeful reminiscing about his old job. "Running STFU was awesome. Though some unfortunate decisions were made and I lost my job, I've still kept doing what needed doing."

"What's that exactly?"

"Preparing the way for you Chosen folks to get the job done when the time comes. I've been gathering intel, laying the groundwork for future operations, stockpiling the special weapons mankind will need in order to beat this chaotic fuckstick, and most importantly of all, building alliances."

I had to admit, my curiosity was piqued. "Where are these weapons?"

"Someplace safe."

"What kind of alliances?"

"Asag eventually wants to tear apart the entire universe down to the molecular level, which is generally frowned upon by everything that lives here. You'd be surprised some of the groups that are willing to fight him, or maybe not. You've met a few of them."

I thought back to some of the things Julie had told me about her rescue mission to Europe. "Susan . . ."

"Among others. Your mother-in-law is kind of a badass."

I bolted to my feet, reached across the table, grabbed him by the lapels, and jerked him out of his seat. "If you had anything to do with my son's kidnapping—"

Someone immediately started banging on the other side of the mirror.

"Easy there, big fella. I had nothing to do with that."

The door flew open and MCB agents rushed inside, ready to shoot me for endangering their prize. It wasn't the first time Feds had pointed their guns at me, and let's be honest, it probably wouldn't be the last. "We were just talking." I let go of Stricken and he slunk back down into his chair.

Mr. Coslow was standing behind the agents. "I do not have patience for foolishness, Mr. Pitt. Get me my signature. The clock is ticking, Mr. Stricken." Then they closed the door and left.

Stricken adjusted his wrinkled jacket and continued like I hadn't been about to body-slam him through the foundation. "Asag offered your kid to get Susan to work *for* him, instead of working *with* me. She's a bit of a psycho grandma. But before you get all in a huff . . . you've fought against her: would you rather have her with us or against us during the final battle for the fate of the world?"

"Trick question. I'd prefer her dead before we get there. Keep talking."

"Glad to. It's not often I get to wax poetic about my life's work. I'm rather proud of it. But wait, there's more." He said that like he was a infomercial pitchman. "Even better than having the second most dangerous master vampire in the world on our side, how about the Fey?"

"I'm not convinced there is an *our side,* but you expect me to believe the trickiest bastards in existence would help us? Are you serious?"

"As a heart attack. I've got some courts on my side, and more I'm working on. And there's others. Those are just the tip of the iceberg of what I can bring to the table. We're going to need a real big tent by the time I get done."

His alliances sounded like a darker version of what MHI had been trying to do with other groups of Hunters. So what Stricken was saying sounded plausible. Insane, but plausible.

"For proof that you should believe the words coming out of my mouth, I give you exhibit A." He reached out and patted the stack of paper again. "In here, all my multitude of sins are forgiven, I get full immunity, and will be given a positively obscene amount of money to become a special consultant for the United States government. When the people with access to all the juiciest secret intel in the world believe in me enough to offer me this sweetheart deal in exchange for my cooperation, literally one minute after I've been taken into custody, that's saying something, because I've done some *evil shit* in my time."

I raised my voice. "Hey, Director Cueto. You strike me as an honest guy. Knock on the glass twice if this weasel is telling me the truth about what's in this phonebook."

Thump thump.

Well, crap. "Okay, Stricken. That's pretty convincing. Good for you. You've hoodwinked the President. Makes me glad I didn't vote for the guy."

"Aw, that's cute how you still think voting matters."

Since we were in the offices of an agency that existed to lie and commit fraud, he probably had a point there. "So you got a deal. Now why did you need to talk to someone like me?"

"Well, Pitt, there's *two* reasons for that." He extended an abnormally long finger to start a new count. "Number one, there is a massive problem looming that only someone of your unique nature can handle—or one of the other Chosen, should your dumb ass get killed in the process. It's not a world-ending kind of threat, yet, but it's a make-life-really-uncomfortable-for-a-lot-of-innocent-people problem, and by uncomfortable, I mean violently dead. Regardless, it's Chosen business. I was just going to nip this little problem in the bud myself. I'd *prefer* to handle it myself, because I don't trust you clowns to not screw it up, but as you can see, I'm currently indisposed."

"Bullshit. You don't care about innocent people dying."

He shrugged his narrow shoulders. "True, that hero nonsense is more your thing. But stopping this crisis would be a favor for one of those aforementioned potential allies, who would be a huge help down the line. I'll fill you in on the details later, but it's nothing that one of Sir Isaac Newton's Ward Stones couldn't handle. Which was why I was trying to buy this one off those stupid reptoids."

So much for me not telling the Feds about what MHI was trying to steal. Ward Stones were so incredibly rare and super valuable, I could only imagine that Beth was making a very frantic phone call right this very instant.

Stricken must have caught the pained expression on my face. "The really sucky thing, Pitt? My former coworkers are probably losing their minds right now. They'd kill for another Ward. A little-known fact is that the strategically placed one that protects Washington DC is dying. It's running out of juice. And the other one we have in inventory, belonging to the Department of Defense? Well, they don't dare move it because it's the only thing keeping something ancient and super nasty bottled up under Cheyenne Mountain, which is the real reason we built the base there to begin with. But that's *super* classified." He put finger number one to his lips and went, "Shhhh."

That was probably one of those secrets that would get me killed one of these days. Wards were strategic assets. Defensively, undead or unearthly beings couldn't cross their boundary without exploding. Offensively, they were the only thing mankind had which could obliterate a Great Old One. Except the secret to making them had been lost to time. What was out there was all that was left, and there hadn't been very many to begin with.

"The lizard people found this one, lost and abandoned, deep underground somewhere. I was going to use it to do something good... Don't laugh. It's true. But if Unicorn gets it first, it's going straight to DC instead, and all those poor orphans and widows and kittens will get mulched. But that's on you now. It's out of my hands, and thousands of people are going to die... unless, of course, MHI agrees to take care of it. I'd sleep a lot better if you promise me you'll handle this problem."

"Fine. I'll look into it."

Stricken had a sly, evil grin. "Excellent." He raised his voice. "I assume you heard him say that, Harold."

"You're such a douche," I said, as the realization sank in that I was getting dragged into someone else's nonsense once again. But if there was even a tiny chance that what Stricken was saying was true, I couldn't let a bunch of innocents get massacred and not at least try to stop it.

"Just a heads-up in the meantime, and this part is really important. The auction contract for this Ward specifies that if the seller failed to deliver the item, there's an entity on retainer to punish whatever party broke the deal. Your wife damaged the Dark Market's reputation so badly that they're adding free insurance to every deal they broker now. And by insurance, I mean they've got some incredibly deadly beings contracted to handle any problems that pop up. So that little scamp who stole my rock, she's about to get wrecked. If she'd just waited until after I had it in my possession, free and clear, she'd be off the hook. But now? This thing will not stop. You're going to need to find her before it crawls up from hell, because once it's on the trail, things are going to get really messy."

"What kind of entity are we talking about here?"

"Powerful shit that even I don't understand what-all it can do. There's thirteen of them to choose from. Which one will get called up, I can't guess, but all of them are bad. These things are the unliving embodiment of the word *relentless*."

"Call it off."

"I would if I could. I can't. It's called a Drekavac. Look it up."

"I will. You could have just sent me an email about all this and spared me from this interrogation." I shoved the agreement closer to him. "Now sign your stupid form so I can go back to work."

Stricken picked up the cheap pen in his left hand and clicked it, poised to sign, but then he paused. "Do you realize, Pitt, that this isn't just mere ink and paper? An agreement made with Harold watching isn't just symbolic. Signing my name to something created by the PUFF Adjuster would be just as eternally binding as making a contract with a Fey queen."

"Good to know. Luckily for me I'm not the one who has to choose between it or the electric chair."

"How morbid!" Stricken grinned. "Only you forget, Pitt, I said there were *two* reasons I demanded to speak to a Chosen before I'd sign this thing."

"What's the second one then?"

Stricken extended finger number two. "For the longest time I thought I wanted my old job back, but I've really enjoyed being freelance, so I'm not signing shit. I just needed to buy some time for my associate to get here." He raised his hand toward the mirror, then he put finger number one down, so that he was flipping off everyone on the other side of the glass. As he did so, a wall of thick black smoke suddenly rose up behind his chair, coalescing into two giant bat wings. "So long."

A form rose through the smoke. It was a voluptuous woman, only with horns, fangs, and a tail. She wrapped her wings around Stricken's shoulders, protectively covering him. Franks or Heather immediately fired through the glass, except Stricken and the succubus vanished in a flash of fire. The wave of heat knocked me from my chair before I was blinded by smoke.

CHAPTER 5

The humans who had been caught near Stricken's demonic smoke bomb exit lurched, coughing into the MCB bullpen. The interrogation room had gotten so thoroughly gassed that it had activated the fire alarm. I felt like I'd been flash-banged and my borrowed MCB T-shirt wasn't a very good gas mask.

The bullpen area was much less chaotic, but the whole place stank of sulfur and it was still hard to see. Luckily, they must have disabled the fire sprinklers to keep from frying all the computers, because at least we weren't getting drenched. The MCB agents who hadn't been nearly suffocated were scrambling, weapons out, thinking they were under attack.

Figuring that smoke rises, I found a corner and laid down on the carpet to try and catch my breath. While lying there, I realized that the flash from the demon had been actual fire because my eyebrows and arm hair were singed and crinkly. I felt like I had a sunburn.

Franks probably had armored lungs or something because inhaling all that smoke hadn't done anything to hamper his ability to shout orders. "Jefferson! Do you have Stricken's signal?"

Grant ran to a laptop that was open in one of the cubicles and started clicking buttons.

"You stuck a tracker on Stricken?" I asked between bouts of coughing.

"Of course. Four of them. There's no way he'll..." Grant trailed off and stared at the screen. "I've got nothing, Franks."

Franks stood there, wearing an expression of absolute disgust on his big square mug. I realized that he was holding a chunk of the table from the interrogation room in his hand, the steel of which was still glowing orange from being magically sheared through. So much for the chains.

Cueto was leaning against a cube wall, tie undone, wheezing. "How'd that thing breach our perimeter? Franks!"

"Yes, sir."

"What was that?"

"Unknown."

I was a little surprised he said that, because Franks was normally super observant. But he had been busy throwing his body through glass after his bullets hadn't worked so maybe he hadn't seen her face. I'd been closer and must have gotten a better look. I pointed at the last picture on the MCB's Most Wanted wall, of the demon woman with the fangs. "That's her right there." I hacked up some brimstone phlegm and spit on the MCB's carpet.

"Maybe," Franks muttered.

"No. I'm sure. You're probably going to want to bump her up a few spots from number ten."

"Damn it," Cueto said. "Alert every agent in the city. Lanoth is in league with Stricken. We don't know how far her kind can shadow-walk carrying a passenger. They might still be near. Get a sniper team on the roof and scramble the chopper. Check the footage from every camera. And somebody open some windows already!"

The director must have forgotten this particular MCB office was in a basement. It took me a second to pick Beth from STFU out of the chaos because she'd wrapped a scarf around her face to filter the smoke. She was only a few feet away. Her ninja skills must have been second only to Gretchen.

"Where's Heather?" I asked her.

"She ran outside to use her nose," Beth said. "If she catches a scent, she'll call for backup."

Considering taking Stricken alive had already resulted in him escaping once today, I very much doubted she'd be waiting for backup. If Heather found Stricken, she'd pluck his heart out, *then* call it in. "Good luck with that."

"We paid those stupid elves to draw their stupid magic runes on all our offices to prevent this kind of invisible magic portal bullshit!" Cueto roared. "How did a succubus get in here? I want answers!"

I sure hoped those weren't the same elves MHI used. "Did any of those elven contractors ever happen to work for STFU while Stricken was in charge?" I asked Beth quietly.

"We used European elves as contractors. They're snoots, but their work is usually solid. The American ones are usually a little too yee-haw, fly by the seat of their pants for us. But if Stricken learned their runes he could have taught his people how to get around them. I'll go check on that. You should stick around, Pitt. MCB isn't done with you yet. If MHI knew there was a Ward up for grabs and didn't call it in, there's going to be hell to pay." The head of Unicorn stomped off to make some calls.

According to Heather, her current boss was actually a moral and decent person, so basically Stricken's total opposite. However, Beth still worked for the uncaring federal leviathan, and I didn't want to wait around to get yelled at or worse. So as soon as Beth was out of sight, I got up and headed for the exit. The MCB was awfully distracted so it would be a real shame not to take advantage of that.

I saw the evidence bag with all my stuff in it, but it was over on the desk next to where Grant and Franks were checking camera views. There was no way to grab the bag without being seen. Everything in it was replaceable except for the pistol. It had sentimental value because Julie had given it to me and we'd been through a lot together. But it was slip out now, or risk getting tied up in Fed BS for the rest of forever while the Ward got farther and farther away. So I walked out.

The air was much more breathable in the parking garage... except the mysterious PUFF Adjuster was standing there, briefcase in hand, obviously waiting for me. Oddly enough, even though he'd been in the hallway where all the smoke had vented, he looked completely unfazed.

"Going somewhere, Mr. Pitt?"

"Yeah, home. I'm not under arrest. I did what you people asked me to. So I'll take the thanks of my grateful country and get out of your way while you guys handle your fugitive business."

"Of course." Coslow looked me over slowly. I couldn't tell if he was disapproving of me in particular or just mildly irritated in general. It could go either way. "Will you be keeping the promise you made to Mr. Stricken?"

I was still a little flustered and oxygen deprived. "What promise?"

"You agreed to deal with the specific events Stricken alluded to. Events which would necessitate a Ward Stone in order to prevent a tragedy of unknown nature. I observed you, speaking on behalf of Monster Hunter International, entering into an agreement with Mr. Stricken. I shall check my notes." He reached into his jacket, pulled out his little notebook, and flipped it open to a page... which appeared to have an entire handwritten transcript of my conversation with Stricken in it already somehow.

"That's a nifty trick," I muttered.

Coslow didn't look up from his notes. "Yes. Here it is. You said, I quote, *Fine, I will look into it.*" He put the notebook away. "That would appear to be a verbal contract. A gentleman honors his contracts. I take contracts very seriously, Mr. Pitt."

"I bet you do. You seemed proud of that big one you printed out for Stricken, but last I saw it had gotten blown all over the room and most of the pages had caught fire." I didn't know *what* Coslow was, with the magical healing and Stricken's vague utterances, but there's only so many times a guy can get kicked around by cosmic forces before he becomes pretty jaded. "I owe you nothing and I owe Stricken even less. Assuming he wasn't just lying his ass off as usual, and there is actually a problem, I'll handle it as I see fit. Now have a nice day, Mr. Coslow. I'm out of here."

I began walking past him.

"Wait, Mr. Pitt."

I paused, sighed, then turned around. "Yeah?"

The PUFF Adjuster was giving me a curious look, brow knitted in confusion. "Your involvement was not part of our initial projections concerning this particular situation. Nor is this the first time your presence was an unforeseen variable in one of our calculations. Once again, it appears you are a *complication.*"

He said the word like it was the most unsavory thing ever. The PUFF Adjuster seemed to be the sort of man...wizard... entity...whatever who really liked to keep things *orderly.* "What's that supposed to mean?"

"I do not know yet. Now that you are involved, we will recalculate accordingly before proceeding. The Subcommittee thanks you for your aid." He popped open his briefcase, reached inside, and pulled out the clear plastic evidence bag with all my stuff in it. "Allow me to return your property."

I took the bag from him. Sure enough, inside was my pistol, phone, and wallet. It was the same bag that I'd seen on Grant's desk while I'd been walking out the door a minute ago, except Coslow had already been out here. "How—" Except when I looked back up, Mr. Coslow had simply vanished into thin air. I'd not heard him move, and the nearest car he could have been hiding behind was like twenty feet away, and he didn't strike me as a sprinter. "Never mind."

In this job, when things get weird you just have to roll with it, so I hurried up the ramp toward daylight.

Once I was free of the smoking federal building, I called in and they sent Hertzfeldt to pick me up with the van. The crew hadn't had any luck catching the shapeshifter. I found out that when Trip had heard my gunshots he had rushed back to help me, but the Feds were already there, so he'd gone after the shapeshifter again. The delay had cost him, so the thief was long gone. Without the big red backpack to spot, Milo and Skippy had come up with zilch. Earl had caught up with Trip and used his werewolf senses to follow her scent for a few more blocks, but lost her in another garage, where she'd either had a backup vehicle stashed, or had hot-wired herself a new ride.

The other Hunters had converged at the Atlanta team's HQ, which was in a nondescript warehouse not too far from the airport. The team room had been the upstairs office, which they'd made into something like a comfy living room, with lots of couches and a ping-pong table. When Hertzfeldt and I walked in, most of the Hunters were sitting around, sullenly trying to figure out their next move. Boone was up front, standing before a great big map of the city, handing out assignments of where we should check next.

Earl wasn't there. From my Alabama team, Trip Jones, Holly Newcastle, and Milo Anderson were there. Skippy, of course, who was uncomfortable around humans, was off doing Skippy things. The rest of Boone's team consisted of James Mundy, who'd been an African bush pilot; and a married couple, the Groffs, both of whom had been Marines; their doc, Kathy Sherlock; and of course Gregorius, the crusty old SF vet, whom I'd known since Natchy Bottom. Hertzfeldt was the only Newbie, so it was an experienced crew.

There was a brief laugh at my stupid MCB shirt, but then it got pretty glum again, and then it went back to sulking and drinking all of Boone's beer. Hunters *hate* losing. Anybody who was okay with losing would make a terrible Hunter. One tiny girl had made our group of badasses look like a bunch of chumps. There hadn't been any reptoids to tail back to their hidey-hole, so even though the city was down two of the carnivorous bastards, there were probably a dozen more in their tribe still out there eating hobos. Then I got to make everything worse by telling the others about how the MCB had managed to let the biggest scumbag in the world escape.

After I gave everybody the quick recap of everything I'd witnessed, Gregorius summed up what all of us were feeling by saying, "Those damned idiots. They should have put a bullet in Stricken the second they confirmed it was him."

The rest of the Hunters all nodded along at that. "I'm kicking myself for not putting a sniper on a roof across the street," Boone muttered. "We could have just popped Stricken and done the world a favor."

"We can't just go around assassinating human beings in the streets," Trip said. "Even Stricken."

"Eh...Can't we though?" As usual, Holly was the most morally flexible of us all. She had a heart of gold for those who deserved it, and zero mercy for those who didn't.

"Franks really wanted to kill Stricken," I explained. "But there was this weird dude there from the government who wouldn't let him. MCB and STFU were both deferential to him. Name of Coslow."

"What?" Boone nearly choked on his beer. "Harold P. Coslow?"

"I didn't catch his middle name, but probably. Stricken called him Harold."

Boone was downright flabbergasted. "He's still *alive*?"

"He looks like he's a hundred and I didn't take his pulse, but yeah. Director Cueto said he was the PUFF adjuster, but the other adjusters I've dealt with have just been regular government employees. This Coslow guy was weird." I didn't like how Boone seemed a little unnerved by that name. Boone was old-school MHI and didn't shake easy. I looked over at Milo, who'd been around longer than the rest of us; not that Milo was that old, it was just he'd been with MHI since he was a teenager. I was surprised to see that Milo had gotten really pale all of a sudden. And since Milo's a freckly redhead anyway, that meant he'd gone downright ghostly on us. "What?"

"You didn't make the Adjuster angry at you? Did you, Z? Because that would be, like, superbad."

"Of course not. I don't think so. Why would you say that?"

"Well, you've kinda got this way of antagonizing people—"

"No. Not me." I already knew I was an abrasive dick who had problems with authority. "I mean why is everybody scared of this Coslow guy? Stricken offered to tell me, but he probably would've just lied anyway. *What* is Coslow?"

Milo shrugged. "Beats me. But he's been around a *long* time."

"Hell if I know either," Boone said. "I was a Newbie last time MHI dealt with him. He was the ultimate authority setting bounties on anything unique we caught back in those days, but beyond that, there are some stories about him that are downright unnerving. I don't think anyone has seen Coslow in decades."

"I figured he was dead or retired." Milo seemed to find all this rather exciting. "But in the old days, the rumor was he only showed up on cases where things could get really catastrophic, like some kinda herald of doom. Sam Haven once told me that he thought Coslow was actually a mummy who could suck your soul out through your eye sockets—"

"Then government work sounds like a great fit for him," Holly interrupted. "Sorry to ruin the speculation, but we need to get back to catching this shape-changing bitch." Holly was pragmatic like that.

"Yeah, any luck identifying her?" I asked.

"She's not anyone that's come up on our radar before," Boone said. "But if she's from around here, or especially a new creature in town, she must have come to someone's or something's attention. I was just handing out assignments. We're going to split up and shake every tree around Atlanta to see what falls out."

"Peaches, probably," Milo said helpfully.

Boone sighed. "Somebody has to know who this shapeshifter is. Groffs, you've got the gnomes."

"Aw, come on," the male Groff groaned. His beard rivaled Milo's, to the point that he looked like an old-timey sea captain. "Not the gnomes. Those little bastards are the worst. Why us?"

"Because Shannon is the shortest one here," Boone pointed at the wife of the pair. "And gnomes distrust tall people."

She was just barely over five feet, so she shrugged. "That's fair. The gnomes will all be busy pickpocketing and generally screwing around with all the Dragon Con people anyway. We'll take Jones with us. He seems to know his way around that world."

"I'll grab my costume," Trip said, because of course he had packed one, just in case. "I've got this really great Captain America... You know, because the cops might have my picture from earlier."

"*Sure*," Boone said, obviously not buying that.

"The mask covers the top half of my face," Trip said.

"Uh-huh. Milo, you still speak gnoll?"

"I only learned a few phrases so I'm not exactly fluent, but I can probably squeak by."

"Gregorius, take Milo to the dump and visit the gnolls."

The big man just frowned, then he sighed, because, frankly, gnolls were *gross*. "Come on, Hertzfeldt. You're with us."

"Why me?"

"Because you're the Newbie, I'm too old to crawl through garbage looking for gnolls, and Milo is our guest. Bring your gas mask and rubber boots. Trust me on this one." Gregorius headed for the door, along the way saying to the new guy, "Are you up on your tetanus shots?"

"Mundy and Sherlock, check all the regular sources around town." The two of them nodded because every town had its oddball places where monsters and the monster-adjacent types hung out. "I'll take Newcastle and we'll see if the APD has had any unsolved crimes that might be explained by a perp who can change faces on the fly. Let's go."

"What about me?" I asked.

"Somebody needs to wait for Earl. When he found out his girlfriend was in town and working this case, he wanted to go talk to her about it."

"I'm glad I'm not there for that conversation."

"Me too. Earl will need a debrief about what the Feds are up to anyway. In the meantime, call headquarters and see if they've ever heard of this Drekavac thing Stricken warned you about. Then get cleaned up. You look ridiculous." Boone just shook his head as he walked toward the stairs. "Bringing MCB swag into my house? That's downright disrespectful. Why don't you just take a dump on my carpet while you're at it?"

"Seriously, man," Trip said as he left. "That look is a huge step down from Cookie Monster."

"Okay, I get it already! I'll burn the stupid MCB shirt. It's not like I bought it in their gift shop!"

While I took a shower, I inspected the cuts Coslow had fixed. I wouldn't call them healed so much as brutally cauterized, and they still hurt like the dickens. Plus from the way my back felt and all the bruises, I don't think Coslow's trick did much to help the part where the reptoid had bounced me off the wall. I probably should have had Sherlock check out the new burn scars, but she'd been a regular doctor so this magical crap was probably outside of her wheelhouse anyway. I'd ask Gretchen to take a look when I got home.

As I was drying off, I got a video call from my wife. Whenever one of us was on the job and the other was stuck at home, we always made the time to check in. I put a towel around my waist because she was probably still at the office, and the last thing I wanted was Dorcas looking over her shoulder.

"Hey, hon." Julie was just as gorgeous as ever. Her long dark hair was currently tied up, meaning that she'd probably been sneaking in some range time. Seeing her always brightened my day. From the pictures on the wall behind her, she was in her office at the compound, so I'd made the right call with the towel. She laughed when she saw how I was dressed. "Did I interrupt your spa time?"

"In my copious free time I figured I'd get a massage. Dealing with the MCB really puts a lot of tension in my shoulders."

"Uh-huh. Sounds plausible. I already got the quick version from Boone earlier. Are you actually okay, or just doing the tough guy thing where you can't show weakness in front of other Hunters like usual?"

"I'm actually okay. It was one little fight with a lizard man. It never even had a chance."

"Sure." Julie was obviously unconvinced, but she'd been doing this sort of thing a lot longer than I had and was no stranger to all the myriad ways Hunters could get hurt. "How are Grant and Franks?"

"Unlike last time we saw him, Franks has all his limbs attached. Grant's Grant, so far too handsome yet still bafflingly annoying."

"Be nice. He tried to help me out for the Europe thing."

"I know. That's why I was nice."

"Really?" Julie was right to be incredulous.

"I was polite *and* helpful. We even made small talk."

"I'm so proud of you," Julie said sarcastically. "That must have been hard."

"I'd rather fist-fight another reptoid. The Feds are on the warpath though."

"I heard about Stricken escaping. I'm sorry."

"Well, maybe next time we'll get lucky and they'll forget to confiscate my guns first."

Julie got it. If all the people who wanted to take Stricken out had to take a number, she'd be further down the list than Franks, Earl, or Heather, but she'd still happily take the shot if given the opportunity. And my wife is an extremely good shot. "I know you need to get back out there, but I've got somebody here who wants to say hi." Julie turned her camera downward to show that my son was crawling up her leg to get onto her lap.

Ray was a happy, chunky, energetic toddler now. His round face lit up when he saw me. "Daddy!"

"Hey, big guy." It didn't matter that I'd just gotten my mission derailed and my ass kicked. You always put on a smile for your kid. That's what dads do.

He started to babble about his day, and I was happy to listen. It was something about Legos.

After Julie had rescued our son, the three of us had gone into hiding for a while. I had needed to recuperate from the Nightmare Realm, and Julie had been a wreck from what she'd gone through getting Ray back. Since Asag had already demonstrated he would go after our families, we'd used fake identities and stayed as far away from the business as we could. It had been a peaceful vacation, but monster hunting was in our blood. And after a few months we'd both gotten incredibly bored and antsy. Since the chaos god we had a beef with had been remarkably silent since Severny Island had gotten nuked, and we couldn't just sit on our asses hiding forever, we'd gone back to our regular lives. It was hard having that kind of a danger constantly hanging over you like a big angry storm cloud, but we'd adjusted as much as possible.

That looming threat was a good reminder that I needed to get back to work. "Be good for Mom. I'll be home soon. I love you guys."

"Love you too," Julie said. "Be safe."

Clean and in a fresh change of clothes—thankfully without any MCB two-headed eagles on them—I went back to the team room and found that Earl had just gotten back. He looked grumpy, cigarette dangling from one lip, sitting on Boone's desk with Trip's fancy camera in hand, mashing buttons.

"How do you make it so you can see pictures on the screen of this damned thing?"

"Give me that." I took the camera from him. "You Luddite."

"Considering I was in my twenties when they invented the television, I think I keep up with technology pretty damn good, kid."

"Says the guy who still uses a Tommy gun." Except after saying that it still took me a minute to figure out which knobs brought up which menus. While I played with the camera, Earl angry-smoked. I swear, if the monsters didn't kill me, the perpetual secondhand lung cancer cloud from my boss would. "Here. Just push the arrows to see the next one or go back."

He took the camera and began flipping through the pictures Trip had taken during our stakeout.

"Any luck finding Heather?"

"Yep." He didn't look up from the screen. "We spoke."

"Wanna talk about it?"

"Nope."

"Okay then." I flopped onto the couch and waited, because I knew him well enough that he was going to vent about his girlfriend anyway. What can I say? I'm a good listener.

"It pisses me off, Z," Earl said as he continued to click. "She's too stubborn to quit Unicorn even though that job keeps trying to kill her. It's because Heather looks at those monsters like they're her kids. She's protective. That whole outfit would probably fall apart if it wasn't for her."

Gee whiz, that sounded familiar. Change monster to Hunter, and it was basically Earl's life story. But I didn't say anything.

"I get that Unicorn can be a force for good. Hell, when I was stuck there, we saved a lot of lives. We did the nasty things regular soldiers couldn't. Which makes it worse, because I know the exact kind of shit she gets involved in. It's hard having your woman disappear for months at a time, because you know she's probably in some third world country killing terrorists because they decided they wanted to summon demons or open a portal or some other evil nonsense. She keeps saying she's going to be done, but then it's one more mission, one more thing where they're counting on her to save the day."

"Yeah, I can't imagine what that would be like."

"Fair . . . But you know what really grinds my gears this time, Z?"

"She got called up because they had a shot at taking down Stricken, but she kept that secret from you?"

He looked up from the camera and squinted at me. "Good guess."

I shrugged. Though I preferred door-kicking and face-shooting, I wasn't a total lummox when it came to this complicated interpersonal crap. "Did you tell Heather that MHI had a line on an actual Ward Stone?"

"Obviously not."

"Well, there you go. She can't tell you her top-secret government business, and you can't tell her MHI business whenever it's something where the government would screw us if they knew what we were doing. You don't want to put her in a tough spot. She does the same for you. You respect her, so you've got to trust her. She took an oath. She's not going to break it."

"Of course not."

"Then you two really need to work this shit out."

"We will." Earl sounded surprisingly certain.

"Good, because it's inconvenient for the rest of us." I didn't add that preferably their solution would mean Heather quitting Unicorn and coming on with us full time, because having another bullet resistant and nonpsychotic werewolf around would really kick ass, but I'm selfish like that. "You want my advice?"

"Not particularly." It was obvious Earl preferred talking about the pertinent business stuff rather than the messy personal stuff. "Enough about Heather. Let's get back to work."

"Best idea I've heard all day." I didn't need to push my luck with the life coaching. It wasn't like I was good at this either. I'd had one successful relationship in my life and had been pretty much been winging that the whole time.

"We don't know what kind of creature we're looking for so we're just guessing where to look. Problem for us right now is that the MCB really wants that Ward, and so will every powerful monster or whacko cult or wannabe necromancer once word gets out there's one up for grabs. Not to mention the reptoids have a shaman with magic that actually works, so they'll be looking for it too."

"If Stricken's to be believed, since the Dark Market auction contract has been violated, something called a Drekavac will be after her too." That name had been a new one on me, but I'd sent a message to Lee to check the archives to see if we had any records on what those were. He hadn't come up with much yet. "The name means screamer or shrieker, but not like a banshee. More like how an animal howls on the hunt. Folklore pegs it as some kind of cursed undead."

"Ghost or physical body?"

"Stories go both way, so unsure, but Albert's working on it."

Earl gave a resigned sigh because we both knew that when it came to monster capabilities, folklore was wrong more often than it was right. Ideally, we'd find accounts by actual Hunters, because those cut through the myth and bullshit and got down to the nuts and bolts about how to kill things.

"We'll deal with whatever that is when it shows up, Z. STFU is after her too. Do you have any idea the kind of nefarious spy shit that outfit could accomplish with someone who can change faces on demand? Unicorn's gonna catch her and make her an offer she can't refuse. If Heather thinks she's doing that girl a favor, she'll find her. Heather's dogged."

"Pun intended?"

Earl looked at me like I was stupid. Then he shook his head and went back to the camera. "We're dealing with something who can change form at doppelganger speed, but with near lycanthrope-level physical abilities. There aren't many things who can do that..." Earl trailed off. He was staring at one of the pictures. Trip had managed to get some great shots of the girl while she'd been fighting. "Aw, hell."

"You know what she is?"

"Maybe. Who I'm thinking of is one of a kind, but this does kind of remind me of her. Hang on." Earl put down his camera and took out his phone. He flipped through the addresses and picked a number that was identified by the initials J.S. He put his finger to his lips to indicate the need for silence, then put the phone on speaker and set it on Boone's desk.

A woman picked up on the third ring. *"Hello?"*

"It's Earl Harbinger."

She was quiet for a long time. *"It's been a few years."* There was no polite greeting, no small talk. She had a really pretty voice. It was downright melodic, like a gentle wind through the leaves of a tree, which made it hard to tell her actual mood. *"What do you want?"*

"I'm really sorry to do this to you. This ain't a social call. I've got a problem with our mutual friends."

"The ones who gave us our silver tags?"

At first I thought she meant one of the plaques from the memorial wall, but then I remembered that Earl carried one that declared him to be PUFF exempt, and that legally he wasn't considered a monster who could just be exterminated on sight. Which meant whoever he was talking to also had to be STFU alumni.

"The same."

"I've got nothing to do with them anymore. What did you do to make them mad this time?"

"It ain't me drawing their ire. Are you currently in Atlanta by any chance?"

"I haven't been in Atlanta since I saw Bob Marley play at the Fox. And no offense, but I'm not going to tell you where I am in case those people are listening in. I prefer to be left alone."

"I don't think they've tapped my phone," Earl said. Since he had shushed me, I didn't want to interrupt to say that he really was a Luddite, because they didn't need to *tap* them anymore. They just collected all the data in the world to scan through at their convenience. Then Earl looked at his phone suspiciously, because even though Heather wouldn't listen in on his private conversations, her employer certainly would.

"Why on Earth would you think I was in Atlanta? Oh no. My daughter is there."

"I was afraid of that."

"What did she do this time?"

"I don't know if it's her or not. It could have been someone else who interrupted a deal between monsters and a spy in order to steal an artifact, who knocked out some Feds in the process, and then led my boys on a chase, doing backflips and jumping through windows like some kinda circus performer while changing faces every few minutes."

There was a long pause. *"Kids can be a real pain in the ass."*

"That they can. Have you heard from her lately?"

"She texted me last week. She's supposed to be working a normal mundane job to pay for her normal mundane education. I warned her not to draw attention."

"It's a bit late for that now."

"She promised me that she'd keep her abilities secret and live like a normal human. I knew I shouldn't have trusted her . . . Is it really bad?"

"It's not just them she's pissed off, but the thing she stole is really valuable to a lot of scary and murderous type beings. They're all gonna be gunning for her too. And none of them are the sorts to be constrained by concepts like mercy or forgiveness, if you know what I mean."

"I should have known she'd get in trouble somehow. She's too proud. She's just as cocky as her father. She was always the most obstinate little brat, picking fights, causing trouble, but I thought she'd been behaving lately. You have no idea how many times I had to bail her out of jail or beg a judge with tears in my eyes not to send her to juvie. She's always pushing the limits, Earl. I knew it was just a matter of time before she fell in with a bad crowd and got hurt!"

"Hold on." Earl tried to reassure the worried mother. "I promised you a long time ago that I would help your family however I could, and I stand by that. I need to find her before they do. Anything you can tell me will help. The presence of the thing she stole, not very many things knew it would be here. Could she have been hired by someone to get it for them?"

"Maybe. I don't know who though. I've done my best to keep her away from that life. I forbid her from associating with Hunters or anything from the other side, but did she listen to me? Of course not! Regular moms have to worry about their daughters experimenting with drugs or dating bad boys, but not me. Oh no. That would be too easy! She never listens. What do I know?

I've just been dealing with this for hundreds of years. She's half human so she knows everything! Oh no, Earl... What if somebody is using my poor baby?"

I'd watched her poor baby beat up some Feds and leap off of the sky bridge earlier, so I was having a real hard time seeing her as the victim here.

"Stay calm. I'll do everything I can to find her before they do. Does she have any friends or contacts around here? Anyone she might have mentioned to you?"

"You know how she is. She's always popular, but never actually close to anyone. She does have a bunch of friends who are into the same music scene though."

I thought that sounded tenuous as hell, but Earl said, "It's something. I'm going to give you another number I need you to call. That's Melvin, my internet troll. He's squirrely, but really good at his job. He'll make it so our friends can't listen in, then you give him every contact of hers you can think of, he'll get them to me, and I'll find her. Okay?"

"Promise me you'll keep my little girl safe, Earl."

"I'll do my best." He hung up, blew out a long breath, then said, "Oh boy."

"So who, and or what, was that?"

"She's someone I made a promise to once. She's a type of yokai."

"Yeah, I know what that is. But how are you friends with something from some spirit realm? Were you two in Unicorn together?"

"Not together. Different teams, different times. We first met when she was one of my Hunters' guests at the Christmas Party."

"*The* Christmas Party?" Which of course meant the *big one,* where a grief-stricken Ray Shackleford had been manipulated into opening a portal that had almost sucked Alabama into another dimension, and a ton of people had died as a result. That mess had gotten MHI shut down for years.

Earl nodded. "Did you ever read those old memoirs Albert found in the archives, from a Hunter by the name of Chad Gardenier?"

CHAPTER 6

We didn't know if this was the same shapeshifter we were looking for, but if so, her real name was Sonya. Her dad had been a Hunter. Her mom wasn't human, but rather convincingly lived as one. She was actually a creature known as a kodama.

Since Earl was the sort of leader who felt eternally responsible for the families of those who got killed under his command, he kept track of all of them as best as he could, helping out whenever possible, sometimes anonymously when MHI's help wasn't wanted. This included the girlfriend and daughter of the man who had given his life so Earl could close the gate at the Christmas Party.

Earl said that even with their shared background of having been in Special Task Force Unicorn, they weren't exactly tight, because it had been Earl who had ordered Chad Gardenier to his death. Something which the mother claimed she understood had been necessary, but I got the impression it weighed on Earl. He had checked in on the two of them periodically to see how they were doing while Sonya was growing up. From the way Earl talked about the daughter, I could tell he was rather fond of her. He had even talked about offering Sonya a job as a Hunter when she grew up, but her mom had absolutely forbidden that, declaring it too dangerous for her little girl. Earl had respected her wishes and never mentioned it again.

His visits had become more infrequent while Sonya was a

teenager, and nonexistent in the years since she'd been an adult. In his defense, we had been really busy, but he was kicking himself for it now, because it looked like she might have turned to a life of crime.

Melvin had called Earl. Our obnoxious—yet surprisingly useful at times—internet troll had set up a secure line and gotten all of Sonya's info from her mother. It turned out she had a bunch of different accounts under fake names on all the social media sites, each one filled with pictures of a different girl, none of which looked similar, but for whatever reason I could sort of see how they could all be the same person. It was hard to get a handle on what Sonya was actually like because each profile was into wildly different things. There was a pretty version, a goth version, a jock, a nerd, and even a cowgirl, but the only thing they had in common was a love of selfies. It was as if she had a different name and face to wear for whatever mood struck her that day. My gut told me none of these public ones were real, and she kept her real personality secret.

Though they all looked extremely different, at least all of her identities appeared to be about the same age, size, and sex. That would narrow our search a bit, but Earl didn't know if that was an actual limit on her shape-changing powers or not. Looking like a twenty-year-old girl could just be her normal comfort zone, and right now she was escaping the country disguised as a morbidly obese eighty-year-old man named Morton Leibowitz or, hell, maybe even Morton's Seeing Eye dog. Earl didn't know all the details about what that type of yokais' powers were, her mother kept the family secrets close to the vest, and he knew even less about which of those powers had gotten passed onto her half-human offspring.

Working backwards through her pages, Melvin had broken into Sonya's private messages and then email. Trolls are *scary.* You'd think trolls were scary because they were huge, nearly unkillable carnivores, but oh no, their ability to get into your private info was the real terror. A troll was way more likely to steal your credit card or Social Security number than they were to eat you. Identity theft was a multibillion-dollar business in this country, and not all of that was done by humans. Melvin had run a trace on Sonya's regular cell phone, but it was still sitting in her dorm room. Hoping that he had the wrong shapeshifter,

Earl had called that number, but it had gone right to voice mail, which wasn't a good sign.

Melvin skimmed through the recent emails and texts, and it turned out there were a few messages from an untraceable source that seemed to be in some sort of code. It wasn't slang either, because trolls are really good at keeping up on that sort of thing. Our troll said he'd try to crack it because, I quote, "Melvin love puzzles!"

By the time we got all that from our internet troll, it was nearing sundown. If Sonya had fled the city with the Ward as soon as we'd lost her, she could be hundreds of miles away by now. So this might be a wild-goose chase, but we decided to hit everyone she had ever associated within the Atlanta area, going in order of how recently she'd had dealings with them. The rest of the Hunters were already busy chasing down other leads, and we didn't even know if Sonya was our actual target, so Earl and I split up to start checking her contacts out.

The first few places I stopped by were total duds. One apartment was empty and for rent. The other was a normal-looking house in the suburbs, but nobody was home, and there was three days' worth of junk in the mailbox.

It was dark when I arrived at a bar on the outskirts of the city. A few of her identities had liked this place, and she had posts about meeting up and partying here. It was not at all what I expected. When Sonya's mom had said that her daughter had some friends here who were into the same music scene, none of her profiles had prepared me for this.

The establishment was named Perdition's Abyss; I kid you not. The sign announcing that name was spray-painted on a rusty old car hood that had been stuck in the ground. There was a chain-link fence around the property. There were bars on the windows, and razor wire on the tar-paper roof. The parking lot was gravel and holes. There were more jacked-up trucks than cars, but motorcycles outnumbered them both. There was even a big-ass Rottweiler on a chain run to dissuade anyone from trying to sneak in the back door.

I parked the company truck and headed for the entrance. Even out here it smelled like stale beer, puke, and weed. I could already hear the music blaring from a hundred yards away. It was heavy metal, and was a cover of one of my brother's songs, which was kind of nifty if you think about it. It gave me a feeling of *connection.*

Inside, it was dim, crowded, smelly, and deafening. One look around told me this was a *rough* bunch. The clientele appeared to be a mix of bikers, rednecks, roughnecks, and that type of youthful belligerent who'd managed to get kicked out of everywhere else respectable. It wasn't a strip club, per se, so I assumed the drunk women dancing on tables were volunteers. This was the kind of place where if somebody got stabbed, they'd just throw some sawdust on the floor to soak up the blood and keep on trucking. If the health inspector ever came for a visit, they'd just murder him and bury his body in the woods out back. I felt right at home. Working in this kind of place was how I'd put myself through college and where I'd discovered the lucrative world of illegal underground fighting. Knocking men unconscious with your bare hands is a great way to pay tuition.

The bouncer at the door was one big fella, like several inches and a hundred pounds bigger than me, far right side of the bell curve, chonky boy. He had cauliflower ears, scars all over his knuckles, and a beard that had probably won more fights than most people would ever see. Tough guys tend to automatically size up other tough guys, and he looked me over, decided I wasn't obviously high or looking for trouble, and nodded. I nodded respectfully back. Professional courtesy.

The band was doing a decent job of recreating Cabbage Point Killing Machine's music, but the sound system in here was painfully distorted. All the regulars had to have permanent hearing damage by now. I gave the room a quick once-over, looking for anyone who might be Sonya. There were a bunch of girls close enough in size and age to be her, though none of Sonya's online profiles had been in the persona of sleazy bar skank. Places like this always attracted a disproportionate number of suburban girls who wanted to live dangerously. I scanned for anybody else interesting. I'd worked in places like this long enough that I easily picked out the resident drug dealer, and also the guy I would talk to if I really wanted to buy a cheap handgun with the serial numbers ground off. So, the usual.

Trying to figure out how to play this cool, I went up to the crowded bar. They were so busy it took a minute before I caught someone to ask for a beer. The bartender was female, had a mohawk, and asked me what brand. I told her whatever was cheap. I didn't intend to drink it anyway. Working in places like this and dealing with alcoholic morons had really soured me on the whole drinking thing, and I'd just never picked the habit back up, but I figured having a bottle in hand would make me look more natural.

I was suspicious enough that I checked out the bartender as she fetched my drink, but she was too tall, too busty, and probably ten years too old to be our shapeshifter. Unfortunately, she caught me staring. Fortunately, she seemed to take that as a compliment and gave me an obviously flirty grin in return. Considering I'm a rather ugly individual, that should tell you how comparatively unattractive most of the other meatheads in here were. I reflexively got embarrassed at her smile and knew that Julie would laugh at my discomfort. Thankfully, they were so busy the bartender had to go right back to work.

As I watched the crowd, I tried to figure out how to proceed. I couldn't just whip out my phone and start asking random strangers "Have you seen this girl?" because, first off, I figured that only worked in cop movies, and second, though I had a bunch of pictures of her, I didn't know which face, if any, Sonya would be currently using. But what the hell, the bartender seemed kind of into me, so it couldn't hurt to ask her first.

I was spared that awkward exchange because that was when I noticed somebody who looked vaguely familiar sitting at a little table in the corner. It was poorly lit and smokey enough that I'd not noticed him during my initial survey of the room. He was average size, maybe a little older than me, dark hair, vaguely Asian, wearing bland clothing, and being otherwise completely forgettable. He was so unremarkable that it was no wonder I hadn't noticed him. He was the living embodiment of the grey man concept. Except something had pinged my radar. It took me a second to remember where I'd briefly seen him before. It was the Vatican Hunter who had found Agent Franks when we had been putting him back together at the MHI compound.

The Blessed Order of Saint Hubert the Protector was the Catholic Church's secret monster hunting organization, though I didn't know if they actually answered to the Pope, or if they were just loosely affiliated—it was really hard to tell with them. It wasn't like a tiny organization colloquially known as the Secret

Guard was an open book. They were supposedly the oldest group of Hunters in the world and didn't really associate with the rest of us. They rarely collected PUFF bounties and didn't compete for contracts, so they weren't really competitors either. Their rep was that of a bunch of mystical warrior monks who went around killing monsters because it was a good deed or God willed it. Which sounded cool and all, though I preferred getting paid obscene sums of money while doing the same thing.

On the Harbinger scale—which consisted of ranking all rival Hunting organizations from Asshole to Alright—he had declared them *alright*. Only I knew that Earl had a soft spot for the Catholics because it had been a former member of the Secret Guard who had helped him learn how to deal with his lycanthropy, so he was probably a little biased.

The real question was, what was one of the Secret Guard doing here? Surely it couldn't be coincidence. You don't accidentally run into other Hunters in random scum holes in a big city neither of you live in. Hunters just aren't that common. I didn't think he had noticed me yet, so I tried to slouch down on my stool to look smaller. There was a mirror behind the bar, so I used that to keep an eye on him, rather than directly staring like a moron.

I got out my phone and texted Earl about who was here, then watched and waited. The Hunter's expression remained neutral. He really didn't seem that into the music either, despite them being pretty talented for a cover band. He idly checked his watch. A minute later he checked it again. He was waiting for someone and they were late. I got the feeling he was annoyed but trying not to show it. Could he be waiting for Sonya? There was a racing jacket over the back of his chair and a long canvas pack at his feet. I really wanted to know what was in the bag. If it was a stack of money, then maybe the Catholics had hired her to steal the Ward for them? If it was weapons or explosives, maybe he was here hunting her too? Either way meant I'd be getting involved.

I should have brought backup. And that thought made me realize that he might have backup too...but I had no idea what any of their other Hunters looked like. For all I knew half these rednecks might actually be able to speak Latin...wait...did the Catholic Church still speak Latin? *Italian. Whatever.*

The band took a break, and the Hunter appeared relieved that the replacement filler music over the sound system was a little quieter. Apparently, he wasn't into metal. His playlist was probably all Gregorian chanting or something.

I thought about trying to take the Hunter's picture, but he seemed way too alert for me to pull that off without getting spotted. Only it turned out it didn't matter, because Earl knew who I was talking about. His reply text told me to hold on, he was on his way. And also, no matter what, for me to not pick a fight with Gutterres—so that was his name—and Earl put three exclamation points after that order. Which I took to mean that Gutterres was probably a badass. Which reminded me that even though the Blessed Order of Saint Hubert were *alright*, they also had a reputation for being a bunch of trigger-happy holy warriors who always thought God was on their side... We really needed to change the Harbinger Scale from a thumbs-up or -down to a system with more range to allow for some nuance. *Catholic Hunters, usually pretty chill, but will cap you without hesitation if you get in their way. Three stars!*

Ten minutes later the band came back from their smoke break. For the band's protection, there was a chain-link fence between them and the dance floor, because crowds like this often consider throwing bottles a form of constructive criticism. After a brief setup, they launched into another song, one I didn't recognize, but the soft opening was catchy. When the singing began, I realized that they had added a new member. They hadn't had a female vocalist before.

I looked toward the stage. Despite the nose ring, the singer was pretty, in a grungy tank top and sleeve tats sort of way... and, wow, she had a great voice. It was so songbird clean that it seemed glaringly out of place in a crap-sack establishment like this. Her voice was so good it transcended the awful speakers. It was like rose petals and a beautiful sunset in soundwave form. All the assembled scumbags and tough guys stopped to stare. She had them downright hypnotized. From the looks on their faces, half of them fell in love with her right there. The women were either jealous, or kind of into her too.

Then out of nowhere the band started to shred, and the singer dropped into a snarling growl that was deeper than I could have achieved on my best day. She shifted gears so fast it came out of nowhere. Beauty died and this was all diesel fumes and primal anger. It was pure distilled rage and the discontent of a generation. A hundred people automatically started banging their heads.

That voice would have been more appropriate coming out of the bearded mammoth working the door than the tiny girl who had started furiously jumping up and down with the microphone.

Then she flipped back effortlessly to smooth and melodic, and instantly had the crowd swaying along to a tragic love story. She was dragging the audience with her, whether they wanted to or not.

Except for Gutterres. Because when I looked back over at him, he'd lost the neutral expression, and was openly annoyed. When the singer looked toward his back corner, he lifted his arm and tapped his wristwatch, as if saying *we had an appointment.*

Only the singer grinned at him, did a sassy little twirl, threw the horns, and went back to the gravel roar chorus that was so low it made Skippy sound high-pitched. The lyrics were about burning churches and looting villages.

I had never heard a human being with that much range before…which made sense, because she was only half human. Even though I knew what I was looking for, she had temporarily clouded my judgment and sucked me along in her musical maelstrom. The singer was the right size, age, attitude, and the secret Vatican dude was obviously ticked off that she was screwing around and showing off rather than talking to him.

I got out my phone and sent Earl another text. *Sonya is here.*

The bartender came up to me. "From the way you're gawking, I guess you haven't heard Debbie sing before."

Debbie? "Yeah. First time. She rocks. Does she play here often?"

"Not really. She comes and goes as the mood strikes her. The regulars love when she shows up though."

"Yeah, I can see why."

The song was done. The crowd went nuts. Sonya soaked up the cheers for a moment, then yelled into the mic, "Thank you, Perdition's Abyss! I love you too! Now this next one is an all-new composition I like to call 'Contract Renegotiation'!"

Sonya's little garage band immediately launched into another song. I recognized the tune, because they had stolen this one from Cabbage Point Killing Machine too, but she'd replaced Mosh's lyrics.

> *I did what you asked,*
> *I took up the task.*

But there's a bounty on my head,
Vengeful lizards want me dead!

"*Time to pay up, bible thumpers!*" she screamed. "*Pass that collection plate one more time!*" Then she switched to the super-rumble beast voice for the chorus while looking directly at Gutterres.

You know the deal,
You gotta pay me to steal.
I didn't want this much trouble,
It's gonna cost you double!

She could certainly sing, but her songwriting abilities were unimaginative crap. I remember Mosh scribbling better lyrics on the back of homework assignments when he was fifteen and going through his emo phase. Yet Sonya repeated the chorus and the audience was so enamored with her, they started singing along, informing the hapless Secret Guardsman that she wanted more money.

Gutterres folded his arms and scoffed. I'd not noticed he was wearing an earpiece before, but he began talking to someone, probably to ask for more money. Being MHI's accountant, I'd been at the other end of the line in a few conversations like that over the years. Whoever he was talking to must have balked because Gutterres began arguing with them. I really hoped the Church's accountant stuck to their guns and told her no deal, because whatever they wanted the Ward for, MHI needed it more.

One last warning,
Or you'll be mourning,
You fuck around with me,
I'll toss it in the sea!

Gutterres passed that message on, and his handlers must have decided negotiating with terrorists would be okay this time. As Sonya wrapped up her song, Gutterres gave her the OK sign. The deal was approved. Sonya would get her money and the Secret Guard would get the Ward Stone.

Except that's when the monster arrived.

CHAPTER 7

I knew something was terribly wrong even before I saw the creature.

There are certain types of supernatural beings that can suck the warmth right out of a room, as if their taking action in our world requires stealing energy from their surroundings. I had felt that effect with soulless abominations before, usually different types of undead. When a master vamp gets really charged up it feels like you got shoved into a walk-in freezer.

This was like that, but *worse.*

It had been uncomfortably warm and muggy inside the bar. The old air-conditioning unit just couldn't keep up with this many bodies. Then out of nowhere it felt like I'd been dunked in ice water.

It wasn't just the sudden cold. It was the unnatural stillness. The bar went from super loud to unnaturally muted in an instant. All the other patrons were still shouting or cheering for Sonya—I could see their lips moving—except what had been a roar dropped to a whisper. Clapping hands and stomping boots were muffled thumps.

I glanced toward the front window. It was so dirty it would have been hard to see through during daytime. At night, looking out into a parking lot where most of the lights were burned out, I could only see shadows and shapes. Yet something weird was moving behind the line of Harleys. I thought it was another

bike, but it was too tall, and the shape was spikey, and vaguely...
organic? It stopped. The rider dismounted. When his feet touched
the Earth the already weak lights in the bar flickered, and when
they came back the place seemed even dimmer. All the hair on
my arms stood up.

"Oh, hell." I hurried and typed another text to send to my
team. *Unknown monster incoming.* The message failed to send.
It said I had no connection. I hit retry, then shoved it back in
my pocket and moved my hand to the pistol under my shirt.

The bar patrons didn't seem to realize what was going on
yet. For some reason they didn't feel the change in temperature,
sound, or pressure, but Gutterres must have been as tuned in as
I was, because he got up and moved quickly toward the stage,
where Sonya was so caught up in her performance and gleefully
fleecing the Catholics out of more money that she seemed oblivi-
ous to the impending doom.

The thing walked through the front door.

It was man-sized and man-shaped, dressed in a long, duster-
style coat and a really tall, wide-brimmed hat, like something the
pilgrims would wear. Beyond that it was hard to tell many details
from where I was sitting because the thing was pitch-black and
obscured by the ghostly fog that rolled in with it.

The big bouncer was the first normal person who saw the
newcomer. He spoke. Of course I couldn't hear it, but if I had
to guess it was something along the lines of *Hey, buddy, wrong
part of town for the costume. The con's that direction.*

Only then an eerie light ignited around the shadowy being as
it slowly raised its gloved hands. Then two massive black hounds
sprang into existence beneath its palms. The dogs were sleek,
powerfully built, and dark as night except for their unnaturally
white fangs.

The gigantic, experienced, ass-kicking bouncer dude took
one look at that obviously supernatural display and must have
had the good sense to decide this dump didn't pay him nearly
enough to deal with that kind of bullshit, because he hopped off
his stool and ran for the back.

Personally, I get paid a lot more than that bouncer, so I'd
be sticking around. I pulled my .45, kept it low at my side, and
started walking toward the monster. There were too many people
in the way for me to blast it yet.

When the thing lifted its head, the eyes were points of blue fire in the shadows beneath its hat. The sound of the bar was still muted like my ears were filled with slush, but I could hear the monster's instructions to his hell hounds, perfectly clear, as he pointed toward the stage. "Time to hunt." When he gave that order, both of the shadowy dog things' eyes began to glow with the same blue as well.

The hounds launched themselves through the crowd, and since each of them had to be well over a hundred and fifty pounds, they plowed right through. Customers yelped in surprise as they got shoved aside or knocked over. A woman fell off her dancing table. They were heading directly for the stage.

Except then, one of the locals made the mistake of kicking one of the demon dogs. I think it was just a surprised reflex, but he placed a steel-toed work boot right into its mastiff snout. The monster dog's head snapped around, but when it came back, it was snarling, fangs bared. It bit the man's ankle, pulled his leg out from under him, and then began savaging him, flinging the poor guy back and forth like he was a chew toy.

The dogs had been given clear instructions, but apparently they were easily distracted, because as soon as the other one smelled blood, it went nuts too and bit a nearby waitress.

For a split second, through all those moving bodies, I had a clean shot on the dog that was biting the man's leg. The victim was being dragged around in a circle, arms flailing, but I punched the gun out, focused on the front sight, and the spinning dog behind it, and tried to time my trigger pull in order to not shoot the poor dude I was trying to save.

The silver hollowpoint went right through the dog's head.

The whole animal exploded in smoke and blue sparks.

The bar erupted in chaos.

Hunters learn a lot about how to deal with the public. Legally, we're required to keep this stuff as secret and low key as possible. However, there are times when we have to act in the open, which means doing it as quickly and decisively as possible, because regular people tend to panic, get hurt, and generally make things worse. Only this wasn't the usual freak out and run and get eaten type crowd. This was the smash you over head with a pool cue and put boot to dog type establishment. And these guys did not take kindly to a hell hound trying to eat the girl who brings out their beers and onion rings. The nearest bikers started beating the hell out of the beast who was mauling the waitress. All the tough guys who had been sitting stood up to see what the ruckus was about. Knives were flipped open. Guns were pulled.

As far as these normies could tell, this wasn't a monster, it was a lunatic in a big hat who'd interrupted their evening with a fog machine, blue glow sticks, and a pack of fighting dogs.

When the monster saw the whole bar was ready to throw down, it said, "You were not to be my prey tonight, fleshlings. I am here to judge the thief. Step aside."

"Who the fuck you think you is?" somebody shouted back.

The monster lifted its hand again. The fog swirled beneath its palm, congealed, became solid, and the dog I'd just killed, re-formed, alive and whole by his side. The beast snarled directly at me, obviously annoyed that I'd just killed it.

"If it be battle you seek, then it is battle you shall receive," the monster said. Then it sprang forward, moving crazy fast, and swatted a biker across the face. He went flying. It grabbed another unlucky bastard by the neck and hurled him ten feet straight up, into, and partially through the ceiling tiles.

Everybody there started at the unnatural monstrosity that had just planted one of their friends headfirst through the roof. "What the shit, man?" one of them shouted as we were all drenched in years of accumulated ceiling dust, because even in a place this seedy, there are certain rules, one being that it's never cool to violate the laws of physics.

Then it drew a *sword.*

When three feet of blue glowing pirate cutlass came out, I think every other armed individual in this place had the same thought that I did, which was *screw that.* Guns rose. Of course most of these guys had guns. This was Georgia after all.

I shot first. At least half a dozen others joined in. Plenty of rounds missed and put holes in the walls, but a lot more hit. The guy standing next to me whipped out a Yeet Cannon and shouted, "Let's dance, homie!" as he held the gun sideways and dumped the whole mag in the monster's general direction.

The thing jerked and twitched as it was riddled with bullets. It bled sparks. I nailed it repeatedly where the brain should be. The body seemed to break apart, into shards of black and blue, before collapsing into the fog.

My ears were ringing. At some point the automatic sound system had turned back on and started playing Rob Zombie's "Lords of Salem." It appeared the monster had vanished. I hadn't seen where the shadow hounds had gone.

"Damn it, Jack! Why'd you let that freak with the dogs in here?" the bartender shouted for her missing bouncer. "You know the cops shut us down for a week every time we have a homicide!"

I retained my partially spent mag, reloaded with a new one from my belt, and then walked toward where the monster had dropped. There was a vortex of fog swirling a foot off the ground with a pale glow coming from the center of it. As I watched, the monster slowly rose from the mist. And I don't mean it stood, I mean it *floated up through the floor.*

The wide-brimmed hat tilted back, allowing me to stare into the horror that was its face. There was no skin. Instead of flesh and bone it looked like barbed wire had been twisted into a sort of human form to make a cage that barely contained the cold fire burning within.

"Amusing."

As it said that, whatever warmth had been lingering in my body fled. I cranked off two rounds into its chest, but then had to dive to the side as the sword whistled past my head. The monster followed. One palm shot out and struck me in the ribs. It was like getting hit with an ice-cold hammer, and I flipped backwards over a table.

Which was when the dogs came seemingly out of nowhere to attack the crowd. Jaws clamped onto the throat of the man with the empty pistol and dragged him down, gurgling. The other bit a biker on the arm, which was unfortunately holding one of those goofy Taurus Judge shotgun pistols, and when he spasmodically jerked the trigger, he accidentally shot another biker in the leg.

As the thing with the sword waded into the crowd, the fog seemed to follow, billowing outward, filling the space. It swung and removed a man's arm. Then spun and took off another man's foot. That was one sharp sword! Somebody smashed a chair over the monster's head, but it simply turned and ran him through the guts, then yanked the sword out in a red spray.

"The prey is escaping," the monster told its dogs. "Get her."

Since I was lying on the sticky floor, I had to sit up to see the stage. Sonya had seemed really cocky earlier, but from the surprised look on her current face, she hadn't been expecting anything like this.

The dogs let go of the men they'd been mauling and bounded across the room directly toward Sonya. One leapt onto the bar and ran down it. I fired at that one, nailing it in the ass and spinning it around in a blue flash. The dog flew off the bar, crashed into the wall of bottles, and shattered a lot of glass.

The other dog jumped at the stage but crashed against the chain-link fence. The fence was meant to keep the band from getting pelted with trash on open mic night, it really wasn't intended to stop a really pissed off demon dog, and it began tearing it down immediately. Only Gutterres came from behind and slashed it with some manner of edged weapon. The dog's neck split open, leaking light, and then the whole beast disintegrated.

Sonya bolted from the stage.

Gutterres went after her.

"Wait!" I got to my feet. "Shit!"

The monster with the sword came at me, looking like a hellish version of Solomon Kane, and I had to scramble backwards to retain my head. My back hit the bar. It swung downward, and I barely had time to get out of the way before it planted the glowing blade deep into the wood. I drove my pistol into its armpit and fired. It grabbed my wrist with one gloved hand and slammed my knuckles against the wood hard enough to leave a dent. I lost control of my gun and the STI went sliding across the bar.

The bartender with the mohawk had ducked down when the dog had gone flying past. She stood up now, having retrieved a sawed-off double-barrel shotgun from under the bar. From only a foot away, she blasted the monster right in its nasty wire face.

The pilgrim hat went flying. The thing collapsed in a shower of sparks and the black matter turned to fog.

The dog I'd shot was still in one piece though, and it collided with the bartender, jaws snapping for her face, but all it got was a mouthful of wooden stock. It tore the shotgun away, but better the gun than her throat.

I slid over the bar, grabbed two handfuls of icy fur, and slung the dog hard into the wall. The mirror I'd been using to spy on Gutterres shattered. The dog popped right back up, but I grabbed a whiskey bottle and smashed it over its head. The first hit made a meaty *clunk* that deformed its head. The next broke the bottle and cut my hand. It didn't even leave me a convenient stabby bit like in the movies.

The bartender was crawling away. Her shotgun was lying in the broken glass. The dog was getting back up, so I scooped up her weapon and turned, just in time to jam the twin barrels into its open mouth. "Choke on this." I gave it the second barrel and blasted fiery magic dog goo all over the wall. The now headless thing dissolved through the floor.

Glancing back toward the stage, I saw that Sonya and Gutterres were gone. The room had filled with the weird fog and a lot of wounded, dismembered, and freaked-out people. Sadly, but expectedly, the blue light had coalesced in the center of the dance floor and the fog had begun to spin around it again. Evil hat guy was coming back.

I picked up my pistol but kept the shotgun too, because you should never turn down a free shotgun. I thumbed the lever and popped the action open. The two spent shells auto-ejected. "More ammo?" I asked the bartender.

She pointed one shaking hand at a cardboard box beneath the counter. I reached in and grabbed two rounds of double aught, dropped them in, and closed the action...but since the monsters were still re-forming, I spent that valuable time shoving the rest of the shells into my pockets. Since I was on my own, I'd probably need everything I could get my hands on because the other professional Hunter was nowhere to be seen. *Thanks for the backup, Gutterres.*

By this point, the assorted tough guys had realized that this *was not normal*, and most of them were beating feet, except for the unlucky few who'd just lost their feet. On the bright side, everybody running away meant there would be fewer people for it to massacre.

The monster rose to its full height. It had even regained its hat, and worse, had two fresh hounds with him.

"You must be the Drekavac," I said.

"A title, rather than my true name." It seemed content to stop slashing people for a moment to talk. "You are a Hunter. We have no quarrel. Once a pact has been broken, it is my obligation to punish the transgressors." The thing had an ominous voice, as bone-chilling as its clinging fog. "Leave in peace, or fight and die."

For me, Plan A when dealing with monsters was *kill it*. But since this one just kept coming back to life, I'd try Plan B. *Diplomacy.* "Wait a minute. Stricken won the auction. He's the contract holder. He asked me to take care of the problem for him. So your work here is done. You can float on back to the scary hat store."

"You have your contract. I have mine. They are not the same. She must be judged." The Drekavac looked toward the stage. "Except our thief has fled. Good. I enjoy a challenge."

Which was when the bouncer came back into the room, except now the big man was carrying an old-school, M60 belt-fed machine gun that had been stashed in back. The bouncer hadn't fled. He had been gathering hardware.

"Get the fuck outta my bar, devil man!"

I hit the deck as the machine gun opened up and hosed down the monsters with hot lead. The bouncer bellowed as he raked the muzzle back and forth, machine gun in one hand, belt in the other, Rambo style. The Drekavac exploded. The monster dogs exploded. The floor around them exploded. The wall behind them exploded. I stuck my fingers in my ears as he kept on hammering the place with what was probably an extremely illegal Vietnam War bring-back. The fog moved like a living thing, rolling out the front door and into the parking lot. A hundred rounds and ten very loud seconds later, the bouncer shouted, "And stay out!"

Through the broken window and Swiss cheese wall I saw two bullet bikes fleeing the parking lot. The first had a female rider, the second, a male. That had to be Sonya and Gutterres. They took off fast, cutting through the mist.

Only it appeared the monster had a method of transportation as well, and it had re-formed ready to ride, because all of a sudden there was a terrible, gurgling roar, followed by a terrible, ear-splitting screech as a giant shadow flew down the road after Sonya.

I went after them.

CHAPTER 8

The parking lot was nuts. There were several wounded, and people were trying to help them, mostly with improvised tourniquets from the look of things. The rest were running for their cars or hopping on bikes to get away. Anybody who had an outstanding warrant was fleeing before the cops get organized, and from the look of things, that was nearly half of them.

I couldn't stick around, but I could still help out a little. When I reached my vehicle, I grabbed the med bag and threw it to one of the helpers who looked like they actually had a clue about first aid. "Here. It's got real TQs and bandages in it." Then I got in the company truck, put the borrowed sawed-off on the seat next to me, and drove off in the direction Sonya, Gutterres, and the Drekavac had gone. They were already out of sight, but I put the hammer down and hoped for the best.

Every MHI team draws from the same fleet of company vehicles. I'd taken the last thing in Boone's garage, which had been a Ford pickup truck. Though it had a big engine, it was a tall, four-wheel drive, with a winch and a snorkel on it, so this wasn't exactly a speedy vehicle. I was downright lumbering compared to the bullet bikes they'd been on. I had no idea what the hell the Drekavac was driving, but it had sounded like it had a friggin' jet engine, so it probably wasn't exactly slow. I suppose I could have stolen one of the bikes at the bar, but let's be honest, if I hadn't gotten shot by the owner in the process, I was a pretty mediocre motorcyclist, and would have ended up in a ditch in short order anyway.

It was a dark, moonless night, and we were heading farther away from the city, on a country road with thick trees all around. If they turned off, I'd have no way of knowing. Except, it appeared there was a stark line of icy fog hanging about a foot above the road, and since it was summer, there was no way that was natural. So I followed the Drekavac's trail.

I got out my phone. "Call Earl Harbinger." But there was still no service. That had to be interference from the monster because we were only half an hour outside of a major metro area. I'd seen certain unnatural beings mess with things like phones or radio reception before. As the needle on the speedometer climbed, I kept trying other members of my team, but kept getting nothing. I was on my own.

They have a pathological hatred of straight roads in the South, so I maxed out at about a hundred before having to stomp on the brakes going into a sudden corner. I made it through without flipping the 4x4 though, but that near miss reminded me to put my seat belt on.

There was no oncoming traffic, but there were multiple sets of headlights off to the side, crashed at weird angles. The monster had been running everyone off the road. Whatever the Drekavac was riding was causing people to swerve out of the way, and here that meant hitting a tree or driving off into the bushes. Some of the occupants had gotten out and were staring, baffled, in the direction I was going.

What the hell was I chasing?

The fog was getting thicker. I was catching up.

There was a blue glow ahead. From the smoke and dust hanging in the air, it looked like one of the bikes had crashed. The thing chasing them had stopped, and the Drekavac had dismounted in order to approach on foot.

I squinted, trying to tell what I was looking at.

It was hard to explain but imagine giving a mad taxidermist the carcass of a giant black horse and ordering him to stretch that over a bunch of bones put together by a maniac with no spatial awareness. Stitch it together with wire, add spikes and then set it on fire. Then make the fire blue, with ghosts and shit dancing in it because, why not? Shoot for the stars. It didn't even have hooves. The thing just seemed to hover on a cloud of fog. And worst of all, the Drekavac's vehicle—for lack of a better term—appeared to be... alive? Because as I rapidly closed the distance, it turned its head to look at me, and the eyes were like blinding headlights.

But before my eyeballs got blasted, I caught a quick glimpse of Sonya, lying there next to her wiped-out bike, and the Drekavac closing on her, sword in hand.

So I aimed for where I thought the Drekavac would be and floored it.

SLAM!

The monster went up over the hood, cracked my windshield, and went flipping over the roof. I saw fiery bits of monster raining down in my rearview mirror as I hit the brakes.

The truck came to a lurching halt. Thankfully, Boone kept up on his regularly scheduled vehicle maintenance, and the brakes worked great, because I stopped only a few feet from driving down a really steep hill.

The Drekavac had been splattered everywhere, but I'd already seen that wouldn't last long. I saw Sonya in my side mirror. She was staggering to her feet. Judging by how trashed her bike was, she'd wrecked hard, so was either lucky to be in one piece, or her inhuman toughness had saved her life. Since her bike's rear tire was twisted and glowing blue, it must have gotten blasted with some sort of Drekavac magic. I threw open the door and shouted, "Sonya! Come on!"

She pulled her badly scraped helmet off and tossed it in the grass, revealing that she was still wearing the same rocker face that she had at the bar. "Who are you?"

I pointed at where the fog was glowing and swirling as the monster came back to life behind my truck. "Does that really matter right now?"

"Nope." She ran to the passenger side door and hopped in. "Go, go, go!"

"Where's Gutterres?" I barely knew the guy, but I wasn't about to leave a fellow Hunter behind.

"He tried to protect me, but glowing angry dude blasted him off the cliff with a fireball. He's dead. Like we're going to be unless you drive, moron! Drive!"

And to accentuate that, the Drekavac's horse thing came

from seemingly out of nowhere and shattered her window with its skull. I stupidly hadn't expected it to act on its own. Sonya cried out as it tried to bite her with its big blunt teeth.

I snatched up the sawed-off. "Duck." Thankfully she had the sense to listen, and I blew a gaping hole through the horse's head. A shorty 12-gauge is *really loud* inside a truck cab. There was a terrible screeching noise as the monster horse fell over. I threw the truck in reverse and drove backwards, fast. There was a *thump thump* as the tires smashed the remains of the Drekavac, then I was back on the road. I put it in drive and accelerated.

A moment later we were clear of the fog and getting away. I took a deep breath and concentrated on not wrapping us around a telephone pole.

"I recognize you. You're one of those dopes who chased me earlier. You're the slower, uglier one."

Only comparatively. It wasn't my fault Trip was a fairly good-looking dude who could also run really fast. "Yeah, you've been a pain in my ass all day."

Then Sonya surprised me by pulling a little pistol out of her pocket and pointing it at my head. "Who are you? Talk or else!"

It's hard enough to speed on a windy country road in the dark without the added distraction of potentially catching a .380 in the dome. "Put that away, kid. I don't have time for your drama." I was still holding the shotgun, and it was still generally pointed in her direction, so I turned it a bit and thumped her in the stomach with the muzzle to accentuate my point. "If I wanted to hurt you, I could've cut you in half already." Then I slowly removed my hand from the shotgun and left it sitting on the center console to show I meant her no harm. Plus, I really needed both hands to drive this fast. "See? Now put that thing down before you shoot me by accident and kill us both."

I risked a glance at her and realized that despite being able to change her face, she really couldn't hide her emotions that well. In the dim lights from the dash, I could see that her lip was quivering and her eyes were watering. She actually was scared. Good, because so was I. She slowly lowered the tiny pistol. "Okay. But only because I want to."

"My name's Owen Pitt. I'm friends with Earl Harbinger."

"You know Harbinger? You're MHI?" That seemed to surprise her.

"I bet you wish you hadn't run from us now, huh?"

"Are you kidding? Earl's cheap. The Catholics just paid me two million bucks for that rock."

"No shit?" Robbing monsters really was lucrative.

"Well, it was one million, but they're pretty desperate, so I made them a counteroffer. Speaking of which"—Sonya got out her cellphone—"I need to check my bank account and see if they wired the money yet."

"Now? You've got other problems."

Sonya scowled at her phone. "No signal? Lame."

"Listen, the Catholics aren't the only desperate ones. MHI really needs that rock. There's an evil chaos god who wants to destroy the whole world, and that Ward might be the only thing that we can stop him with."

"Sounds like a personal problem."

There was a Y in the road. I went right. The Drekavac was out of sight. If we were lucky maybe I could shake him.

"Where's the Ward now?" I demanded.

"So you can swipe it?" She barked a sardonic laugh at me. "It's somewhere safe. I'm not telling you."

"Then I should pull over and you can get out and walk home."

"You wouldn't leave me at the mercy of that thing. I know MHI is a bunch of goody two-shoes."

I started slowing down.

"Whoa...Hey. What are you doing?"

"Letting you out. Maybe that glowing pirate can give you a lift." I braked. "He seems nice. Or you can tell me where the stone is."

"But the Secret Guard already paid me a bunch of money for it!"

"Pay them back." But then I saw two blue lights in my rearview mirror, growing rapidly. Tough talk aside, I couldn't actually leave her to get murdered by the spectral terminator. "Shit."

As I sped up, Sonya smugly said, "Called it." But then she turned around and looked out the back window, to see the rolling wall of doom fog closing fast. "You'd better step on it."

"I am." But from the way those lights were gaining on us, ghost horse was rocket powered. "How's he tracking you?"

"I have no idea."

Oncoming cars zipped past, but then they careened wildly out of control as the Drekavac's ride struck them. He was coming down the middle lane and catching up fast. The only thing that seemed to briefly slow him down was actually killing him, and even that only seemed to help for about thirty seconds. "Can you shoot?"

"Duh. I'm an expert. Better than you probably. Didn't Earl tell you who my dad was?"

"So shooting ability is genetically inherited now? Spare me the cocky bullshit, you friggin' orphan."

"I've got a mom."

"And she seems nice. You should call her more often. She's worried about you. There's some gun cases in the back seat. Do me a favor and pop this guy."

Sonya rolled smoothly into the back seat. My bigger guns were on the floor. I could hear her unzipping the top case. That would be my shotgun, Abomination. It had a short enough barrel it wouldn't be too awful for her to maneuver back there.

"Okay. Got one. Now what?"

I checked the mirror. Ghost horse was within fifty yards and closing. "Shoot him!"

"Uh…" There were some metallic noises as she ineffectually fiddled with various things. "How?"

"Expert my ass. See the big lever on the right side? That's the safety. Flip it down."

"Got it…" She must have yanked on the trigger. "Nothing's happening!"

"You've got to chamber a round."

"I've not seen one of these before, okay?"

"It's a Kalashnikov! Third world goat herders use these!"

"Quit yelling at me. Jeez!"

Twenty yards. And objects in the rearview mirror are closer than they appear. "Pull back the charging handle all the way and let it go. That's the handle that sticks out the right side." The familiar noise told me that she'd just successfully loaded it. "Now—"

There was a thunderous roar as Sonya yanked the trigger. Unfortunately, the combination of my rushed instructions and her gun illiteracy meant that she had flipped Abomination's selector from safe to full-auto, and a full-auto 12-gauge loaded with magnum buckshot, you really need to hang on and know what you're doing. Which Sonya clearly didn't, because she blew out the rear window, shot the tail gate, launched about fifty bucks' worth of silver down the road, and then blew a hole in the truck's roof in one burst.

"What the shit, Sonya?" My ears were ringing and none of those had been anywhere near the Drekavac.

"It's empty."

I leave a short five-round mag in Abomination when it's in the case. The bigger mags were all too long to fit and still zip it shut, but I kept a ton of those on hand. "Pockets on the side of the case." Then I saw a road sign warning me that there was a twenty-five mile an hour curve. I was going a hundred. "Hang on!" I hit the brakes on the way in. The truck managed to keep two whole tires on the road, but Sonya bounced off the back of my seat.

We made it around that turn at close to triple the recommended speed, but the Drekavac was right behind us, and we were deep in his fog bank. My headlights could only illuminate a few feet ahead, so I had no choice but to slow down.

All I could see of the Drekavac was its black silhouette in a blue halo, sitting tall in the saddle, using both hands to control its mount. Except then he reached down and pulled a weapon from a scabbard. From my vantage point it appeared to be shaped like an old-timey blunderbuss with a big bell end.

"Stay down." I swerved hard.

There was a brilliant flash as a crackling ball of lightning burned down the side of my truck. It zipped past, hit a tree, and blew it into splinters.

"What the hell was that?" My passenger-side mirror was gone. The paint had caught on fire.

"That's what he blasted the Catholic dude with."

In one smooth movement, I grabbed the sawed-off shotgun with my right hand, turned back, craning my neck to see, pointed it out the broken back window, and nailed ghost horse. It let out a terrible metallic wail and pulled hard to the side.

"That's how you do it." I'd been aiming for the rider, but Sonya didn't need to know that. I broke open the shotgun, fished two more shells from my pocket, and dropped them in, which was a lot harder than it sounds while steering a speeding truck.

"I think I've got it reloaded," Sonya said as she sat up. "There's another trigger on the front of this—"

"Don't touch that. You'll blow us up. That's the grenade launcher."

"Who puts a grenade launcher on a shotgun?"

"A genius." That had been Milo's handiwork. When I checked my mirror, ghost horse had corrected, and was gaining again. But worse, glowing fog was swirling in the bed of the pickup. "Look out!"

One of the demon hounds appeared in the truck's bed, and immediately started climbing in through the back window, snapping at Sonya. She shrieked but grabbed it by the ear and forced its head away. The girl had to be incredibly strong to shove that beast around like that, but she couldn't maneuver Abomination into it. "Bad dog!"

I leaned back and shot the dog right between the shoulder blades. It ruptured, spraying fire all over the truck. Thankfully, the blue fire burned cold rather than hot, because that would have been awkward. This way we'd just have frostbite instead of third-degree burns.

The Drekavac was right behind us, and it was aiming the blunderbuss again. "Hold on." I hit the brakes.

The monster fired. The lightning ball danced across the truck, burned a hole in the passenger seat, blew out the front window and rolled down the hood. But my sudden stop meant that ghost horse smashed right into my back bumper.

It must have weighed a lot more than it looked, because the impact shoved the truck sideways. We went spinning around, tires squealing, glass flying, right off the road. The horse was pulverized. The Drekavac was thrown violently from the saddle. I tried to steer out of the spin but the nose of the truck dropped suddenly as we crossed the edge of the road, and then we were going sharply downhill. A single thought went through my mind as we started sliding through the underbrush. *This is going to hurt.*

I stood on the brake pedal but it didn't matter. We might as well have been riding a sled. We shot down, crashing through branches, and just kept going. I nearly bit my tongue off as we bounced off a boulder. It was a miracle we didn't flip. Then the front end clipped a big tree trunk, hard enough to bounce the whole vehicle into the air. My air bag deployed and smacked the snot out of me.

We were stopped. I was dizzy. It took me a few seconds to

bring myself back to reality. Everything ached. We were sitting at a really weird angle. That was because the driver's side was partially submerged in a stream. I shook my head and safety glass fell out of my hair.

"Sonya? Are you alive?"

"You suck." She sounded muffled because she was lying on the floor, partially squished beneath my seat.

"You can thank me for rescuing you later." I looked around. I had no idea where we were, other than *forest*. Thankfully, my door still opened. When I unbuckled my seat belt, I slid into the stream and got soaked up to my knees. I splashed over to the back door and opened it. "Come on. We've got to go."

The unnatural fog was slowly rolling down the hill after us.

CHAPTER 9

Sonya crawled out of the truck and landed in the stream. *"Ooof."*

"Can you walk?"

"Of course I can walk." She swatted my offered hand away and got to her feet.

"Hopefully better than you can shoot."

She looked up the trail of destruction and saw that we had ended up probably two hundred yards from the road. "Way to go, jackass."

I grabbed my go bag, tore it open, and pulled out my vest. There was no time to fully armor up, but I wanted the pouches full of mags and grenades on my body. I threw it over my shoulders. I'd buckle everything up on the move. Then I took Abomination in one hand and the bag in the other and started walking. "There's another shotgun on the front seat if you want it." At least the borrowed one had fewer levers to confuse her.

"That's it? We're just going to hike through the woods until it catches us?"

Strangely enough, I actually had a lot of prior experience at evading monsters on foot through the wilderness. And Georgia was much nicer than the Nightmare Realm. I didn't know how the Drekavac had found her. I didn't know if it could track us. Maybe we could shake it. Maybe not. But we had to try. I set out, double time.

Sonya grabbed the sawed-off and followed.

I waded down the stream. I didn't know if his hell hounds had noses like normal dogs, but if they did, maybe this would throw them off our scent. Once we were on the other shore, we ran along the stream's edge for about a quarter mile. I knew we needed to turn off. This path was too obvious. The temperature had returned to the normal, muggy, summer heat. I could no longer see the fog. However, losing that pale illumination meant that I couldn't see shit. I stopped to get my bearings.

"This would be a lot easier if you hadn't wrecked your truck," Sonya whispered.

"What's your excuse? He caught you when you were on a bullet bike."

"I didn't know he could shoot fireballs."

The darkness made it really difficult to move, and the woods here were thick. I had multiple flashlights but turning one on would make us a huge target. I also had my night vision goggles in the bag, but I only had the one pair. "Can you see in the dark?"

"Why would you think I could see in the dark?"

"That seems like a reasonable thing for a half-human shape-shifter to be able to do. If you've got other abilities, now isn't the time to be coy about them."

"Sorry. I didn't inherit that gene. I can't see any better than a regular human."

"I've got night vision goggles, so stick close and follow me." I reached into the bag and found one of my rechargeable Surefires and handed it to her. "Take this. But don't turn it on unless you absolutely have to if we get separated." Then I gave her the last of the loose shotgun shells from my pocket. "You should be able to figure that one out."

I fished out my PVS-14 night vision setup and strapped it around my head. I much preferred using this mounted to my helmet, because worn on my head I had to cinch it brain-squeezingly tight to keep it from flopping around. Still, it beat tripping and impaling myself on a sharp branch. I turned the goggles on and the murky woods became perfectly visible in pixilated green. No matter how many times I used these things, that moment was always James Bond supercool. "Let's go."

Once we got away from the stream and beneath the trees, there was zero light, but I was fine. It takes a while to get used to walking with such a narrow view that you can't really see your feet, but I had a lot of practice. Sonya kept one hand on the drag strap on the back of my vest. She had to be totally blind right now.

We kept moving, but there was no sign of the Drekavac. Maybe rear-ending the truck had actually killed it once and for all. That would be nice. Which meant it was unlikely. Monster Hunters never expect nice things to happen to us. If you expect the worst, you're often pleasantly surprised when some things don't suck. With no sign of our pursuer, I crouched next to a tree, to watch and listen.

"What's going on?" Sonya whispered.

"Shhh."

That warning lasted about twenty seconds, before she went, "What do you see?"

"I don't see anything. I'm trying to listen to the woods."

"What do you hear?"

"You. Because you won't shut up."

"Oh." She was really good in her element, but Sonya wasn't striking me as the outdoorsy type. I glanced back at her. Everybody looks unnatural in night vision, but the difference was plain. Ditching us through the urban crowds earlier, she had been on top of the world. Out here, squatting in the dark, being hunted by a scary unkillable monster, she was a bundle of nerves. And she kept turning her head, waiting for something to pop out and kill her.

I couldn't see the Drekavac's glow or its fog, but the woods were too still. A night like this there should have been a lot more noises. Warm summer night in a Southern forest, there's always insects chirping and frogs croaking and general animal noises. Except it was eerie silent. The effect wasn't as pronounced as when the Drekavac had arrived at the bar, but I could still sense it. That thing was out there, searching.

Since it was hot again, maybe that meant the supernatural interference was gone. But when I got out my phone to check, there was still no signal. Either the monster was still close, or his weird energy field had permanently fried my phone. There was a GPS tracker on the truck and on my armor. I didn't know if those would still be working, but if they were, my friends would be coming after us.

"Why are you helping me?"

I sighed. "It's my job."

"I'm not paying you."

"Holy shit, kid, how mercenary do you think we are?"

"Don't act like you're not in this for the money. I know how Hunters work. I know what I've got. You want the Ward. You'll have to outbid the Church boys. They're up to two million. Do I hear three?"

"What's your *I didn't leave you to get chopped up by a Drekavac* discount?"

But then Sonya twitched and looked straight up. She'd seen something. I glanced up to see what had caught her attention. The bird was super bright on night vision, far too bright to be natural. And sure enough, when I flipped up the goggles out of the way, I could see that was because the bird was glowing with that same ghostly light as the fog.

The Drekavac didn't just have hunting dogs and a mutant horse—he had a falcon.

"Don't move," Sonya whispered. "I heard birds can't see you if you don't move."

She was probably thinking of the tyrannosaurus in *Jurassic Park*, but what the hell. It was worth a shot. We held perfectly still as it circled high above us, then it let out an unearthly shriek, banked hard, and began flying back toward where we'd wrecked. Apparently, Sonya's Wild Kingdom hot take about magic-bird vision had been incorrect.

Just like Skippy and Milo had tracked Sonya across Atlanta, the Drekavac had done the same thing to us. This was just the low-tech, supernatural version. Low-tech problems require low-tech solutions, so I shouldered Abomination, led the falcon just a bit, and pulled the trigger. There was a flash followed by a rain of blue-fire feathers.

Except the bird must have had some sort of telepathic connection to its master and didn't need to make it back to report. There was a horrible, echoing shriek back the way we'd came. It was a sound of *delight*. Then the hounds began barking.

"We've got to move!" The time for slow and stealthy was over. I flipped up my goggles and turned on the tac light I had mounted on Abomination, which was a scalding thousand lumens bright. It turned the night into day as we ran for it.

It was easy to forget just how supernaturally athletic Sonya was, until she easily got ahead of me. Then she turned on the light I gave her and quickly left me behind, running effortlessly, leaping over logs and ducking beneath branches fast as a deer. We made it less than a quarter mile before I had to shout after her.

"Hold up. We need to stick together so we can cover each other."

She stopped, way ahead, perched on top of a rock, turned back and called, "You know that old joke about how if you're chased by a bear, you don't need to outrun the bear, just your slowest friend? It's like that. Sorry."

I thought about demonstrating my favorite version of that bear joke by shooting her in the knee, but instead I said, "Go ahead then. You've got a handful of shotgun shells left and a pocket pistol, while he's got two dogs, a horse, a bird, a death ray, and keeps coming back to life. So I'm sure it'll work out splendidly for you."

"It always does." But Sonya hesitated, torn, but the sound of barking must have convinced her I was right. "Fine, but try to keep up."

"Except you're going the wrong way." I pointed the direction I thought the road would be. If I did have reinforcements coming, they'd find us faster by the road than blundering deeper into the woods.

We kept running, and Sonya's light stayed ahead of me, only at least now she was stopping to let me catch up once in a while. Thankfully, the underbrush wasn't too horribly dense here, so I only tripped half a dozen times. From the noise, the dogs were getting closer, and every time I crossed a gap without trees, I could see that damned glowing bird had re-formed and was above us again. Only it had learned its lesson and was flying high enough that it would be really hard to blast out of the sky again.

I was going as fast as I could, sweating, my face and arms continually scratched by thorns, yet the hunting dogs were getting closer. Then I realized that there was only one animal barking behind us. The other had gone silent. Instinct told me the quiet one was circling ahead while the loud one herded us toward it.

"Sonya! Wait!" Except she had gotten too far ahead of me again and didn't hear me that time. Her light kept bouncing away. I'd tried to warn her to stay close, and now she was going to get eaten by a demon dog. "Damn it."

Behind me was a new noise, and it was a sound that brought back memories of running from the Fey. *The thunder of hooves.* When the Drekavac's horse had re-formed, it must have lost the high-speed ghost hover and come back in a more terrain-appropriate form. It turned out the Drekavac liked to make a lot of noise, because it let out a sound that sounded like a higher pitched wolf's howl. It was a frightening noise because you could feel the savage joy of the hunt in it, like the monster wanted its prey to know it was having a good time.

I shined my light back the way I'd come from and, sure enough, the fog was getting closer. I assumed the thickest part represented where the monster was coming from, and there was really only one spot here wide enough to ride a horse through.

"Okay, you want to play, you son of a bitch?" I dropped my pack and pulled out the experimental device Milo had given me. "Let's play."

Milo didn't have an official name for his new, nasty little smart mine yet. He was still trying to think of a cool acronym featuring the words Explosive, Quick Deploy, Area, and Denial. The rest of us just called them Milo's spider mines on account of all the legs. I stuck the bottom spikes into the packed trail dirt, aimed it where I thought the Drekavac would have to ride through, pulled the safety pin, hit the arm button, and then ran like hell to get away from the evil little machine before it went nuts.

Thirty seconds after I pushed the big red button, the IR targeting lasers turned on. They served the same purpose as trip wires, only there were eight of them, instantly. And as an added bonus, if our monster didn't set it off, the lasers were on a timer, so it would go inert fast, hopefully before some innocent hiker tripped over our unexploded ordnance. Milo was considerate like that.

I think the default on the timer was thirty minutes but it could be turned up or down, depending on the mission. I didn't need thirty minutes though. I barely needed two before the Drekavac's mount broke one of the lasers.

BOOM!

It was only a pound of C4, but it had pre-segmented wire wrapped around it for shrapnel. One coil silver. One coil iron. I couldn't see them because of the trees, but from the awful noise radiating through the whole forest, I'd nailed the horse.

The scream abruptly died, and somehow I knew it was because the Drekavac had put it out of its misery.

Not that it wouldn't just come back to life again anyway, but at least it bought us some time. I kept running, trying in vain to catch up with Sonya before the dogs got her. And they were definitely after her rather than me. The noisy hound had passed by on my right and was now ahead of me. I never even saw it through the brush to get a shot. I'd bet anything it was chasing her right into a trap.

"Sonya, look out!" But then I lost my footing on a steep downhill and ended up sliding on my back through the leaf scatter, light bouncing crazily through the trees, unable to stop until I caught a log with my boot.

"Face me, Hunter."

I looked back and saw the Drekavac standing on the crest of the rise above me. He hadn't waited for his horse to come back to life but had pursued me on foot. The monster had its sword in one hand and the blunderbuss in the other.

"You will pay for meddling in my—"

He didn't get to finish that sentence because I shot him with Abomination's grenade launcher.

The 40mm round got him square in the chest. The resulting explosion flung flaming monster pieces every direction.

I got up and ran after Sonya, hoping I could reach her in time. I heard her surprised cry over the barking. The trap had been sprung. There was a gunshot, and then another. One of the dogs yelped.

I crashed through the brush until I blundered into a clearing. The flashlight I'd given Sonya was lying on the ground, still on. There was a glowing blue spot, still flickering with weird fire, where one of the dogs had gotten blasted. The other one was at the base of a tree, snarling and leaping, scratching at the bark because Sonya had climbed up into the branches. She had dropped the empty shotgun but fished the little .380 out of her pocket and was trying to get an angle to shoot the dog below her.

I saved her the effort and put a load of buckshot into the back of its head.

"About time," she shouted as the dog dissolved. Then she hopped off the branch, which had to be ten feet up, to land effortlessly on the ground. "I thought you said you could protect me."

"You're not making it easy." I looked around, trying to get my bearings, and it was then that I realized that she hadn't just run off without me, but she'd done it in the wrong direction again, and taken us farther away from the road. "You've got a horrible sense of direction in the woods."

"That's kinda embarrassing actually, considering my family tree. It's a long story."

"Save it. Come on." I pointed. "*This* way."

Sonya retrieved the light and shotgun. "What was your name again? Opie?"

"Owen. Now stay close because I can't help you if you're running off like a—"

There was a hissing crack as the lightning bolt hit the tree Sonya had been hiding in. The trunk blew apart, throwing chunks of wood in every direction. The shockwave put me on my ass.

I sat up, blinked a few times, and realized the newly re-formed Drekavac was stalking through the trees toward us, manipulating its archaic weapon, probably to reload. *How do you reload lightning?* But I didn't have time to think through magical weapon logistics. "Run!"

Getting to my feet, I cranked off several quick shots in the Drekavac's direction. Rather than let me kill it, this time the monster ducked behind a tree trunk. Maybe it only had so many lives, or maybe it was just tired of having to pull itself together. Either way, it wasn't shooting at me for a second, so I fled.

I crashed through the forest as fast as I could. Sonya's light was bobbing along ahead of me. At least this time she was heading in the right direction. It wasn't until I'd gone too far to go back that I realized I'd lost my gear bag when the lightning had struck. Most of my kit was back there in the clearing. I kept my light pointed straight ahead so I could see the ground, because if I stumbled here, I was probably going to get flash-fried.

There was another *hiss-crack* as the Drekavac fired. The lightning hit a stump next to me and ripped it to pieces. I could feel that impact in my lungs. Dirt rained from the sky. I vaulted over a waist-high boulder, turned around, and snapped off two more shots at the Drekavac, forcing it down. It probably expected me to run, but instead I waited a second, sight on the spot where I'd last seen the Drekavac. And the instant the pilgrim hat rose into my vision, I pulled the trigger.

The hat went flying and the Drekavac stumbled out of view. He hadn't disintegrated into sparks that time, so I'd probably only winged him. I moved up on him, aggressive, searching for the glow, looking for a shot.

And then his damned falcon hit me right in the head.

It had dropped out of the sky like a bomb. The only reason I didn't lose an eye to a talon was that it struck my flipped-up night vision first. The PVS-14s got torn off, but better them than my face. It screeched, pecked, and scratched at me, wings beating around my head. It was a lot bigger than it had looked in the air, with a wingspan longer than I could stretch my arms.

I punched it out of the air.

The ghost falcon hit the ground. I shouldered Abomination and fired. I was so close the buckshot dug a hole in the ground right through the bird.

Then one of the dogs came out of nowhere and bit my arm.

I roared in pain as its fangs sunk into my flesh. Searing cold crawled up the limb. It hit right near where the reptoid had gotten me earlier, so it really fucking hurt. The jaws clenched and the dog pulled, dropping its haunches, trying to drag me off my feet.

My left hand was on Abomination's foregrip. I hit the button to pop out the bayonet and stabbed it right through one burning eye. I shoved the silver blade through the dog's head until the point popped out its opposite ear hole. The jaws unclenched as it dropped dead, black skin crumbling to nothingness.

Then the other dog jumped on my back.

I went down hard enough to catch a mouthful of trail dirt. It was on me. I managed to roll over as it snapped at my face. I managed to get one hand on its head, trying to hold it back, but it was like wrestling a block of ice. Its teeth were going for my throat.

And then its head popped and all I could see for a moment was a shower of blue sparks.

Sonya was standing there, with smoke rising from the end of her double barrel. "Quit dicking around and let's get out of here."

I was actually surprised that she'd not kept running. I grunted as I got to my feet. "Thanks for coming back."

"I'm not going to make a habit of it."

We stumbled through the woods. The teeth marks in my arm burned. I could still move all my fingers so it hadn't severed any tendons, but I switched Abomination to my left hand because it hurt less that way. We kept on for a few more minutes, as the fog seemed to dissipate a bit, and there was no sign of the animal menagerie from hell.

"You're not going to bleed to death, are you?" Sonya asked.

"Not anytime soon I hope." I shined my light on my arm and winced when I saw it was a bloody mess.

"I don't see any more glow. Do you think he's gone?"

"Not a chance."

CHAPTER 10

Running for your life through a dark and unfamiliar forest kind of sucks. But after a few breathless minutes I saw a glimmer of light just ahead. That had to be the road. We had to splash across a stream, and then scramble up a steep moss-covered embankment. There was a metal guard rail at the top. Sonya hopped right over. Because of the angle I had to kind of crawl up, and flop over the rail onto the asphalt.

It turned out the lights I'd seen through the trees had been for a little country gas station and convenience store. It was the only building in sight. There were a couple of cars parked there. Sonya started toward the store.

"What do you think you're doing?"

"His aura is jamming our phones. I'm going to see if they have a wired phone that works to call for help," she said. "Like what do you call the old-fashioned kind?"

Was she trying to make me feel old? "You mean a landline?"

"Yeah, like a landline or whatever."

"And involve some more innocent people so they can get murdered by that thing? Hell no."

"I'm not going to endanger anybody."

"Did you miss all the severed limbs back at the bar or the guy it put through the ceiling? Everyone around you is in danger. This creature is here because of *you*. You interrupted a deal between some really evil assholes, and this Drekavac thing is their insurance policy. The guy you stole it from, Stricken, he's bad news and has seen shit you can't even imagine, and even he called this monster relentless. It's not going to stop until it kills you or we figure out how to kill it permanently."

Sonya scowled at me, then looked back at the convenience store, which appeared well lit and relatively inviting when compared to our ominous patch of shadowy roadside. "What are we supposed to do then? Keep running until it catches us?"

"Or until my friends find us." That was honestly my only real hope. I could keep killing this thing all night, but it only needed to get lucky once and I was toast. We could keep trying to stay ahead of it, but I didn't even know if this was the kind of entity that would stop at dawn, or if it cared about daylight at all. I checked my phone, but still nothing. My radio was in the bag I'd lost, so I couldn't even try that to see if my team was close. "I've got a GPS tracker on this vest and help was already on the way to the bar when this thing showed up."

"What if the thing is messing with the GPS signal like it is our phones? Then what, huh?"

I sighed. That was likely. The air had been clear for a little while, hot and fog free, so it was possible we'd lost it, or maybe it needed time to recuperate or something. This could be our best chance. "Okay, but we make it quick, and then we get out."

We hurried over to the gas station. The car that had been fueling up at one of the pumps drove off. There was only one other vehicle parked at the side, probably from whoever was working. There were clouds of bugs flying around the overhead lights. The night felt normal and alive, which was a good sign.

Through the window I could see that there was a kindly looking woman in her fifties working behind the counter. Since I was huge and scary, even when I wasn't filthy, bleeding, and wearing a tac vest, I was probably going to frighten her, and then have to calm her down, which would take precious time. Sonya was a little dirty but looked relatively unthreatening, even with the heavy metal vibe going on. "I'll stand guard out here and watch for the fog. Call that bottom number." I handed her one of my business cards. The second number on it was to MHI headquarters, and with a Hunter currently MIA it would certainly be manned. They would be able to vector my team and all of Boone's guys right to us. "Try not to freak that poor lady out."

"Will do." Sonya handed me the sawed-off. Then she brushed the leaves out of her hair, and *poof*, just like that, she was a totally different person. One second, she was the nose-pierced rocker, the next she was a cherubic little blonde girl with rosy cheeks and a pixie cut. Even the intricate tats on her arm had vanished, leaving just pink skin. "I used to use this face to sell Girl Scout cookies. I totally killed it."

"I bet." Though come to think of it, I really could go for a box of Samoas right then. "Hurry up."

Sonya went inside. I went to a shadowy corner and watched for sign of the Drekavac. So far, each time I'd run into the monster, I'd been warned by the temperature swing. Hopefully, that wasn't an effect that he could just turn off at will or I was screwed.

I had to remind myself this was worth it. All I had to do was keep this obstinate little thief alive despite the best efforts of a spectral bounty hunter, then we could get the Ward from her, use it to destroy Asag once and for all, and then my family would be able to live without constantly watching over our shoulders for assassins every second for the rest of our lives.

I'd given away my good med kit, but I still had my little emergency blow-out pouch on my armor. After I secured the sawed-off through some of the straps and slung Abomination, I did a quick wrap around the dog bite to control the bleeding. It still needed a good cleaning, but hopefully hell hounds didn't carry rabies... hell rabies? *Wow. That would be bad.* While I worked I told myself it looked worse than it probably was.

What was taking her so long? I started walking back toward the window so I could look inside, but then I saw headlights approaching. Thankfully they were regular, normal headlights, and not blue fire beams coming from a horse skull. They were pulling into the gas station, so I moved back around the corner to stay out of sight until I could figure out who this was. Hopefully, it was one of my coworkers, but then I saw that it was a battered old minivan, which certainly wasn't one of MHI's fleet vehicles.

But it turned out that it was a Hunter after all.

Gutterres winced as he stepped out of the minivan's driver seat. The Vatican Hunter's clothing was charred and burnt in spots. There was a bright red burn mark crawling up his neck and ashes on his face. Battered, covered in dust and blood, it looked like he'd had a much worse time than I had. Gutterres started limping toward the front door, but then he paused, as if he sensed something, and then spun and aimed a handgun my way. "Show yourself."

I moved slowly out from the corner. "Rough night?"

Gutterres lowered his pistol when he recognized me. "You can say that. It's not often I get knocked across a forest and then have to carjack a vehicle to go for help. Pitt, right?"

"Yep . . . Gutterres?"

"The one and only. Is the girl safe?"

"She's safe."

He glanced at the store. "Is she inside there?"

"She's in there supposedly calling my people for help. Did she call you instead?"

"I wouldn't know if she had. My coms are down."

"So are mine." The two of us stood there beneath the hum of the fluorescent lights. This was where it got sticky, because my track record for diplomacy with other groups of Hunters was decidedly mixed. "Here's the thing though. That deal you had with her? MHI really needs that Ward Stone."

"That's unfortunate. So do we."

"I figured. Only we need it to save the world."

"Isn't that a coincidence." Gutterres didn't budge. "Perhaps you can petition my superiors to borrow the Ward, *after* we're done using it to save the world."

"We could compare notes over which one of us has the bigger problem and prioritize from there."

"A reasonable proposition. Or I could just claim the property my organization has already paid for and go on my way."

"You could try . . ." I let that threat hang, like he'd have to go through me first. Except that only seemed to amuse him, which I'll admit was kind of annoying and also a little worrying. Earl warned me not to pick a fight with this particular dude. "Look, man, I need that rock to kill Asag. I'm sure by this point you've heard of him."

Gutterres nodded slowly. "Disorder. The chaos demon who was leaving his mark at massacres around the world, who has been oddly silent since your siege of the City of Monsters."

"He's not just any old demon. He's a world-ender. But yeah, you guys should have come to that party. You really missed out."

"We like to do our own thing. But okay, Pitt. Killing Asag is a worthy goal. I'll give you that. Except that attempt would require destroying the stone, and do you have any evidence it would actually work?"

"I killed a Great Old One that way."

"From my understanding you're the only man alive to ever do so."

I shrugged. "I guess that makes me kind of the expert."

"Too bad the Old Ones hail from an entirely different reality, working on an entirely different set of rules than Asag's species—"

"There's *more* of them?"

Gutterres openly scoffed at my ignorance. "I'd assume so. How could there not be?"

I'll admit, I hadn't really thought about that much. One of them was bad enough. "So what does the Pope need another Ward for? Don't you guys already have one?"

"I'm not at liberty to discuss what we need it for. My assignment is to retrieve this one, and time is of the essence...So please, step aside."

Neither one of us was pointing our guns at the other, but we were both still holding them. I didn't like the idea of harming a fellow Hunter, but I had no doubt this particular holy warrior was dedicated enough to his order and mission that he'd shoot me in the head and sleep like a baby tonight. Only I couldn't back down because this was bigger than either of us, so if he lifted that pistol I'd fucking end him...though unlike Gutterres I'd probably feel remorse afterwards. A very tense few seconds passed.

Only I never got to find out which one of us was more committed because our standoff was interrupted.

The lights flickered. The buzzing insects scattered. It was suddenly very cold.

"Not this guy again."

"We should continue our debate later," Gutterres suggested.

"Truce," I quickly agreed, because he didn't strike me as the sort to shoot me in the back as soon as I turned around. The Vatican guys couldn't possibly earn an *alright* on the Harbinger scale if they were dishonorable back shooters. I started looking for targets. "Let's blast this jackass."

"That's a bad idea. I'm guessing you've not fought one of these before."

"This is my first time on the Drekavac express. Would not recommend."

"How many times has he been destroyed so far tonight?"

"Uh . . ." That was a good question. I'd kind of lost track during all the excitement. "Does his petting zoo count?"

"They're all facets of the same being, but only the humanoid form ultimately matters."

"Five or six probably?"

"Then you've only seen him at less than half his might. Shooting him is a waste. He can be reborn thirteen times before the cock crows, and each time he'll simply come back stronger. The last few forms are incredibly deadly. The only way to keep him from re-forming is to take his head as a trophy."

"Decapitation. Got it." I could work with that.

"It has to be clean. That's got to be the killing blow. If he's killed before his head comes off, he'll just come back. Got it?" Gutterres was staring at the fog bank that was curling along the edge of the road. It was skulking along like a living creature, low and hungry. "How are you with a blade?"

"I can Lizzie Borden the shit out of stuff, but it isn't exactly graceful. I'm way better with a gun." I wished Edward was here. He loved decapitating things. "You?"

"Superb." And the way Gutterres said that obviously wasn't boasting, it was simply an honest assessment of capabilities in the brief moments before battle. "Only I lost my main blade when I got hit by lightning. All I've got left is this little fellow." He spun a hooked karambit around in his left hand that he'd kept hidden from me before. There were two kinds of men who carried karambits. Morons who liked to spin them around and show off who were more likely to cut themselves than their opponents, or psycho knife fighters who were really good at hooking limbs and severing tendons. Gutterres didn't strike me as a moron. He'd probably been intending to surprise me with that nasty thing if we had thrown down.

I drew the massive kukri from the sheath on my vest, flipped it around, and extended it to him, handle first. The blade was twenty-one inches of wickedly curved steel, specifically designed for happy little Gurkhas to lop off limbs.

Gutterres hefted my kukri. "This will do."

"I want that back. Okay, I'll be the distraction. When he's concentrating on murdering me, circle around and take his head."

"Will do." And then he turned and ran toward the woods. Even injured the dude was so quick that he vanished within seconds, like some kind of Catholic ninja.

Since I needed to draw the monster out, I walked away from the building and out into the open. It didn't make sense to hide behind a bunch of gas pumps to fight something armed with a blunderbuss that shot lightning bolts.

There was movement inside the country store. Sonya was banging on the glass, shouting something that looked like "What are you doing?" and "Are you insane?" I waved my hand downward, trying to tell her to stay low.

The fog was hanging like a solid wall a hundred yards ahead. I was going to feel really stupid if Gutterres doubled back and grabbed Sonya while I was busy getting hacked to pieces, but sometimes you just have to go with your gut. I started walking toward the fog. "Here goes nothing."

Just in case my stupid plan didn't work, I picked out some things I could take cover in or behind quickly. Then all I could do was hope that Gutterres was as good as he thought he was.

There was a growing glow ahead. The eerie light made the trees on both sides of the road look like towering monsters. The Drekavac appeared. The wide-brimmed hat bobbing up and down as it strode toward me. I think he'd been trying to duel me once before, so drawing him out seemed like the thing to do.

"I'm challenging you, Drekavac!" I shouted. "Come over here and fight me."

I had a feeling the strange being might have been willing to go *mano y mano* earlier, but that was before I'd hit him with a grenade, because this time he simply pulled his cannon out from under his coat and started blasting.

I ran for the tree line.

Lightning struck. It blew a hole in the road behind me. Flaming chunks of the asphalt rained down as I dove into a drainage ditch and landed face-first in a pile of weeds. Some asshole had thrown some beer bottles in here, and a couple had broken, so I got cut *again*. Gutterres hadn't been lying about the Drekavac coming back stronger, because it took a lot less time between shots now than it had before. I crawled forward as the monster blasted the dirt above me. The impact was so close it rattled my teeth and I could feel the pressure in my eyes. I popped up long enough to fire two shots in his direction, but I aimed low on purpose, skipping silver buckshot off the road, because I didn't want him dead, I wanted him distracted. I was subjecting myself to this abuse in the hopes of making the monster perma-dead.

The Drekavac stumbled as I clipped it in the leg, but then I ducked back down as its gun belched blue fire. Its aim was off, way high, because he missed the ditch entirely and nailed a big tree behind me.

Or at least I assumed he had missed his target, until the top half of that tree landed right on top of me.

I got hit everywhere. The dirt walls of the ditch caught the trunk, but the smaller branches filled the space. My body was shoved hard into the mud. There were so many leaves, I couldn't see a thing. I tried to move, but I was squished. The harder I struggled, the more branches got stuck. "Damn it!" I thrashed my way forward, trying to find an angle so I could shove the smoking trunk away, but I was hosed.

The Drekavac used that time to walk up to the edge of the ditch. I looked up to see those two fiery eyes staring down at me through the leaves, and there was no pity in the flames. As the creature pointed his gun at me, his face was a twisted metallic facsimile of humanity, but its sliver of a mouth turned into an all-too-recognizable sneer . . . because it knew I was doomed.

Gutterres proved it wrong.

There was a flash of steel. The Drekavac's head flew from its neck. The body slowly fell to its knees, and then came apart at the seams, melting into blue fire and ashen bits. The big hat caught a gust of wind and floated a little way before it disintegrated too.

The other Hunter went over to the severed head and picked it up. Weirdly enough, the Drekavac's head still appeared to be alive. It didn't move or speak, but the fire was still burning in his eye sockets, and the expression frozen there was *really pissed off.*

"Is it dead dead?" I shouted.

"This should stop him for tonight. Though the head will turn to ash at dawn, enabling the creature to re-form again tomorrow night."

I'd volunteered to be a punching bag to buy Sonya one night? "That's it?"

"I don't make the rules, Pitt. You have to put down a Drekavac thirteen times before the cock crows to banish it once and for all, but its last few evolutions are so powerful that pulling off that feat is rather legendary. I'll deliver this head to the local priests and maybe they can do something to slow him down a bit more." Gutterres walked over to the edge of the ditch and looked down at me. "Are you wounded?"

"Only my dignity." The tree falling on me had really sucked, and I was going to have bruises everywhere and the cut from the broken bottle, but nothing felt broken or punctured. I tried to wiggle free, but there was just too many branches pressing against me. "I could use some help here."

"You're really stuck, aren't you?" That seemed to amuse him.

"Yeah." There were probably eight hundred pounds of big fuck-off tree on top of where I was squished. The only reason I wasn't dead was because the biggest chunk had hit the dirt first, and the leafy branches that were trapping me had spread out the impact. "Give me a hand."

"That looks like it'll take you a little while to get out. Here's your knife back." He dropped my kukri. It stuck point down in the dirt, well out of reach. Then he began walking away. "Thanks for the assist."

"Hang on!" I shouted, but Gutterres kept walking. "What the hell, man?"

"Sorry. Sonya made a deal with us. If the Ward survives our mission, maybe we can work something out with MHI. I'll be in touch."

"Gutterres! You son of a bitch!" But my yelling was in vain, because he wasn't coming back. Not that I could blame him, because if the tables were turned, I'd probably have done the same. It beat having a shoot-out to see who got the Ward. I went to work trying to pry myself free.

It took me a minute of fighting, snapping branches, collecting more scratches, and covering myself in sap, but finally I scrambled out from underneath the fallen tree. I snatched up my knife and ran back to the country store.

Oddly enough, I was surprised to see that Gutterres hadn't used that time to escape with Sonya. The minivan he had stolen was still there. Minivans are always depressing to look at, but this one looked even sadder than usual, since it was sitting on four deflated tires.

The Catholic Hunter was standing there, looking nearly as

ticked off as the severed head he was still carrying. The convenience store lady had come outside to see what all the commotion was about, which was when I noticed that the only other car that had been parked here—which I assumed belonged to the convenience story lady—was missing.

I started to laugh when I realized that Sonya had slashed Gutterres' tires so he couldn't follow her, and then stolen the store lady's car. She'd screwed us all.

"This is not funny," Gutterres snapped.

I had to disagree. I found the situation hilarious.

CHAPTER 11

Gutterres and I ended up hanging out at the country store until our rides showed up. Once the Drekavac's severed head got stuffed into a cooler, our phones started working again. The convenience store lady had made Gutterres pay for the cooler and the bags of ice too.

It turned out her name was Bonnie. She was short, plump, cheerful, and I hadn't needed to hide from her either. Only a tiny minority of people know about the world of professional monster hunting, but as soon as Bonnie saw the patch on my vest, she had brightened right up and said, "Oh, it's Monster Hunter Incorporated. You boys come in and rest up." It shouldn't come as too much of a surprise that she knew who we were, because if anyone was going to know monsters are real, it's someone who works the night shift at a hole-in-the-wall stop and rob just outside Atlanta. She asked me if that nice man from South Africa was still around because she hadn't seen him for a few years—he used to get his morning coffee and doughnut here—but I had to tell her that Priest had transferred to our Colorado office.

Bonnie was genuinely upset however, not because of the monster shooting lightning bolts—those things happened—but because that *nice young girl* had stolen the car keys from her purse and taken Bonnie's Hyundai Sonata. And it was nearly paid off! I talked her into not calling the police and reporting it stolen by promising Bonnie that we'd get her car back ASAP.

I got ahold of Earl and he was sending someone to pick me up. My colleagues had already found the wrecked truck. Earl had used his nose to follow my trail. When I had called, he had been in the clearing where I'd lost my bag. It might take a few minutes for them to get here though. It turned out the reason we hadn't seen very many cars driving by was that a crazy thick fog wall had formed around the area as the Drekavac had grown more powerful, and there had been several car accidents which were now blocking the nearby roads. It was a real mess.

After I got that straightened out, I needed to tend to the dog bite. To disinfect you need pretty strong alcohol, but all Bonnie had for sale was beer and wine. Probably a legal thing. "You got anything stronger?"

"Oh, hon, of course I do." Then she pulled something out from under the counter. "Personal stash. Help yourself."

I took it, and nothing screams quality like vodka in a plastic bottle.

Bonnie called after me, "Don't bleed all over in there. I just cleaned it!"

The wound wasn't too deep. Pouring the alcohol over it hurt more than getting bit, but I dealt with it as good as I could with what I had on hand. There were lots of monsters with infectious bites, like zombies or lycanthropes. I had no idea about ghost dogs, but one perk about being Chosen was that I was apparently immune to that sort of thing, so I wouldn't be turning into anything. However, I was still human and could get a nasty infection as easily as the next guy, so hopefully a hundred proof would kill any germs that got in there. Then I washed the sink because it's rude to leave blood all over the bathroom. When I returned to the main room, Gutterres was still there. Bonnie was grilling him about what had been outside her store throwing lightning bolts and what was in that cooler, and he was being vague but also trying to reassure her that it wasn't anything she would ever have to worry about again.

Gutterres appeared to be in a sullen mood. Which was understandable. He was about as beat-up as I was and was holding a towel full of ice from the soda machine against the burn on his neck. In addition to getting swatted across the forest, his organization was out a bunch of money he was probably accountable for, and Sonya wasn't answering his calls.

"Leaving me stuck under a tree was a dick move." I sat next to him at the end of the little lunch counter. Then I slid the half empty bottle of Popov in front of him.

"Sorry about that." He took a swig of the vodka and grimaced.

Bonnie got two hot dogs off the roller, stuck them in buns, and dropped them in front of us. "On the house, boys."

"Thank you, ma'am," Gutterres said. Then he grumpily went about eating his plain hotdog as Bonnie went back to work.

I squirted ketchup all over mine. I've got the constitution of an ox and a gut that can digest anything so I actually kind of like gas station hot dogs, and this one hadn't been on the roller long enough to turn to jerky, so it wasn't bad. Gutterres drank more of the vodka. For a moment, we were just two tired Monster Hunters who'd had a hard day at work.

Gutterres spoke in a way that would let him blend in anywhere in America, but there was just enough of a rough edge to it that suggested English wasn't his first language, and something else that made me think he'd not learned it here. "Where are you from?"

"I grew up in Macao."

"Huh. Neat." I'd kind of expected him to say Rome.

"You?"

"Military brat. We moved a lot. So how do you know Sonya?"

"She reached out to us last year. She said that her father was of the faith and had been a *holy warrior chosen by God.*" Gutterres chuckled at that.

I'd skimmed those memoirs. "Wasn't he?"

"He certainly believed he was. Was he really? How should I know? Sonya was interested in following in his footsteps. She approached us, told us of her abilities, and then asked to join our order."

So much for Sonya's mom trying to keep her sheltered from this line of work. "And you hired her?"

"Of course not. We shot her down. Politely, but firmly."

"Ouch." In the extremely brief time I'd known her, she hadn't exactly struck me as the humble type. "How come?"

"You don't *apply* to my order. My order observes, and then approaches the rare person it deems worthy. Some of us were raised from birth for this work, and even then there are years of training and testing before we are offered knighthood. We are few in number. When we need more manpower, we call upon the Swiss Guard, but the order itself is rather select. How can I explain this? MHI is a job. *This* is a calling."

That was my turn to laugh. He obviously didn't get why I thought that was so amusing either. I had drawn the galactic short straw and had been getting my ass kicked ever since. "Dude, I know a lot more about callings from higher powers than you'll ever guess, but never mind. Please, continue."

"In this case, Sonya took it personally, and said a few rather unkind things about our order, our leadership, and the chastity of their mothers."

"She strikes me as having a bit of a chip on her shoulder."

"You think?" Gutterres snorted. "However, when we learned about the auction, we didn't have sufficient resources in the area—my flight just arrived this afternoon—my superiors remembered Sonya approaching us, knew she was living here, and since they were desperate, they made her an offer. Retrieve the Ward for us, and they would reconsider her previous application."

"I take it that didn't go over well?"

"She was still offended about how we rejected her previous advances. She said her father knew Saint Peter personally so how dare we, so on and so forth."

"Heh. I can't really relate. When I came back from the dead the first time, my guide was Jewish."

Gutterres gave me an incredulous look, but then continued. "Sonya said she would do it, but only if we paid her a very large sum. Despite my objections, my superiors agreed to her terms. I was supposed to meet her, confirm the Ward was real, and take possession."

I made sure Bonnie was out of earshot before asking, "Okay, level with me. What world-ending crisis do you guys need the stone for?"

"I'm not supposed to talk about it with outsiders." But then he sighed, realizing that we were stuck here together for a bit, so he might as well say what he could. "What I can tell you is that there's been a serious incident in South America."

I wondered if that might be the event Stricken had been alluding to. "Where?"

"In an area where the people have few resources, so their pleas for help are usually ignored. Their government has no PUFF equivalent for a threat of this magnitude, so it's nothing your company would be interested in."

"We might surprise you on that. We do some pro bono killing on occasion. I hear you Secret Guard guys are big on charity cases."

Gutterres nodded. "There's a network of the knowledgeable among the local priests. People come to them with their problems, so word of monster trouble always gets back to my order eventually. One of us was dispatched to check on the rumors. What he found was extremely troubling."

"What kind of troubling?"

"Evidence of Old One activity. Not minions either. The real deal."

"No shit?" In that case *troubling* was a serious understatement. The Great Old Ones were bad news, though the world had seen a lot less activity from that particular faction since Franks and I had obliterated their Dread Overlord.

"They are mobilizing, reasons unknown. Anyone who gets in their way has been killed or worse. The Secret Guard has tried to stop them, but it appears a major offensive is brewing. At first we just thought it was cultist and some minor summonings, but there is a *major* entity involved. Some type of very large creature from their dimension, which had been hidden and dormant for hundreds or perhaps thousands of years in an odd cavern deep beneath the ground."

I nearly choked on my gas station dog as Gutterres described something I had once seen in the centuries-old memories of a conquistador.

"Are you okay, Pitt?"

"A cavern where it's almost like the walls are made of living tissue, and the wind is its breathing, with mystical pillars made of obsidian inside, that's way out in the jungle in Brazil, beneath an ancient lost city? Or at least it used to be out in the jungle, but that was a long time ago. I don't know about now."

His eyes narrowed suspiciously. Some of that must have matched with their scout's reports. "How do you know about that?"

That was a really long and complicated story, and I didn't have time right then to tell him about how as one of the Chosen I was sometimes granted the power to read people's memories, including the times that I'd seen some epic weirdness from the point of view of a conquistador who had been cursed. "That's where Lord Machado got turned into a monster five hundred years ago. I thought the big thing would have slithered off after that, but..." It was obvious that I'd confused the hell out of the poor guy. "Look, I'll explain everything, but you need to know right now, the big thing you're dealing with? Assuming we're talking about the same thing, it's not just the thing in the cave you've got to worry about. It's connected to this other being, she's some sort of herald, messenger, string-puller, instigator for the Old Ones, and she's been around for a *long* time. She's been out there for thousands of years impersonating goddesses and screwing with mankind. I knew her as Koriniha, and she's insanely dangerous."

My honest fear must have been coming through because Gutterres simply said, "I believe you."

"That demon bitch seduced and manipulated Lord Machado into nearly killing us all, she stabbed my girlfriend—now wife—in the neck, and then tried to trick me into blowing up the whole world to try and save her life. She vanished after we defeated Lord Machado. If Koriniha is back, very bad things are about to go down." I took a deep breath. And here I'd been so certain that I needed the Ward more. "This sucks."

Gutterres and I were both silent for a long time. Then he said, "This thing is gathering its forces for unknown purposes *right now*. So...about which one of us needs Newton's device?"

"I don't honestly know." I'd accidentally woken up our world-ender while trying to stop their world-ender several years ago. "One wants to enslave us and use humans for food and entertainment, and the other wants to obliterate the whole universe. It's like choosing would you rather have lung or colon cancer?"

"I'd prefer neither, but one threat at a time."

"Flip a coin?"

The Vatican Hunter ate the last of his hotdog and thought about it while he chewed. He swallowed. "Sadly, the decision will be made for us if someone else, like your MCB, gets to Sonya before we do, and then neither of us will have it."

I looked at the wall clock. It was almost midnight. "And the Drekavac will be after her at sundown again tomorrow?"

"Perhaps. When I leave here, I'll go directly to a church

where I can perform some rites over this head." He thumped the cooler with his shoe. "That might slow it down a bit, buy us a few extra hours maybe, but I wouldn't bet on it. Cursed beings of this nature are tenacious. They are only set free when they have a contract to fulfill, so they take a great deal of perverse joy in their work. We need to find Sonya before he does." Headlights pulled up out front. Gutterres looked over, saw that it was one of those tall Mercedes-Benz vans, and said, "These are my reinforcements. I must go." He stood up.

I gave him one of my cards. "I'll have our archivist pass on everything we know about Koriniha in case she's connected to your problem."

"I appreciate that, and we'll do the same for the Drekavac. I recognized this one from the descriptions. This particular creature has been around since the 1600s."

"Not shocking, considering his fashion sense."

"The first time my order encountered him was in the aftermath of the Salem Witch Trials. As a man, he was a judge, trusted to be righteous, who instead made a pact with evil in exchange for immortality. What you saw tonight is only a fraction of his capabilities. He'll only grow stronger the more you kill him. We're all in great danger. My organization isn't very keen on working with others, but in this case, I will strongly suggest to my superiors they may want to make an exception."

"I think that would be wise."

"We'll be in touch." A bell rang as Gutterres walked outside. The van door slid open, and there were two really tough-looking guys sitting inside with carbines slung over their plate carriers. I'm pretty sure those weren't local clergy. Gutterres got in and they immediately took off.

"That half-Chinese fella seems kinda high strung," Bonnie declared from behind the cash register.

"He doesn't work for us. Different...company." We'd shaken on it, but that didn't mean I could trust him. They were almost certainly going to grab Sonya as fast as they could and not tell us a thing. I waited until Gutterres' van was down the road a bit. Then I got up. "Could I see that phone you let the girl use?"

"Sure, hon." She reached beneath the counter and pulled out an old plastic phone. "Here you go. But I thought your cell was working again?"

"It is. But I'm going to hit redial and see who Sonya called."

"Oh, the girl didn't call nobody. It was the weirdest damned thing. Somebody called her."

"Really?"

"It was funny timing too. Nobody ever calls here at night. It's pretty dead usually. Anyways, as soon as she picked up the phone to dial, there was somebody talking to her. She must've picked up before the first ring, but anyways, whoever it was got her to stop and listen to them."

That didn't sound like a coincidence at all. "Did you hear what she said?"

"Oh yeah, sure. She seemed real confused, but then she got all excited, perked right up and said that was way more than she'd already gotten paid so far."

Son of a bitch...Somehow—I looked at the security cameras suspiciously—someone had known where Sonya was, and made her an even better offer for the Ward. "Are your cameras connected to the internet?"

"Oh, those aren't hooked up to anything. The cameras quit working years ago. I leave them up to scare off shoplifters."

It had to have been some form of magical scrying then, which narrowed down the possible suspect pool considerably. I was going to be extremely pissed off if it turned out I'd been tailed by an invisible gnome all night. "Did she say anything else?"

"She said she knew where that was, it was a bit of a drive, but she was on her way and then hung up. Too bad I didn't realize she was about to steal my Hyundai, bless her heart."

"We'll get your car back, I promise. I'll even get it detailed."

"What if you don't find it?"

"Then my company will replace it with a new one as an apology for inflicting her upon you." I mainly didn't want Bonnie filing a police report and complicating matters. MCB monitors that kind of stuff.

"I'll take your word, on account of the other ones of you I've met being so damned courteous."

I stared at the phone in my hand and tried to remember what the old trick was so you could call the last number that had called you on landlines. Bonnie must have read my mind.

"Star six nine, hon," she said helpfully.

"Thanks." Once I heard the dial tone, I punched that in.

Except it didn't do anything. The number was probably blocked, or maybe that service didn't work anymore. I memorized the number written on the tape attached to the phone though, in the hopes that maybe Melvin could somehow look up who had called that recently.

I texted everything I'd learned and Bonnie's license plate number to the other Hunters. Then, with no other investigative leads to follow, I used what time I had left to buy a whole bunch of snacks and sodas for the road. I had a feeling it was going to be a long night. I paid for my snacks just as another car pulled into the parking lot and honked. That had to be my ride. I passed Bonnie one of my cards. "Thanks for your help and call me if you think of anything else."

"Sure will. And tell that cute South African fella to stop by when he's back in town. I do love his accent."

While Holly Newcastle drove, I sat in the back seat with Doc Sherlock so she could fix up my arm. If you've never gotten five stitches put in you while riding in a moving Suburban in order to close a gash from a hell hound fang, you aren't really living. Or so I told myself while Sherlock ran the needle through my arm. She missed a few times because Holly kept hitting potholes. Luckily, that hurt way less than pouring vodka on it.

When I said that out loud, the doc scoffed at me. "There are so many things that work better and hurt less."

"I know, but I left my med kit at the bar and I lost my go bag in the forest."

"We found it. Your gear is in the back," Holly said. "You're probably going to want to armor up."

"Why? Where are we going?"

"Long story short, the gnomes told Trip and the gnolls told Milo basically the same thing, that there's something crazy evil holed up in an old farm west of here. When word got out that the Ward was up for grabs, that thing started putting out feelers to all the supernatural creatures saying it would pay them a reward for information about the stone's whereabouts."

"What kind of evil are we talking about? Because if it's something that can do magical scrying, somebody found us and called Sonya out of the blue to make her an offer she couldn't refuse."

"The city gnolls said the country gnolls said it smelled *dead but not*, and they were scared of it, which doesn't narrow it down much because they're scared of everything. And the gnomes, those greedy little shits, didn't know what it was either, they only cared that it was offering to pay a reward." Holly was distracted, mostly focused on the road, because we were going way too fast in the dark. "The rest of the guys are on their way there now."

I was kind of surprised. That was more fly by the seat of the pants than was normal for MHI. Usually, if there weren't any lives in immediate danger, we'd at least try to find out what kind of creature we were dealing with. Blundering into the unknown was a great way to get killed. "That's not a lot to go on."

"I know, and Albert's doing a rush job on the research right now, but fifteen minutes ago a state trooper buddy of Boone's who was at one of the fog wrecks said that he let through a young woman in a car that matches the description you gave us, going in that same direction."

Considering how long it had been since Sonya had ditched me, that meant she'd probably had time to retrieve the stone from wherever she'd hidden it—and it made sense that her stash would be somewhere near Perdition's Abyss—and now she was on the way to meet her new buyer.

"And don't forget the other complication," Sherlock said, as she wrapped my arm in medical tape. "That's the best part."

"Oh, yeah. The stupid-ass gnomes told the lizard cult the same thing they told us. So the reptoids are more than likely on the way too. I wish Trip would've clocked the little thug who told him that but Trip's too merciful. I would've kicked him right in the beard."

Holly really didn't like gnomes.

"Friggin' gnomes." I reached over the seat and grabbed my bag so I could get my armor on. This night just kept getting better.

CHAPTER 12

Thirty minutes later we reached the location. The property was in the middle of nowhere and consisted of a couple hundred acres in its own little valley stuck between some heavily wooded hills. It was almost MHI compound-level hidden. Easily secluded enough to be a home for some kind of secretive monster, assuming the gnomes weren't lying to us and this was just their attempt to have us take out a rival meth cook or something.

The other Hunters were parked in a field off the main road half a mile from the farm. We were the last to arrive. The other vehicles were out of sight and hopefully we weren't close enough yet to tip off whatever it was that owned the property.

The other Hunters were already gearing up. Mags were being checked, rounds were chambered, and night vision tested. A couple of Hunters had already gone up the hillside to set up sniper positions. Earl—who was by far the stealthiest one among us—had gone ahead to reconnoiter the farm. That left Boone in charge. The Atlanta team lead had a laptop out and was using Google Earth to map the property and give assignments to everybody else. It appeared there was a two-story farmhouse and a big barn, as well as a bunch of smaller sheds and outbuildings.

After an evening being chased by a horrific evil without much in the way of help, it felt really good to be with my team again.

Boone saw me get out of the truck. "I heard you had a rough night, Z. You up to fight?"

"Hell, yeah. This is just a scratch."

He looked to Doc Sherlock, who wasn't about to lie to her boss, and raised an eyebrow. Luckily, she covered for me. "It looks like a regular dog bite. He'll be fine."

"You sure?" Boone asked.

"How many Vicodin have you taken for your bad back today, Boss?" Sherlock responded.

"Point taken." Hunters working while messed up wasn't exactly an oddity. We spent a lot of money on painkillers and energy drinks. "Jump in."

Holly checked her phone. "Incoming email from Lee. He's scrounged up what he could about this place. Let's see what we've got..." She started reading. "Okay, for tonight's location, who had murder-suicide in the pool for what the awful backstory would be?"

"I did," said Mundy.

"Then Mundy wins it. Albert says thirty years ago the farmer who owned this place went bankrupt, then went insane and stabbed his wife with a pitchfork before hanging himself in the barn."

"Hey, I had suicide," declared Gregorius.

"But not *murder*-suicide. Pay up, suckers," Mundy crowed. Because, of course, Hunters always placed bets on what the awful backstory would be of the horrible, haunted places we had to visit. I usually put my money on it being the home of a weird cult that had conducted acts of unspeakable evil there, because I'd had really good luck with that one over the years.

Seriously though, not to get all metaphysical or anything, but there's just something about places with bad energy attracting bad entities. The worse the history, the worse the occupants it drew. Milo always bet on *nothing bad ever happened there, it's just misunderstood*—because he was an optimist—but I don't think he'd ever once won the pool.

Holly continued reading off her phone. "The bank repossessed the farm. The locals considered it cursed, the usual. It lay fallow for decades, rotting and falling apart, and it looks like ten years ago the land was bought by an obvious shell company—Albert can't track down any actual real people behind it yet. There're no weird police reports. The number of missing people in this county is about in line with the demographic average for rural America, so it can't be anything too hungry." Holly put her phone away. "So what are we thinking moved in here? Vampires? Necromancers?"

Trip said, "If it's either of those, then Sonya is probably already dead."

I'd tried to warn her not to run off. "Lack of missing locals indicates it's not vamps."

"Unless they get their food delivered," Gregorius said. "People are always vanishing in Atlanta."

"I'm hoping for three kobolds standing on each other's shoulders in a trench coat trying to look big," said Boone. Then he went into command mode. Whether leading soldiers or Hunters, the man had a lot of practice giving orders. "Time to shelve the guesswork. I hate going in blind, but we work with what we've got. Earl's already snuck up close and has eyes on. It looks like that car Pitt reported as stolen is parked between the barn and the farmhouse. There's no other vehicles in sight other than some old rusted tractors and junk. I've put the Groffs on the hill providing overwatch. Skippy is on standby with the chopper in case we need a medevac. The rest of us will move in nice and quiet, up that field." Boone pointed at the weed patch that had probably once grown crops. "We get into position and then breach at the same time. My team will hit the house. The Alabama team will take the barn. Once those are cleared, we can search the rest of the smaller structures. Questions?"

"What about Harbinger?" Hertzfeldt asked.

Though that was a perfectly reasonable question—you really don't want your allies to be in your backstop—Holly and I shared a knowing look. *Poor Newbie.*

"Don't worry about Earl." But then Boone unconsciously glanced up to see how full the moon was, but it wasn't even close. "Earl will do whatever he wants. You stick with me and don't worry about him. Anybody else?"

"I've got a bad feeling about this," Milo said. "We don't know what's hiding in there."

"You want to just camp here while that shapeshifter gets eaten?"

Milo shook his head. "I didn't say that. She's the daughter of an old friend. We have to try. Just be careful, everybody."

"Noted. Anybody else?" Boone asked again.

There was nothing. Most of us had done this kind of thing a lot. The Hunters were energized, but it was a casual sort of dangerous. You can be confident in your lethality and simultaneously aware of your mortality without getting all worked up about it.

"Move out."

The path we took through the fields had already been scouted by Earl, so there weren't any booby traps—mundane or magical. The worst thing I bumped into was some stickers that attached themselves to my armor like Velcro. We moved, single file, quick but quiet, everyone scanning side to side with their night vision. Whatever they had grown here before had all been replaced by weeds. The trees around the farm buildings were so ancient and overgrown that even if there had been sentries posted, they wouldn't have been able to spot us through the leaves and dangling vines.

We all heard Earl whispering in our earpieces. *"I'm a hundred yards to the northwest of you lying under the old tractor."* The rusting hulk was so covered in moss that it took me a second to pick it out. *"I've got no lights or movement. No sign of anyone, including Sonya."*

That was worrisome. Earl should have at least been able to catch her scent. The fact he couldn't meant she wasn't actually here, or worse, she was, but whatever lived here had a way of obscuring its presence.

"This is Shannon," said half of our sniper team on the hillside. *"The only thing we have moving on thermal is you guys. The car's still hot though, so it hasn't been stopped for long."*

We passed a scarecrow in the field, but it was just a regular old boring scarecrow. Not the "built from dead bodies so it can reanimate and murder you with a hay hook" kind of scarecrow. That was the first thing Earl would have checked. But just in case, Holly poked it with the muzzle of her gun to make sure it wasn't filled with cursed bones.

There was an odd noise. Almost like a high-pitched child's voice. Every Hunter froze. The noise came again. *Eeeeeen.* I slowly shifted Abomination in the direction I thought the eerie call was coming from. Milo pointed his rifle that way, cranked up the magnification on his scope, and scanned. A moment later he whispered, "It's just an owl." That got relayed down the line and guns were lowered.

That owl had no idea how close it had come to getting blasted. This kind of shit is *tense*. Even when you spend a lot of time in the country at night, sometimes normal animals can sound really odd. I had almost shot a regular old coyote once on a hunt because it had sounded like it was speaking in a foreign language.

We reached a barbed-wire fence, but it was so floppy and loose that it really wasn't much of a fence at all. Even our shortest Hunters made it over without getting snagged. Boone started giving hand signals. This was where the teams parted ways. His guys went toward the house. I took point for my team as we headed for the barn.

It was me, Milo, Trip, and Holly now. Earl would join us when he felt like it. I'd worked with these Hunters so many times that we were damned near telepathic with each other. We walked through the pitch-black, stepping carefully, because there was a lot of old wood scattered everywhere. There were piles of ancient garbage, empty paint cans, and scattered tools rusted beyond recognizability. We followed a fence line and stayed low until we got close to our target. The barn was huge, easily big enough to park a couple of combines inside, but it had a slight lean to it. The beams looked soft and were coated in patches of moss like a cancerous growth.

There was a big sliding door, but the rollers were probably rusted solid. Luckily, it was stuck open enough that even I would be able to get through without making too much noise. That was a fortunate break. I'm a big dude anyway, but covered in armor and mag pouches, I'm downright thick.

I peered through the gap, but even with the night vision, all I could see was more old junk piles and dust particles floating between them. I signaled for my team to stop and wait for Boone's signal. I clicked my radio twice to let the other team know we were in position. There wasn't anything new from Earl. The Groffs were in an elevated position with precision rifles, but they'd stay quiet unless there was something they needed to warn us about.

Boone clicked three times. They were going in.

I signaled for Trip to follow me, and he passed that on. As soon as it popped off, everybody would go to hyper-speed face shooting, but until then we'd proceed quietly for as long as we could. I moved into the barn.

My team was smooth, practiced, and we went quick, even

in the dark. As each of us swept in, we covered a sector. I went right with Abomination shouldered. Trip came in behind me and went straight ahead with his LWRC .45 subgun up. Then Holly with her shorty 300 Blackout, and then Milo with his JP mini-Cazador hooked left. In normal life I'm kind of a clumsy giant but put a gun in my hand and I turn into a tactical ballerina and these guys were my choreographed backup dancers. The idea of Milo in a tutu made me giggle.

It was a big open space, but it was filled with old cars, farm equipment, and piles of assorted junk. The floor was hard-packed dirt. It stank like moldy decaying hay. My eyes immediately started to itch. This was going to be hell on my allergies. I should've put my gas mask on.

We moved through the trash, heads on a swivel, checking up and down too, because the things we routinely had to deal with had no problem hanging from ceilings or popping up through floors.

"*This is Earl,*" he whispered in all our ears. "*There's something talking in the back of the barn.*"

We were in the very front of the barn. I looked to my teammates, confirmed they were ready, and we headed for the rear of the building. It was getting really hard not to bump into anything though. The interior was a hoarder's delight. There were a bunch of rickety shelves close together here, and they were so full that the aisles between them made for a snug fit. There were cardboard boxes melting into squishy mush on the floor, spilling their contents of rusting nuts and bolts. I got spiderwebs all over my face. I bet this place was full of brown recluses and black widows.

There was a loft above us and ladders leading up. Normally I would've cleared the high ground before proceeding, but there was no way we'd make it up there without alerting whatever it was that was waiting ahead of us. I pointed it out to Holly. She lifted her gun to cover the loft and watch our backs as the rest of us moved forward.

Then we heard what Earl had gotten through the cracks in the walls. The voice was raspy and barely audible. "Who sent you?"

"I already told you!" That was Sonya, and she sounded like she was in distress. "I got a call. I was told to come here because you wanted to buy the Ward."

"Do you think I'm a fool? You brought that weapon here to destroy me." Even though the voice was quiet, I recognized the accent. You don't spend as much time around the Shacklefords as I have without being able to recognize an old-school Southern accent real fast. "Who sent you against me, child?"

"Nobody," Sonya cried out. "Wait! Don't kill me, please!"

I carefully moved around the edge of an old cattle trailer until I could see the conversation. I noticed Sonya first, and she was still wearing the face of the cherubic bubbly blonde girl from next door. Only now she was hanging upside down, five feet from the ground. Her ankles were bound with a thick rope, which had been tied to a ceiling beam.

Then I saw what Sonya was talking to.

The creature's back was toward me. It was naked and shaped like a man, but way too skinny. Not just emaciated but dehydrated to the point that all the moisture had been sucked out of the tissues, until all that was left had the consistency of jerky. Bones were visible through gaps in the leathery skin. It was like a body that had been left out in the desert sun to blacken and shrivel, only it was moving around just fine.

I turned back to Trip and mouthed the word *undead.*

Trip shrugged, like what was he supposed to do with that? Undead was a big catch-all term with a wide variety of capabilities.

I spread my hands like *beats me,* because I had absolutely no idea what kind it was. It didn't *feel* like a vampire. It was obviously intelligent, but that could still be a bunch of things. If it was a revenant we'd be able to put it down with a few bullets and go home. If it was something like a lich, we were in deep shit. So we'd just have to proceed with caution. I peered back around the trailer.

"Last chance, child. Who sent you to kill me?"

"I told you nobody! I mean, somebody sent me, but not to kill you. They told me you were going to give me five million bucks in cash for the stone."

"I live in a barn because I have to hide from Hunters. I have to pay degenerates to steal bodies from funeral homes to continue my work," the thing snapped. "Does it look like I've got that kind of money?"

"I thought maybe you were laying low." Sonya was quiet for a moment. The only noise was the creak of the rope holding her up. "Okay, so obviously there's been a big misunderstanding here. How about you let me free, I'll take the stone away, and get it out of here? Your secret's safe with me, Mr. Phipps."

"That's Colonel Phipps to you."

Earl must have caught that exchange. *"Aw, hell. It's Buford Phipps."* And from the way Earl said that, it was bad news. If Earl had covered this particular undead asshole during Newbie training, it must have been on a day I'd fallen asleep during class. I looked back at Trip but he didn't seem to know either. *"Give me one minute to change, then distract him. I'll take Phipps. You free the girl and run."*

That was not good. That sounded like Earl was going to wolf out on us. He had the control to force a change whenever he wanted, but he rarely did it this far from the full moon, and only if we were dealing with something crazy dangerous. Shit had just gotten real.

The abnormally gaunt form of Phipps was walking around Sonya. He didn't look like much more than an awkwardly thin zombie, but Earl wouldn't risk transforming around other Hunters unless it was absolutely necessary. Phipps was appraising Sonya like she was a hanging side of beef. I could see the profile of his face now. There were patches of skin and hair stuck to it, but most of it was bone. It turns out a skull can still look hungry.

"It's too late for your conniving ways now, girl. You got spirit-world blood in you. It's been a long time since I've had a feast like that. I'm going to bleed you slow, because spirit blood has so very many uses in my work. Then I'm going to eat you alive, piece by piece. It'll hurt more than you can imagine. Or you can tell me who sent you, and I can put you out of your misery quick and clean, no suffering. I promise."

The undead monstrosity didn't sound particularly trustworthy as he said that either.

"I don't know. I swear!"

"That's fine. I'll ask again after I eat your hands. We've got all the time in the world." He grabbed her wrist and tugged. Sonya shouted and thrashed. She hit him with her free hand, and from the solid noise it made, even hanging upside down, Sonya packed a right like a heavyweight boxer, but it did nothing to the monster. The rope creaked as he dragged her over to his mouth. Phipp's jaw hinged open. The jerky skin stretched.

The mouth got bigger and bigger until it could have fit Sonya's whole arm inside.

Earl hadn't gotten his requested sixty seconds yet, but I couldn't let Phipps bite her limbs off. "Hey!"

Phipps spun toward me. My boss had asked for a distraction. Figuring that nothing was quite as distracting as a magazine full of silver buckshot to the face, I put the IR targeting laser on the monster's skull and fired.

So did Milo. Half a second later so did Trip. The monster let go of Sonya and staggered back until he hit the wall. Multiple lasers danced across his body as sparks filled our night vision. Sonya was sent spinning back and forth like a punching bag that had just gotten violently kicked, and I just hoped that none of us plugged her by accident. Milo's and Trip's guns were suppressed, and quiet. Mine was the only one that was loud as hell.

We had probably pumped a pound of silver and lead through Phipps, but as the smoke cleared, he was still standing. Splintered bones immediately fused back together and the dangling bits of jerky sucked back into place. Our projectiles hadn't accomplished shit.

Buford Phipps roared, *"Kill the trespassers!"*

Which caused all the many corpses buried in shallow graves around the farm to wake up. Hands erupted through the floor. Bodies that had been hidden on the loft flopped over the edge. Shelves of junk toppled over as the dead rose. Milo yelped as claws grabbed his boot.

The lead monster pointed one bony finger at me, the jawbone moved, and sanity-rending arcane words spilled out. He was casting a spell. *Phipps was a lich!*

But before he could finish the incantation and rip my soul out or turn me into a frog or some other awful fate, a hairy werewolf arm punched through the wall. Claws sank deep into Phipp's rib cage, and Earl yanked the lich right through the planks and into the night.

Holly moved up, stubby carbine shouldered, nailing undead in their heads as they crawled toward us. Her gun was so quiet the impact of the bullets made more noise than the action. Skulls popped and the bodies went limp. From their sluggish move-ment, mummified appearance, and rotten clothing, these were old zombies, stashed here for who knew how long. But there was a *lot* of them. It was like the entire floor of the barn was moving all around us.

"Mundy might not have won the pool after all," Holly said. "I had serial killer burial ground."

"Great," I shouted back. "I liked his better."

Earl had the lich. We needed to rescue Sonya and get the hell out of here. But that was easier said than done, as the ground split open between me and her, and there was suddenly a sea of grasping hands and snapping teeth between us.

"Hang on, Sonya," I said as I reloaded Abomination.

"What's going on?" Sonya was still swinging back and forth and couldn't see in the dark, so all she probably knew was that there had just been a lot of gunfire and chaos. "Is that you, Opie?"

Her getting my name wrong again made it awfully tempting to just shoot the rope holding her up so she'd fall on her head, but there was a zombie crawling out of the ground directly beneath her. "Can you climb up? There's zombies under you." Sonya bent at the waist, caught the rope, and with a couple quick tugs, propelled herself to the ceiling, where she grabbed the beam and hung there, far out of reach of the undead. The move was impressive. It must be nice to be half yokai. She'd probably be fine up there while the rest of us down here got devoured.

Milo stomped on the hand holding his boot until enough bones broke that the zombie had to let go. Then he stuck the muzzle of his carbine close to the lump of a rising head—*Whump!*—and pierced the skull. The experienced Hunter took one look around the barn, realized we were about to be swarmed, and said, "We'd better boogie!"

He was right. Our position was indefensible. "Sonya, can you get free?" A zombie lunged at me, coming seemingly out of nowhere through the dust, but I blew its head off. "We have to go—now!"

"The knot's too good." She had moved into a sitting position on the beam but was clearly struggling with the rope around her ankles. She was supernaturally athletic but good luck hopping out of here with her feet tied together. "I need something to cut it."

Trip had that covered. He ripped the RMJ tomahawk from the sheath on his belt. At first I thought he was going to say *catch* and toss it to her, but instead he just hurled it. The hawk flipped end over end and the head got planted into the wood next to Sonya with a *thunk*. It hit so close that she flinched in surprise.

"There's a tomahawk by your hand, kid! Hurry up!"

"Nice throw," I said as I used Abomination's buttstock to brain a zombie that was reaching for Trip.

"Cheryl and I have been going to this ax-throwing place on date night," Trip said. "It's fun and practical."

Sonya wrenched the hawk out of the beam and slashed at the ropes. Trip kept his blade sharp enough to shave with, so she cut right through. "Got it!" She flung the ropes away.

Now for an orderly, fighting retreat. "Head for the exit." Holly and Milo crowded in next to us, and the four of us fought our way toward the door, shooting and moving.

Except then Phipps hurled Earl through the wall. Our werewolf crashed through several zombies, broke through two big support beams, and then bounced off a third. Decades of dust and owl poop rained from above. It was like our night vision turned to static as swirling dust filled the air. We were blind.

The already leaning barn shuddered. Earl's body had broken the supports. The whole structure groaned.

The barn was going to fall on us.

I flipped up my goggles and turned on my light. That wasn't much better. The choking dust was reflective. I could hardly see, hardly breathe. That crazy impact would've killed most things, but there was a flash of pale fur as Earl leapt up and rushed past me to get back into the fight. Werewolf Earl is *terrifying*. Even with some bones sticking out, he was fast as lightning, and I was super thankful that he had the self-control to not accidentally disembowel me on the way. He jumped out the hole his body had just made in the wall and went after the lich.

Sonya leapt from the beam to the loft. It was a good ten feet but she made it, and disappeared from sight.

Nails popped like gunshots. Boards splintered. "Run!" I screamed.

The suddenly awakened dead struggling up from below shoved over the shelves in front of us. More zombie hands burst through the ground, clawing. All they had to do was slow us up for a second and we were doomed. There was a mob rising ahead of us and more behind. We were still a few feet from the door when the back quarter of the barn came crashing down, crushing zombies beneath tons of wood and shingles. And it kept collapsing in sections, coming for us like a slow-motion train wreck.

We riddled the zombies ahead of us as we rushed for the door. Trip and Milo dove through the gap. I could barely see through the dust, but I knew Holly was right next to me.

"Where's—" But before I could finish shouting for her, Sonya seemed to fall out of the sky. She landed and nailed a zombie right in the forehead with the tomahawk's back spike. She ripped the spike out and congealed black ooze sprayed out of the hole like its head had been pressurized. "Go! Go!" I blasted zombies until Sonya and Holly were outside, then I hurried and squeezed through the door after them.

As soon as I was clear, Trip and Milo immediately began trying to force the rusted roller door shut, but a pile of dead flesh crashed against it. Several arms shot through the gap, and the only reason the barn didn't barf out an army of zombies was because the stupid things were temporarily getting in each other's way. It was five zombies trying to fit through a one-zombie hole.

But while we were plugging the hole, the barn was still falling down, and if the front fell over on us...

Holly yanked an incendiary grenade off her vest. I realized what she was trying to do, so I stepped back and immediately blasted a couple rounds of buckshot through the door. This close the buckshot pattern just chewed a single big hole through the wood. "Grenade!" Holly yanked the pin and shoved the grenade through the hole. The canister bounced across bare zombie feet. "Move!"

The rest of us didn't need much encouragement. As soon as Trip and Milo let go, the door burst open and zombies piled out, but that only mattered for a second, because then they were all bathed in chemical fire. The whole front of the barn was consumed in a flash. The zombies were so dry they went up like kindling.

Fire leapt up the walls. Just as it reached the last remaining section of roof, the whole front of the barn collapsed. Heavy beams landed where we'd just been standing. The impact launched a cloud of choking dust outward.

I turned back and gunned down one of the burning zombies which had made it through. Milo head-shot the last one. Zombies don't feel anything, but it never seems right to let something that was once a person wander around burning until it quits kicking.

The barn was just a pile of wood now, and most of the stuff buried beneath must have been extremely flammable, because it went up fast. Zombies who hadn't gotten their heads smashed were still struggling to get free. Arms poked through the debris but the fire was spreading fast. All those buried zombies would get burned to a crisp. We had to move away because the heat was becoming too intense.

Boone got on the radio. *"What is your status, Alabama?"*

Milo responded. "Watch out for zombies. Their boss is a lich. Earl is fighting him. We don't know where they are. We've recovered the hostage and are falling back."

"Gregorius, ready the SMAW. Milo, we're headed your way. Come in, overwatch."

"This is Shannon."

"If you see a werewolf, do not shoot the werewolf. I repeat. Do not shoot the werewolf."

"Don't worry. We already know about him. Make sure you warn the new guy though."

Milo keyed his radio. "Boone, the lich is Phipps."

"I didn't catch that. Say again."

"Colonel Buford Phipps."

"Oh shit. Not that asshole! Everybody prepare to fall back. Hit the lich with the biggest guns you've got and retreat toward the vehicles."

Boone was clearly scared, which didn't happen very often.

"Milo, who is Phipps?" Trip asked.

"A total freaking whackadoodle jerkface. I'm talking eugenics, mad-science nutball stuff *before* he discovered necromancy."

"Is he powerful?"

"Crazy powerful. This is why we shouldn't go on rescue missions without doing our homework." Then Milo pointed. "There's Earl!"

I turned my flashlight that way just as our werewolf boss got hurled across a field. Phipps must hit like a truck because Earl was airborne for fifty feet before he hit the ground and rolled through the weeds. He lay there, a great hairy mass, breathing hard, and bleeding from several deep lacerations. Werewolves regenerate crazy fast, and Earl made a regular werewolf look like a wimp, but as he started to get up, he wobbled, then sank back down into the grass. Even the king of the werewolves needed some time to heal.

"That's bad," Holly said, because anything that could kick the ass of Earl Harbinger, could eat us mere mortals for breakfast.

The lich came out of the forest. His slender form didn't look that physically dangerous, but there was a frightening energy building in the air. Phipps wasn't walking. He was levitating a few feet off the ground, and he slowly began rising higher in the air. The plants around us wilted and crumbled to dust as he sucked the life force out of them to power his magic.

We opened fire. Dozens of bullets smacked into the hovering form, but they seemed to zip right through with little effect. A rifle bullet shattered one of Phipp's arm bones, tearing the thin limb right off. Only instead of falling, the arm seemed to hover for a moment before suctioning back into place.

Phipps gave us an almost dismissive gesture, and my entire team got knocked off our feet by a wave of telekinetic energy. I crashed into a fence. Milo ended up in an old horse trough. Sonya ran away.

"Hunters!" Phipps voice was loud enough now that it could be heard even above the crackling flames of the barn. "I despise Hunters. I only wanted to be left alone, to continue my study of unnatural philosophy in peace. I was at the cusp of ridding mankind of its impurities when that cur Sherman burned my first laboratory. And every time I have tried to rebuild since, you damnable Shacklefords have been nipping at my heels. When will you subhuman filth learn to let me be?"

I struggled to my feet and launched a grenade at the lich, but he merely floated to the side as the 40mm projectile zipped past. My grenade exploded out in a field.

Phipps looked down at his burning barn. "You've destroyed all the subjects of my anatomical study! Do you have any idea how long it takes to collect this many cadavers without being detected? I'll have to find a new home and start over. Oh, you will pay dearly for this trespass." He was twenty feet in the air now, and violent winds were whipping through the farm. Then the skull snapped toward the road as Phipps sensed a new danger. "You cowards even brought reinforcements."

I turned to see what had gotten the lich's attention. There were a bunch of headlights racing down the dirt road directly toward us.

"Lizard folk," the lich muttered, clearly disgusted. "So the

Hunters have allied themselves with the Lacertian Cult. I should have known you inferior types would eventually commingle with reptiles."

The reptoids and their followers were the opposite of allies, and if the lich didn't kill us, they certainly would...But for once I was really thankful that gnomes were a bunch of loudmouth reprobates, because if they hadn't blabbed to the reptoids, we wouldn't have gotten this great distraction. Everybody on my team used the opportunity to get up and run like hell.

Buford Phipps pointed both of his hands at the road, bony fingers splayed wide, and started chanting. The ground began to shake so much that I lost my footing and fell on my face. The earthquake increased in intensity. The smaller buildings collapsed. Fissures were torn in the Earth. Real magic is some scary shit.

The cultists were inbound fast. The maniacs hung guns out their windows and started blasting, only the growing earthquake was bouncing the vehicles around so much that they weren't in danger of hitting anything. The lead car suddenly slewed sideways, and the next one in line clipped it. The convoy came to a sudden, dusty halt. Cultists bailed out. Among them were the hulking, shrouded figures of actual reptoids, and there was so many that this had to be the entire Atlanta cell.

The lich clapped his hands.

A terrible magic was unleashed. The ground rippled and came alive. It was almost as if the soil became liquid, and the entire field along the side of the road rose into a wave, rolling and growing, racing toward the vehicles. The cultists screamed as it crashed over them. Cars flipped. Bodies were crushed. Then the wave broke. Tons of rock and soil fell, burying them instantly.

As the dust cleared, fifty yards of road was just *gone*. Other than one pair of headlights sticking straight up out of the dirt, it was as if the reptoids had never been there at all.

Milo hadn't been kidding about crazy powerful. We needed to take Phipps out fast or his magic was going to smoke us all. I looked toward the car Sonya had stolen from Bonnie. The interrogation we'd overheard had made it sound like Sonya had brought the Ward with her, so it was probably in that car. If I could reach it, I might be able to power it up just long enough to obliterate Phipps.

The insanely dangerous lich turned his attention back toward MHI. "Now, where was I? Ah, yes…" He began floating in my direction. "I was about to twist the blood from your bodies like wringing out a sponge."

As the other Hunters started shooting at the lich again, I got up and ran for the Hyundai.

Sonya was already there, messing with something in the front seat of the car. At first I thought she was trying to drive away, but then I realized she was struggling with some object inside a plastic grocery bag. It was the Ward.

"Turn it on!" I shouted.

"I'm trying to figure out how." She got out of the car holding a black rock about the size of a softball. The Ward that MHI had used before had a strange mystical code imprinted on it, where bits of the rock would actually become pliable to be moved into shape. Align the right code and it would activate. This one had to be something like that as it seemed to come to life in Sonya's hands. "I think I've got it."

The Ward flared with a blinding white light.

When I blinked myself back to reality, all of the windows on Bonnie's car had been blown out. Sonya was lying on the ground. For a second, I thought that she must have activated it, but then I heard Phipp's insane cackling. The lich was still alive. It hadn't worked.

Sonya bolted upright, gasping for breath. I ran to her. She still had the rock in her hand, only now it had turned a bright angry red color, so she'd done something.

"Let me see it." I tried to take the stone from her but she wouldn't let go.

"It's stuck," she said in disbelief.

I was so much bigger and in such a rush that I hoisted her to her feet and she still wouldn't let go.

"No! I mean it's stuck *to* me!" She turned her hand upside down and shook it, but it was like the Ward was glued to her palm. "Get it off."

"Hold still." I grabbed her wrist and turned it so that I could see the Ward better. It was smaller than MHI's old one, the designs on it were a little different, and it was clearly stuck to Sonya's hand. Not stuck. *Fused.* Like welded to her skin.

"Uh…"

"What the hell, man?" Sonya demanded. "The dead guy's looking right at us. Make it go, Opie."

"Working on it." I touched the markings on the stone, but they seemed stuck in place now. I tried to force them to move, but they were totally frozen. "How do you *jam* a rock?"

The lich was ignoring all the bullets smacking into it and floating our way. "How *dare* you bring such dangerous alchemy into my presence?" He made a dismissive gesture. A gust of hurricane-force wind smacked into me. I planted my feet and managed to hold onto Sonya for a couple of seconds before she was torn away and I got tossed over the hood of the car.

"Curious. It appears there has been an unexpected interaction between Newton's natural science and the spirit mongrel. Bring the device to me, child."

Sonya tried to run, but Phipps clenched one bony fist, and she was instantly frozen in place. The look stuck on her face was one of absolute terror as she began to float up toward the lich. Phipp's licked his nonexistent lips with his jerky tongue. Not only could a skull look hungry, it could also look greedy.

"A fascinating development. Perhaps this new discovery will make up for tonight's inconvenience."

Boone's voice was in my ear. *"Everybody duck and cover."*

The other team had taken advantage of the lich's distraction. I realized what they were doing, but I also knew that the results would probably kill Sonya too. Without hesitation I sprang up, sprinted forward, and tackled her. We both hit the ground hard.

Then Buford Phipps exploded.

CHAPTER 13

When I say that the lich exploded, I'm not talking a little explosion, like I could get from Abomination's grenade launcher. Oh no. I'm talking a big-ass literal fireball, with a deafening roar and a shockwave that bent the air around it and made me eat dirt.

"That was a direct hit, Gregorius," Boone said over the radio.

"You know I love me some thermobaric warheads, Jay."

I lay there, ears ringing, coughing, really thankful that Gregorius had used a round that relied on heat and pressure in the biggest gun we'd brought tonight, as opposed to a warhead with a bunch of shrapnel, because I'd be dead. Instead, I probably only had brain damage. But a lich was a terrifyingly capable foe, so even hitting Phipps with a bunker buster was no guarantee that he was finished. I rolled off Sonya and looked in the direction the lich had been levitating, but there was no sign of him.

"Are you alive?"

"Yeah. Quit shouting in my ear." Sonya glanced around, obviously stunned. The blast had flattened several of the outbuildings. A few more fires had started and the barn was a mighty blaze by this point. Boone's guys must have set the farmhouse on fire too, because it was burning. There were brain-shot zombie corpses scattered everywhere. "You MHI guys really don't mess around."

"Are you injured?"

"Just this stupid thing stuck to my hand." She shook the Ward but it wouldn't fall off.

"Okay, stay down while we finish this son of a bitch." I got up, checked Abomination to make sure it was ready, and stumbled in the general direction I thought the monster would've ended up.

Since we'd gotten separated when the lich had given us that telekinetic bitch slap I looked around for my team. The spot where Earl had been was empty. He'd run off, which was good, because even though he had far more self-control than most werewolves while transformed, he was still a werewolf and would need to stay away from people until he changed back. I spotted Milo and Trip already up and moving, searching the charred area for the lich. I couldn't see Holly though. I keyed my radio. "Come in, Holly, status?"

"I'm fine, Z. I'll catch up in a minute."

Boone's team had moved up on the barn and began searching the ground with their flashlights. Gregorius was there with the gigantic SMAW launcher over one shoulder, grinning. Which was a pretty common expression among Hunters whenever we had the opportunity to set off a truly glorious explosion.

"Got one of his arms here," Mundy shouted. "It's still crawling."

"Hurry and throw it in the fire," Boone ordered.

Mundy picked up the lich's arm with a look of distaste. That was understandable since the fingers were frantically grasping. He tossed it on the bonfire. A moment later Sherlock found a leg, and Hertzfeldt found a pelvis stuck beneath the tractor. Apparently, there were some limits on how far apart Phipp's severed bits could end up and still pull themselves back together. A thermobaric warhead gets the job done.

"Put the parts in different woodpiles and burn them all," Boone directed his team.

I joined Boone. "You think that'll work?"

"Probably. Even really tough supernatural bodies can only take so much physical punishment. The real problem with liches is that they pluck their heart out and leave it in a magic jar that their spirits retreat back to when their bodies get destroyed." Then he noticed a rib stuck in the dirt near his boot and bent over to pick it up. "Where's the girl?"

I'd been kind of distracted. "I left her back at the car."

Boone looked at me like I was stupid. "The one who has

already run away from you a couple times?" He grabbed his radio. "Anybody got eyes on the shapeshifter?"

"Way ahead of you guys." I turned around to see Holly and Sonya walking toward us. Holly looked smug, while Sonya looked guilty. Holly had her carbine casually pointed at Sonya's legs, and her gun handling was good enough that the angle certainly wasn't on accident. "Our little shapeshifter here was about to make a run for it."

"I was not."

"Uh-huh..." Holly said. "I bet you were getting in the car to drive for help, right?"

Boone scowled at me and shook his head. "Moron."

I felt like such a sucker. I turned toward Sonya. "I can't believe you stole that nice woman's Hyundai."

"I was going to return it. It got kinda trashed though."

I sighed. A promise was a promise, so it looked like I was buying Bonnie a new car. "Let me see the Ward."

Sonya held out her hand and showed us the stolen treasure. "Yeah, about that..." She turned her hand over, spread her fingers wide and then shook it hard, but the Ward still wouldn't let go. "Since I've got all you occult experts here, is it supposed to do that?"

I signaled for Milo. "Hey. Magic rock check."

Milo came over from where he'd been gathering lich parts to take a look. He tossed Phipp's jawbone in the nearest fire. Then he approached Sonya and politely said, "May I?"

"Knock yourself out." She held the stone out to him. "I touched it before and it didn't do anything, but when I tried to turn it on it got all weird and bright for a second, and now it's glued to me or something."

Milo squinted through his glasses. "Huh... Part of it actually disappears into your palm. It's got to be fused with her bones."

"What?" Sonya sounded really worried.

"Does it hurt?" Milo asked.

"No."

"*Cool...* Sorry. I imagine that's kind of horrifying, but it's also kind of amazing what those inventors came up with back in the old days." Milo ran one gloved hand across the numbers visible across the top of the Ward. They seemed to quiver with a life of their own, but just like when I tried, they wouldn't move to a different setting. "Yep. This is the real deal alright. A little more compact than our old one, and that one never bonded itself with anyone's flesh as far as I know. Nifty."

"That is not *nifty*. Make it come off."

"I don't know how." Milo reluctantly let go of the Ward. "Sorry. We'll have to research that."

Boone cut in. "This chick and her pet rock sound like an Alabama team problem. Now if you'll excuse me, I'm going to go make sure this lich is really dead and then try to figure out how many reptoids got buried. This PUFF check is going to kick ass."

"But the lich killed the reptoids, not us," Trip pointed out.

"The MCB doesn't need to know that."

After Boone left it was just those of us who'd been in the barn clustered together. Milo stopped examining the Ward long enough to ask, "You guys okay? Anybody bitten?"

Everybody checked. We were professional Monster Hunters. There wouldn't be any of that "hide the bite until you suddenly turn on your friends" nonsense with us. If a Hunter got zombie-bit, then it was time to take Old Yeller behind the barn, or go out in a suicidal blaze of glory, depending on that Hunter's last wishes. There was no cure for a zombie bite . . . Well, except for me once, but to be fair, I'd been trying for the blaze of glory way out at the time.

We all trusted each other. As everyone said they were fine, we all believed them. However, none of us trusted Sonya.

"I didn't get bitten." She was filthy, covered in dust and cobwebs, but didn't appear to be bleeding. "I don't know if that would work on me anyway."

"Bummer. I was hoping for an excuse to shoot you," said Holly.

"Who are you anyway, lady?" Sonya snapped. "Have we met before, or are you just this bitchy to everybody younger and prettier than you?"

"Oh, look at that, the shape-shifting skank wants to catch an ass beating."

"No. I just want this thing off of me, so I can sell it and get paid. I stole it first, fair and square."

"You're not selling shit." Holly wasn't in the mood for her nonsense. "My people have had to stick our necks out twice to save your stupid life today."

"I wouldn't be sticking that old turkey neck of yours out anywhere people might see it."

Holly just laughed, because she was smoking hot and knew it. "I've got a PhD in Mean Girl Politics, twerp. Nothing that comes out of your fake-ass face is going to get a rise out of me."

"My face and ass are less fake than those tits."

"You mouthy little shit..."

I briefly wondered if I'd have to tackle Holly to keep her from murdering Sonya. Trip and I exchanged a nervous glance, but he whispered, *"Not it."*

"Ladies, there's no need for confrontation." Milo—ever the gentleman—stepped between Sonya and certain death. "We can work this out like civilized—"

Sonya moved with supernatural speed, caught Milo by his long red beard, and spun him around to use as a human shield. She was so fast that poor Milo never even had a chance. She must have had Trip's tomahawk hidden on her the whole time, because she stuck the blade under Milo's neck. "Back off!"

I was tired and possibly concussed, so it took me a moment to realize what she was doing. "Are you kidding me?"

"I'm taking the stone out of here. If you can't fix this, maybe the Secret Guard can. Once we're down the road, I'll let him go."

"Uncool," Milo said. "Very uncool."

Sonya began backing Milo toward the stolen Hyundai.

"Oh, come on, you idiot," Holly said as she casually aimed her carbine at Sonya's face. "We just nuked a lich. You really want to try us?"

"Don't make me hurt him."

I sighed. This was probably the most pathetic hostage situation ever, with about a zero point zero percent chance of success for the hostage taker. Boone's Hunters had heard the commotion and were spreading out and shouldering weapons. Sonya struck me as someone young, brash, and in a situation way over her head, but I really didn't want to see her get that head blown off, so I keyed my radio. "Everybody be calm." Then I addressed our overachieving hostage taker. "Think this through. This can't possibly work. If you hurt him, everybody here is going to shoot you. A lot."

"Yeah, we all really like Milo," Holly said. "You should have taken Z hostage. He's way less popular."

"True that. I'm not nearly as cuddly as Milo."

"It's all in the beard," Milo squeaked.

Sonya's eyes were darting back and forth, taking in the many well-armed Hunters prepared to shoot her, and surely realizing that she done fucked up. "Wait. Milo? The Milo? Milo Anderson?"

"That's me."

"Oh, shit! You were one of my dad's best friends."

"Yep. I sure was."

"Which would make you slicing his head off before being cut down in a hail of gunfire extra tragic." I slowly stretched my open hand out, trying hard to not make a tense situation a whole lot worse. "So how about you give me back Trip's happy little murder ax and we chalk this up to a big misunderstanding."

She wasn't ready to give up quite yet, so she played the desperate negotiation card. "I really need that money, Opie. Let me sell the rock to the Catholics."

"Money's not worth dying over."

"Somebody is dying though. That's why I need a lot of cash fast, to save her."

"Who?" I asked.

"It's a long story."

"You didn't mention that earlier."

"Why would I tell you people anything? It's Hunters who made her sick to begin with."

"Sure. This is all because her grandma needs a spleen transplant or something. Those copays are killer." Holly turned on her laser and a bright green dot appeared on Sonya's forehead. "Scrunch down a little, Milo."

"Hold your fire," Milo ordered.

"Why?" Holly asked. "You actually believe her?"

"Kind of, and maybe we can help. Chad was my friend. If his family is in need, helping them is the least I can do. Plus, no offense, Holly, but I was one of the people who taught you to shoot, remember? If any of you guys are going to be launching bullets around my head, it should be Z."

That was quite the compliment coming from Milo. "Thanks, man."

"Well, all things considered, I'd prefer Julie, but she's not here."

"Fine." Holly slowly lowered her gun. "I did warn you to scrunch down first."

"Do you people ever shut up?" Sonya shouted, exasperated. "Okay. Don't shoot. I'll let him go—"

Except Sonya's impending surrender was moot, as Earl Harbinger suddenly appeared behind her and grabbed the tomahawk by the handle. Luckily for her, Earl was back in human form. If he'd still been in werewolf form, he probably would've swatted her head off her neck. Instead, he just roughly shoved her and Milo to the ground and kept the weapon.

"What the hell are you thinking, girl?" Earl stood there, angry, wearing nothing but the mud and leaves stuck to him. That wasn't shocking for most of us. When your boss is a werewolf, you learn to expect the occasional incident of workplace nudity. "These Hunters risked their lives to save your fool ass, and that's how you thank them? That's downright disgraceful."

"Sorry, Earl." And shockingly enough, either Sonya was the best actor ever, or she really did feel sheepish about it. "I didn't know that was Milo."

"Because threatening to kill one of my other people is somehow better?" He extended a hand and helped his old friend up. "You okay, Milo?"

"Only thing hurt is my pride," said the humblest man any of us knew. "She got the drop on me."

"Yeah. She does that to folks."

"I said I was sorry. This is a desperate situation, okay? I wasn't lying about a life being at stake. I'll explain everything." Sonya covered her eyes. "But, eww, could you at least cover up or something?"

"Oh, you'll live." Earl tossed the tomahawk back to Trip, who caught it. "Trip, would you mind getting my gear? I left it on the back side of the barn."

"I'll get your pants," Trip said.

"I mostly need my smokes."

"I'll get your pants," Trip reiterated as he walked off.

"Is your little friend going to do anything else stupid?" Boone had circled back toward us, probably to get a good angle on Sonya with his rifle. "Because my guys really need to get back to work."

"Naw, she's done screwing around," Earl glared at Sonya. "Ain't you?"

She nodded sullenly.

"Good. Alright, Hunters, we should be clear to burn all of old Buford here, but the only way to get rid of a lich once and for all is to destroy his phylactery. His nasty spirit will fly right back to it to hide. Considering his history, I doubt we'll find it here though."

"Sounds like you guys have met before," I said.

"Afraid so. Buford Phipps has been a nuisance since the Civil War, when he was just a mortal jackass who found a spell book and started raising zombies. Last time he popped up, Ray and Susan took him out. Before that, Leroy Shackleford destroyed him. I've killed him once before, way back when. Hell, it's practically a family tradition. First time one of us killed him was Bubba Shackleford himself hitting Buford with a cannonball. If luck holds, we won't see old Colonel Bone Head for another twenty or thirty years, when some poor bastard finds his phylactery and gets possessed again. Hmmm... about that, just in case..."

"You heard the man," Boone shouted at his team. "If you find a cursed artifact, do not play with the cursed artifact."

Regular family traditions were things like do you open presents on Christmas Eve or Christmas morning, but I'd married into the Shacklefords, where the traditions were things like fighting a Confederate lich every few decades. Someday little Ray would probably get to blow up Phipps too. Good times.

Most of the Hunters went back to scouring the area for body parts, but the Newbie, Hertzfeldt, was still staring at our naked boss. "Wait. Harbinger is..." He trailed off, astounded. "So *that's* why we weren't supposed to shoot the werewolf."

"Yeah, kid," Boone patted him on the shoulder. "That's one of those company secrets covered by that NDA you signed in training. Now come on. Let's go count how many reptoids got buried so we can collect us a big-ass bounty." Boone led the bewildered Newbie away.

"It's not as much of a secret as it used to be after the siege," Earl muttered. It was really hard to turn into a werewolf every full moon when you're stuck at the top of the world with hundreds of other Hunters in close proximity for a year. Trip returned with Earl's gear. "Thanks." First thing he did was fish out a pack of cigarettes and lighter to get his nicotine fix. He lit one and then started getting dressed. "Milo, call Skippy for an extract. Boone can clean this mess up without us. We've got to get this Ward somewhere safe."

"What about me?" Sonya asked.

"Call a taxi. Or one of them Uber things they've got now.

I told your mom I'd try to keep you safe, and we've more than fulfilled that promise. Then you paid back that kindness by threatening one of *my* men. After that behavior I'm not in the mood for any further bullshit. You're on your own." But then Earl saw the pained expression on Milo's face. "What?"

"You missed that part. The Ward has *merged* with her. I don't know how to remove it. It has to be something to do with her not-human half messing with magic designed to be used by humans. We can probably figure it out, but we have to take her with us."

Then it was my turn to deliver more bad news. "From what the Vatican Hunter said, that Drekavac thing is going to be coming after her again in..." I checked my watch. It was just after two in the morning. Sundown this time of year was around seven. "...about sixteen hours at the earliest."

"Sucks for her then," Holly said.

Earl took a long angry drag off his cigarette. "You sure about that, Z?"

"I've got no idea, but Gutterres seemed pretty certain of it. That Drekavac is going to keep coming back, stronger and stronger, until we manage to kill him thirteen times in one night. I probably got about halfway there and it was already one scary son of a bitch." I gestured toward the road. "Not burying a bunch of cars in a dirt-tidal-wave-level scary but getting there. He's fast, mobile, has really bitey spirit-animal helpers, a blunderbuss that shoots lightning bolts, and he strikes me as the highly motivated type. On her own, she's as good as dead."

"You've got to help me, Earl," Sonya begged.

I cut her off. "What was it you said to me earlier when I told you MHI needed the Ward Stone to stop an ancient chaos god from destroying the whole world?" I feigned confusion trying to remember a distant memory. "Oh, yeah. 'Sounds like a personal problem.'"

"I didn't mean it *that* way." Sonya batted her eyes and tried to look innocent for Earl. I wasn't sure but she might have even shifted her face a little bit to look more victimized and forlorn, and she was already wearing her Girl Scout cookie dealer face. "So I stole a thing from a bad guy to try and help some good guys, and in exchange I was going to use the reward money to help a loved one in need."

"And then everybody clapped," Holly said sarcastically. "So she's the real hero, but I've got a suggestion. We could just saw her hand off. We keep the stone, and then maybe she can find Stricken and apologize enough that he'll call off his attack dog."

"Hang on," Sonya shouted.

"She's kidding," Trip said. "We wouldn't do that."

Holly shrugged.

Of course this offended Milo's sense of chivalry. "We can't abandon her. Her dad was a fellow Hunter!"

"And my dad was a construction worker, Milo," Holly said. "That doesn't mean everybody else owes me a free house. She just threatened to cut your throat."

Milo grimaced because Holly had him there. "Yeah, but—"

"No buts. We've got what we came for. You want to find a nicer way to get the rock, great, do surgery, whatever, but then kick her to the curb. If princess here wants us to save her ass, she'd better talk to the accountant." Holly jerked her thumb toward me. "Maybe she can work out a payment plan."

"What's the PUFF on a Drekavac anyway?" Trip asked me.

There was a sudden crash as a bunch of the burning barn beams split, dumping more shingles into the inferno. A giant cloud of sparks rose into the night sky.

"I don't think that monster is on the tables. I'd have to fill out a request form and send it to the MCB for a special one-of-a-kind ruling. Judging by his abilities and annoying ability to keep coming back from the dead, it's got to be a pretty good payout."

"Give me your best guess, Z." From Earl's tone, he was asking that question as the man who had to pay for all this stuff. SMAWs and attack helicopters aren't cheap.

"Well, specials are all over the board. Like this lich. They're all different based on their danger and history. MCB will look at their criteria and then decide the payout. What did MHI get paid for Buford last time?"

Earl thought about it for a second. "I can't recall exactly, but since he's been annoying the Feds for over a century, it was pretty good. I remember the company cleared seven or eight hundred thousand after Leroy parked that bulldozer on Buford's head, and that was back in the Eighties."

I said, "With inflation, it'll be a lot more than that. You know, Gutterres told me this Drekavac has been around since the 1600s. If we could document that—and he said the Church would share their records—that creature could be one hell of a lucrative PUFF bounty for us."

My boss was clearly thinking the same thing I was. Though with Earl, it probably wasn't about the money. My guess was that he'd angrily said he was going to ditch Sonya, but he was far too honor-bound to leave her to her fate, and it was easier to act tough but mercenary in front of his Hunters than it was to be a big softy. Except a seven-figure PUFF was a seven-figure PUFF, so even Holly, as much as Sonya clearly rubbed her the wrong way, was interested in getting paid. We did a lot of good things, but we were ruthlessly practical about it whenever we could be. It took a lot of work to pay for this rock-and-roll lifestyle.

"I do like when the paycheck comes to us," Holly muttered. "Beats chasing them down. I made bank on the siege, but I sure didn't like having to go to the ass end of the Earth to do it."

We all looked down at Sonya, who was still sitting on the grass, trying to look helpless and forlorn. Except she was too cunning to make that stick for long. "Hang on now. You're thinking you could potentially make millions of bucks for scary hat guy. Only in order for you to ambush him, you need me for bait. If I don't cooperate, you're out of luck."

"If you don't cooperate, your head is going to end up mounted on the Drekavac's wall." That monster struck me as the kind of thing that would decorate his lair with taxidermy.

"Maybe. Maybe not. I've still got a few tricks up my sleeve."

"What're you going to do, kidnap Milo again?" When Holly said that we all laughed. Well, except for Milo. It was hard to tell in the firelight but knowing him he was probably blushing.

"I'm always happy to help MHI," Sonya suggested, innocent as could be. "Okay, I volunteer. I'll go with you. Only I get a percentage of the bounty. Like half. Like I should for this lich too, because you wouldn't have come here if it wasn't for me."

"Wow. You really are greedy," Trip said.

"Not greedy. Just desperate."

Earl looked toward the sky. His superior senses could hear Skippy's chopper long before the rest of us. Our ride was almost here.

"One other thing to think about," I said to my boss. "From what the lich said, he's not the one who called Sonya and told her to come here. It was a trap. Somebody else had eyes on us. They might be watching us right now."

"I was thinking the same thing. And why did they send her here? We'll talk about it later." Earl looked down at Sonya and sighed. "Let's go."

"So we have a deal then, half the bounty?"

"Not a snowball's chance in hell of that happening. But I did promise your mom I'd try to keep you alive. Don't make me regret it."

CHAPTER 14

Skippy landed in a nearby field to pick us up. As soon as we were airborne Earl handed out assignments. Messages were sent and plans were made. I also noticed that Earl didn't give Sonya a headset so that she couldn't listen in. Unless she was excellent at reading lips or had supernatural hearing, she would be shit out of luck. I knew Earl liked her, but I could tell he was genuinely pissed off about her threatening Milo. That had crossed a line. I was still curious what her sob story was going to be about why she needed the money so bad, but that could wait.

We talked strategy during the first part of the helicopter ride back to Alabama, but after that I took a nap. I'd had one hell of a day. Once the adrenaline wore off, the aches and pains started. I was so exhausted I could barely keep my eyes open. Sleeping this soon after being that close to a thermobaric warhead going off probably wasn't good for my brain, but I'd see Gretchen when we got home. She'd grind up some roadkill and leaves, make a smoothie, do some orc magic on it, and I'd be good as new. Probably.

The inside of a Russian MI-24 Hind is extremely loud and not exactly comfy, but I had a lot of practice getting sleep whenever I could squeeze it in. The trick when riding with Skippy was unplugging your headphones so you could no longer hear his heavy metal playlist. I managed to get a power nap in before waking up as we reached the MHI compound. I love flying home at night, because out the window it's just miles and miles of pitch-black forest, until all of a sudden, *boom*, there's this huge fenced-in paramilitary compound, with multiple buildings, hangars, and a world-class shooting range. It's amazing what you can hide in the Alabama woods. Skippy put us down with his usual gentle touch at the end of the runway.

There was a contingent of masked orcs waiting there to meet us. That was Skippy's ground crew. Thankfully they had one of their healers with them, and she took a look at my arm. She wasn't Gretchen—Skippy's head wife and all-around best healer ever was otherwise occupied—but I'd take an orc healer over a regular hospital any day. She growled at the cauterization Coslow had left on my arms, pronounced it "trash magic," gave me a paste made out of smashed-up bugs and flowers to rub on the dog bite, a gag-inducing vinegar with some dirt in it to drink to "make bone crack fix" and told me to take some Ibuprofen for my headache. While she worked on me, she complained in broken English about how humans were squishy and our skulls were soft, not "strong like urks." She might not have been Gretchen, but she certainly had learned Gretchen's no-nonsense bedside manner.

Sonya was escorted to one of the guest rooms, and Holly discreetly woke up some of the other Hunters who were currently staying at the compound and put them on guard duty, probably with the orders to shoot Sonya if she tried anything suspicious. Earl ordered the rest of us to get some sleep and we'd reconvene tomorrow. Most of my team had homes in nearby Cazador, but they were tired enough that they just crashed in their rooms at the compound for the night.

Not me. I drove home. The old Shackleford estate was only a short distance away. I missed my wife and wanted to give my son a hug.

I was about a mile out of the compound, the headlights of my truck cutting through the dark of the winding country road, when a man walked out into the road right in front of me. I had to slam on the brakes to keep from running him down. The truck came to a halt, front bumper only inches from the legs of PUFF Adjuster Harold Coslow.

He gave me a polite nod.

I probably shouldn't have stopped.

"What the shit, man?" I bailed out, pistol already in hand. Just because it looked like Coslow didn't mean it was Coslow, especially out in the middle of nowhere on a country road at four in the morning. "I could've killed you."

"Calm yourself, Mr. Pitt. It is pointless for you to threaten violence against me."

"Don't take it as a threat, just an abundance of caution." I had my gun at the compressed ready position, not aimed at him, but back by my chest. Which meant that I could punch it straight out and drill him in the heart really fast if I needed to. "How'd you get here?"

"The same way I get everywhere," said the mysterious little man.

"Where'd you come from?" There was nothing but trees as far as I could see, no cars, no other vehicles, zilch.

"Most recently, the MCB offices in Atlanta, Georgia, where I have been overseeing the efforts to find the fugitive, Stricken."

"How's that working out?"

"Not well. Stricken is even wilier than our projections indicated. When given ample opportunities to prepare, he is a rather formidable foe. However, we are adjusting our strategies based upon recent developments and have made new projections. Which is what brings me here, to speak with you now."

"Oh, good. I was really hoping for more cryptic pronouncements." Coslow was still wearing the same, worn old suit, and no parachute, so he hadn't dropped out of the sky. So he'd either teleported, or fast-roped out of some invisible silent stealth helicopter...and it wouldn't surprise me in the least if the MCB had one of those. "What the hell are you anyway?"

"I am the PUFF Adjuster. That's all you need to know."

Stricken had offered to tell me. I probably should have taken him up on it. "Fine. Talk."

"You were an unforeseen variable in this affair, yet now it appears your involvement has become pivotal. You will either heed this message—or not. Our projections have taken both possible responses into account. I will warn you, however, that the pathways branch rather dramatically based upon how sensible you are. Should you listen to me, the odds of your success, though slim, will go up dramatically. Should you disregard my advice, the resulting number of civilian casualties will be rather high, even by my admittedly jaded standards."

"As far as government assholes go, you make me miss Franks. At least he says what he means."

"Yet, he rarely says anything at all."

"That's a perk. What's the message, Coslow?"

He cocked his head to the side. "Simply this. It is of the utmost importance that you keep the verbal contract you made with Stricken."

It took my very tired brain a moment to process that. "I said I would look into his mystery problem."

"That is correct. Our projections now confirm that your doing so will be of vital strategic importance."

"What's the crisis then?"

"We do not know."

"Is it the thing the Secret Guard is worried about in South America?"

"We do not know. You would have to confirm that with Stricken."

I took a deep, calming breath. The calming part didn't work. "But Stricken's currently hiding from you guys. How am I supposed to contact him?"

Coslow shrugged. "We do not know."

Him saying "We do not know" was like a more honest, but just as annoying version of Franks' *classified*. "What *do* you know?"

"Only that this particular crisis is not an extinction-level event. Mankind will survive this no matter what."

I laughed. "Oh, good! You had me worried there for a second."

Coslow gave me a curious look, and I noticed that his eyes had a bit of a red shine in the headlights. "However, if you do not deal with this crisis in a timely manner, approximately two million human beings will lose their lives in the upcoming weeks. The resulting refugee crisis will kill at least another million over the following year."

"*What?*" I was stunned. "Millions? That's insane."

"No. It is simple math."

"Based on *what*?"

"The ratios generated by the predictive futures market of the soul feasters." And then Coslow blew right on past that before I had a chance to unpack it, like that wasn't the weirdest damned thing I'd heard in a while. "The numbers may actually turn out worse. Tumultuous events like this often lead to wars, famine, and breakdowns in society."

That sounded suspiciously like Asag's MO. "Is it—"

"Despite the guilt you feel for waking that monster up, not everything is caused by your white whale, Mr. Pitt. We do not believe it to be Disorder's doing, though he may be peripherally involved. If the models are accurate, the ultimate cause is most likely the Great Old Ones. Though the most likely reason they have gone on the current offensive may be in response to Asag's recent awakening. Those two factions are ancient enemies."

"They hate each other as much as they hate us."

"Oh, the Old Ones do not hate mankind, Mr. Pitt. They see you as too insignificant to hate. You are merely minor obstacles to be overcome on the way to their inscrutable goals. Nor does Asag *hate*, for hate implies a fiery emotion. He is instinctually driven to destroy everything, and he will work toward that goal with complete dispassion. However, as I was saying before you rudely interrupted me, this event could cause more ripples, but each waveform becomes harder to predict the farther it gets from the inciting incident. For now the expected casualty number has been set at three million."

I stood there dumbfounded and not really knowing what to say. Since I now knew without a doubt that this was the real Coslow—no illusion or doppelganger could be this frustrating—I slowly reholstered my gun. "So I'm on the hook to finish Stricken's mission, even though nobody knows what it is..."

"That is correct. You made a verbal contract with him—"

"Bullshit."

"Irrelevant, Mr. Pitt. I say you made a contract. You can deny that, however everything we have in our records about you indicates that you would be psychologically incapable of *not* trying to stop this kind of event once made aware of it. You would be compelled to come to the aid of those people regardless. Heroic meddling is encoded in your very DNA. So now that you are aware, your involvement from here on is a foregone conclusion. I am merely educating you about the stakes and the necessity of heeding the one called Stricken. Now that you know these things, you are trapped."

Okay, this fucker had my number there. "If I'm supposed to stop this thing, how do I proceed?"

"That is up to you. Those are answers I do not have. I do not know the details, merely the cost should you fail."

"Three million people." Talk about the weight of the world on your shoulders. "If you guys catch Stricken, can you at least beat it out of him, and then give me a call to tell me where to go?"

"Gladly. I was offended by the way in which he mocked the extremely generous contract which was offered to him. However, I would not count on the MCB or STFU finding Stricken in time. He is rather clever and has a great number of allies to call upon, facts which have caused us a great deal of consternation."

If somebody were to drive by right then, we would probably look like two men stupidly blocking one lane of a narrow country road, but one of us was mortal though drafted by cosmic forces beyond his understanding, while the other was some weird-ass supernatural entity that was worrying the shit out of me while simultaneously not providing much in the way of actionable intel.

"Since you don't know for sure what I'm supposed to do, can you at least guess?"

"I do not guess, Mr. Pitt."

"Humor me."

"I do not 'humor' either. The only thing which I am able to confirm, which may be of some use to you, is that your presence was not the only unforeseen variable which forced us to recalculate. The half-kodama, Sonya, is not numbered among the Chosen. Do not be surprised that we already know her identity. STFU pieced together who the thief was and they are fully aware that she is in MHI's custody. However, I told them to leave her be for now so as to not interrupt your work. Their efforts will be focused elsewhere. As I was saying, Sonya has not been Chosen. To the best of my knowledge no faction has picked her. She is what we adjusters refer to as a *free agent*. However, her involvement in these matters was no accident. Like you, or the Shacklefords, she is the product of a pivotal bloodline. History was manipulated to bring these forces to bear in this age. The actions of her ancestors foreordained that she would be drawn into this conflict."

"We talking her human side or the other one?"

"Both. We could not ascertain the reason she was brought into these events, because some ripples are harder to read than others. Hers was appreciably more chaotic than usual. However, I would encourage you to do your best to keep her alive until the role the universe has for her is revealed. On that note, an entity of extreme power and unrelenting vengeance will be coming to kill her this evening, so you should get some sleep."

I laughed because, sure, tell me that I'm responsible for millions of lives and then expect me to be able to sleep ever again. "Yeah. I know about him. Any advice about how to deal with Drekavacs?"

"No. I know this one was once mortal, a judge and executioner who was corrupted by evil. Since then our paths have not crossed. Should you defeat him, you will need to fill out form 875-G for a *Cursed Super Being*, and form 62-F for subcategory *Unrelenting Killer*. Do not forget to check the reason box as *Contracted Hellish Vengeance*."

"I totally would have done that anyway."

"See to it. There is no excuse for sloppy paperwork."

Now that was getting personal. "Whoa, back up. My PUFF paperwork is fucking meticulous. I might not be the best Hunter MHI's ever had, but I'm pretty damned sure I'm the best accountant this company has ever seen."

Coslow grudgingly nodded. "Your statement is accurate. Of the many financial specialists I have seen Monster Hunter International employ over the last century, you have by far the lowest error rate of them—a fact my auditors find most vexing." The PUFF Adjuster abruptly turned and started walking down the road.

"Do you need a ride or something?"

"Thank you but I will be fine. Good luck, Mr. Pitt."

I turned back to my truck, then remembered something. Coslow might know who it was that called the country store to trick Sonya into nearly getting herself killed by the lich. "Hey, what about—" But when I turned back, there was nothing but empty asphalt. The only movement was from a few moths fluttering through the headlight beams.

"That is one freaky little dude," I muttered to myself as I got back into the truck to drive home.

Julie woke me up by opening our bedroom curtains. Photons flew over and punched me in the eyelids.

I groaned. "Ugh...What time is it?"

"Time for you to get up. It's almost noon and apparently we've got a busy day." My wife sounded chipper. "Or night, I guess. Since apparently you guys decided to invite some sort of murderous ghost to the compound for some inexplicable reason."

Squinting, I sat up in bed and shielded my eyes. "He's kind of a cowboy pirate murder ghost. I would have told you all about it when I came in, but I didn't want to wake you." She had been sleeping peacefully, and honestly, it had felt nice to just lay there and listen to her breathe during the few minutes before I had passed out. "It's a long story."

"I gathered that from the email Milo sent on your flight home. For a super genius he sure does struggle with being concise. From Milo's mad ramblings it sounds like we've got a real fight on our hands." Julie was standing at the foot of the bed, still as radiant as the day I'd first met her. Except that time she had been professionally dressed and acting very proper and put together. Currently she was wearing workout clothes and was breathing and sweating like she'd just got off the treadmill. But that was one of the perks of a good marriage, you see each other at your best and your worst, but you still like each other anyway.

"You're beautiful."

"You're just delusional because you've been on the road too long. I need a shower." Julie smelled her armpit and then made a grossed-out face. "But anyways, I've got a team of smart people trying to figure out how to remove the Ward from that girl's hand. I called for backup Hunters and everybody else is prepping the compound's defenses now. The Catholics sent us their file on Drekavacs. We're breaking the good stuff out of the armory. It's all hands on deck."

"Hang on a second." I knew her moods way too well. "You're actually *excited* about the prospect of this thing attacking us tonight, aren't you? You're pumped for this."

Julie flashed me a sly grin. "What do you think? I've either been playing mom or running this company while you've been flying around to exotic locations having stakeouts and car chases. You're damned right I'm looking forward to doing some real monster hunting. I've already arranged for a babysitter."

"Atlanta's hardly exotic." Well, Dragon Con was actually kind of nuts, but I didn't need to go into that. "How's the Chunk?"

"He's taking a nap. Speaking of which"—Julie peeled her shirt off—"hurry and get naked before he wakes up."

Actually, being married has several perks.

✧　　✧　　✧

For the first time in decades, the Shackleford family estate wasn't actively under construction. Most of the time I'd been here, we had been fixing the old mansion from one crisis or another. Julie was actually good at home repair and power tools. I was good at heavy lifting and reaching things that were high up. Between the two of us, and a few complicated things where Julie's pride had actually allowed for us to hire contractors, we'd finally gotten the place fixed. Which meant that now we could actually sit in our kitchen and eat in peace, not surrounded by tools and drywall dust.

Julie and I sat at the table, eating sandwiches, while we waited for Ray's sitters to arrive so we could go to work. Ray played on the floor, brutally whacking his toys with a plastic squeaky hammer, a useful skill that he had probably gotten from me. Dispensing blunt force trauma had come in really handy in my career.

"So who did you get to babysit?" I asked, because after your kid has already been kidnapped once by the forces of evil, you tend to get kind of paranoid about that sort of thing.

Before Julie could answer, the black blob that was lying beneath the kitchen table declared, "No need babies sat. Mr. Trashbags protect Cuddle Bunny's Cuddle Bunny."

"Shhh...He gets sensitive about that," Julie warned.

I sighed, because I had once again inadvertently hurt the feelings of the Saint Bernard-sized eldritch abomination that lived in my house. "Sorry, Mr. Trashbags, but you need backup."

The blob rolled out past my bare feet and looked up at me with seven blinking eyes. He loved Julie and Ray unconditionally, but he was still kind of suspicious of me. "Mr. Trashbags nanny."

"I hired Shelly to be the nanny, but you get to be *assistant* nanny." Julie took a handful of potato chips and dropped them on the floor for her loyal pet shoggoth to devour. "We know Mr. Trashbags is the very best at protecting us."

Two mouths full of weird-looking teeth formed on Mr. Trashbags' amorphous form to gobble up the chips. He formed a third mouth to keep talking. "Shelly Nanny good. Mr. Trashbags more gooder."

It had taken me some time to get used to having Mr. Trashbags around, since the first time we'd met he'd been a multiton killing machine who had tried to steamroll me. He was from a different dimension, but he had demonstrated his total loyalty by saving Ray's and Julie's lives on multiple occasions in Europe. Plus Julie was really fond of him, so now he slept in one of the downstairs bathtubs and ate our trash.

"You're both good," Julie assured him. "Just good in different ways."

"Shelly Nanny is biped. WEAK."

"But she also has opposable thumbs, can reliably operate a telephone, and can cook human food for Ray," Julie pointed out.

Mr. Trashbags made a strange gurgling noise as he thought that over. "Mr. Trashbags procure nourishment for Cuddle Bunny's Cuddle Bunny."

"You tried to feed him a dead mouse," I shouted.

"Tiny mammal was food," Mr. Trashbags stated without irony, which also explained why we no longer had a vermin problem around the house.

"Ray didn't even have that many teeth yet!"

"It's okay, I've got this." Julie reached over and patted my hand to get me to chill out. "Just remember, Mr. Trashbags, who's in charge when Cuddle Bunny isn't here?"

"Shelly Nanny," Mr. Trashbags said with resignation. "Mr. Trashbags serve Shelly Nanny."

"And what do you do if anyone tries to hurt Ray?"

"CONSUME!"

"Good boy," Julie dropped some slices of lunch meat on him, because she knew that Mr. Trashbags would straight up eat anybody who tried to mess with our kid.

Once we finished eating we started staging the gear we wanted to take for the night in the living room. The rows of Shackleford family portraits looked down approvingly as the pile of guns grew. To be fair, I was anthropomorphizing the paintings because not all of the Shacklefords had gone into the family business, and the ones who had stuck with Hunting, most of them were dead now. Julie came from a big family, but the paintings hadn't been updated since she was a kid, and she didn't really keep up with any of the multitude of uncles, aunts, and cousins who'd bailed out to lead normal boring lifestyles. For Monster Hunting royalty, the Shackleford family's numbers were getting a little thin on the ground now.

Long before the doorbell rang, we were alerted that someone was coming. After the events of the last few years, we had really beefed up this place's security system. There were motion sensors everywhere. The cameras were in regular and thermal, which was especially handy for undead beings that didn't radiate body heat. If something was moving with an unnaturally low body temp, that was a huge red flag. Since we were on much better working terms with the elves since Tanya had joined the company, there were protective and warning runes inscribed all over the property to alert us to any supernatural presence. There were armored shutters that would drop down over the doors and windows, and we had one concrete, fireproof panic room sufficient to contain a werewolf, that Shelly could take Ray into to wait for the cavalry, or until Mr. Trashbags digested whoever was bothering them. Did I mention he was kind of terrifying?

I let Shelly in. Like most of Skippy's tribe she was shorter than average, squat, and wearing a mask to hide her features among humans. But even with the mask she was easy to pick out from the other orcs, because she had a really obvious lazy eye.

"Hey, Shelly."

"Brother of Great War Chief," she greeted me with a bow. Because even though I'd saved the world, to the orcs I was still basically chopped liver when compared to my brother, the former rock star.

Once inside, the orc girl took off her mask, revealing her tusks, snout, and pointy ears. Then she hung her coat on the rack. She had a hand-tooled leather gun belt around her waist, with a Super Blackhawk magnum revolver holstered on each side, and shells in little loops all the way around.

All orcs were born with gifts, where they were supernaturally good at one thing. Shelly's was blasting stuff. The teenager could toss a handful of quarters in the air and draw and shoot them all before any hit the ground. She was to six-guns what Edward was to stabby things. Shelly was near the top of my list of people never to get into a gunfight with. I'd tested her when she'd applied for this job, and I could say without a doubt that she was like a one-orc Secret Service detail. Plus, Ray really liked her. As an orc she was too honor-bound to invite her boyfriend over to mess around like a human babysitter might, so she was basically perfect for the job.

Julie came in carrying a rifle case over each shoulder. Mr. Trashbags was squishing along at her heels. Ray was riding the shoggoth like he was a pony and giggled with delight when he saw Shelly. She was his favorite, probably second only to Mr. Trashbags. The blob gently lifted Ray with two tentacles, and Shelly took the happy toddler from him and immediately squished his chubby cheeks. She may have been a stone-cold badass, but she really loved kids.

"Okay, we're not going to be back until really late. We'll set the perimeter alarms when we leave. There's a meatloaf in the fridge for dinner. You'll just need to warm it up."

Shelly nodded along to Julie's instructions. "Shelly will nourish junior war chief and bring great honor to tribe."

"Of course you will." Julie looked down at Mr. Trashbags. "Remember, Shelly is in charge."

"Mr. Trashbags NANNY!"

"Wrong," Shelly said, giving him one suspicious eye. The other eye was pointed at the wall. "Mr. Trashbags blob pet. Shelly the nanny."

Mr. Trashbags gurgled a bit before agreeing. "Orc is nanny. Orc has opposing thumbs."

Shelly looked down at her hands, suspicious about this revelation. I gave my son a hug, and then grabbed my gear bags and headed out the door with my wife before either of us could worry about the wisdom of once again leaving our progeny in the care of a gunslinging orc and a domesticated shoggoth.

CHAPTER 15

The compound was about as busy as I had ever seen it. It's a rare opportunity for MHI to have a monster come to us, and even rarer to actually be able to schedule it in advance. The last time there had been this much excitement here was when Hood had dropped off a few truckloads of undead monstrosities. We'd learned a few things from that experience and invested in some improvements. This would be the first time we'd give them a real-life workout.

On the flight back from Georgia, Earl had put out the call for help. Everybody who wasn't working an active case—as in monsters were going to eat somebody if we weren't there—and who could get to Cazador before sundown, was on the way or already here. Luckily, we were between Newbie classes, so we wouldn't have any untrained people getting underfoot. By the time the Drekavac arrived, we would probably have a few dozen experienced Hunters on hand, which is one hell of a welcome committee.

In addition, the orcs and the elves had agreed to help. Since the orc village was really close to the compound, it would be evacuated. Their noncombatants would be camped by the Shackleford estate. The elves were sending a few of their best trackers down from the Enchanted Forest to help.

Elves and orcs working together? Crazy, but true. If a historian—assuming he was cleared to know about the secret existence of monsters obviously—ever looked back on my life, he'd be forced to say that my greatest achievement had been helping broker a peace treaty between those two groups. And I'd saved the world and killed a god once. That's how much orcs and elves usually despise each other. They had even worked together the whole siege without a single murder occurring. As much as I'd like to blame all this newfound peace and harmony on my brilliant diplomacy, in reality the current peace was the direct result of Princess Tanya being a bossy force of nature and her browbeating the rest of the elves into not being judgmental pricks. Meanwhile, Chief Skippy still didn't trust the elves, but with his beloved brother and right-hand orc, Edward, hooking up with Tanya, he was kind of stuck. MHI was happy, because it meant we had access to orc muscle and medical, and elf magic at the same time.

And we were going to need that magical edge too. From what Albert had been able to look up, and what the Secret Guard had sent from the Vatican's archive, I'd only scratched the surface of the Drekavac's full capabilities last night. Stricken's contract with the reptoids must have had the Really Scary Bastard Clause in it to make sure nobody backed out because the Drekavac's later forms were supposed to be terrifying.

Only with this many Hunters, this much prep, and all our resources, it shouldn't be anything we couldn't handle. Provided that we didn't accidentally sever his head before we got to the thirteenth death, because then we'd just have to do it all over again the next night, and according to Coslow's predictions, we couldn't afford to be dicking around with this thing.

So while the others got ready for tonight, I tried to figure out what Coslow thought was about to kill a few million people. Albert, our regular researcher, was up to his eyeballs in Drekavac lore, so I couldn't bug him. The other big-brain Hunters who had arrived were trying to figure out how to get the Ward unstuck from Sonya. Melvin, our internet troll, might be of use to me, but that would have required me to visit Melvin's office-cave in the basement, and he was a real pain in the ass to deal with. Giving him this broad of a topic to look into would be an exercise in futility and whining, so I'd save Melvin until I had something more specific for him to drill down on.

The interior of the MHI archives looked like a very large, very full used bookstore, with floor-to-ceiling shelves, jam-packed with books and papers throughout. The room took up a large chunk of the basement and had been filled by Hunters bringing back anything they found which was monster-related. It had been a mess before it had gotten blown up during the Christmas Party, and that had made it a whole lot worse, but Albert Lee had devoted himself to caring for this place, and after years of labor it was actually pretty well organized now.

To begin my mission, I decided to learn more about the guy who had stuck me with it. Not Stricken, because we already knew he was a complete mystery, but Coslow.

I pulled up Al's topical master database on one of the computers and typed in *PUFF Adjuster*. It referred me to a bunch of other documents, including the scan of the official—yet nebulously useless definition—provided by the Department of the Treasury, about how that office was the final ruling authority over all PUFF bounties. The term was mentioned in several reports and journals, but those all seemed to be referring to normal human bureaucrats. So I typed in *Harold Coslow* and was rewarded with several other hits. I wrote down the shelf numbers and went to look for the documents.

The first one I found was from the Boss, Raymond Shackleford the Third, may that total badass rest in peace. It was one of his journals and he mentioned Coslow showing up to oversee a case involving an unidentified transdimensional being in West Virginia in 1967. Boss Shackleford said Coslow had given him the quote "heebie-jeebies" but hadn't known what he was either.

The next mention of Coslow I pulled turned out to be a handwritten diary that dated clear back to the founding of the company, before it had been renamed Monster Hunter International, and had still been known as Bubba Shackleford's Professional Monster Killers. I kicked myself for not sorting by date, because this one was so old that at first I thought it had to be a mistake, but Al seldom made mistakes, so it probably had to be a different Harold Coslow. But Hunters have flexible minds, so I checked anyway. The journal was written by a Hunter named Hannah Stone, which was kind of surprising for that era. I'd not known Bubba had employed any female Hunters. The old books were kept in plastic bags to protect them, and I put on some of the disposable gloves Al kept on the reference desk before handling the pages because I didn't want him to yell at me. Like all good librarians, the dude was rather protective of his books.

The journal was about a case where the Professional Monster Killers, led by Bubba himself, had tracked down a traveling circus run by a powerful necromancer, that had been moving from town to town secretly taking victims, because all the things in the freak show were actually real monsters. That sounded like an amazing case, and I was bummed I didn't have time to read the whole account, but I skipped to the one page where Coslow was mentioned. After Stone described him as "an elderly fellow of somber words and obnoxious condescension who was the chief administrator for the Federal's new bounty program for monsters," I had to admit that it sounded like the same guy. Which meant that Coslow had already been an old man over a century ago.

The next number I'd written down was for a Hunter's memoirs from the 1980s. It had been filed a few rows over. Except when I walked there, the spot on the shelf was empty. *Well, crap.*

Except then I heard somebody . . . weeping?

I moved around the end of the shelf to see who was making the noise. There were a few comfy reading chairs in the back corner. One of them was occupied by a young woman I'd not seen before, and when she saw me coming she quickly wiped her eyes and composed herself. "Hey, Opie."

"Owen," I corrected her, immediately knewing I was talking to Sonya. Today she looked like a gawky teenager, Asian, and kind of awkward and nerdy, like she wouldn't be allowed to sit at the cool kids' table in the lunchroom. I noted that her left hand looked perfectly normal, and the Ward wasn't there anymore. Somebody must have figured out how to remove it already, and in such a way that it hadn't even left a mark. "What are you doing here?"

"I was just reading."

"Were you crying?"

"No. Of course not." Sonya was clearly lying and doing her best to hide the fact that she really had been crying. She wiped her nose and sniffed. "It's dusty in here."

"You're supposed to be confined to one of the guest rooms but, let me guess, you changed your face again so you could sneak past the guards unnoticed?"

"Yeah, dude, I totally risked getting shot by some trigger-happy goons just so I could go to the library."

"I'll pass that on to our librarian. He'll take it as a compliment. Let's go."

"Wait. Earl gave me permission to wander around the main building, as long as I didn't mess with anything or get in the way. And this is my real face. I was born with this one."

If she wasn't lying, she was actually a lot more unremarkable-looking than most of the masks she wore. I thought it over, trying to decide if she was telling the truth, or if I needed to escort her back to her room. My gut told me she was lying. After the stunts she'd pulled, Earl wouldn't let her wander around our basement unsupervised. We had some scary shit stored down here and secret tunnels that could be used to escape.

"Come on, Sonya. I've got a finely tuned bullshit detector."

"Just give me a few more minutes, please?"

I looked to see what she'd been reading that was so important. I could read the numbered sticker on the side. Coincidently, the notebook in her hands was the very same one I'd just been looking for. Then the realization slowly dawned that the memoirs she'd been reading had been written by *her dead father*. She saw me looking at it, and then she knew that I knew. Sonya got embarrassed and put the book on the table. This had just gotten awkward.

"Have you read your dad's stuff before?"

"Sure. Earl made copies after you guys found them and mailed them to Mom, but I wanted to see the originals because . . ." She trailed off for a moment. "Never mind. I don't really know."

"Yeah, you do." I picked up the book and handed it back to her. "And there's no shame in that."

She took the memoirs, looked at them, and then sighed. "I guess it's because my dad touched these pages, so it's different. You know?"

"I do, kinda." It hadn't been that long since I'd lost my dad, and sometimes I still forgot he was gone. It wasn't like we'd been super close most of my adult life, but I suppose I'd just taken for granted that he'd always be there. At least I had known mine. Sonya had never had that chance. And thinking about that made me feel a little bad for her, and the next thing I knew I was trying to be helpful.

"I looked at those after Lee found them. Your dad seems like quite the character."

"You think he's full of shit."

"I didn't say that." Some of the guys had, but I didn't say that part out loud. "Hunters tend to be a little colorful in our recounting of events is all. Some more than others. Earl and Milo vouched for him. That's good enough for me."

"All I ever knew about Dad was what my mom told me. She always said he was the brightest and bravest human she'd ever seen. She really loved him, which you've got to understand is a big deal for one of her kind to fall for a human. As I got older I always thought she might be exaggerating. You've got to understand that my mom's kind of a hopeless romantic. She's addicted to Scottish time travel romance novels. She's a little flighty, so I take her stories with a grain of salt. But after reading his memoirs, it's like I'm hearing his voice. I don't know, it changes things, makes him seem more real to me."

Sonya and I had gotten off on the wrong foot, but she was basically a scared kid who'd gotten pulled into some crazy business, so there was no need for me to be a jerk when she was being vulnerable. I pulled up one of the other chairs and sat down.

"I get it. I didn't really understand my dad most of my life either, and mine was around. Sometimes you think you know somebody, but then it's not until you get older that you really understand what makes your parents tick."

"Was your dad cool?"

"Cool?" I snorted. "If you mean cool as in nice or fun, oh, hell no. But he was a *good* man. And probably the toughest man I've known, and I work *here*. Look, there's nothing wrong with wanting to connect with your past. Even if you didn't meet him, he's still part of you, and part of where you come from. You should take that memoir and keep it with you during your stay. But just make sure you put it back before you leave, because Albert will lose his friggin' mind if somebody messes up his system."

She laughed, but did keep the book on her lap. "Thanks... About the whole thing with yesterday, I really am sorry about how that went down. I kinda stepped in it, and you guys have done nothing but try and help me. I even threatened to shoot you."

"Hey, I'm fine. Though you should probably take it up with Milo. He's a nice guy and gets kind of sensitive about being taken hostage."

"That wasn't my finest moment." She seemed genuinely contrite.

"It really was a douche move. But Milo is honestly about the kindest and most forgiving person in the world. He's like Mr. Rogers but with more guns. Talk to him. You'll see."

"I'll apologize to him," she promised.

I gestured at her hand. "I see the Ward is gone. Was Milo the one who figured that out? He's remarkably good at that kind of thing."

"Oh, no. They're still stumped." Sonya reached up and pulled down the neckline of her hoody, revealing that the stone was now *embedded in the top of her chest.*

I cringed. That didn't just look painful, it looked like it should be fatal. "How'd it get *there?*"

"Beats me. When I went to sleep it was on my hand. I woke up and it was there. The thing is just kinda swimming around or something."

Only a quarter of the Ward's surface was visible, and the part that was embedded in her would've been cutting off her subclavian artery, so she should've been dead. You can't just move a softball-sized rock through a body and not wreck a lot of systems. "Does it hurt?"

"I feel fine. It's like it's not even there."

"You seem remarkably calm, all things considered."

"If I'm being honest, I just hide it well. My mom's an immortal from a spirit realm, so by human standards I've seen some weird things in my life, but this one has got me a little freaked out."

That was probably why she'd turned to her dad's books. He'd been a smart guy, good at this kind of thing; she'd probably been looking for comfort. "Since you're not dying or screaming in agony, that's got to be some sort of effect that's enabling both it and you to exist in the same space at the same time."

"You get that idea from one of these books about magic?" She waved her hand toward the shelves.

"Sorry. I just pulled that theory out of my ass. I've got no idea what's going on. Anything like this ever happen before to you?"

Sonya shook her head in the negative. "I guess Isaac Newton never thought someone like me would try to use one of his magic weapons." She covered the oddity back up. "That big lumberjack-looking grandpa who flew in earlier messed with it but didn't know what to do to get it out either, but he assured me they've got an elf princess on the way who will be able to fix this right up."

From that description the old lumberjack in question had to be Ben Cody, who had a wall full of PhDs and knew more about crazy super science than anyone else in the company. He'd retired from heading our New Mexico team after the siege, but Julie must have called him up and asked him to come in for a consult as a favor. If he was stumped, that was really bad. Plus, I knew Cody had zero faith in elf magic so if he was talking up Tanya's abilities, he had probably just been trying to make Sonya feel better. That wasn't a good sign.

"Cody's right. Tanya is the expert on magic. She knows all the old ways." That was a huge exaggeration, but I didn't want to scare her. "She'll know how to get it out."

"I sure hope so. I never should have taken this job, but I was desperate. It's just that I really do need a whole lot of money—and fast."

"You mentioned that. What kind of life-or-death thing makes it so a college student suddenly need millions of dollars? I know tuition and books can be a pain but stealing something that puts a giant target on your head is kind of extreme. You got gambling debts with the mob?"

"I didn't know about the target at the time. It's my problem, I have to be the one to deal with it."

"Because that's worked out so good for you so far." My chair creaked as I leaned forward. I might not be able to do much about the Newtonian superweapon stuck in her chest, but I could maybe help with the nuts-and-bolts stuff. "Level with me, Sonya. MHI can't help you if we don't know what's going on."

She thought it over for a long time. I did my best to try and look sincere. Apparently, it worked, because she relented. "Okay, you know what my mom is, right?"

"A little. Japanese folklore isn't my area of expertise."

She patted the book. "My dad loved that stuff."

No kidding. I'd read some of Gardenier's records. The guy had been a total weeaboo, from the mystical spirit of the sword stuff, to dressing in kimonos. If he was still alive he'd probably have one hell of an anime collection, but I just said, "I heard he was knowledgeable in that area."

"It was his knowledge on the subject that got Mom interested enough to date him, but she never told him what she is. Humans tend to get a little twitchy about that kind of thing. He died never knowing that my mom is a yokai. But that's a really big category. They come in all sorts of different shapes and sizes. I know it sounds hard to believe, but they're not from Earth originally, but from one of the realms that's connected to Earth."

"I got it." She gave me a curious look when I said that, because it was the sort of concept that baffled regular people, but I just shrugged. I'd visited more dimensions than the average American visited other countries. "Trust me. Our world being connected to others is not something I personally struggle to believe in."

"Okay, but my mom has lived on this planet for a long time, so she's not as connected to the spirit worlds as some of her relatives. Some yokai are good, some are evil, just like people. Specifically, her family come from the kodama family."

"Forest spirits, right?"

"Yeah. Sorta." Sonya seemed a little surprised that I'd known that, but it was only because I'd gotten to know some members of Strike Force Kiratowa while training for the siege, and they'd told me a few stories about what monster hunting was like in Japan. "The kodama are connected to forests. Like nymphs are connected to bodies of water. You've got nymphs here, right?"

"Not that I know of."

"Oh, come on, Georgia is lousy with nymphs, those stuck-up bitches. Alabama has to have them too. But anyways, even kodama come in different forms. Yokai aren't like humans in that they've got a sort of fixed shape with some variations. Yokai can get *weird*. Mom's branch of the family can easily pass for human, so they live among them and usually like them. They traditionally try to protect people and do good. But she had this one cousin, who was kind of psycho from what I hear, and he'd gone on this revenge-fueled murder spree in New York City. She was trying to stop her cousin, and it turns out my dad and MHI were trying to catch him too, and long story short, they totally hooked up."

"It's the classic love story, boy meets yokai. Boy gets yokai pregnant. What's all that got to do with why you need millions of dollars fast?"

Sonya became deadly serious. "I have to save my family's forest."

She let that hang, like I was supposed to be shocked by this revelation or something, but I was just confused. "What?"

"It's the forest my branch of the kodama are connected to. It's my ancestral homeland. It's the place that links the two worlds. Don't you get it? It's in danger. Humans used to leave it alone because they thought it was haunted, but the Hunters there chased off the last of the evil yokai in the area so people weren't as afraid as they used to be, and they started moving in. Big business doesn't care about the local superstitions anymore. They're going to develop it. Log the trees and bulldoze the stumps and put strip malls on it. I have to buy all the land to keep them from doing that."

I rolled that over in my mind. "Huh..."

Now it was her turn to say, "What?"

"That's way more Fern Gully of you than I expected. No offense, but you just struck me as the pragmatic type."

"I'm not some hippy, you big dope. I'm doing this for my mom. She's connected to that land. It's her anchor to the spirit world. If it goes, she goes. Not fast, like instantaneous death, but she'll weaken and become mortal, and start to age like a human. She tells me she's okay with that. Like 'it's the way of things. All things change. Blah blah blah.'" Sonya made quote marks with her fingers. "Screw that! Most of the kodama in Japan have already faded away, same as most of the spirit beings that used to be super common on this continent. I can't let my mom wither away like that."

"So you need a few million bucks to buy a bunch of trees?"

"Have you priced Japanese real estate lately? I need that much to *start!*"

For someone descended from forest spirits, her blundering around in the woods earlier hadn't exactly struck me as someone who was *one with nature.* Sonya saw my incredulous look and must have realized what I was thinking.

"Yeah, I know. I'm a city girl, born and raised. My mom tried to keep me away from the natural world as much as possible. I think she was afraid I'd hear the call of the wild and go feral or something. I guess kodama do that once in a while. No danger there. I like electricity and showers."

"Have you ever even been to this family forest?"

Sonya got a little defensive. "Not really. See, there's...well... let's call it clan law that kodama aren't supposed to ever mix with humans, so Mom has been declared an outcast, eternally banished—only she likes living in America better anyway so she's fine with the decree—but I'm considered a half-breed disgrace and would be destroyed on sight by the old kodama. So I've never actually *been* there. The pictures make it look nice though."

"Dang. Your mom's family sound like racist assholes."

"It's more speciesist than racist. But I'm not buying that land to protect those crusty, stuck-up, decrepit old losers. I'm doing this for Mom. Now do you understand why it's so important that I sell this stupid rock for as much as I can get?"

"Which is why you slashed Gutterres' tires and ran off when somebody made you a better offer. That sure worked out well for you. So who was on the phone?"

"I don't know. She didn't say her name, but she made a real compelling argument with a lot of zeroes on the end of it."

"She?" That was curious. There weren't very many things which would know where a monster like Phipps was hiding in order to send Sonya to a certain doom, which would also be keeping tabs on MHI's affairs, and be motivated to screw with us, so I immediately thought of my mother-in-law. "Did she have a Southern accent and call you hon?"

"No accent, though she had one of those smokey voices. Sultry, you know? But it wasn't an affectation for right then either; I bet she always talks seductive to everyone. That's her default."

That made me scoff. "And you made that psychological workup based on one short phone call there, Criminal Minds?"

"Trust me. I can change voices like I can change faces. Accents, inflection, tone, piece of cake."

"Yeah, I heard you sing."

"Now, that I do for fun. But one of my gifts means that I can tell a lot about people just by looking at them or listening to them. I figure it's genetic. Mom's people survived thousands of years because they could watch humans and then blend in with them. It doesn't do much good to be able to look like anyone if you aren't good at pretending to be them too. So I can get a read on someone fast."

"Yet you were still gullible enough to walk into a trap."

"Rub it in, why don't you? Whoever she was, she's a super-good liar."

Susan Shackleford was cunning, but this didn't sound like her MO. She would've just killed Sonya and kept the Ward for herself, not farm that out to some other monster and risk losing something so incredibly valuable. "We'll figure out who it was.

In the meantime, you should probably just tell Earl about your mom's ancestral land and ask for his help."

Now it was her turn to be incredulous. "Like Earl has that kind of money."

"Are you kidding? He's not big on flash, but the man bought stock in Ford back when horses were still the big thing. Do you know how compound interest works? Because Earl sure does, and he's over a hundred."

"Mom is *way* older than he is, but she's not exactly good with money. She's more ... *artistic*. Dad actually had a fortune when he died, but Mom opened a new age bookstore and went broke trying to sell healing crystals to housewives who do yoga." Sonya sighed. "Look, I know he's probably got *some* money, but just because Earl feels guilty about my dad sacrificing his life so he could save the day, doesn't mean that this is anyone's problem other than mine. My family, my solutions. I'm not going to beg for handouts. I've got gifts, I've got skills, so I'm going to use them to handle my business. You got a problem with that?"

I could respect the stubbornness. "Naw, that's cool." I was also going to tell Earl about this, even if she wasn't. Knowing his sense of honor, he'd probably pay her out of his own pocket for the Ward and call it a finder's fee. It would actually be charity, but neither one of them would call it that, so they could both keep their pride intact. "I bet you've always been like that—tough, dedicated, standing up for what you believe—even when you were a kid."

"Why would you guess that?" she asked suspiciously.

"I read that book you're holding. Earl wrote the ending. He wouldn't have called you a badass otherwise. He's got high standards. Coming from him, that's one hell of a compliment."

"Oh." Sonya actually blushed, then she tried to blow that off. "I figured he said that because when I was a freshman in high school, I kicked the shit out of a vampire who was eating our cheerleading squad."

"Probably that too ... So now that I know you snuck out—because if Cody came out of retirement to figure this puzzle out, there's absolutely no way he'd let you wander around unattended with that Ward stuck to you—let's get you back to your room. We can concentrate on keeping you alive through the night, and then you can worry about saving your magical forest tomorrow."

"When you put it that way, it sounds dumb."

"Whatever you say, tree hugger. Let's go."

Sonya stood up, but kept the memoirs clutched tight. "Just a heads-up, *tree hugger* translates to a really serious insult to the kodama. Don't say that in front of my mom or she'll smack you."

"Duly noted." I'd once gotten my ass kicked for not realizing how offensive garden gnomes were to real gnomes. Hunters had to be culturally sensitive like that.

CHAPTER 16

There were over thirty members of MHI at the compound, which by our operational standards, was a lot. We would also have twelve orcs, five elves, four Secret Guard, two MCB, our internet troll, and a partridge in a pear tree, but I'm getting ahead of myself.

The Secret Guard arrived late that afternoon in the same big black van that I'd seen them pick Gutterres up in the night before. I wasn't surprised to see them show up for the party. It was less than a three-hour drive from Atlanta to Cazador, and they really wanted that stone for themselves. They were stopped by the guards we'd posted at the main gate but asked for me by name. When I got the call from the guard shack, I said to let them through and went outside to meet the Catholics in the parking lot.

The van stopped and four men got out. Gutterres I knew, but the rest were strangers. Two of them were big, bald, tough-looking dudes, one as tall as me, the other just over six foot. The last one looked kind of like a young Charles Manson with the beard and hair. In the brief moment their van doors were open I could see piles of modern gear, armor, and guns, but they also had things like swords, crosses, and a big silver thing on a pole that I assumed was some kind of holy water sprinkler. The door slid closed before I could figure that one out.

Gutterres was carrying the same cooler from last night. "Good afternoon, Pitt."

"Let me guess, the head melted at the crack of dawn?"

"Despite my best efforts, yes." He opened the cooler lid to show me that the interior was filled with black ashes. "However, I should be able to use these remains to perform a rite which might help us turn the tables on the creature."

"What kind of rite?"

"The kind which will make it so that he doesn't reset the clock each night. Thirteen lives total, no matter how long it takes us to get through them, and then he's done, forever. I've also confirmed the Drekavac's mortal identity."

That sounded like a pitch. "Are you officially offering a trade?"

"I am. Our expertise and help in return for access to the Ward."

"On that, you'll have to make your case to Earl Harbinger, but he's a reasonable guy. What happened to *we prefer to work alone*?"

"I made a convincing case to my superiors," Gutterres said.

"If you'll let us, we'll help," the tall one said. I was a little surprised when he sounded American. I'd thought that all their muscle was Swiss. "The Combat Exorcist made a very compelling argument to the council about the value of cooperation. They're not used to him asking for help. They called us up and said we should escort him to scenic Alabama to offer our services."

I looked at Gutterres and raised an eyebrow. "Seriously, your actual title is *combat exorcist*?"

"That is one of the titles bestowed on me, yes."

"Dude, that is so badass."

"It is. These are my associates." Gutterres gestured at the big one, "Messina." Then the average height one that could probably still easily bench-press me, "Warrington," and then the skinny one. "LoPresto."

None of them struck me as particularly priestly. They seemed more soldier than clergy. "Are you the junior exorcist squad then?"

"Hell no," said Warrington, who also sounded like an American. "If somebody's head starts spinning around and projectile vomiting, that's his problem. We got recruited for this because the Church couldn't get a contingent of the guys with the pikes and stripes here fast enough."

"Don't let the festive colors on their dress uniforms fool you," Gutterres said. "The Swiss Guard are an elite force, and trained to deal with the supernatural, but they are few in number and have other duties as well. After the incident with Franks, the council decided we needed to be able to bring in reliable agents for rapidly unfolding situations around the world. We've been keeping tabs on members of the faith who have applicable skill-sets in case of need."

I looked over the three, and they all had that air of no fucks to give, all in a day's work, been-there-done-that attitude culti-vated by professionals in the fields of applied violence. I'd have bet good money that each of them was some kind of combat vet or their regular day job required door kicking. I'd have to see how they did tonight, because if the Church was using unpaid volunteers for this weekend warrior stuff, MHI was always hiring, paid good, and had medical and dental.

"You guys getting paid for this?"

"We're just thankful for the opportunity to serve the Lord," Messina said.

"Their check had still better cash though," LoPresto muttered under his breath.

"All you need to know is that these men have been briefed on the basic mission of the Secret Guard, so they will do. It is rare for us to utilize outsiders, and then they only work under Secret Guard supervision."

"Like how you supervised Sonya?" I asked.

Gutterres sighed. "It's a new program. We're still working the bugs out...So how is our tire-slashing delinquent?"

"She's alive, but only because MHI rescued her from a lich who was about to eat her."

"And the stone?" Because of course Gutterres wasn't offering their services out of the kindness of his heart.

"Well, that's complicated. She's got it. Only it's been somehow magically fused to her body and our smartest people can't figure out how that happened or how to undo it."

The Catholics shared an incredulous look between them.

"You're screwing with us," said LoPresto.

"Nope. You can go see for yourselves. Last time I talked to her it was floating around inside her chest but somehow miracu-lously not stopping her heart. Your Order happen to have any rites for that sort of thing?"

"I can check the handbook," Gutterres said.

"We get a handbook?" Messina asked.

"I was being facetious."

Then I heard an incoming helicopter. It wasn't ours. The Hind was parked in its hangar while Skippy and crew bolted on a bunch of illegal weaponry for the night's festivities. Because what was the point of having an attack helicopter if you couldn't bust out the good stuff for special occasions? I listened to the distinct sound for a moment.

Warrington identified it first, I was guessing because he'd ridden in one a lot working for Uncle Sam. "Sounds like a Blackhawk."

Gutterres frowned. "Unless MHI called up the National Guard, it appears your Monster Control Bureau is on the way. From your pained expression I'm assuming you weren't expecting them?"

"Nope." After Coslow had told me he'd called off STFU, I'd gotten my hopes up that we could complete this job without the government sticking their nose into our business. Optimism is for suckers.

A pitch-black helicopter with no numbers stenciled on it came into view over the trees. Only the MCB leaned that hard into conspiracy theory stereotypes. I was disappointed they were here, but not surprised. The government could always be counted on to make life complicated.

"Our debate over which of our organizations needs the Ward more becomes moot if the MCB simply seizes it for themselves," Gutterres said.

"Tell me something I don't know." The MCB's arrival could screw up everything. Plus I'd need to call Skippy and warn him to stop committing felonies. "I'll deal with them. Head inside the main building, ask for Julie or Earl, they'll figure out the best place to use you. I'm going to go see what these douchebags want." I started walking toward the runway. Since the parking lot was full, that was the only place that made sense for the MCB to land.

The noise drew a bunch of other curious Hunters out. I saw Milo standing in the doorway of his workshop, but as soon as he saw who it was, he ran off, probably to hide the evidence of whatever anti-Drekavac projects he'd been working on. MHI paid a lot of taxes and did a lot of paperwork for our regularly purchased explosives, but that didn't cover some of our off-the-books exotic weapons we'd gotten out of storage, or any of the homebrew stuff of questionable legality Milo was currently mixing together. At least Milo would have the sense to conceal Sonya and the rock and to warn Skippy to hide the missiles.

It was doubtful that this was a random yet unfortunately timed inspection by our governmental overseers. Somebody must have tipped them off about what was going on tonight. Regardless, I couldn't let them know about the Ward Stone because they'd seize it. And considering how heartless the Feds could be they wouldn't even care if it was currently stuck to some kid.

I had to shield my eyes from the stinging dust particles as the helicopter got closer. Before it had even touched down all the way, Agent Franks had already hopped out and started walking my way. They'd sent the big man himself, which was a bad sign. Franks had ditched the suit and was geared up for battle, wearing a suit of the MCB's sleek new body armor that looked like something out of a sci-fi movie. Another armored Fed got out after Franks, but he was a lot slower because poor Grant Jefferson was having to serve as Franks' gun caddy, laboring under the weight of several rifle and gear bags.

The helicopter immediately lifted off and soared away. Which was an even worse sign because it meant Franks was planning on staying for a while.

The really loud helicopter was still pretty close, so they probably didn't hear me say, "What the hell are you dorks doing here?"

Franks' ugly mug curled into a scowl, which meant his stolen ears had heard that just fine. Grant hadn't heard me and shouted back, "What?"

The helicopter was farther away now so I could speak normally. "I asked what can MHI do for you upstanding gentlemen today?"

"Where's Stricken?" Franks demanded.

It took me a moment to process that, because of the many things I expected from Franks right then, that question had not been among them. "What? I don't know."

"Where's Lana?"

"Who?"

"The succubus who broke Stricken out of our interrogation room." Grant had caught up with his much more intimidating partner. The look on the junior G-man's face warned me that Franks wasn't fucking around. Franks was legit angrier than usual. "This is serious, Pitt. Have you seen any indication that either of them has been here at the MHI compound since the escape?"

I was honestly baffled by this turn, but I could also tell that this was not the time to be a smart-ass to Franks, because he appeared even shorter tempered than usual. "No. We've not seen them."

"Are you absolutely certain?" Grant asked.

"Yeah. The weird-looking creep who everyone here despises and wants to murder and a smoking hot chick with bat wings would probably stick out a bit. We're not that unobservant." I looked to Franks. "Just because we helped you when you were a fugitive doesn't mean that MHI takes in every stray asshole on the run from the law. What's going on?"

"We got intel," Franks said in his usual terse way that explained absolutely nothing.

"What kind of intel?"

"Classified."

"Come on, Franks."

"It's a reliable tip," Grant interjected.

"MCB already shot their wad on that whole informant-inside-MHI thing with you last time, Grant. Even if you've managed to sneak another rat into our ranks to tattle to mommy whenever we break the rules, I can guarantee they're full of shit on this one, because if Stricken had shown up here I'd have already capped him myself. Never mind what Earl Harbinger would do to him. I can guarantee that if we saw Stricken, it would be shoot, shovel, and shut-up time. There's a track hoe in the garage and we've got a lot of acreage." Though come to think of it, if we simply fed Stricken's body to the wargs there would be even less evidence. The idea of Stricken ending up as warg poop made me smile.

"It's not an informant, it's...something else."

"Coslow?"

The two Feds exchanged a knowing glance, which meant I was probably right.

"I can't say. But the information is good. I can't tell you how, but it looks like Stricken is really interested in whatever it is MHI is prepping for tonight. He's up to something. He'll be close, or it'll at least be one of his trusted allies."

"Like the succubus," I said. Franks' reaction after the prison break had seemed a little off to me. "Do you two know each other?"

"No."

"Too bad. She was strangely attractive for a lady with horns. But don't worry. If this obvious demon woman shows up in a compound full of extremely well-armed Monster Hunters and we don't just immediately cap her to collect the PUFF for some baffling reason, we'll be sure to call the MCB."

"She's not always obvious," Franks corrected me. "Lana can alter her form."

Great. Another shapeshifter. Just what I needed complicating my life. "You sure you don't know her? Because I'm kind of getting the vibe that you know her."

"No." Franks' denial was perfectly flat.

A little too flat maybe. And the fact I could tell that was a testament to how much quality time I'd gotten to spend with Franks over the years. "Sure...We'll be on the lookout then. Thanks for the warning. You can go now."

"If it's all the same to you, we're going to stick around here and observe for ourselves," Grant said. "And by 'all the same to you,' I mean we're going to do whatever we want anyway because we're the law and can make your life miserable until you cave, so you might as well get over it and cooperate."

Franks simply grunted in agreement.

"Wow, Grant, you're remarkably good at throwing your weight around and being a total dick. Government work suits you."

"My high school guidance counselor told me I'd be good at public service, but I decided to waste a few years being a dumbass MHI employee first." Grant gestured toward the main building. "After you."

"Fine." I started walking toward headquarters. They followed me. Earl was going to hate this, but Grant wasn't bluffing. If we fought the MCB over this, they'd just hit us over the head with a big legal hammer. And instead of just these two we'd be up to our eyeballs in meddlesome Feds. At least I knew Grant was good in a fight, and Franks was a virtual wrecking ball of monster-killing destruction. We could use the help. "But I'll warn you, we've got something really nasty incoming. It's the contract-enforcing monster Stricken warned me about during our meeting. So if you did your observing while shooting back, that would be handy."

"We're here to watch for Stricken," Grant said. "As for this other business, our orders are to not interfere."

"We're gonna interfere," Franks told his subordinate.

"Never mind then." Grant passed his boss one of the heavy gun bags. "I guess we're interfering."

There were so many people at the compound that Julie moved the ops meeting from the conference room to the cafeteria. As the new official CEO since the death of her grandpa, Julie was in charge. Earl was there—with his nearly a century of practical experience—to gently correct her if she got anything wrong, but he mostly sat there looking tired. Earl didn't need to say much because Julie knew what she was doing and transforming into a werewolf off the calendar always left Earl exhausted and gaunt. Normally he spent a month gaining weight just to lose it all at the full moon, and he'd burned even more calories than usual because Phipps had really worked him over.

The compound's defenses were already solid, and a bunch of Hunters had spent the day making sure everything was ready. Julie handed out assignments to everyone else where they could join in as soon as we were done here. The plan had already been presented, and she was trying to make the rest of this quick. The more we could accomplish before the Drekavac arrived, the better off we'd be.

The assembled Hunters gave Franks and Grant a wide berth. No matter how many times MHI worked with the MCB, that general feeling of animosity between our organizations would probably never change. Half of their job seemed to be making our lives miserable. The other half was keeping monsters secret, which made our lives complicated. To the MCB we were the messy cowboys who kept blowing shit up in public making it harder for them to keep monsters secret.

Speaking of secret, the guys who were so secret that they literally had secret in their name were there too. Gutterres hadn't even introduced himself yet, but all the Hunters already knew what he was. It turns out that in a business where most of us work for money or glory, mystical warrior monks develop something of a rep. The soldiers he'd brought looked a lot more like regular Hunters, but the exorcist was an oddity. I caught Gutterres looking at Sonya a few times, probably annoyed that she hadn't just delivered the rock like they'd hired her to do.

Sonya struck me as somebody who normally enjoyed being

the center of attention, but not today, not like this. All of the big-brain Hunters had taken a look at the Ward stuck to her, and they were treating her almost like an afterthought. I don't think they were being dicks on purpose. It's just that a good bedside manner wasn't normally that important to what we do.

Cody was watching her like a hawk. After the mentally and physically grueling siege, he had been happy to retire. After decades of leading MHI's team that handled all of our mad-science contracts with various research labs, he'd been happy to buy a fishing boat and a little place on the beach in Gulf Shores to live out the rest of his days in peace and quiet. Except as soon as Julie had told him *another Ward Stone*, he'd probably broken a whole lot of speed limits to get back here. He'd been baffled at how Newton's weapon was interacting with Sonya.

Our young shapeshifter was probably pretty good at hiding her emotions behind various faces, but it was obvious that she was really bothered when Tanya—who she had been promised would surely know how to fix this—had been confused too. It turned out there wasn't a lot of overlap between elf magic and Newton's alchemy.

Unfortunately, one thing Cody and Tanya had both agreed on was that it couldn't be good for Sonya's long-term health to have an artifact crackling with magical energy embedded in her body. Too bad she was basically shit out of luck until they could figure out how to fix it.

"Some of you may have noticed that we've got a few guests who will be helping us tonight," Julie told the cafeteria full of Hunters. "Most of you know Agent Franks and Agent Jefferson of the MCB."

I was impressed. Nobody booed. But that wasn't out of respect so much as fear of Franks.

"Do you have anything you want to say to everyone, Agent Franks?" Julie asked.

Franks slowly looked around the room, surely trying to decide if he wanted to regale us mere mortal Hunters with his copious wisdom. "No."

Julie wasn't surprised or disappointed by that answer. "Great. Moving on—"

"I'd like to say a few words," Grant interjected.

"Of course you do." Julie sighed. "Agent Jefferson."

Grant stood up to address his former coworkers. MHI is a pretty tight bunch. When one of our own ditches us, joins the hated MCB, and then comes back to spy on us, it leaves some hard feelings. So of course there was some muttering from the crowd. Among that I picked out the words, *traitor, Judas, backstabber,* and *dickhead*... Okay, I'll admit, that last one might have been from me. But I was sitting in back so not too many people heard it... probably.

"I just want everyone to know that the MCB will in no way hinder MHI's operations tonight. We are merely acting as observers. I'm fully aware of everyone's feelings about the Bureau and about me personally. However, we're going to set that aside because we all have more important things to worry about. Officially, all I can say is that if you have any knowledge pertaining to the whereabouts of the man known as Stricken, the MCB is offering a reward for any information leading to his capture. Thank you."

That was a remarkably non-dickish message by Grant standards. Holly golf-clapped for him.

"Thank you, Agent Jefferson," Julie said, a little surprised that Grant had managed to keep it that professional. He must have been bucking for a promotion. "And over here, we've got some representatives from the Blessed Order of Saint Hubert the Protector, who have agreed to share their intel about tonight's threat."

"In exchange for access to the Ward Stone," Gutterres specified. "We have a rather pressing need for it."

"After we figure out how to get it unstuck from our other guest, sure," Julie said. "But please, continue, Mr. Gutterres."

The combat exorcist stood up. "The creature you will be facing tonight is known as a Drekavac. It is a rare power bestowed by the devil himself to only the vilest of human beings to have ever lived. Men and women willing to sacrifice their souls in exchange for immortality and terrible abilities. This offer is only made to the most unrepentant mortals who have become the living personification of some terrible sin. This creature in particular is the embodiment of *unrighteous judgment.* His mortal name was Silas Carver. He was once trusted to protect the innocent, a killer of monsters, burner of witches, but who, in his search to punish sinners, became everything he hated and more."

"Sounds like a real asshole," Earl said.

"Grade A," Gutterres agreed. "He was so focused on destroying evil that he embraced it."

"One of yours?"

"Protestant, thankfully. But if you want to throw stones about our organizations' various embarrassments—"

Earl held up one hand before Gutterres could bring up someone like Julie's dad or Martin Hood. "No need. I didn't intend any offense. You can't do what we do without having some bad apples once in a while."

"Of course." Gutterres nodded politely. "Silas Carver was relentless in life, and that hasn't changed in undeath. Each Drekavac is a unique being with differing abilities. We have not dealt directly with Carver before, so I can't tell you how his abilities will manifest the more he dies. However, I can assure you of one thing: He will become increasingly dangerous until his thirteenth form is defeated."

Albert Lee was sitting near the front, taking notes so that he could update MHI's files. "How has mankind beaten these things before?"

"Usually, they don't," Gutterres answered. "They try...fail... and eventually hand over the Drekavac's target to appease it so that it'll go away."

Holly, who was sitting next to me, leaned over and whispered, "So that's Plan B."

"In the times that mankind has defeated one the full thirteen, it has cost a great number of lives. However, they also lacked modern firepower, which hopefully will make up the difference. I can make certain that once Silas Carver enters these grounds, he is committed, so that this will be finished tonight, and he can't strategically retreat and come back to attack again when you least expect it."

"We appreciate that," Julie said.

"In return, I will require the Ward, whether it is still with the girl or not."

"Hey, now," Sonya said. "I didn't agree to that."

"You've already demonstrated your agreements mean nothing. If you'd simply kept your word, you wouldn't be in this predicament and I would be on the way to finish my real mission. Instead, because of your greed and dishonesty, we are here, risking all of these Hunters' lives. Every minute we delay my mission costs more innocent lives. You might not care about those people, but I do."

Gutterres was so blunt about it that Sonya actually shut up. The man had a gift for guilt-shaming people. It must be a religious thing.

"You going to expound on this ongoing crisis of yours, Mr. Gutterres, or leave it to our imagination?" Julie asked.

"I'm not authorized to give all the details yet, but thousands of lives are at stake. I recognize that MHI's goals for the stone are worthy. Mine are more so. I could try to persuade you that this is bigger than any of us. Instead I'll say this. Most of you don't know me, but you know Agent Franks." Franks had gone back to sullenly ignoring everyone, but he lifted his head when Gutterres invoked his name. "You may not like him, but you recognize that he is, by nature, accurate in his assessments. Agent Franks knows me, my office, and my organization. So I pose the question to him to answer before all of you—do I exaggerate this threat?"

Franks thought it over. "No."

And that pretty much settled it, because even though Franks was an asshole, he was an extremely straightforward one.

Julie was the official boss, but she still looked to Earl for wisdom. He sat there, pondering on it for a moment. Then he nodded at Julie, knowing that she'd do the right thing. That said a lot about how much faith he had in her.

"I'm fine with you having first access to the Ward, Mr. Gutterres." That had to be a harder decision than most would realize, because Asag had targeted our family personally. "But only on two terms."

"Name them."

"We deal with this monster first. Then we figure out how to remove the Ward, or you work it out with Sonya before you drag her along. Because I'm not letting you kidnap a kid, no matter how much you think you need the thing stuck to her."

Sonya seemed a little surprised that Julie was standing up for her. She shouldn't have been.

"Agreed." Gutterres sat down without another word. He probably recognized arguing with my wife would be fruitless. *Smart man.*

Back to business then. Julie knew how to run a meeting, short and to the point. Put the plan out there, let the experienced Hunters poke holes in it, fix the problems, and then get back to work. Except there was one potential problem she wasn't addressing directly, which was the fact we had a bunch of untrustworthy outsiders here, each with their own goals that didn't necessarily coincide with ours... except I had an idea how to keep an eye on them.

CHAPTER 17

MHI has quite a few secrets. Even in a business that runs on secrets there were some things that needed to be kept from our rank and file for various reasons, like the fact our IT department was a PUFF-applicable troll or our boss was a lycanthrope. I'm about as inner circle as you can get at this company, and there were probably still things that I didn't know about. For example I still had a deep and troubling suspicion that Milo Anderson actually had a functioning nuclear weapon stashed somewhere.

So while most of the Hunters and our various houseguests were distracted prepping for tonight, I snuck down to the sub-basement to the janitor's officer to have a word with one of those company secrets.

I liked our janitor. Though I couldn't really tell if he liked me or not. Sid was one of those tough-as-shoe-leather types it was hard to get a read on. The little dude was a scrapper and a hard worker, so Earl had offered him a job as a Hunter after he'd beaten a zombie to death. Sid had no desire to be a Hunter as far as I could tell, but all our support staff needed to be read-in on the supernatural too, and he turned out to be a great janitor. The previous guy had been an idiot.

Sid wasn't in his room, but with all the battle space prep work being done around the compound that wasn't a surprise. He'd probably jumped in to do manual labor on one of the projects because that was his nature. We'd warned all the noncombatants and support staff away because of the Drekavac, but I'd be willing to bet Sid would stick around just to get a jump on the cleanup. He was stubborn like that.

There wasn't anything secret about Sid though. He was just another regular human being. However, the things he'd met and made an alliance with a little while back weren't human at all, and since they'd escaped from a secret government lab, we had made a deal to keep their existence on the downlow as much as possible. Only me, Sid, Earl, Julie, and Milo knew about Justinian's legion. Even the veterinarian I'd taken a few of them to had been kept in the dark about their intelligence. In exchange for letting the legion live here and the occasional request for supplies, they served as our subterranean early warning system and took care of small problems for us.

One of the heating ducts had been marked with red tape. I went over and knocked on it with the specified pattern that indicated I needed to parley. Since Justinian had a phone, I could have just done this via text, but asking for a favor, it seemed more respectful to do it in person. Knowing that they'd need to dress up their honor guard—because every visit with Justinian was a formal one—I sat on the concrete floor below the vent and waited.

A few minutes later I heard music coming from the duct. It was some grand military marching tune. The vent popped open, and the honor guard filed out in an orderly row of five rats wide, four ranks deep. Each rat had a little red shield and X-acto knife spear on his back, secured with Christmas ribbons and fishing line. They came to a halt in a perfect phalanx right in front of my knees. It would've been cute if it hadn't been so disturbingly militant. Those knives were razor sharp and these little dudes were disciplined . . . and also probably smarter than a lot of the humans I knew.

Next came the band, which in this case consisted of two rats carrying a cellphone that was playing a marching song from YouTube. Then Justinian himself appeared. His armor had been painted gold, and he was wearing a plastic crown that had probably come off of a toy. Justinian gave me an adorable little bow. I returned the gesture and resisted the urge to pet him, because then I'd probably die a minute later from hundreds of tiny stab wounds. Justinian stopped next to the phone-carrying rats as another phalanx of warrior rats brought up the rear. They were very big on pomp and circumstance. Justinian may have been tiny, but the rat emperor had gravitas.

As the song finished, the rats maneuvered the phone so that I could see the screen. Justinian swiped the screen to a different app and began to type.

GREETINGS MR. PITT. ALL IS SECURE IN THE LANDS BENEATH MHI. TO WHAT DO WE OWE THIS PLEASURE?

I still couldn't get over how weird this was, even by my jaded standards. Some mad scientists had decided to genetically engineer smart rats, they'd escaped, heard about somebody named Earl Harbinger who might give them sanctuary, so now I was basically their landlord. Life comes at you fast.

"I have brought a gift as a demonstration of MHI's continuing friendship with the legion." I reached behind me and picked up the grocery bag I'd brought down with me. "It is a selection of dried meats and quality cheeses from around the world, which my wife picked up on her last trip to Costco."

EXCELLENT. THANK YOU FOR THIS BOUNTY. MAY OUR ALLIANCE ENDURE FOREVER.

Not only was the rat unnervingly intelligent, he was also an excellent typist. His tiny fists were punching the letters on the screen as fast as I could work a heavy bag.

YET IT IS NOT FINE CHEESES WHICH BRINGS YOU TO THE SUBBASEMENT TODAY. YOU ARE CLEARLY TROUBLED. HOW MAY WE AID YOU?

"There's a very dangerous creature coming to attack the compound tonight."

DIRE TIMES. DO YOU WISH US TO AID YOU IN BATTLE?

"No. This thing is crazy dangerous. It would be best if you stayed out of sight." They were smart, but also proud of the warrior ethos they'd adopted, so I had to tread carefully here so as to not give offense. "I mean, obviously you would be very helpful but MHI has need of your skills in a different way."

THERE IS NO NEED TO MINCE WORDS MISTER PITT. THOUGH FEARSOME MY SOLDIERS ARE APPROXIMATELY 1.5 POUNDS EACH. I AM AWARE OF OUR LIMITATIONS IN BATTLE. EVEN BOUNDLESS COURAGE WILL NOT OVERCOME PHYSICS.

"You are wise. The reason I'm here is that there may be untrustworthy people among us."

DO YOU WISH FOR US TO ASSASSINATE THEM IN THEIR SLEEP? Judging by the fact these guys could sneak in anywhere and were armed with razor blades, I could see how that would work frighteningly well. "No. Nothing like that. They're supposedly our allies. I just need you to keep an eye on them for me during the chaos tonight." Come to think of it, last time I'd worked out an arrangement like this, it had ended up with a gnome being stuffed in a toilet. Intelligent rats were easier to deal with than gnomes, with way less ego, but nearly as invisible. "I'm afraid some of our enemies or even some of our so-called friends might try to take advantage of MHI while we are concentrating on the monster."

Justinian studied me with tiny black eyes which were unnervingly astute. He gave me a small nod, and then typed, THAT IS WISE. WE SHALL SERVE. YOU SHOULD OPEN THAT CHEESE AS WE DISCUSS THE DETAILS.

With all the preparations going on, Milo was probably the busiest guy in the company right now. He was our go-to expert on all things mechanical or chemical, which meant most of our defenses. So when he called and asked me for a favor, I dropped everything and got to it as fast as I could. Which meant grabbing Sonya from the "guest's quarters" to escort her to Milo's workshop on the far side of the compound.

I had to talk Cody and Tanya into letting me temporarily borrow her first. That odd couple were still fighting over how to get the Ward out of Sonya without killing her. Edward was also there, serving as Tanya's bodyguard and moral support. Not that he got involved in the magic versus science arguments. Ed was the strong silent type.

Sonya and I walked fast. The sun would be setting soon, and we didn't know how soon after that Silas Carver would show up.

"What do you think Milo wants?" Sonya asked me.

"I don't know."

"You think he's going to yell at me for the whole threatening to kill him thing? Because I really do feel bad about that."

"Milo's not really the yelling type." Seriously, by Monster Hunter standards that guy had reached some sort of Zen one-with-the-universe level of chill. "But I'm sure it's important or he wouldn't have asked for you."

Hunters were running every which way, moving guns, ammo,

and medical supplies into the main building. Sonya took note of all the activity, but nobody had any time to pay any attention to our guest. "You guys are serious about tonight, aren't you?"

"This thing is bad news. So we hope for the best but prepare for the worst."

"They're doing all this for me..."

"You could look at it that way, but honestly they don't even know you. They'd take this risk for anybody, well, anybody and a paycheck. This is just the kind of thing Hunters do. It's our job."

"Yeah, I know your spiel. You're the good guys, recruited from survivors who find out monsters are real. I've known about the supernatural my whole life. Too bad Earl Harbinger never thought I was good enough to be one of you." She muttered that last part.

I stopped walking so suddenly that Sonya nearly crashed into me. "That's some bullshit. That's not what happened."

"My mom told me all about it. I talked about trying out to be a Hunter, like my dad, but Earl Harbinger didn't think I was good enough so don't even bother."

I couldn't believe my ears. "Earl was *excited* to make you an offer. He barely tolerates most Newbies. He already *liked* you. Plus, shapeshifter powers. Duh. Your mom forbade him from ever bringing it up because she was trying to protect you from this life. She was worried about you getting hurt. Hang on. Is this why you've got such a chip on your shoulder about us?"

"No...I..." Sonya scowled. "Shit."

"Your mom straight-up lied to you." I laughed, and then started walking again. No wonder she was grumpy at Hunters. She'd thought she had been rejected by us and the Secret Guard. "So how long have you been butt-hurt about this imagined slight?"

"I'm not butt-hurt." She followed, silent for a long moment. "But that does make more sense than Mom telling me that a half-kodama wouldn't be welcome here, considering I just met your trailer park elf employee, and she's kind of nuts."

"Kind of? And we've got a troll and a ton of orcs too, but oh yeah, our werewolf boss is supersensitive about keeping this outfit humans only. Damn, you're gullible."

"Like you've got room to talk, Mr. Self-Righteous. Gullible like back in the meeting, when the lady in charge was telling everyone about how she wouldn't let the Vatican kidnap me, which is kinda funny while I'm being held prisoner."

"First off, that lady in charge is my wife, so check yourself before you say anything about her to piss me off."

"*She* married *you*?"

"Yep." I wasn't even offended. When a five hooks up with a ten you get that kind of reaction a lot. "Second, as for you being our prisoner, the gate is that way. Ain't nobody stopping you. Have fun with the Drekavac." Of course, rather than run for the hills, she kept following me toward Milo's workshop. "Didn't think so."

"A girl has to weigh her options."

"Yeah, you just keep on looking out for number one," I said.

"It's not like anybody else is going to do that for me. It's a cold, cruel world out there."

We were silent for the rest of the long walk. Milo's workshop was far enough away from everything else that if one of his experiments went horribly wrong, the resulting explosion wouldn't get the rest of us. There were several Hunters working there today. Bombs were being carefully loaded into the back of a pickup while Milo supervised.

"Careful...gentle...oh, hey, Z." And Milo immediately forgot about the ultra-deadly explosives being handled so he could wave at us. "Sonya! I'm glad you came. Welcome to my workshop. Come on in. I've got something for you."

We followed Milo into the chaos. There was a table full of hydraulics and hoses, then another full of circuit boards and wires, then boxes and boxes of gun parts, and then past something that looked like a riding lawn mower had a baby with a tree trimmer except it had a machine gun mounted on it and the whole thing appeared to be remote-controlled.

"What does he do here exactly?" Sonya whispered.

"Whatever he feels like. Milo goes where his muse takes him. I just pay the invoices and try to stay out of the way."

Milo had heard me. "Oh yeah. If monsters hadn't eaten my family when I was a kid, I'd probably be building Mars rovers now, or maybe working at a Ren Faire. Could've gone either way, I think."

"He's a mechanical genius," I said.

"Naw. I just get ideas and then poke at them until they work or blow up. That happens a lot too. Anyways, I'm really sorry about how it went yesterday."

"I'm the one who attacked you."

"Yeah, but it was a heated situation. You roll with it, sometimes you make a dumb decision, but we all learned from it, and nobody got shot, so no hard feelings." We reached the back corner where Milo had set up his forge. There was a big anvil and a wall full of hammers and tongs. Milo had all the modern tools for metalworking, like lathes and drill presses, but sometimes he felt like going old school. "Hey, Z. You mind giving me and Sonya a minute?"

"Sure thing, man." I looked to Sonya. "Promise not to take him hostage again?"

"I'll try not to," she said sarcastically.

I nodded and walked around the corner to give them some privacy. I didn't wander off too far though, not because I was worried, but because I was curious. Milo was being kind of weird. Not his regular weird-weird this time, but awkward weird. There was a pair of electronic earmuffs hanging off one of Milo's power hammers, so I put them on and then cranked up the volume on the microphone so I could listen in on their conversation. It was probably rude of me to spy, but I was trying to look out for my friends, and I still didn't entirely trust the shifty shapeshifter to not stab us in the back again.

Sonya was apologizing, "I really am sorry. I know you and my dad were tight and—"

Milo stopped her. "Yeah. We were. Which is why I needed to apologize to you."

"But I . . ."

"You screwed up one day, Sonya, but I screwed up *years*. Your dad was one of my best friends. I should have helped more after he was gone, just because of that. I owed Chad that. Only I was never there for you."

"I remember we met once," she said, sounding hesitant. "Or did I imagine that?"

"A few times actually, only you were little."

"I just remember somebody who made me laugh who had a big fluffy red beard."

"That was me. The beard's greyer now, but yeah. I used to stop by to check on you guys. Me and my buddy Sam, he's gone now too . . . but your mom . . . well . . . we'd get to reminiscing about your pop, and the whole thing just kind of made her sad."

"She does struggle with depression."

"I think it's because she longs for her home. There aren't too many things that make Earth okay for her. You're one. Your pop was another. Only whenever I'd visit, it was like reminding her of what had been taken from her, what could have been. She'd end up in a funk afterwards, and it was my fault. I was doing more harm to your family than good. I tried to be a good uncle, and instead I was a painful reminder. I'm not good at *not* talking about things. Now, Earl, he's great at never talking about emotional stuff. So he kept visiting, but I stopped. I don't think your mom liked being reminded of the old days."

"Yeah...I'm finding out that my mom was a lot more selective about telling me about things than I ever thought."

"Don't get mad at her. It's a parent's duty to protect their kids. She did what she thought was right. But either way, I wasn't ever there for you, and for that, I'm really sorry. Meeting you makes me feel like I let your dad down."

"Because I'm a thief and a screwup?"

"I didn't say that. I think you're a young woman who made the best choices she could and ended up dealing with some really bad people."

"Yeah, when the Church guys asked me to grab the package, I didn't know Stricken was—"

Milo cut her off. "I'm not naïve, Sonya. You don't suddenly know how to steal things, beat up a bunch of Feds, and have preplanned escape routes the first time you do something like that. You've been up to some *shenanigans*."

Sonya gave an embarrassed laugh. "Okay, yeah, you got me. It seems like a waste to have powers and not use them to have some fun."

Milo used his *dad voice*. "Who else have you robbed?"

"Drug dealers mostly. Okay, yeah, I haven't always made the wisest decisions...Please don't tell my mom."

"I get it. I was a teenager when I started doing this stuff. You wouldn't believe some of the stupid crap I did! When we have more time, remind me to tell you about me and your dad playing zombie golf."

"Zombie golf?"

"Long story and no time. I've got a lot of work to do before sundown, but I would love to talk more later."

"I think I'd like that, Milo."

"Cool." Milo sounded relieved that he might actually get to fulfill some self-appointed-uncle responsibilities. "Anyways, I wanted to give you something." There was some noise as Milo started moving items around on a shelf. "Now, I'm no samurai bladesmith whose family has five hundred years of experience folding meteor steel ten million times and all that metaphysical bushido, soul-of-the-sword stuff that Chad liked to go on about, but I did win the competition on the one episode of *Forged in Fire* I was on."

Now I was really curious, so I poked my head back around the corner to see what Milo was giving her. There was a sheathed sword in his callused hands.

"Is that..."

"Mo No Ken. The Sword of Mourning." Milo seemed rather proud as he handed it over. "I found all the parts in the wreckage after the Christmas Party. It had got bent really bad before the blade snapped off. I salvaged what I could and tried to make it look exactly like how it used to."

Sonya slowly, reverently, drew the katana. It was a relic, reborn.

"Careful. It's crazy sharp. I mean, obviously, you'd know that. Not much point otherwise. Like I said, I'm not into all that mumbo-jumbo, but this was a hero's sword, so treat it with respect. Okay?"

"Milo, it's beautiful."

That made him grin, because Milo showed love through giving away weaponry. "I hoped you'd appreciate it. It's been waiting for you for years."

"Really?"

"Oh, yeah. I was going to give it to you on your sixteenth birthday, but I asked your mom and..." Milo trailed off as he realized he'd said too much. "Well, it didn't go over well. So I honored her wishes and put it away."

Sonya had teared up. "Sorry."

"It's okay. Better late than never."

Then Sonya hugged him.

I walked away and hung up the electronic muffs where I'd found them. Then I picked up a gun magazine off a table and pretended to have been reading it the whole time. When Sonya appeared she had dried her eyes and was showing no weakness, but she was proudly carrying her father's sword.

"Ready to go?" I asked.

"Yeah."

"What did Milo want anyway?"

"None of your business."

I was happy to let it go.

CHAPTER 18

The fog rolled in about midnight.

I was on the roof, braced against the ledge, watching my sector, when all of a sudden it got uncomfortably cold. Since I was wearing all my armor and gear I had been uncomfortably warm and sweaty because all that weight on your chest and back really traps the heat in, but then *zap*, within seconds I was chilled to the core.

"You feeling that?" Julie asked.

"Yeah. He's here."

Julie keyed her radio. "Wake up, everybody. This is Julie on the roof. We have a supernatural temperature drop outside. Get ready. I think this is it."

Honestly, being a spotter with nothing to spot for several hours can be terribly boring, to the point that I'd been in danger of falling asleep. There were six two-man teams stationed on the roof of the main building, because it was our best elevated position. Everybody else was waiting at their designated battle stations.

The main building had already basically been a fort, but we'd done extensive renovations and put in improvements since Martin Hood's attack. The walls had been reinforced and every window had armored steel shutters now. We'd installed more cameras and every kind of sensor you could think of. Tonight would be the first real-world test of Milo's new point defense system, and he was downright giddy about that.

Tanya and her elves had checked and rechecked the magic markings they'd inscribed around the property to weaken the Drekavac. She assured us they'd used their most powerful magic— also known as "Mama's special recipe" on the main building itself, which should theoretically keep the Drekavac from porting in or re-forming his body inside the walls. If the Drekavac wanted to come inside, he would have to do it the old-fashioned way. Since Sonya, the target of his unholy wrath, was hiding in Earl's concrete cell in the basement, he'd certainly try.

Sonya had wanted to be outside, to be quote, *where the action is,* except Earl had told her to take her scrawny ass to the bunker, which was also a direct quote. That hadn't been up for debate. Cody was with her and a bunch of books from the archives, still trying to figure out how to get the Ward detached.

Gutterres had walked us through what he knew about other Drekavacs' thirteen manifestations. The Church's records were spotty, and since each Drekavac was unique, possibly inaccurate for ours. Nobody had fought all the way through against this particular one and lived to tell about it that they knew of. So we'd prepared for everything we could think of.

I listened over my radio as the Hunters watching our video feeds reported in. There was something moving fast along the private road heading directly for the front gate. As I watched, that same thick, oily fog as last night oozed out of the forest and began poking through our chain-link fence.

"Alright, Hunters. It's time to get to work. You know the plan." Only as Earl spoke over the radio, the signal started breaking up. "Expect to lose coms. Hold your fire until after the exorcist does his thing."

There was a lot of static. Something about the Drekavac's aura screwed with our radio the same way he'd killed my cellphone, but we were prepared for that.

A single vehicle pulled away from our main building and started driving toward the gate. "There goes Gutterres," I muttered. "I hope his little ritual works."

"They're the oldest Monster Hunting organization in the world," Julie replied. "They didn't last this long by being stupid."

"Maybe they lasted this long because they can coast on tithing money while leaving the heavy lifting to companies like us?"

"If it's used for the ritual application of holy water, it's called an aspergillum," Julie said.

"How'd you know that?"

"Art history degree, remember?"

"Ah..." And there was another example why other couples would only play Trivial Pursuit against us once. We were undefeated. The only other couple that had given us a good challenge was Trip and his new girlfriend, Cheryl, and that was because they got all the sports questions. Julie and I both sucked at sports trivia.

Gutterres finished his ritual just as the horse and rider came into view. The horse thing was so big it could have easily crashed through our gate, but it slowed down. As it slowed, the horrible sound tapered off. It came to a stop and the Drekavac dismounted to approach the gate on foot, his long coat nearly dragging along the ground behind it. The big black hat hid his awful face. I'd already dialed in the range so I put my crosshair on his chest. Gutterres opened the channel so we could hear the thing's eerie voice.

"*You know why I have come.*"

"I do," Gutterres responded. "*Only I know who you are, Silas Carver.*"

"*You know my mortal name. Then you must also know that I will never stop. To stand in my way means certain doom. Move aside, Hubertian. My oath must be fulfilled. The transgressor must be punished. The auction must be retrieved.*"

"No. I will not. For I too have taken an oath. Your oath is to the prince of lies. While mine is to Almighty God. I have invoked the *exilium aeternum.*"

The Drekavac's angry hiss temporarily shorted out all of our radios.

"*Which means however many lives we take from you after you cross this threshold, they are gone forever. Upon taking your thirteenth life after you enter these grounds, you will be banished from this mortal plane for eternity. Like most things who think they're immortal, you've grown complacent. Break your oath, turn back, and relinquish this contract, or we will rid the world of your foulness once and for all.*"

"*You offer a false choice. There is another option. Kill you all before you can kill all of me and claim my prize. Your threats do not sway me.*"

"I don't know how big their memorial wall is, so 1 crossed. You're just sore he left you stuck under a tree."

Maybe I was a little indignant still. Hunters are a p bunch.

The car stopped by our front gate. Gutterres got out passenger side. One of his guys was driving and stayed l the wheel, ready to get them the hell out of there. Gu walked by himself to the unmanned gate shack.

"Okay, that's a little disappointing," I said as I watched tl Cazador's scope, that I had turned all the way up to twen times magnification.

"What?" Julie asked.

"He's just dressed in normal clothing. I figured a c exorcist would at least rate some cool robes or a big funn

"Focus, dear."

The unholy screaming noise of the Drekavac's ride appro The fog hovering around the front gate began to glow. "Tl guy is approaching the main entrance." I didn't need to tel the range to the front gate—five hundred and fifteen—b she had the yardage of every possible shot across the com memorized. "Zero wind." In fact, it was eerily still.

"Got it," Julie said as she peered through her scope. F Cazador was chambered in 6.5 Creedmoor, which had better ballistic coefficient than my .308. It had a trajector a laser beam. Hitting someone at that range would be c play for her.

"Can you hear me, MHI?" Gutterres asked.

"Barely," Earl responded. He was in the command cente all the cameras and had the most powerful receiver and ant *"Lots of static."*

"I'll leave this transmitting so you can hear what the Dre says, but I will stop while I perform the rite. No offense."

"None taken. I understand. Trade secrets."

"More sacred than secret." Gutterres let go of his radio. (ously, he was still talking, but from way over here we cou hear him. He lifted something silver in one of his hands flicked it at our gate. Oddly enough, as Gutterres chante(fog seemed to pull back from the fence a bit.

"I think that's the sprinkler thingy I saw in their van."

"Only the vilest sinners to walk the Earth have been offered your mantle, and only thirteen have ever been foolish enough to accept it. Mark my words, Hell Spawn. If you cross that fence, Satan will be down to twelve."

"Okay, that is pretty metal," I said.

"No kidding," Julie responded.

"I shall slay everyone who stands against me until this place is soaked in blood."

"You can try." Gutterres turned his back on the Drekavac and started walking to the car. *"All yours, MHI."*

"Dibs," Julie shouted so everyone else on the roof could hear her. And since she was the CEO now, nobody was going to argue with that. She aimed, slowly exhaled, and fired on the respiratory pause. The suppressor mounted on the end of her Cazador turned the muzzle blast to a muted *whump*. The Drekavac's head snapped back and its hat flew off.

"Hit," I confirmed for her as the body turned into sparks and melted into the ground. "Looked like right in the face."

"One down," Harbinger told us all. *"A dozen to go."*

Then, for good measure, Julie brained the horse monster too.

Gutterres got back in the car and the driver floored it, trying to get back to the cover of the main building as fast as possible. *"Good shot, MHI. Keep the Drekavac on the other side of the fence for as many lives as you can. Once he crosses the threshold, his body will be able to re-form inside the perimeter."*

There was a lot of noise from the runway as Skippy fired up the helicopter's engines. We'd kept him on the ground in order to save fuel so that we'd have him when we needed him the most. Now that it was on, Skippy could do what Skippy did best. Even though Franks was here, Earl's executive decision had been to leave the munitions on the Hind. We'd risk the charges. That had made Skippy's day.

Besides, Franks wouldn't snitch. Grant, on the other hand, might. I'd jokingly offered to frag him, because *accidents happen*, but Julie had given me a disapproving look so I'd dropped the topic.

A few tense minutes passed. Surely the Drekavac had re-formed by now. The fog was floating back toward us. Every light in the compound was burning so that we could see better, and we had several giant spotlights mounted on the roof, but the bulbs by the front gate flickered and died. The eerie glow was growing again. "He's coming up the road again. He's going to crash the gate."

The Drekavac appeared, riding hell-bent for leather. The horse's legs were moving so fast that they were a blur. It had to be going about seventy. Milo had floated the idea of installing some of those big hydraulic car bomb barricades last year, but Earl hadn't thought we'd ever need them. Usually monsters just walked or flew in.

"Open fire," Julie said, and everybody on the roof was happy to comply. We had even mounted a 7.62 minigun on the roof earlier. At six thousand rounds per minute, it made a hell of a racket, but they walked a line of red tracers right into the fast-moving target. The Drekavac veered hard to the side, hit a tree, and went up in a big—very unnaturally blue—fireball.

Everybody on the roof cheered.

"That's two," Earl said from the control room. *"Round three, fight."*

"Did Earl just make a Mortal Kombat reference?" I asked.

"I highly doubt it," Julie said. Then she raised her voice so the roof crew could hear her. "Don't celebrate yet. You heard the Vatican Hunter. We've got to keep this monster on the other side of the fence as long as possible."

"There," someone shouted. "Light on the main road again."

That had been fast. The Drekavac wasn't messing around. This time the monster had gotten a running start and was moving much quicker. The horse had to be doing at least a hundred miles an hour by the time it came into view. Every sniper on the roof shot him and then the minigun shredded the Drekavac and an acre of forest behind him. Only this time he got hit dozens of times before losing control. The horse flipped, end over end, tumbling toward the gate. It skidded to a halt, just barely touching the metal. As the bodies disintegrated, the fog seemed to close in a bit more.

"That was too close," Julie said.

"That's three," Earl said. It was hard to tell with all the static now, but he wasn't sounding nearly as confident.

"He's getting too much momentum for us to stop him from crossing the line." Julie keyed her radio. "Skippy, hit him farther out."

The Hind roared toward the gate. There were orcs hanging

off both sides, manning door guns. They threw the horns at us as they passed. MHI owned thousands of acres around the compound, so that was our land, and we could blow it up if we felt like it. If somebody had blundered into the area by accident, they were about to have a real bad night, but this was a perfect example of why we had all those NO TRESPASSING signs posted.

The Drekavac must have re-formed a thousand yards down the road to get more acceleration, because lines of tracers shot from the Hind were firing at something that was out of our view. From the way Skippy had to turn and chase his target, the Drekavac was moving even faster than before. Rockets lanced down from the chopper, causing a rapid chain of explosions along the road. But then Skippy stopped firing and banked away.

Skippy transmitted something, but I could barely make it out. It sounded like *"Monster get blowed up."* That would be four down, only Earl didn't confirm the count because that was when even our most powerful radios went out entirely.

Thirty seconds later, the Drekavac must have already re-formed, because I could see blue fire racing down the road. One of Skippy's door gunners started shooting, but our orc wasn't going to be able to swing his nose around in time to track the monster down with his big guns.

Julie saw it too. The compound had an old-school intercom system installed in it that dated back at least thirty years. The Drekavac messed with air waves, but it probably wouldn't be able to do anything that was hardwired. Julie let go of her rifle and picked up the handpiece. "Milo, crater the road."

We'd buried some gigantic charges around the perimeter today, and Milo had them all wired to where he was stationed in our ad hoc compound defense center. Except there was no response to Julie's call. The Drekavac was getting closer.

Maybe Milo had heard her and just not responded. Maybe he was working on it. But just in case we had a couple of bullhorns up here to relay orders, and if that didn't work, different color flags to wave and flares to shoot to relay messages to the other Hunters. I picked up the gigantic industrial bullhorn and raised it to my mouth. Milo was only one floor down, so hopefully this would work.

"MILO." Holy shit this thing was loud. I was glad I had my hearing protection on. *"DETONATE THE ROAD BOMBS."*

The Drekavac came into view, and I couldn't even tell you how fast he was going this time. I'm talking jet-aircraft-flyby speeds. Our roof-mounted minigun couldn't even swivel fast enough to hit him. Except Milo must have heard one of us and pushed the big red button because all of a sudden the entrance was *gone*.

BOOM!

I don't know how many pounds of ammonium nitrate Milo had buried there, but it was a lot. It made a visible shockwave that flattened trees for fifty yards. It blew the guard shack away. It broke a bunch of windows around the compound. It was so big that everybody on the roof felt it in their eyeballs.

"There go my rose bushes," Julie said.

There were a bunch of spotlights pointed that direction already, but somebody angled one upward so that we could see the mushroom cloud, which was two hundred feet tall and growing rapidly. It began raining debris.

And the Drekavac fell out of the sky.

His mangled body landed *inside* the fence.

The perimeter was breached. "Oh, shit." The body dissolved within seconds, but his fifth death came a moment too late. The evil fog moved with a hungry suddenness into the compound. I got on the bullhorn again. "THE MONSTER IS INSIDE THE WIRE."

He had eight lives left to use against us, and no more do-overs. When those were gone, they were *gone*. It was going to be tooth and nail from here on out.

A dread quiet fell over the compound as everybody waited for the next shoe to drop.

The silence was broken. "South side, south side!" The sniper team on that end of the roof began shooting down toward the barracks. I ran in that direction, but there was a sudden *hiss-CRACK* as a bolt of lightning smashed into the building. The two Hunters were flung back from the ledge. We were all hit by stinging bits of concrete, and then everything was obscured by smoke.

As the two stunned men were dragged away by the others, a few of us reached the damaged edge, peered over, and saw the Drekavac walking toward us, blunderbuss in hand. He was less than fifty yards away, so he basically filled my entire cranked-up scope when I aimed at him. I nailed him twice in the chest with Cazador. He barely even twitched. Then the Hunter to my left opened up with a 240B and stitched him from knee to throat, before the Hunter on my right dropped a 40mm grenade right at his feet.

The Drekavac fell apart. That was six.

"Man your positions! Cover your zone," Julie shouted. As we moved back to our stations, more Hunters ran up from the stairs to grab the wounded, and others took their place watching that direction. Since the Drekavac was going to be close now, I hurried and cranked Cazador's scope down to the lowest setting of five power. I went back to watching the front of the compound for danger before I realized that I didn't even know which of us had just gotten hit. There hadn't been time to look.

A few nervous seconds passed. The fog was everywhere in the compound now, thick as soup, and really hard to see through.

This time the Drekavac was smart. He didn't re-form in the open where our lookouts could see him. He re-formed behind one of the outbuildings on the east side. Our first warning was when a bolt of lightning hit one of the antennas on our roof. It came crashing down, spraying fire and sparks everywhere. The Hunters on that side returned fire, but the Drekavac fired again. The impact shook the roof and tore a burning gouge through the concrete ledge. There were only a few seconds' delay between lightning bolts now.

Then the fucking birds came out of nowhere and hit us.

I'd dealt with one ghost falcon last night. This time there was a flock of the damned things. They dropped out of the sky like meteors, screeching and clawing for our eyes. I reflexively clubbed one out of the air with Cazador's suppressor, then stomped on its head with my boot. Then I watched in horror as another bird nailed one of the Hunters, who was distracted shooting at the Drekavac, right in the back of the helmet. He was already hanging dangerously far over the edge of the roof, off-balance, in order to get a good angle. The impact was enough to shove him over. He went over the side with a scream.

I ran over, looked down, and discovered Vaughn Spencer about two feet down on the other side hanging by his fingertips. The drop probably wouldn't kill him outright, but it was enough to break some bones, and then he'd be lying there in the open in the line of fire of an angry Drekavac. He saw me and shouted, "Give me a hand."

"Hang on."

"No shit, Pitt!"

I let my rifle dangle by the sling so I could hold onto the ledge with one hand and lean way over to grab his wrist with the other. Spencer was one of the out-of-town Hunters who had flown in earlier to help. Luckily for both of us, he was only about 5'9" and 170, but with the armor and ammo, heavy enough to make this a challenge. I pulled hard. He managed to get his boots against the wall enough to find some purchase. I almost had him, but then one of the damned birds was flapping around my helmet, wings smacking me in the face.

"Hold still," Julie ordered, which is a lot harder to do than it sounds when a ghost bird is trying to peck your eyes out. But I did. A bullet whistled right past my helmet to smack the blue falcon out of the sky. Bird gone, I went back to lifting.

The building the Drekavac was hiding behind was being riddled with bullets. The monster was surely getting nailed too, but he'd gotten tough enough that he was shrugging most of the hits off now, and I watched, horrified, as he swung around the corner and aimed his blunderbuss at us again.

I pulled Spencer over the edge and we both dropped as the monster fired. The bolt slammed into the spot we'd just been occupying. The impact shattered the concrete wall, pelting both of us with hot fragments.

Luckily, Skippy had seen where the lightning bolts were coming from, because the Hind tore past, firing rockets, and the Drekavac and the outbuilding he was hiding behind were obliterated. Which was too bad, that building was where we parked the bucket tractor we used for range maintenance. I was going to miss that little Kubota.

Julie had drawn her pistol and was shooting ghost birds. When she saw that our cover was being obliterated by the Drekavac's gun, she ordered, "Fall back. We're abandoning the roof."

It was the right call. We were hanging out in the open here, and this asshole just kept developing new abilities. If his next trick was lobbing a fireball like a mortar round, we were all dead.

"Covering," I said, as the other Hunters headed for the exit. Abomination would've been perfect for skeet shooting all these damned birds, but I'd brought my rifle instead because of the expected range. But at least I had a micro red dot optic offset mounted on Cazador for this up-close and personal stuff. So I twisted my rifle at an angle and started blasting falcons with high-powered rifle rounds. It wasn't efficient, but it was satisfying.

The Hunters all rushed down the stairs. I was the last one out and made sure the roof was clear of good guys before I ducked inside. Spencer slammed the heavy steel door on a ghost bird hard enough to cut it in half, then dropped the big crossbar to lock the door. Immediately a bunch of birds started thumping against the other side.

"Hold this entrance," I told Spencer, and then I went after my wife.

CHAPTER 19

Julie was in the hall, giving orders to the roof crew to take up their secondary positions, when Earl walked into the hall and spotted us. "You two. Command center. Now."

"We couldn't hold the roof, Earl."

"I know. Come on."

As Julie and I followed Earl to our so-called command center, I could hear heavy gunfire through the walls. Skippy was laying down the hate. We passed a bunch of Hunters who were manning the narrow firing slits through our armored shutters along the way. Everybody stumbled as the entire building shook. Dust rained from the ceiling. Lights flickered. That had felt like artillery. The Drekavac's gun was getting kind of ridiculous.

We'd already had a room in the basement for monitoring all of our surveillance feeds, but it was too cramped for more than a couple of Hunters to work, so Milo had taken over one of the empty storage rooms on the top floor. When we got there, Milo was standing in the middle, giving orders to our technically minded Hunters who had been drafted for this job. Melvin had set up a bunch of computers for them. In addition there were a whole lot of rough-looking switches that looked like they'd been hastily wired together.

In addition to our guys, Franks was there. None of the Secret Guard were though, which made me a little suspicious, because part of me still expected Gutterres to make a move for the Ward. They'd been honorable so far, but I'd been screwed over too many times in this business for trust to come easily.

Milo saw us enter. "Hey, Earl. You want the good news or the bad news first?"

"Spit it out."

"Skippy just bagged number eight for us. Bad news, it took about twenty direct hits with his 30mm nose gun to do it, so this jerk is getting really resilient."

"That *is* bad," Earl muttered.

"Oh no. That was the good news. The bad news is that he is already coming back and it looks like he's ten feet tall." Milo pointed at one of the screens, which showed the now gigantic Drekavac swirling into existence in front of our building.

"If he breaches the walls, Tanya's spell will be broken, and he'll be able to re-form in here with us," Julie warned. "Where's Skippy?"

"Coming around for another fast pass because he almost got fried by a lightning bolt when he was hovering," Milo said. "So can I try out my system now or what?"

Earl thought it over. "Is everyone inside and out of the line of fire?"

"They're supposed to be. If they're not, they're gonna want to duck."

"Do it," Earl ordered. "But if you wreck the whole damned compound I'm taking it out of your paycheck."

Milo pumped his fist in the air. Our mad genius had been waiting for this moment for a long time. "Alright, boys, you heard the man. Hinerman?"

Dave Hinerman was a beefy, bearded Hunter from our New York team, who'd been a software engineer before we'd recruited him. "The program is running fine. Ready when you are."

"Vivier?"

Eric Vivier was a tall, spikey-haired guy from Paxton's team in the Pacific Northwest. He'd been an engineer. The two of them and a few of our other mechanically adept Hunters had helped Milo on the project while he'd installed it over the last year. Vivier checked his screen and reported, "All systems are go. Everything hardwired is still responding."

"Let's light this candle." Milo sat down in front of a computer.

"We're living in the future, Earl. Today is one small step for MHI, one giant leap for Hunter kind." Then he giggled, because Milo truly loved his work. "Activate turrets one and two."

"Activating turrets one and two," Hinerman said.

Screens were one thing, but this I needed to see with my own eyes. There was one window on the far wall of the command center, and luckily it was oriented in the right direction. The armored shutters were rolled down, but I'd still be able to see through the firing slits, so I walked over. Earl followed me, probably because he'd allowed Milo to spend a lot of money on this and wanted to see how much of it had been wasted. Agent Franks was already there, watching, and he appeared mildly curious as below us two armored boxes rose up through the ground, lifted by hydraulics. As the turrets rotated, bits of dirt and grass slid off of them. Ports slid open and barrels extended through. From up here, one looked long and skinny, the other short and fat.

"The first is an M2, and the second is an Mk19," I told Franks. "Turrets three through eight cover the other sides."

"Your project?" he asked me.

"I made the budget spreadsheet."

Franks just grunted, unimpressed.

The Drekavac was fully formed, and he'd grown. The proportions were the same as before, but he was easily ogre size now, and he started toward our front door, determined to kick it in.

"Fire!" Milo shouted.

The two turrets opened up. Fifty-cal rounds zipped right through the monster. The Mk19 rhythmically and ponderously slammed 40mm grenades into his chest.

Shockingly, the monster just lowered his head and kept walking through the onslaught. The Drekavac lifting his hand to protect his face seemed like an almost human reaction, except instead of blocking a punch, he was absorbing high explosives and armor-piercing shells. The turrets slowly turned, tracking him, pounding away. They just kept hammering. He got hit hundreds of times and was shredded down to what looked like a flaming wire skeleton before the Drekavac collapsed and disintegrated back into the fog.

"Gutterres wasn't kidding about it getting tougher as the night goes on," Earl stated flatly. "That's nine."

That had been scary impressive, and we still had four to go. "How'd mankind handle these things in the old days?"

"Send a thousand pikemen," Franks said. "Expect to lose nine hundred."

"Or they gave them what they wanted, and then hid in their huts hoping for suckers like us to come along," Earl said. "Milo, status?"

"Status level awesome," Milo exclaimed. "Okay, guys, go ahead and activate the other turrets and put them on standby in case he hits the other walls. Watch the cameras. Hey, Julie, would you warn everybody to yell as soon as he pops up? There's no way he's getting in here now."

I know Milo was really giddy about being able to play with his new toys, but I wasn't feeling as confident as he was. "You got an ammo counter on those things?" I asked Vivier.

"That used about half of one and three quarters of two's belts," he said. "And the only way to reload them or clear a malfunction is manually."

"Don't worry, Z," Milo said. "We've got defense in depth. That's just the first layer. Like a big lethal onion of doom."

Franks was squinting through the gap in the steel shutters, studying the fog. I'd thought that once it had broken through the fence it had filled the whole compound, but from this vantage point I could see that the fog hadn't covered everything yet. There was a clear circle around the base of our building, like the substance was being held back by something, either Tanya's runes or maybe the warm lifeblood of all the Hunters inside, but something was keeping him from appearing right at our door.

"You feel that?" Franks asked me and Harbinger.

All I was feeling was unnaturally chilled to my core and a sense of unease.

But Earl said, "Yeah...He's not *in* the fog. He *is* the fog. It's got weight to it. It's where his physical forms are coming from."

I grasped what they were getting at. "It congeals, becomes solid. Like how things work in the nightmare world, only he's doing it here on Earth."

"Kind of like what we saw at the Last Dragon." Then Earl looked out over the vast area covered by the soupy substance and frowned. "He's got a lot of material to work with still."

Then I spotted where the fog was swirling together. The circle was huge compared to what I'd seen before. The Drekavac was returning to the exact same spot he'd just died, probably to continue heading right for our front door. "He's coming back even bigger."

"We've got to burn off some of this fog fast, deprive him of mass..." Earl said. "Milo! Did you get your sprinklers hooked up?"

"Sure did, Earl. I switched the pipes over this afternoon just in case."

"Time to water the lawn."

Milo leapt up from the computer, went to a nearby table, and started flipping switches.

"Is that like a metaphor for spilling blood or something?" I asked, because I'd missed this part of the plan visiting rats and had no idea what they were talking about. Except then below us, the compound's sprinkler system came on. So Earl had been speaking literally, which made me even more confused. The sprinklers were a relatively new addition. When I'd started working here, everything had just been dirt, gravel, and natural plant growth. Only Julie had gotten tired of looking at that mess and declared that we could afford some real landscaping.

The Drekavac stood where he'd fallen just a moment before. He was still wearing the coat and hat, but they seemed stretched over his now hulking form. He had to be fifteen feet tall and broad as a bus. He started for the front door.

Then I smelled the gas fumes.

Milo wasn't *watering* the grass. He was soaking it with gasoline. Sprinklers were spraying all the way around the main building. I didn't know how big our system was, but it had to be pumping hundreds of gallons a minute.

Julie got on the intercom. "Everybody move back from the windows. I repeat, move away from the windows."

The Drekavac drew his sword. It was long enough to slice an elephant in half. In his other hand was the blunderbuss, the muzzle of which was now big enough to drop a bowling ball down. He started toward the front door.

Milo's turrets started blasting the monster. Shockingly enough, the impacts didn't ignite the gas. The blue sparks flying from the Drekavac's wounds weren't real fire, and the turrets were far enough away from the lawn that their muzzle blasts didn't ignite the rapidly expanding fume cloud yet.

However, when the Drekavac lifted his blunderbuss to take out turret two, all hell broke loose—because his lightning was flammable.

A lot happened in a few seconds. The turret was ripped apart in a violent flash, and it still had a bunch of grenades inside of it. They rapidly cooked off in a chain reaction of explosions. It was a good thing our headquarters building was basically a hardened fortress, because that would've ruined our night otherwise.

The lawn ignited. A rolling wall of flame rapidly spread across the grass, consuming everything in its path. The sprinklers turned to flamethrowers, spinning twenty-foot streams of flaming hot death. Within seconds the main building was surrounded by a ring of fire. The Drekavac's fog actually *shrieked* as acres of it were burned away in a flash.

The Drekavac's glowing eyes could be seen through the wall of fire, glaring directly at our window as it turned to ash.

Ten.

"He sensed where that order came from somehow..." Earl warned. "Put your killer robots on autopilot and then everybody out of this room."

"Even the Claymore Roombas?" Hinerman asked hopefully.

"If you can do it in less than thirty seconds, then sure, whatever that is too, then fall back. Everybody else evacuate the command center. Now."

Me and Franks stayed by the window, me because I was trying to catch a glimpse of where the monster was going to come back, and Franks, probably because he didn't like being told what to do.

Milo was staring at the monitors in shock. Our Newbie barracks had caught on fire. "Were you really serious about this coming out of my pay, Earl?"

"Of course not," Earl said as he grabbed Milo by the strap on the back of his armor and dragged him toward the door. "I don't pay you enough to cover this. Move!"

It appeared that the heat from the fire had driven the fog back, but on the other side I could see the glowing stuff moving, glowing, flowing like it was alive and angry; it almost looked like a giant snake. It was gathering in one spot.

"He's already back," I shouted. The monster rose on the other side of the fire, easily over twenty feet tall now. The puritan affectation was gone. The coat and hat were missing. Now it was just a giant sort of man-shaped skeleton made of twisted wire and powered by blue flames. "Main parking area, about two hundred yards out." Then I watched in horror as the Drekavac bent down and easily lifted a car by its front end. He began to spin the vehicle around like he was doing a hammer throw. Even Franks decided that was a good time to back away. I did, too, because the car was gaining speed until it was whistling through the air around him. Then Drekavac let go and whipped the car toward MHI HQ.

It sailed through the air like it had been launched by a catapult. It was a white Audi R8, and it managed to even look good while flipping end over end through the sky. The Drekavac's aim was good and he hit the command center wall. The impact shook the building so hard it knocked me off my feet. Dust filled the air. The window I'd been standing by was gone, replaced by mangled metal and broken concrete with rebar sticking out of it.

Holly ran into the command center carrying an AT-4. She pushed past Franks, saw me lying on the floor, then she saw the remains of her new car sticking through the wall.

"You motherfucker!" she screamed. Holly went over to the hole in the wall and aimed the smoothbore anti-tank weapon at the monster. "I just paid that off!"

The command center was a really big room, but the back blast on an AT-4 was still a bitch, so I got to my feet and fled to not get burned by the overpressure.

Holly fired. The concussion was insane. Anything in here that hadn't been ruined by the Drekavac got scorched or blown away by that instead. This kind of hostile work environment bullshit was why I had tinnitus.

The Drekavac had picked up a pickup to toss at us when Holly's 84mm warhead hit him in the midsection. The explosion cut him in half. Both halves melted into the parking lot as the truck burned on top of him.

Eleven.

The fog immediately flowed back into that same spot. But I couldn't even call it fog anymore. It was more like the ectoplasmic slime we'd seen in Las Vegas. And this time it was *all* of it. Every bit of the unnatural substance crawled beneath that bonfire. And a mere five seconds after its last death, the Drekavac sat up. The burning truck went bouncing away. The monster stood, covered in chunks of molten asphalt, bigger than the frost giant we'd fought during the siege, and he let out a roar of such intensity that people must have heard it in Birmingham.

Earl was in the hallway, bellowing, "Big guns on the parking lot now! Hit him with everything we've got!"

All along this side of HQ, Hunters threw open the armored shutters. We had a variety of man-portable heavy weapons ready to go, including bunker busters and anti-tank weapons. The Hunters started firing. It was like being inside a metal drum being beaten with hammers as multiple SMAWs and Carl Gustafs went off.

The Drekavac was rocked by so many explosions that I couldn't even see it. This was an order of magnitude of more firepower than we'd used to obliterate Buford Phipps. The explosions staggered the monster but didn't drop him. We'd been warned that the last few manifestations were powerful, but this was madness. We were hitting him with enough munitions to sink a battleship. Instead of dying, he reached down, scooped up a car that had caught on fire, and flung it at us.

The flaming wreck spiraled through the sky and landed on our roof. The gas tank must have ruptured because the next thing I knew, the roof was caving in and barfing fire everywhere.

Julie was shouting for every Hunter in the building to run to this side to concentrate fire on the monster. And whoever didn't have a heavy weapon picked up a fire extinguisher or carried the wounded out of the way. Franks was firing a 20mm rifle freehand.

The Drekavac started running toward us, covering vast amounts of ground with every step. Milo's secondary turrets lit him up. Mines went off. Warheads punched through his chest and head. Big chunks of monster were flung in every direction. Our Hind flew past, hitting the Drekavac with everything, but he didn't even slow. The monster crashed through the towering wall of fire, falling to pieces but still pushing forward, until a lucky hit got him right in the knee. The bottom half of his leg came off. The monster stumbled, but he was so big that falling brought him nearly to the front door.

He was too close for big explosives without injuring ourselves in the process, so every Hunter there hung out the nearest window or fresh hole in the wall and shot at him with small arms. I ran to the remains of Holly's car, clambered up the crumpled hood, hung Cazador out the gap and dumped a magazine as fast as I could pull the trigger. He was so big I couldn't miss.

The Drekavac was dying, but not fast enough. He didn't draw the sword this time. It was more like he willed it into existence. The crackling blade hit the first floor and sheared right through the concrete like it was a laser beam. I sure hoped the Hunters at those windows had gotten out of the way in time.

The floor beneath my feet rumbled. It felt like this whole side of MHI's HQ was about to collapse beneath us. It was odd. Nobody screamed. Nobody panicked. We all just kind of froze for a moment, staring at each other wide-eyed, not even daring to breathe, as the building groaned below us.

It didn't fall down.

We all started to breathe again. It was a good thing Grandpa Shackleford hadn't skimped on the construction of this place.

The super-giant Drekavac slowly sank to his knees, too damaged to continue. And died. *Twelve.*

By my count, he still had one life left.

Franks appeared next to me, reloading the 20mm cannon that was longer than I was tall. "Hmmm...make that five thousand pikemen."

"The main doors have been breached!" Julie shouted. "Tanya's spells are broken. He can come inside. Get ready for anything."

I looked down at the Drekavac. As he died this time, he didn't dissipate back into fog, because every bit of fog was already compressed into this one huge form. The body had been burning with that evil supernatural blue, but it looked like the fire was hardening into ice.

"Something weird is happening," I warned.

The body crystalized. Cracks formed. The cracks began to spread, faster and faster.

Franks scowled, looking out into the night as if he'd sensed something. "Lana's here," he muttered.

"That's your takeaway from this?" I flipped out. "That's what you're worried about right now? Are you fucking kidding me?"

"You got your mission. I got mine," Franks said as he ignored the giant super monster that had suddenly turned into crystal, sounding like somebody had just turned a garden hose on ten million bags of Pop Rocks. Franks walked away. I looked down again to see that the Drekavac's corpse was shaking with building energy.

"Everybody get back."

For a second I'd thought the monster was going to go off like a bomb. What actually happened for his thirteenth and final form was a whole lot worse.

The giant shattered into an army of Drekavacs.

CHAPTER 20

There had to be hundreds of them, each the size of the original being. Every bit of the monster's mass was converted into new bodies all at once, and it had been *huge*. The kneeling giant collapsed in an avalanche of skeletal blue bodies. The parts that had just been blown off by the explosives split into monsters too. All of a sudden, I was looking down at a concert-sized crowd of glowing horrors. The ones who had been born in the middle of our lawn inferno insta-died. The rest charged MHI HQ.

"We've got lots of monsters incoming!"

The Hunters opened fire. Only ghostly flintlock pistols materialized in about half of the Drekavacs' hands and they shot back. Tiny blue bolts smacked into the walls around us as Hunters had to duck down. The pistols seemed far less powerful than the blunderbuss, but each impact still left a glowing blue hole.

While we were being pinned down, the other half of the army formed spectral swords or axes and charged our front door. I tossed a grenade out the window, and by the time I'd reloaded Cazador, it had detonated. Then I stood, picked out a Drekavac with a gun, and shot him in the face. I swiveled, picked up another monster, and shot him through the side of the head. Both of the creatures dropped. Which meant that they were probably only about as tough individually as the Drekavac's first iteration. Too bad there were piles of them now. I had to duck as half a dozen ghost bullets clanged into the wrecked Audi.

The monsters may have all been aspects of the same being, but they sure didn't act that way. It was like each one had an independent mind because they were moving in every direction and trying multiple lines of attack. Some were breaching our doors. Others were climbing up the walls to get in the opened windows. A bunch were taking cover and shooting at us. Milo's turrets were slicing them down, but then groups of monsters began targeting the turrets. It was nuts.

Julie was shouting orders, sending most of us downstairs to reinforce the first floor, while she kept a crew up here to pick off the monsters in the open and climbing up the walls. "Owen, go with them."

"On it," I said as I jumped up and rushed to the stairs. My wife knew me well. Close-range face smashing was my specialty. I was wearing rifle pouches, but I'd left Abomination leaning in a corner with a belt full of drum mags, so I grabbed my shotgun along the way. There were several other Hunters ahead of me, including Milo and Holly.

Earl was in the lead. "These sons o' bitches ain't getting through us." He shoved another mag in his Tommy gun and yanked back the bolt. "We kill as many as we can and leapfrog back as we need to. They'll be heading for the vault."

"We've got a problem," Milo warned.

"No shit?" Holly said sarcastically.

"No, I mean a math problem. I don't know his original density, but square cube law and all that, figure that big fella had to weigh one or two hundred tons at least."

"That's a lot of fog," I said.

"Magic fog, so I'm assuming it's less dense than something solid like a kaiju, and he looked kinda wispy so I'll guess a hundred tons. The baby Drekavacs look pretty skinny all thin and wiry like that, but he's probably heavier than he looks because of the strength displayed, no wonder he wears the big coat and hat, really bulks him up—"

"Milo," Earl shouted. "Get to the point."

"Quick math, if each of these little guys are between a hundred and two hundred pounds each, there might be up to a couple thousand of them out there right now. But that's assuming a perfectly efficient system, and even magic recycling can't be that good, but still we've probably got a thousand of them at least."

"That's your *low* estimate?"

We reached the ground floor and ran for the reception area.

The giant Drekavac's sword had chopped our heavy reinforced door in half, but the Hunters stationed here had dropped the emergency portcullis to block the way. A bunch of the man-sized monsters were currently hacking and tearing at it. And from the way the steel bars were popping, these things were still freakishly strong.

Several Hunters were already here, using the wall corners and our big reception desk for cover. They were shooting down the hall through the gaps in the portcullis... and from all the glowing holes in the walls, the monsters were shooting back. One Hunter was being dragged away by his friends, screaming because of the smoking hole that had just gotten punched through his thigh. He left a red trail on the tile.

I wasn't surprised to see that Dorcas was there, even though she was a one-legged senior citizen, whom Earl had specifically told to go home because she was too old for this kind of roughneck shit. She was leaning on her desk, shoving 12-gauge buckshot shells into the mag tube of a Mossberg 590. "About damned time, Earl."

"I thought I told you to sit this one out."

"Oh, stick it. This is my turf." Dorcas pumped the shotgun. Over the decades those two had known each other, he had only aged a few years but she'd gone from young girl to crusty old lady, so Dorcas was one of the few people around who gave Earl lip. "Ain't no assholes gonna run me off. Now get to helping. That gate ain't gonna hold them for long, and they're hitting the other doors too."

Earl started grabbing various Hunters and sending them in different directions to reinforce those entrances. I flipped over the table next to the memorial wall, braced Cazador over the top, and started flinging .308 rounds down the hallway. Milo crouched next to me and started shooting too. Ejected brass bounced off my armor. There were so many bodies throwing themselves against the gate that we couldn't hardly miss. All I needed to do was not accidentally hit the portcullis.

We killed a pile of them and they just didn't care. Bars bent. Welds snapped. The portcullis was down. They were coming in.

Dorcas picked up a clacker. "Fire in the hole!"

We got down as she set off the claymores.

MHI's entryway was shredded by hundreds of projectiles. Dozens of monsters were torn apart. The air was filled with smoke and drywall dust. Then there was only the briefest delay before the bad guys came pouring in.

There were several of us shooting down that narrow channel. It was a fatal funnel filled with flying silver and lead. The Drekavacs pushed forward anyway. The wire strands of their thin limbs unraveled beneath the high velocity impacts. But not every aspect of the monster was suicidal because some of the creatures used cover and fired back.

There was a blue flash as the table Milo and I were hiding behind was struck. Splinters flew. Milo got hit and the impact knocked him down. He landed on his back and clutched at his chest. As more bullets hit the table, I grabbed Milo by the drag strap on his armor and pulled him down the hall and around the corner.

"Ouch! Ouch!" Milo was struggling to get one of the pouches open on his armor. He yanked out a magazine that was dripping molten plastic from the glowing blue hole burned through it. The spring shot out of the damaged mag and rounds went rolling across the floor.

"You okay?"

Milo grimaced as he shoved one hand inside his armor. "Oh, that hurts." He pulled it out. *Clean. No blood.* "Oof. Low velocity. Not enough penetration to punch our armor. Lots of energy dump though. About like getting kicked by a horse."

"You can analyze the ghost bullets later. Can you walk?"

"Sure." Milo staggered to his feet and winced, clearly in a whole lot of pain. "Uh-oh. You know that feeling when you put a rib into one of your lungs?"

"No."

"It's not pleasant."

I glanced back toward my previous firing position. It had been turned into Swiss cheese. The reception desk was a smoking wreck. Hunters were falling back. Earl had picked up stubborn Dorcas and was carrying her over one shoulder. She wasn't wounded. She was just too pissed off to retreat. In fact she was still shooting her shotgun as Earl ran. One of the blue streaks nailed her in her fake leg and blew her foot clean off. "Not again!"

Dorcas tossed the now empty Mossberg and pulled out her hand cannon. She managed to crank off a couple of shots before Earl got her out of the line of fire.

I leaned out to cover them and dropped another monster with Cazador. They were close enough I just twisted the rifle to the side and engaged them with the micro dot sight instead of the much more powerful scope.

Earl passed our angry little receptionist off to Milo and Holly. "Get all the wounded to the cafeteria."

"That looks like most of us, Earl," Milo said.

"I know. Holly, keep them alive. There's only one way into the pantry. That's the choke point. Hold it." Then he clapped my shoulder and gave me orders even as I was shooting. It was a good thing my rifle was suppressed so I could still understand him. "Basement, Z. We're gonna reinforce them."

We had only sent a small crew down to guard Sonya in Earl's cell. Trip was in charge and he had his shit together, but if this many bodies came at them at once, they'd be overwhelmed.

"Got it." I dumped my last few shots the Drekavacs' way and then followed Earl, reloading as I ran. I had a rifle in my hand, my shotgun bouncing at my side, and a bunch of drum mags slung over my shoulder, so it wasn't exactly smooth. These were tight quarters so I threw Cazador around my back and switched to Abomination.

It was just the two of us and there were monsters swarming everywhere. Earl had point, I kept looking back, which turned out to be smart because a couple Drekavacs crashed through a door behind us. I immediately wheeled about and started blasting. Silver buckshot ripped through their thin bodies, except this time I had to put several rounds into both of them before they came apart.

It was like each of these shattered aspects was getting tougher. That was troubling.

I got my confirmation of how that was happening a moment later as a Drekavac blundered around the corner right into Earl's path. He ripped a long burst from his Tommy gun into the monster's chest and head. It went down and ruptured into pieces as it hit the floor. The bits melted into glowing fog...which then flowed quickly along the ground and around the corner, to congeal around another Drekavac.

Earl shot that one at least a dozen times before it went down. Only the monster was still alive and crawling by the time I got there and put an anchor shot in its cranium. It came apart, and this time the fog oozed up the wall and disappeared into a vent.

For each of these we killed, some of their strength was being fed into the others. Each surviving Drekavac would get stronger and stronger, until there was just one left, who would probably be as powerful as the epic thing we'd just had to hit with a shit ton of anti-tank weapons to kill.

Oh, shit.

We reached the stairs to the basement before the Drekavac who'd breached the front door did. I could hear lots of gunfire coming from above and to a lesser extent below, which was a bad sign. Some of the monsters must have found another way into the basement.

"Aw, hell..." Earl looked back the way we'd come from. There was a lot of fog flowing in that direction and the eerie ghost light was growing. There were a bunch of Drekavacs heading this way and this narrow stairwell was the best place to delay them, but it sounded like the Hunters below needed our help too. "Alright, Z, I'll stay up here, you go to the bottom of the stairs and kill anything that gets past me. But no matter what, help Trip and Cody protect Sonya. I made a promise to her mother."

"You going to wolf out?"

"Probably have to in a minute." Twice in two nights not even close to the full moon *and* around friendlies? That showed how incredibly desperate our situation was. "I sure hope their glowy shit don't work like silver."

"I've got to warn you first. I think each one of these we kill, it feeds into the others. They're getting stronger as they go."

"You got a better idea than killing them?"

"Not yet."

"This job ain't ever easy." As Earl said that, a bunch of Drekavacs rushed around the corner. It was an angry mob of cold-fire skeletons, and they shrieked when they saw us. "Go, kid."

I went down the stairs as fast as I could.

This part of the building was mostly storage rooms and the entrance to the archives. On the other side of that was a straight shot to Earl's cell. There was gunfire coming from that direction. I wanted to help, but they had a defensive position, and I'd help them a whole lot more by not letting another squad of Drekavacs down the stairs to join in.

I could hear the chatter of Earl's Thompson. Then a grenade went off. Then six fast shots from a revolver. During all that was a bunch of the *hiss-cracks* of the Drekavacs' magic guns. Thankfully from the rate of fire, Silas Carver's idea of guns was limited to the single-shot types that he was familiar with from when he'd been alive. Earl appeared, stumbling down a few steps. There was a glowing impact on his leather jacket, but it hadn't penetrated the incredibly tough minotaur hide.

Then Earl got shot in the cheek. His head snapped around. Blood hit the wall as the bolt tore through him.

"Earl!"

Except my boss didn't fall. He grabbed onto the railing to steady himself, shook his head like he'd just taken a punch, and spit out a tooth. There was a bloody, smoking hole right through both sides of his face. He reached up and touched the ghastly wound.

"Nope. It ain't even close to silver." I could see the white of his jawbone through the dangling flesh as he talked. "I tell ya, that's a relief!" Then Earl Harbinger leapt up the stairs and got right back into the fight. A second later a Drekavac was hurled violently down the stairs. I put a round of buckshot into its head as it bounced.

The next few seconds really sucked, as I stood there, useless, not helping anybody, torn over which direction I should go, but also knowing that I was supposed to hold this spot. From the sound, Earl was going all savage werewolf on them. He'd been doing this so long, a full transformation only took him a few seconds, and he could fight while doing it. The Drekavacs were shrieking and Earl was roaring. I don't know which one was scarier. Wire body parts were being thrown down the stairs: arms, legs, heads.

And the whole time that damnable fog was drifting past my legs and into the archives. It was going to buff the monsters who were attacking the vault.

Then the Drekavacs started pushing past Earl. They didn't bother taking the stairs, they just vaulted over the railing and started dropping straight to the bottom. I opened up Abomination, nailing them before they even reached the ground. I went through a twenty-round drum in a few seconds, and by the time I got another one rocked into the gun, more Drekavacs had hit the ground. I blasted those at conversational distance. I took an arm off at the shoulder, and the ax it had been wielding still hacked into the doorway I was using for cover. Ghostly or not, those blades could cut.

Our werewolf came tumbling over the edge. There were four Drekavacs wrestling him. One got its skull flattened on impact. Earl wrapped his claws around another monster's neck and slammed him into the wall hard enough to put a crack in the concrete. He bit the third one on the neck and shook him. The fourth one ran Earl through the guts with his sword. I shot that asshole in the chest. Then Earl backhanded the wounded Drekavac and sent him flying. There was blue fire and red blood all over the stairwell.

But then I had to concentrate on keeping myself alive. Monsters were cascading over the edge, and then getting right up to fight their way through me.

I flipped Abomination to full-auto and dumped the rest of the drum into the mass of creatures. One made it through and I had to leap back as he swung a sword at me. I transitioned to my pistol and shot it in the eye. It still tackled me and we fell into the hall.

The monster was on top of me. It was squirting ghost fire out of its shattered socket as it clawed for my throat. The thing was so damned cold that it felt like it was sucking the life right out of me. Good thing I had my anger to keep me warm. I caught its arm, levered it hard to the side, jammed my .45 into the spot where its ear would have been and shot it dead.

I leapt to my feet as more monsters reached the door. I dumped them with my STI. I fired to slide lock, did a speed reload, and downed another Drekavac with a pair of hollowpoints to the head. There was a brief delay, so I holstered, grabbed Abomination and the last of my drum mags, and retreated.

A few seconds later, monsters were pouring through the doorway. Some of them had already been deprived of limbs or were wearing claw marks, but they were leaving just enough bodies in the stairwell to keep Earl occupied while the rest headed for the Ward.

I was standing in a T intersection. There was zero cover here, so I ran for the library. At some point the power had gone out, but I could still see by our dim emergency lights. Some of the Drekavacs went after me, but more veered off down the other halls. Those would also get them to the vault, it was just a longer route.

There was a series of blue flashes. I dove behind a bookshelf. Precious tomes were hit by bolts. Antique paper was turned into confetti. I tossed my last grenade into the hall. It landed and rolled between the feet of a bunch of Drekavac. The explosion took out the glass wall in front. Lee was probably at the vault with the others, but when he saw this mess, he was going to be furious.

I got up, shouldered Abomination, and moved out. The Drekavacs were spreading out through the stacks. The instant I saw blue fire moving, I killed it, so these had learned to keep their heads down. They were crouched, shooting, moving. I moved behind another shelf. A couple of monsters thought that meant I couldn't see them so they got up and moved my way. They were going to flank around both sides of the shelf, but I shoved a bunch of books off to make a gap in the shelf and gunned them down through it.

There was a terrible impact on my back. It spun me around and sent me crashing into the books. My shoulder blade was on fire. A ghost bolt was lodged in my back. It hadn't punched through my armor, but it was stuck there, cooking me. The weird blue fire that powered their bodies wasn't hot, but their bullets burned like a motherfucker. I reached back, dug it out with my fingers, and then had to drop it on the carpet because it was making my gloves sizzle.

The Drekavac who had shot me willed a sword into existence and chased after me. I turned around just in time to stick Abomination into his face. It was a good thing that the severed-head thing didn't reset the process now, because I literally blew his head off. That had been way too close.

Moving into the aisle, I methodically worked my way toward the vault. It was look, shoot, move, duck, repeat. Monsters kept coming at me and I kept blasting them. Abomination ran dry and I yanked out my last drum. I was nearly out of shotgun shells, but on the bright side, I could toss my super-awkward bandolier. I flung a couple rounds at the monsters pursuing me, and then sprinted for the rear door.

Except a Drekavac appeared before me, pistol already raised. *CRACK.*

It punched me in the sternum so hard it swept me off my feet. The pain was incredible, but I sat up just enough to cut that monster's legs out from under it with Abomination. He fell facedown, and I put a final round through the top of his skull.

Gasping for air, fire radiating through my torso, I stumbled upright. But the other monsters had caught up. I got shot again. Just a bit higher than the last one and I ended up flipping over Albert's desk. My body took out his computer monitor and collection of Funko Pops before I landed on his office chair. The little wheels shot out from under it and I spilled onto the floor.

I lay there for just a second, stunned, but having two molten slugs scorching your chest brings you back to reality fast. Unfortunately, I didn't have time to pull them out because the Drekavacs were approaching, swords and axes raised. I climbed up, rested Abomination on the desk, and started shooting as soon as my sight covered blue.

MHI must have killed a slew of these things, because the remainder were getting *really tough*. I ran through the rest of Abomination's ammo to drop three of them. There was still one left, and it was coming at me with only one arm and half his face torn off, so I dropped Abomination and picked up Albert's chair. I hurled it. The monster slashed the chair out of the air with his sword. I used that time to draw my pistol. The Drekavac lunged at me but I pumped six rounds into him before he fell to pieces.

Every monster in the archives was dead.

CHAPTER 21

Shit. Shit. That hurts. I put my STI on the desk, grabbed one of Al's nice metal pens, and used that to pry the ghost bullets out of my armor. They were probably going to leave some severe little burns under there. But I couldn't worry about that because there was still a lot of noise coming from Earl's cell. Unfortunately, there was also a river of evil fog flowing in that direction. From the amount, there couldn't be that many monsters left topside. The stuff was so thick and gave off such an unnatural vibe that it reminded me of the substance that had fed the Nachtmar at the Last Dragon. I really hated monsters who operated beyond our understanding of the laws of physics.

Taking a quick inventory, I still had Cazador and about a hundred rounds for it. I was down to a couple pistol mags. I didn't know how many monsters were between me and the vault, and it was taking an ever-increasing number of bullets to put each one down. I topped off my guns and moved out. All I had to do was follow the fog stream.

The back of the archives was clear, but when I turned the corner there were a bunch of Drekavacs clustered around the corridor that led to Earl's vault. The monsters were popping out and snapping off shots, but then having to duck back to keep from getting shredded by what sounded like a M240. Judging by the number of holes in the walls and gun smoke in the air, some-body had already run through a couple of belts to hold them off.

"You never take Melvin alive! Come at me, scrub lords! Melvin is ripped!"

It must have gotten pretty desperate down here for Trip to give our troll a machine gun.

One of the Drekavac leaned out, shot, and must have gotten lucky, because Melvin let out a startled yelp.

"It burns! It burns!" And then there was a clatter as he dropped the machine gun.

The Drekavac immediately took advantage of that lull and rushed the vault.

"Crap." I went after them. They hadn't seen me yet, so I popped a Drekavac in the back of the head. They'd absorbed so many lives that braining it didn't even put it down, and the monster turned around, whipping blue fire across the wall from the exit wound where his nose had been. It shrieked. Two of its brothers heard and turned around to join it in charging me. The other dozen or so continued toward the vault.

I kept hammering the lead Drekavac with Cazador until its body came apart, but the other two were nearly on me. A sword thrust meant to pierce my guts got knocked aside at the last instant by Cazador's metal handguard. I kept shooting from the hip, but I wasn't going to stop the other one in time.

Only that Drekavac stumbled as it got shot in the back. Four Hunters were moving up the opposite direction, also converging on the vault. They were doing the combat glide, moving fast and smooth, carbines shouldered. So I dove for the floor to let them have a clear shot. It was more of a desperate instinct than a clear tactical decision, but either way, it was the smart play as those Hunters lit the two monsters up. Blue sparks rained on my head as the monsters twitched and jerked until they disintegrated.

"Friendly!" I shouted, even though that should be obvious since I wasn't a glowing skeleton.

"Pitt?" It turned out to be Gutterres and his men. I wasn't surprised to see them down here since they made no secret that they were in this for the Ward. "You hurt?"

"I'm good." I got up and immediately started reloading. There was a bunch of gunfire and shouting coming from down the corridor. "We've got to protect the vault."

"There's another wave right behind us," the big guy, Messina, warned. He was covering their rear with a Para SAW. "But there's a friggin' werewolf eating them!"

"Don't mess with the werewolf. He's a friendly."

The mercs all gave me an incredulous look, but Gutterres took it in stride. "Very well."

"Seriously?" LoPresto asked.

Gutterres shrugged. "The greatest knight in the history of the church was a werewolf."

"Sonya's down this way." I pointed. Judging by the way the fog from the monsters we'd just capped was heading past the Secret Guard guys, toward that next unseen wave, instead of the ones who were already hitting the vault, any of those Drekavacs who made it past Earl were going to be really nasty.

"We'll clear these first." Gutterres signaled for his guys to halt. The corridor to the vault was between us. The corners the Drekavacs had just been using for cover had been chewed to bits. Melvin had done a real number on the drywall. "Warrington, LoPresto, first, then me and Pitt. Messina, watch our backs."

"Hang on." This part was going to be really dangerous, not from the group of monsters we were about to box in, but because we didn't want to get shot by our friends at the other end, and we didn't want to shoot them through the monsters. So I shouted as loud as I could, "Hunters coming in!"

I could barely hear Trip's response over the gunfire and monster screeching. "Hurry up. Hold your fire, Melvin." A long burst of machine-gun fire zipped between me and the Catholics. "No. Bad Melvin! *Bad!* Put that down."

"Melvin sorry."

"You're good, Z!"

Man, I hate this chaotic part. At least the teams were color-coordinated. The Catholics were all wearing regular street clothing with just plate carriers thrown on top. MHI armor was all various earth tones. "Only shoot the blue ones."

"Fuckin' Smurfs," Warrington said.

"Move," Gutterres ordered.

His men might not have been full-fledged Secret Guardsmen, but I had to hand it to them. They knew their shit. They were quick and smooth, sweeping into the hall and immediately engaging the monsters as they moved. Because storage space was always at a premium at MHI HQ, there were a lot of boxes and crates here, and the two used those for concealment as Gutterres and I moved in next.

Trip had piled up a bunch of crap as a barricade, and the Hunters were hiding behind it. Between us there were half a dozen Drekavacs in the open. We shot them in the back. The vault crew shot them in the front. By some miracle we managed not to shoot each other. Thank you, Saint Hubert!

Ten seconds of rapid but very carefully aimed fire later, the corridor was filled with the fog of dead Drekavacs. Unfortunately, it immediately went zipping down the hall past us, past Messina, and out of sight. It must have found the next batch of monsters to strengthen, because an ungodly screech came from somewhere inside the archives.

The screeching didn't stop. It was getting closer. And this time it sounded like it was only *one* voice. The might of hundreds of monsters, collected into one. And that made it so much worse. The noise suddenly ceased, but it didn't matter. We knew it was coming for us.

"This way," Trip said. We rushed over to his improvised barricade. It looked like he'd piled up all of Earl's old army crates and filled them with bricks to use for cover. Now that was showing initiative.

Albert Lee raised his head over the edge of a crate. "Welcome to Fort Kickass."

When Melvin stood up to his full seven feet of hideous, green, bumpy ugly, I had to bellow, "Hold your fire! He's on our side," before the Catholics could waste him.

"What the hell is that?" Messina shouted.

"It's a troll." Gutterres was perplexed, like werewolves were one thing, but trolls were *annoying*. "You've got a troll? *Why?*"

"He's our IT department. He's cool."

Melvin looked at the newcomers with his beady little eyes. "Melvin cool. You cool?"

"We cool," said Warrington, though he kept his gun at the ready, because Melvin had that effect on sane people.

I surveyed the crew of Fort Kickass. Trip and Lee appeared uninjured. Melvin was missing one hand, but trolls were pretty ambivalent about amputations since they'd just grow a new one. "Where's Cody?"

Trip jerked a thumb at the bank-vault-style door in the back of Earl's room. "He went inside to try one last time to figure out how to get the Ward from Sonya so we could turn it on and maybe kill all these things."

"Silas Carver was born on Earth," Gutterres said. "The stone has no power over him. It wouldn't work."

"Cody figured it was still worth a shot."

"As long as your man doesn't destroy it," Gutterres said. "If we lose that stone—"

"Yeah, yeah, I know, millions dead. Got it." I pointed down the hall at where the ghost light was building. "We've got more pressing matters right now."

A single Drekavac lurched into view.

As more and more power coalesced into fewer bodies, they weren't getting any bigger, but this one was giving off an aura of sheer wickedness. It made the hair on my arms stand up. The temperature *plunged*. All the Hunters could see our breath. Melvin spit out the Red Bull he'd been drinking, because this thing felt *evil*. It hadn't just gathered up the life essence of the ones we'd killed, but who knew how many hundreds more from above.

The Drekavac started toward us. All eight of us started shooting.

I watched in horror as our bullets shattered against the monster's body. A weapon materialized in the monster's hand. It wasn't one of the tiny pistols. Oh, no. It was that damned blunderbuss that had nearly torn the roof off of our headquarters.

"Down!" Gutterres and I shouted at the same time, because we'd both seen that thing in action.

Everybody but Melvin listened.

Lightning hit Fort Kickass. I was pelted by splinters and wet troll chunks.

Melvin hit the wall. His legs were *gone*.

Most of us popped up and started shooting again. The Drekavac was manipulating its weapon to obliterate the rest of us and only seemed mildly inconvenienced by the dozens of bullets hitting him.

Maybe it was the whole Chosen thing, but I could see what was happening. The ghost fire had collected around this body to strengthen and protect it. Each time we hit it, more of that energy was being used up. Each time it attacked us, more energy was expended, which was why when there was a bunch of them, they were only using the little pistols, and now he'd broken out the big stuff. Give us enough time and we'd break him, and he'd disintegrate like the rest.

Except this one had gathered so much energy that we'd be dead long before that point.

"Get inside the vault!" I shouted.

Trip rushed to the door and started opening it. Lee got there a moment later because of the bad leg. Trip spun the wheel and then the two of them started swinging the incredibly heavy thing open.

I ran to Melvin. He'd been splattered against the wall. Our troll looked down at where his body abruptly ended at the pelvis, then at me. "That is bullshits!"

"Hang on." I grabbed Melvin by his remaining arm and dragged him toward the vault. He'd lost so much weight suddenly that I could actually do that easily now.

Trip got the door open. "Inside. Go. Go!" Only Trip didn't go in himself. He'd hold his ground, covering the rest of us, until he was sure we were inside, and only then would he get to safety. Because that was just the kind of hero he was. Except as I went in, I grabbed him by the armor and dragged him and Melvin both inside. Heroic or not, Trip wasn't going to accomplish shit shooting at a bulletproof monster until he got flash-fried by a lightning cannon.

The mercs were laying down fire, especially Messina with that SAW. LoPresto's carbine went down and he immediately drew a DWX and kept shooting as they made an orderly retreat into the vault. If we survived, I was definitely going to see if these guys wanted full-time jobs.

Gutterres was the last one in. And he must have been freakishly stronger than he looked by the way he pulled that giant door closed by himself so fast. Lee was waiting and spun the wheel to slam the massive steel locking bolts. There was no way to open it from this side. We were now locked in. Lee quickly let go, which was lucky because he was one second away from possibly getting electrocuted. The whole room shook as the Drekavac blasted the door. It held.

For now.

We all stood there in the emergency lighting, breathing hard, looking at the door, kind of surprised to still be alive.

"Uh, Hunters?" Melvin said. "Where'd hole come from?"

I turned around to see what Melvin was talking about and dropped our poor dismembered troll in surprise. Ben Cody was lying on the floor, either dead or unconscious. There was no sign of Sonya. Earl's full moon prison cell was just a plain concrete room with a drain hole in the middle of the floor, just big enough to contain a furious werewolf. Earl was like a beacon of calm compared to most werewolves, but even he turned into a bloodthirsty psycho when he transformed during the full moon, so this place was for his protection and ours. Except now the back wall was missing, and there was an eight-foot-wide earthen tunnel leading off into the darkness on the other side. And by missing, I don't mean torn down or excavated, I mean a big circular section of the concrete had just disappeared. And it had happened so recently that the edges that had just been sheared through were still smoking hot.

"Ben!" Trip knelt next to Cody and checked his pulse. "He's alive."

There was a bunch of blood in his hair and beard. My guess was that he'd gotten clubbed, or maybe thrown down in such a way he'd banged his head on the floor. Had Sonya sucker punched him and bailed? Or had something else done it?

"She screwed us again." Gutterres started toward the tunnel.

"You don't know that," I said.

"What else could it be?" he snapped. "She probably got a better offer again. She's played us before."

"Yeah, but I don't think she knows how to do *this*." I gestured at the hole, which had obviously been made by magic. Then I remembered what Franks had said before he'd run off. *Lana is here.* Despite Stricken's words about trusting me to handle his mystery problem for him, he was still grabbing the stone for himself. "But I know what could. Stricken has a succubus who works for him. I saw her do something like this when she teleported him out of MCB custody."

"That can't work here though," Lee said. "Julie had Tanya's people put spells up all over the compound. None of that stuff should be able to operate on compound grounds anymore."

"That's what the MCB director thought about their offices too." Except Tanya was too proud of being MHI to do a half-ass job for us like those other elves clearly had. Which meant that if Lee was right, Lana might have grabbed Sonya, but she'd have to travel on foot until they got outside the range of the elves' enchantments.

BANG.

We all flinched and looked toward the vault door. It had just gotten hit *hard*. And it wasn't the big gun either. From the amount of force, my guess was that he'd willed a sledgehammer into existence and had sucked up enough dead monsters to give himself superstrength.

BANG.

The vault door shook. Little cracks formed in the reinforced walls around it.

"They're getting away," Gutterres said. "Let's go."

"Give us a minute to get our wounded to safety."

"There's no time, Pitt. That stone is more important than any one of us."

There was no way I was going to leave Cody. And yes...even Melvin. "You'll get lost without us."

Gutterres glared at me, but he was a man on a mission. "Stick around if you want. I'll pluck that Ward out of the shape-changer's corpse if I have to."

"You wouldn't dare," Trip said.

"Test me and find out." Gutterres entered the tunnel. His men shared an uneasy look, but they followed.

A moment after the Secret Guard were out of sight Melvin said, "What's got up his ass?"

"He's just trying to save millions of lives. Pressure makes you cranky. Are you okay?"

"Melvin will grow new legs. Old ones had rash anyway."

BANG.

"We can't stick around here though," Lee said. "We've got to follow them."

"Hang on." The thing that Gutterres didn't realize was just how much of a maze the old tunnels beneath the compound were. If the Vatican Hunters didn't pick up a trail, they'd probably take the wrong path. Lana—or whoever had broken Sonya out—had a few different tunnels she could choose to get out and if we didn't know which one she'd taken, we'd never catch her in time.

SCREEEECH!

A glowing blue sword point slowly punched through the vault steel. The Drekavac had given up on smashing his way in, so he was cutting his way in. The tip was glowing like a plasma arc. It had to be using up a ton of the Drekavac's remaining power, but he was shearing through the locking bolts.

"There's too many tunnels to cover even if we split up, and we've got two wounded to carry." I checked my radio, but still got nothing but static. Not surprising, considering the source of the distortion was on the other side of the door.

"We'll just have to pick a route and hope," Lee said.

Cody was a big guy, but even missing three limbs, Melvin still weighed more. So I scooped up our troll. "You're going to have to ride piggyback."

"Melvin's ego not fragile."

Trip and Lee dragged Cody to his feet and each of them got one of his arms over their shoulders. That Drekavac was making unnervingly steady process. The door was dripping molten steel. An incredible amount of heat was coming off of the metal. It wouldn't hold for long, but at least whatever was left of the Drekavac would have been weakened by such an expenditure of energy. We were about to make a run for it when the sword tip suddenly disappeared. There was a muffled *crash* and a *crunch* on the other side. For twenty seconds we heard the sounds of violence but couldn't really tell what was going on. The Drekavac screeched, but that sound was abruptly cut off.

Whatever had just taken out the Drekavac must have known the exterior combo, because a moment later the wheel began to spin. The door swung open.

Earl Harbinger staggered into the room. He was human, or at least mostly human, but still in the process of turning back. His body had been savaged. He was covered in so many rapidly healing bullet holes it looked like he had the chicken pox. One eye was still werewolf yellow; the other was filled with blood. He'd burned so many calories regenerating that all his still twisting bones were visibly poking through his skin. The blood-soaked figure made it a few halting steps into the cell, and then slowly sank to his knees.

"Damn, man," I said. "You look like shit."

"That's the last of them," Earl gasped, exhausted. He was so tired he sounded drunk. Then he looked past his battered Hunters and saw the hole in the wall. "The fuck you do to my room?"

"Sonya's been taken. I think by Stricken."

"Oh..." Earl said as the fog of the last Drekavac he'd just taken out swirled by him, past my legs, and flew down the tunnel out of sight. "Thought we were done, but that slime's going somewhere."

The Drekavac wasn't stupid. He hadn't sacrificed all of his thirteenth form against us. He must have left a body hiding somewhere in the compound to fall back to, and it had collected who knew how many monsters' worth of power. Lana was going to carry Sonya right into that thing's arms.

Earl tried to stand up, but then flopped over on his side, too injured to keep going. "Gimme a minute." Then he promptly passed out. Which was saying a lot about how badly he'd been torn up, because Earl Harbinger was a tank.

I dropped Melvin again, who made a very disgruntled noise when he hit the floor. "Lee, stay with Earl and Cody."

Trip knew what was up. We were Sonya's last chance. "Better. Get to the intercom, alert the others, then stay with these guys."

"Will do. Good luck."

At least I wouldn't be here when Lee found out that I'd had a gunfight in his library.

CHAPTER 22

Trip and I ran through the tunnels.

This section had been dug clear back in the Bubba Shackleford era. They were seldom used now because they were prone to cave-ins. Our weapon-mounted flashlights revealed crumbling brick walls. Obnoxious spiderwebs got over my face. We reached a fork in the tunnel, and when I aimed my light down each, it revealed more side tunnels ahead. The floor was mostly small rocks so we couldn't even see tracks to tell which way Gutterres had gone. Even though we were on our home turf, we were just as lost as the Catholics probably were.

"How are we going to find her?"

"I've got a secret weapon." Then I raised my voice to shout as loud as I could. *"Justinian! I need your help."* The sound echoed in the narrow space. I had one hell of a loud voice. You get a lot of practice when you have to be heard over gunfire. The key was to speak from the chest. *"Justinian or any of his legion, if you can hear me, MHI needs your aid."*

"Who?" Trip asked, confused.

I held up a hand to shush him. *"Which way did she go?"*

"What was that about?"

"Sorry. I'll explain later. Just listen."

"Is that . . . ?"

I hadn't heard it, but Trip had less hearing damage than I did. "What?"

259

"Something's *squeaking*." He pointed down the left fork.

"Go! Follow it."

To his credit, Trip didn't question. He trusted me and acted. Like Harbinger had taught us, a Hunter's greatest weapon was a flexible mind. But I also knew that he was a bit of a germaphobe who kind of freaked out about stuff he thought was gross. "Don't step on any rats!"

"What—" He suddenly leapt to the side. "Yikes!"

There was a big brown rat standing in the middle of the tunnel, and Trip had nearly run over him. I knew right away that this was one of Justinian's tribe because of the way he stood there on his rear legs, defiantly rather than scurrying away. The rat began squeaking rapidly and gesturing down the tunnel.

"Which way was the girl taken?" I pulled out my phone and flipped it to the notes app. Then I knelt and held the phone where the rat could reach it. Without hesitating he quickly began typing a message.

I AM ATTICUS SON OF CIPRIAN SON OF JUS

I temporarily moved the phone away. "Great. Owen, son of Auhangamea. Nice to meet you, but we're in a hurry." I moved the phone back.

The rat began typing again.

"Wait... That rat can *write*?"

"Yes, Trip," I said while Atticus wrote. "Big-brain rats, escaped science experiment. Long story."

THE CHANGELING WAS TAKEN BY A SUCCUBUS BUT SHE SURPRISED IT AND ESCAPED. THE DEMON SEARCHES FOR HER.

That sounded like Sonya. And it wasn't like her getting snatched was good news, but it was better news than her betraying us and knocking out Cody. "Where is she now?"

While Atticus rapid-fire punched the letters, Trip said, "Why didn't you tell me we had smart rats?"

"I made a promise to their emperor and Sid to keep them as secret as possible."

"Sid the janitor?"

"Yes, Sid the janitor." But Atticus had stopped, so I flipped the phone around to read.

GO LEFT, THEN RIGHT, THEN GO STRAIGHT PAST TWO TUNNELS, THEN RIGHT AGAIN AT THE THIRD. SHE HIDES THERE.

Trip read over my shoulder. "The little dude is good with mazes."

Atticus was gesturing for me to give him the phone back.

BEWARE. THE EVIL YOU WARNED US ABOUT HAS ONE BODY LEFT. TWO WERE KEPT IN RESERVE BUT WE TOOK CARE OF ONE OF THEM FOR YOU WHILE IT WAS WEAK. THE LAST HAS GROWN IN STRENGTH BEYOND OUR DEATH BY A THOUSAND CUTS TECHNIQUE.

Even taking one was really impressive. "You guys rock."

WE DO ROCK. ONE MORE THING. THE HUMANS YOU WANTED US TO WATCH DID NOT BETRAY MHI YET. BUT THE CHANGELING INTENDED TO.

"Sonya? What do you mean?"

WHILST FLEEING THE DEMON SHE REVEALED THAT HIDDEN UPON HER PERSON WAS A PAGE TORN FROM A BOOK. IT IS A MAP OF THESE TUNNELS. SHE IS TRYING TO ORIENTATE HERSELF NOW IN ORDER TO ESCAPE.

"Son of a bitch." So that was what Sonya had been doing in the archives when I'd found her. She must have ripped it out of a book in the library and had been planning on bailing the whole time. Looking at her dad's original memoirs had been a handy excuse. She'd probably turned the tears on when she'd heard me coming and stuck the map in her dad's book to hide it. I'd even sent her back to her room with that book! "Thanks, Atticus."

The rat bowed to us.

I bowed back. Trip bowed too, because that seemed like the thing to do. Then we rushed in the direction the rat had indicated.

"What else do we have down here that I don't know about? Ninja turtles?"

"You say that like it's not a possibility." I was forced to crouch because the ceiling was getting lower. It was a good thing I was wearing my lightweight helmet, because otherwise I'd have banged my head on the bricks a lot. When the Shacklefords had dug these tunnels, there hadn't been very many 6'5" Hunters.

When we took the next turn, I saw something that made me freeze in my tracks. A hole had been ripped in the ceiling. Bricks and dirt had been spilled everywhere. From the dust hanging in the air, it was fresh. I went over, looked up and saw the night sky above. This must have been where the river of ectoplasm had zipped upward to join with its final host through an existing crack, and the now empowered monster had clawed its way down.

"The last Drekavac is in here with us," Trip whispered.

"Yep." And the second-to-last one had been damned near

indestructible and cutting his way through a bank vault until Earl had surprised him and, unfortunately for us, the king of the werewolves was currently indisposed. "Be careful."

We moved cautiously, following our rat guide's directions. Sonya had told me that she couldn't see in the dark. Assuming that wasn't a lie like everything else, she must have had a flashlight on her to make it this far.

Trip held up one fist. I froze. He tapped the muff of his ear protection, and then pointed at the last tunnel we were supposed to head down. He'd heard something. Rock music and guns had left me half deaf. I'd have to take his word for it. He kept moving that way, weapon shouldered. I was right behind him with Cazador at the ready. A moment later I could hear what he'd heard. A woman was talking. As we got closer, the sound got clearer.

"Come out, Sonya. I know you're in here. I can smell you. *Sonyaaa*." There was something about that voice that made me mighty uncomfortable and set off all sorts of warnings deep down in my caveman brain, because it was sensual and predatory at the same time. Like she'd screw your brains out but then eat your head like a praying mantis. That *had* to be the succubus.

I'd dealt with a few different kinds of demons over the years, but never that kind. Harbinger had warned us about the seductive ones. It didn't matter how mentally strong you were. They were telepathic and designed to get into your head. I'm talking lust-based mind control shit. A succubus could supposedly charm her way through your defenses, mess with your thoughts, show you one hell of a good time, and then leave you as a desiccated corpse with a big smile on your face.

"Wish Holly was here," Trip whispered.

"She'd be in danger too." I was pretty sure succubi swung both ways. "No talk. Just shoot."

"Got it. She can't flirt if she's dead."

I didn't want to correct him on that, because a couple of undead things had flirted with me over the years, but that was just semantics. I motioned for him to follow me, and then crept forward as quietly as possible. This tunnel was familiar. I knew where we were now. The voice was coming from the room where we'd stored our old Ward Stone. It was one of the bigger spaces down here.

"Why are you hiding, Sonya? I'm not trying to *hurt* you. I'm trying to *save* you. If you stay here, you're gonna die. Come with me and I'll get you someplace safe. I promise."

A promise from a demon was about as trustworthy as gas station sushi. We stacked up on the entrance. Trip put his hand on my shoulder to signal he was ready to move. Silver worked better on traditional demons than lead, but cold iron supposedly worked the best. Sadly, I don't think either of us had packed any iron bullets. So silver would have to do.

It was too quiet. The succubus had stopped talking. Had she heard us approach? Was she going to ambush us? But the longer we waited, the more likely it was the Drekavac would show up. *Shit.*

Cazador at my shoulder, I turned the corner. The beam from my flashlight filled the room.

Nothing. *Where is—*

I should have looked *up.*

The succubus kicked me in the head.

My helmet saved me from getting my skull cracked, but I still went headfirst into the brick wall. There was a crashing of wings. Trip got off a couple of shots, but then he cried out as he got flung across the room. I rolled over, lifted my rifle—only to have the succubus stomp on the muzzle, pinning Cazador to the ground.

She stood over me and, say what you will about demonic mind control, she was smoking hot, in a super deadly, wings and horns and fangs and red eyes, about to rip my face off kind of way. I drew my pistol. She swatted it from my hand.

On the other side of the room, Sonya crawled out from a crack in the wall, saw all the bouncing flashlights as an opportunity, and ran for it. The succubus saw her go.

"I don't have time for this shit." Lana promptly balled up one lovely fist and slugged me right in the face.

As Newbies we had been taught that succubi were dangerous because of their seductive powers, but physically they were one of the weakest kinds of extradimensional beings. Apparently this one hadn't gotten the memo, because she had a right like Evander Holyfield. I saw stars.

Trip was staggering to his feet, so the succubus got off me, took a couple of steps to reach him, and then spin-kicked him so hard that Trip did a flip. Then she went after Sonya.

I lay there for a moment, dizzy. I think she might have broken my nose.

Trip groaned. "That didn't go as expected."

"I'm getting really tired of magic kung-fu bitches this week." I sat up and waited for the room to stop spinning around. "You okay?"

"Yeah." He shakily stood up. "She's getting away."

That's what I liked about Trip. Quitting never even entered his mind. "Let's go." I didn't have time to look for my pistol, but I still had my rifle, and worse come to worse, a knife, and I was in a mood to shank somebody. Trip took a step and then cried out.

"What?"

"My ankle."

"How bad?"

"Sprained." He winced as he put weight on it. "Don't worry. Even hopping on one foot I can keep up with you."

That was probably true. I hurried after the succubus. It was a dazed wobble of a hurry, but at least I thought we were going in the right direction . . . which, unfortunately, was away from the main building. Once we were away from the elf runes there would be nothing stopping the succubus from magically whisking Sonya and the Ward away.

Gunfire echoed through the tunnels. The Drekavac screeched. A man roared in agony.

"Vatican guys?" Trip shouted.

"Probably." But I couldn't tell from what direction that had come from.

There was another Y ahead, but we didn't have time to wait for a rat. We had to be getting close to the compound's edge.

"We have to split up," Trip said.

"You're hurt."

"So are you. Pick one."

There wasn't any time to hesitate. *Shit.* I went right. "Be careful."

"You too." Trip limped down the left fork.

This stuffy, dark, claustrophobic place got even more unnerving once I was alone. Last time I screwed around down here I'd almost been eaten by some werewolves and had shot Franks by accident. I moved as fast as I could crouched over, because the tunnel got smaller until it was only about five feet tall and wide enough that my shoulders were scraping brick on both sides. That stirred up a dust cloud that made it hard to breathe. I could taste copper and was blowing bloody snot bubbles out of my damaged nose.

The tunnel felt like it was sloping upward though. No. I was sure of it. I was climbing toward the surface. I could smell smoke. There had to be an exit to the compound nearby. There was a light ahead.

Except the light wasn't the compound, it was a flashlight lying on the ground. The combat exorcist was still alive, sitting on the floor, bloody hands pressed against his stomach.

"Gutterres." I knelt next to him. "What happened?"

"We had to split up. The Drekavac surprised me. That doesn't happen often." He coughed and I got hit in the face with bloody droplets. "This last bastard is very quick."

"How bad are you hit?"

Gutterres moved his hands to show me the puncture wound in his abdomen. It was slowly leaking. "I'll probably be fine."

There was blood everywhere. From the angle, it looked like the sword thrust would have pierced his liver. Surely, he had to know that kind of wound was going to be fatal. "I'm sorry."

"No, really. I'm no Franks, but there are some blessings that are bestowed on those who hold my office. I'll heal, but not in time to get the stone."

He might be lying to himself because he was in denial, but I'd seen enough weird, implausible shit in this business that I took his word for it. "I warned you you'd get lost down here."

"Yeah, yeah, I know. But you still don't understand how badly we need that Ward." Gutterres started pulling the gloves off his shaking hands. "Is it true what the rumors say about you, about you having the gift of being able to see other people's memories in times of desperate need?"

It wasn't something I liked to blab about to strangers, but these were exigent circumstances. "Sometimes. If the stakes are high enough to concern the big cosmic beings who're calling the shots, I can."

"Good. I bet this qualifies." Gutterres smacked one bloody hand against the side of my face. "Then witness."

The evil that moved through the jungle below was like nothing I'd ever seen before. The entity filled the valley, flickering in and out of our reality. Everything touched by its tendrils became tainted...plants, animals, even people, all cursed and twisted into horrible parodies of what they'd once been.

"What is that thing?" I asked Fedele.

The ancient warrior crouched next to me, carefully watching the distortion in the distance. "I don't know its name, if it even has one. But it's of the Great Old Ones, Michael. Of that much I'm sure."

Fedele would know that better than anyone. I was sure he could feel their presence in his bones.

We had tracked it from its lair, through ruined villages picked clean. We'd found the spot where it had fought the Brazilian Monster Hunters, but all that had been left of them was bloody scraps. The trail was easy to follow. Simply look for death and then go in the direction that damaged your sanity the most. The creature was collecting biomass, growing, but for what purpose we did not yet know.

The squad of elite Swiss Guard who had accompanied us deep inside the corrupted zone were dead. Our priest had committed suicide during the night. Fedele and I were the only ones of the recon party left. I hadn't slept in days. Fedele didn't need to sleep, but even he had been pushed past the breaking point. We needed to return and report, to beg for help, to gather resources and assistance, but still we watched, hoping to figure out some way to damage the thing.

Our minds could barely perceive it, let alone harm it. How do you kill a color?

At the end of the valley was a small town. From the look of things, it hadn't been fully evacuated yet. A military encampment had been set up there. The troops were unaware that this danger couldn't be stopped by bullet or bomb. There was no way for us to warn them what was coming, and that made me sick to my stomach.

I had seen how it took its victims. Some it took quickly, warping the very fabric of reality, bending biology and chemistry to its whims, to remake them in its image. Such spawn were what had killed most of our escort. Yet we'd seen that it could be insidious as well, gradually influencing minds with dark thoughts, subtly changing people for its mysterious purposes. We'd learned the hard way that it had sunk its tendrils deep into this region long

ago, converting many of the locals to worship it in secret. Our expedition had been beset with treachery, sabotage, and murder from the cultists.

Only instead of flooding in and consuming all the living matter like it had last time, this time the thing crept in and settled into place—almost gently—around the encampment. Its latest victims didn't even know it was there.

"What's it doing?" I asked.

Fedele was somber. "It's recruiting."

I slammed back into reality. Only a few seconds had passed in the real world.

"Did you see it?" Gutterres asked.

"You should've told me."

"Oath of secrecy. You know how that goes. But if I die, someone has to stop it."

"I thought you weren't going to die."

The warrior monk looked down at his wound. He should've already been dead. "It might be fifty-fifty. What you just saw, that was almost a week ago. It's still spreading, but very slowly. I went for help. Fedele stayed to observe. He's not like us. He's incorruptible. Our wisest scholars think a Ward Stone might be the only thing that can destroy a being like that."

"Did you figure out what that thing was doing to those people?"

"It's building monsters." Gutterres coughed again, so hard that I cringed in sympathy. "Only then its creations vanish into the jungle. We don't know where they're going or what it is using them for, but it can't be for good. Now go. Please. Get the Ward to Fedele. He'll know what to do."

I left him there bleeding and went after Sonya.

CHAPTER 23

The tunnel got narrower and narrower until I was really struggling to fit. The bricks stopped and it was just dirt and rocks and tree roots, but there was night sky ahead. I noticed something white on the ground and snatched it up. It was a piece of notebook paper with a map on it, like what Atticus had told me about. Sonya must have dropped this on her way out. I'd gotten lucky.

I shut my light off to not give away my position. There had been a metal grate over this exit to keep the racoons out, but Sonya must have knocked it open because it was lying in the weeds. The tunnel exit was on a little hillside covered in bushes. I crawled out and gasped in a lungful of fresh air. Blessed, blessed air.

Standing up, I got my bearings. I was about ten yards on the other side of the fence, but at the far end of the compound, out of sight of the main building where all the Hunters were. However, if the cameras were still working, they'd see me for sure and send help.

It was *cold*. I'm talking that same unnatural super cold as when I first ran into the Drekavac. It was like we'd come full circle. He was *close*. At least there was no fog this time, but that was because he'd sucked it all in to become crazy powerful. On the bright side, his still being here was a good sign. If Stricken's succubus had already whisked Sonya away, he was too mission-oriented to stick around. He'd go after his prize. This meant Sonya was here somewhere.

There was an angry shout deeper in the forest. It sounded like Sonya. I ran in that direction.

Crashing through the trees, I saw a blue fire glow ahead. I stepped into a clearing and into the middle of a standoff.

Sonya was stuck in the middle. In front of her was the last Drekavac, and his twisted, metallic caricature of a face burned with fury. Behind her was the bedraggled succubus who was clearly tired of chasing her through the woods, because she lifted one hand to unfurl a bullwhip. When she snapped it, the whole thing burst into orange flames.

I couldn't figure out why neither of the two monsters had made a move yet, until I realized that Sonya was holding a hand grenade to her chest and had already pulled the pin. The only thing keeping her from blowing herself and the Ward up was her hand pressure on the spoon.

I slowed down. I'd done something like that once as a bluff because I'd only been armed with a smoke grenade. That was a frag. Sonya wasn't about to get dragged down to hell alive. Couldn't say I blamed her.

"She's coming with me," the succubus said.

"You are nothing to me, minor spawn," the Drekavac rumbled as he pointed his blunderbuss at Lana.

"Oh, I'm no pushover," the succubus said. "This body has gotten some serious combat upgrades recently. I'm working for this human who has got some serious connections."

Sonya glanced nervously between the two creatures. "Do I get a vote where I go?"

"No," said the Drekavac. But he didn't get any closer to her, because as much as he wanted to punish the thief, his contract must have specified that he had to retrieve the Ward undamaged.

"Either of you come any closer and I swear I'll blow this thing to bits! I'm not messing around!"

"I'm trying to save your life here," said the succubus.

"I can't imagine why she doesn't trust you," I said as I walked into the clearing with my rifle on the Drekavac. I probably could have just started shooting, but I didn't know how tough the final body would be so I didn't know if I could drop him by myself or not. I was really hoping my friends were on the way and needed to buy them some time to get here.

"Owen?" At least Sonya had gotten my name right that time.

She was now boxed in on three sides, but MHI was by far her best option. We were mildly inconvenient and didn't want to give her bags of money, while the blue guy wanted to condemn her to eternal torment, and the sex demon with the flaming whip worked for the spy Sonya had robbed. In that equation my team seemed downright boring in comparison.

"Yeah. Let's all remain calm."

And then things got even more complicated as Agent Franks stepped into view across from me, which meant Sonya had no direction left to run. From the looks of him, he'd had about as rough a night as Earl, with his armor covered in scorch marks and bullet impacts. Despite going after the succubus, it appeared that Franks had taken care of a whole lot of Drekavacs for us along the way.

"Franks!" Lana didn't seem too upset to see him. "I was really hoping you'd show up in time for this."

Despite her enthusiasm, Franks aimed his rifle at her. "Where's Stricken?"

"Well, this is awkward," she said, coy. "You wouldn't shoot me."

Franks just grunted in annoyance. I figured the list of all the sentient beings in the universe Franks wouldn't shoot would fit on a Post-it note, and I sincerely doubted any of us assembled here had made the cut.

"Alright. No need for you to get all huffy. I'll tell you where Stricken is, but you're probably going to be upset as usual . . . because he's right behind you."

There was the *clack* of a shotgun bolt being dropped.

Stricken had seemingly materialized out of nowhere, about twenty feet behind Franks. The man must have had gnome-level ninja skills to have gotten that close without any of us seeing him. He had a semiauto shotgun pointed at Franks' spine and had ditched the suit in exchange for some MCB-style body armor, though he had kept the shades. Of course he'd retained that trademark affectation, even though it was pitch-black out here.

"Don't move," Stricken said. Franks was fast, but there was no way he'd be fast enough to not get plugged in the back. Except Stricken must have known that Franks wouldn't mind getting shot if it meant killing him in the process. "I know what you're thinking, but I had these armor-piercing slugs made special after our little Project Nemesis debacle. The shells I've got loaded in here are filled with a neurotoxin harvested from a jellyfish that is the nastiest poison on Earth. Even as tough as you are, all those redundant organs of yours will basically melt."

"It's even lethal to Franks?" Lana said. "Nice."

"Sugar, this shit would nuke a T. rex." Stricken looked around the very nervous clearing. He saw me, but I didn't dare take my gun off the Drekavac in order to shoot Stricken. "So the gang's all here. Pitt, meet Lana."

"We met earlier. She kicked me in the head."

"You told me Pitt was ugly, but I think he's kinda cute," she said.

"You say that about everybody... And you've all met Silas Carver." Stricken nodded toward the Drekavac. "Cursed witch burner turned whatever the fuck he is now, but we're going to need a nearly unkillable super monster where we're going."

The monster was still staring at Sonya with unquenchable hate, except she was keeping the live grenade pressed against her chest so he didn't dare move without risking his prize. Sonya was wearing the same face as earlier—her supposedly real one—and she looked downright defiant. It wasn't that she was unafraid to die. She was obviously terrified. But if you were going to die anyway, better to do it on your terms than on the terms set by some cursed monstrosity determined to punish you for your sins.

"And I believe you've all met Sonya, who I originally hadn't planned on bringing along on our little quest, but I guess Isaac Newton never figured a half breed with spirit blood would dink around with one of his devices and cause a phase shift anomaly either. Trying to make two incompatible types of matter coexist in the same space? What are the odds?"

"Does that mean you know how to fix it?" Sonya asked.

"I do. And I will get that out of you, provided you cooperate. When I looked into your genealogy, it turns out you're a perfect fit for our endeavor and you've got some useful skillsets to boot. So I'm going to roll with this complication and invite Sonya to join our little fellowship. Think of me as your badass Gandalf."

"Fun," said Lana. "I don't have to be the only girl on the team."

"What team?" Franks growled, probably still thinking about whether getting melted by a jellyfish slug was worth it or not.

"I'm talking about the crew I put together for a very important mission. It took a lot of effort to get you all here. I needed to recruit representatives of certain specific offices and bloodlines in order to tackle one hell of a job. It's kinda like how I used to put together special teams for the government, only without as much red tape."

"You're gonna want to listen to him, Franks," the succubus warned.

"What are you all jabbering about?" I demanded, because our Mexican standoff had somehow morphed into Stricken's insane pitch meeting.

"Which brings us to Owen Zastava Pitt, who is contractually obligated to help me save the world because of what he said in front of Veles. Sorry, you know him as Coslow. Same pain in the ass, different millennia. Either way, you really don't want to go back on your word to somebody like that. Trust me on this one. Along with Franks, that gives us multiple Chosen, and we only need one to survive to fulfill the mission. I love having built-in redundancies."

"Enough!" shouted the Drekavac. "Be silent, wretched mortal. There is work to be done."

"I agree with the evil ghost thing," I muttered.

"Easy there, Mr. Carver. Your work is done for now. Unfortunately for you, I'm no stranger to how your all-important contracts work. I paid for the insurance. You failed to secure my property in the specified time frame. So now you *owe* me."

That actually made the Drekavac look away from Sonya. "I grow tired of your words."

"Read the fine print and then check the clock. You work for me now."

"Lies," the Drekavac hissed. But he lifted one hand, and a glowing scroll formed in it. He unfurled it and read, eye beams flicking back and forth. I was tempted to use this distraction to shoot him in the head, but I didn't know if that would be enough, and I was kind of curious where Stricken was going with this.

"It can't be." I hadn't thought the Drekavac could get any angrier, but I'd been wrong. The blue fire flared up. "What manner of trickery is this?"

"That's right," Stricken said. "I insisted on that addendum. You failed to uphold it, so you owe me."

"These Hunters caused my delay. You must have aided them to deceive and enslave me!"

Stricken laughed. "File a complaint. The Dark Market can

send its auditors to check but they'll discover I'm in the clear. I didn't give MHI shit. They're capable of being shockingly meddlesome all on their own. I only stepped in here once you were out of time. Now, in order for you to atone for failing to retrieve the Ward for the rightful auction winner, i.e. me, before the deadline, which was two minutes ago, you now owe me one season of loyal servitude. I only need you for a week, tops. Your other option is your boss punishes you with a thousand years in a fiery pit. I need spectral muscle, and I know how to undo the Vatican Hunter's little ceremony thing with the ashes so you can be at full strength in time for our mission. You don't want to spend centuries suffering unimaginable torment. It's a win-win."

The Drekavac glared at Stricken. I thought that I'd seen hate on his face for Sonya, but that had been nothing compared to the contempt and loathing the wires curved into now. "You think you can trap me in your web of lies, mortal? You believe that I am some mere pawn like the pathetic monsters you enslaved before? Nay... The Hubertian's rite has temporarily taken me to my final life, but it did nothing to weaken my pride."

Stricken didn't dare take his eyes off of Franks even for a second, but for the first time I saw just a crack in the chess master's calm façade. His pitch wasn't going the way he'd hoped. "Be smart, Silas. You need me more than I need you. You're my first-round draft pick, but I've got a backup super monster on tap. You're on your last legs. I'm offering you a really good deal here."

I could hear Skippy's helicopter closing in. Search lights were flicking through the trees. My friends were almost here. Franks looked at me and gave a small nod. I think I knew what Franks wanted. I'd shoot Stricken to try and save him. He'd probably shoot the Drekavac. The Drekavac would shoot somebody, hopefully the succubus. And between all that, Sonya would probably do something stupid with that live hand grenade...

I shook my head *no*.

Franks angry nodded *yes*.

The next couple seconds were going to get *really interesting*.

Except then Drekavac said, "This affair has insulted my honor. It would be better to be damned to an eternity of suffering than to bend my knee to a serpent like you. I will accept my punishment and suffer a thousand years, *content* knowing that I killed you all first."

The monster tore his contract in half.

"So much for being reasonable," Stricken said as he tossed something on the ground.

The world was consumed in a blinding flash.

CHAPTER 24

I couldn't see. It felt like the ground had disappeared from beneath my feet. I dropped. Panicked, flailing, only then it felt like gravity changed direction, and I was falling *up*. I suddenly hit the ground, only from an entirely unexpected direction, and bounced off it with my shoulder.

Facedown, I lay there, dizzy, trying to get my bearings and trying to blink the purple blotches from my vision. The world was spinning but beneath me was smooth concrete, so I held onto that bit of stability, even though I couldn't understand how the forest had suddenly grown a concrete floor.

Last thing I'd known, the Drekavac had been about to attack, so I rolled over and shifted my gun in the direction that I thought he was in, except I still couldn't see. Stricken must have used one hell of a flash-bang.

"Franks! Sonya!"

Sonya shouted from somewhere off to my side. "I lost the grenade!"

Fuck!

I couldn't see a damned thing but I started smacking my hands around on the floor, desperately looking for the deadly little thing before it went off.

"Calm your tits," Stricken said. "I've already taken care of it. If you're going to be on my team, you've got to learn to handle your ordnance better."

Focusing on his voice, I could sort of make out the shape of Stricken standing there. The surprising part about that was Franks hadn't immediately shot him. Except when I craned my head in that direction, I saw that Franks was surrounded by several figures who all had guns on him. When I looked behind me, there were more men pointing rifles at me. I was still having a hard time focusing, but they looked like soldiers.

We were no longer outdoors. There was a roof overhead. We were in some big room...a garage. There were several trucks parked inside. The succubus extinguished her flaming whip and hopped up on a truck to sit on the hood. There was a really loud AC unit running and no windows on the cinder-block walls. There was no sign of the Drekavac. When I saw that we were all inside a big circular scorch mark burned into the floor, I realized what had happened. It was some variation of the portal rope magic I'd first seen used by the Sanctified Church of the Temporary Mortal Condition.

"You teleported us?" No wonder I was feeling motion sick.

"Well, it was either that or stand around there waiting for old Carver to try and murder everyone, and trust me, he still had plenty of horsepower. You wouldn't have been able to shut him down in time. You can thank me later." Stricken had Sonya's grenade in one hand and the unscrewed fuse in the other. That must have been *close*. They only have a four or five second fuse. Stricken was faster than he looked. "Take care of that for me." Stricken tossed the grenade to one of the soldiers, but luckily the surprised man caught it, though he fumbled it, wide-eyed and terrified, a few times before he got it under control.

Sonya threw up. I didn't know if it was from her almost blowing herself up, or the nausea of falling through a portal to who knew where, but it was an understandable reaction to either event.

I slowly moved my hands away from Cazador so none of Stricken's guards got the wrong idea. "Where's the Drekavac?"

"Alabama, for the moment. Hopefully your buddies take his final body out. Otherwise he'll be coming after us soon. How soon, I don't know. I'm a little fuzzy on the details of how he travels long distance." Stricken sighed. "What a waste. Silas is a real talent. I would've killed to have him on Unicorn. My backup-pick monster isn't as impressive, though they're probably equally as annoying."

"I'm gonna kill you, Stricken," Franks stated in a very matter-of-fact manner that was still convincing, despite the six dudes with assault rifles aimed at him.

"I know. You're going to kill me. Which is why I should just take you out now and get it over with. It's not like I *need* two Chosen." Stricken picked up the shotgun that was supposedly loaded with the special Franks-killing slugs, except rather than aiming it at Franks, he rested it over one shoulder. "The fact that I haven't popped you, even though I could, should indicate that this is way bigger than our little feud. You're really going to want to hear me out, Franks. You can get back to hounding me to the ends of the Earth after we keep the Old Ones from tearing the planet a new asshole. You know I wouldn't reach out to the likes of you for help if it wasn't that serious."

Franks made an angry *hmmmm* noise. Because there really was no way Stricken would turn to someone who wanted to end him that much unless something really bad was going to go down otherwise.

Now that I could mostly see, I slowly took in the details of the garage. There had been at least twenty men waiting outside the circle for us to arrive. They were dressed in woodland camo fatigues with mismatched load-bearing gear. Most of them seemed pretty freaked out about the portal magic they'd just seen, which meant they were new to this kind of thing. They were armed with a variety of weapons, including a couple I didn't recognize, which was saying something because I'm a huge gun nut. Among the soldiers were a few gringos and black guys, but most of them were about as tan as I am, but they were on average a whole lot shorter.

"Where are we?"

"Brazil," Stricken said.

Well, shit. I sure wasn't going to get home by the time we'd told the babysitter. "Send us back."

"Sorry. Only had the one rope. Those things are not cheap. You ever been here before?"

Only in other people's nightmares, but I didn't say that. I thought about what Gutterres had shown me. There was no way our new location was a coincidence. "This is about the thing in the jungle the Secret Guard have been fighting."

"Well, it's good you're not a total idiot, Pitt. Yes. Now we're going to finish what they started. Think of this as the forward operating base for our upcoming expedition." He gestured around the garage. "Welcome to Rio. Sadly, I doubt any of us will have time to hit the beaches."

"Rio is nowhere near that part of the Amazon," I said.

"So you're an expert on South American geography too?" Stricken said. "No shit. We're over a thousand miles from the heart of the disturbance, but we've got an important meeting to attend here first. You'll see."

There were twice as many guns pointed at Franks as there were at me, which meant that Stricken had briefed them on which one of us was more dangerous. However, there were only two of them ready to shoot Sonya, which showed a real lack of judgment on their part. I was worried she might be thinking about trying something stupid, so I caught her eye and gave her a little negative head shake.

Only Sonya gave me one right back, and she tapped one finger to her chest. She wasn't going anywhere until she could get that rock out of her. *Fair enough.*

Franks slowly stood up, and it was obvious the soldiers were scared to death of him, which was smart. Especially since Franks was still armed. He slowly and purposefully dusted himself off but left his rifle hang from its sling as he glared at Stricken menacingly. The soldiers looked so nervous and there were so many twitchy fingers resting on triggers that I was kind of surprised Franks didn't get shot by accident.

"I'd order these guys to disarm you, but we both know that would be insulting and pointless. It's not like the legendary Agent Franks needs a gun to kill anybody." Then Stricken looked at me. "Hothead McChosen One, on the other hand, I should probably have them disarm you and pat you down, too, for good measure."

There was no way I could do anything without getting shot, but I wasn't about to give Stricken the satisfaction. "From my cold dead hands, motherfucker."

"Well, they would be room temperature and dead if I have my men kill you, which is kind of the point, Pitt."

"I'll pat him down," the succubus offered. "He's a sturdy one."

"Lana, you really need to quit creating a hostile work environment for the new recruits."

She shrugged and went back to inspecting her claws. She'd painted them festive colors.

"In the spirit of cooperation, everybody can hold onto their guns, but let's keep it polite. I didn't bring you here to be prisoners, but rather *partners*. Besides, my Portuguese is kind of rough when it comes to giving instructions and I don't want all these jumpy paramilitary types I hired to get the wrong message."

I looked to the nearest soldier, who had an FAL pointed at my heart, and said in Portuguese, *Whatever this asshole is paying you, I'll double it.* My Portuguese was archaic crap gleaned from a dead conquistador, and more recently beefed up with some Duo Lingo lessons, but I was pretty sure he got the message. He looked to Stricken.

And of course, Stricken was lying about his language skills, because his accent was so good he probably sounded like a native Brazilian when he told them, *"Nao preste atencao a este doido. Ele fale mentiras e pobre demais,"* which I was pretty sure translated to: *Don't listen to this idiot. He lies and is poor.* Then Stricken looked at me. "We done?"

"We're done." I had nothing but loathing for the man, and the only reason I hadn't shot him myself was all his goons, *but . . .* Gutterres' memories had confirmed that the situation was dire, and all of Coslow's mystic pronouncements had encouraged me to get involved. I walked over to Sonya and offered her a hand to help her up. She didn't need it. I was just trying to keep my friends close. Not that *friend* wasn't a questionable term in this case.

"Hey, what about me?" Sonya said to Stricken. "You said you could get this rock out of me? Let's get to getting."

Stricken chuckled. "I should clarify. I know someone who can. But don't worry, we're going to meet with them shortly. You'll just have to wait until then."

"You son of a bitch," Sonya said. "You promised."

"No. I made an offer, and then moved you to a different hemisphere in order to save your life even after you robbed me. Don't mistake my recent benevolence for patience, because you're the least necessary member of my new team, rookie. So we'll get around to fixing your problem in due time. Don't like it—"

"I walk?"

Stricken actually seemed surprised by how naïve that was. "No. We shoot you and throw your corpse in a ditch. You had your chance with squishy and benevolent MHI, but now you're with me. Playtime is over. We've got shit to do. Screw with my timeline anymore, and I'll just kill you." Stricken could ooze menace when he wanted to. There was no doubt he'd have her capped in a heartbeat. "Understood?"

"Got it," she said sullenly.

"Good. Then you can shut up and wait until we meet with the expert."

"We wouldn't be in this mess if you hadn't run off, princess," I whispered to her.

"Don't want to hear it."

"So how about it, Pitt? Are you in or not?"

"I'm only interested in stopping that thing in the jungle."

"Good. Because I'm the only one who knows how to finish the job. I need someone Chosen, like you or Franks. You need my knowledge."

Until I could figure out how to handle it myself, or Gutterres seemed to think his friend who had stayed out there knew what to do, then I could arrange for Stricken to accidentally fall on some bullets. "I'll work with you for now."

"That'll do." Stricken nodded. "You hear that, Franks? I really only need one of you to cooperate."

Franks grunted. "So I should shoot Pitt?"

"He's joking. I think. But if you harm Franks, then you might as well kill me too. Then good luck scrounging up another Chosen in time."

Stricken grinned and turned to Sonya. "See, kid? Now that's how you bargain."

"You mind if I call my wife to tell her where we all vanished to?" So that Julie could send in the cavalry.

"Aw, you two have such a wholesome and caring relationship, it makes me want to barf...but your phone won't work in here. We've got a jammer on this site."

"Mr. Stricken." One of the white guys walked up next to his superior. His guns were newer and his kit was fancier. His accent suggested East Texas. "We've got a problem, sir."

"What is it?"

"The VIPs still want to meet at sunrise, but we've spotted some tangos poking around the perimeter."

"Cultists?"

"Looks like it." That one had to be Unicorn alumnus who'd stayed loyal to the old boss, which meant he was either a human handler, or something else that could pass for human. "We don't know if they're with the Old Ones or Asag though."

That made me perk right up. Both of those wanted me dead. "What's this got to do with Asag?"

"Those factions hate each other more than they hate us. They're at war. That's what's actually going on out in the jungle. That's the main reason Asag has been too busy to step on you. If either of them win this particular battle, mankind loses."

I glanced at Franks, but from the grim look on his big flat face, he was still trying to decide if he could kill Stricken before he was shot to pieces. Having seen Franks in action, the answer was more than likely yes, and the fact that he hadn't done so yet meant that he was weighing Stricken's words. Franks was big on never failing a mission and killing Stricken was a mission. However, protecting mankind from the forces of ultimate evil was also his mission. I figured saving a few million lives outranked ending one really odious one. But most importantly, the MCB's primary mission was keeping monsters secret from most of mankind. It was their vaunted First Reason, because they truly believed that the more regular people know about the supernatural, the more powerful the supernatural would become, until our world was doomed. From what Coslow had said earlier, if this came to pass, it would be catastrophic enough that even the best bullshit artists at the MCB might not be able to cover it up.

Conflicting missions was probably going to confuse Franks, and a confused Franks was more dangerous than a regular Franks, so I said to him, "You cool with this, Franks?"

"Yeah," he growled, but I wasn't sure I believed him. Clearly, the men prepared to shoot him didn't either.

The man from Texas wasn't done with his warning. "We tried to bag one of the cultists for interrogation, but they disappeared back into the crowd. The way they knew this area, they've got to be locals."

"Thank you, Mr. Curtis," Stricken said. "So you think they know we've been hiding here?"

"We've tried to keep a low profile, but probably. Should we scratch the mission, sir?"

"No. Time isn't on our side and I've already wasted too much as it is getting these clowns assembled. Don't tell the VIPs' security detail anything either. I don't want to scare them off. If the cult makes a move against us, we'll deal with them, but having their lives threatened will just demonstrate to them how much they need us..." Stricken started walking away. "Alright, everybody, get freshened up so we look presentable when we meet the rest of our illustrious alliance."

The succubus hopped off the truck hood and followed Stricken. She winked at Franks as she passed him. "You're not going to want to miss this, Franks. Trust me."

"Who're we meeting?" Franks demanded.

"I'm not about to ruin the surprise," Stricken said. "Our convoy leaves in ten."

Sonya whispered to me, "This guy is a real piece of work."

She had no idea.

CHAPTER 25

I used one of the filthy bathrooms to clean up. I took my helmet off and my hair was damp with sweat, salt in my eyes. My hands were shaking from coming off the adrenaline rush. I was covered in grit and sticky blood, a lot of which I wasn't even sure who I'd gotten it from. I splashed some water on my face from the sink. I was dying of thirst. I'd not worn my CamelBak to save weight—I hadn't thought I'd need it fighting in our own backyard—but since the water turned out to be kind of rust-colored and smelled funny, I didn't dare drink any of it. Everything hurt. I really wanted to take my armor off and check the burns from the Drekavac's bullets, but since there were a bunch of armed guards still watching me, that struck me as a bad idea.

True to his word, Stricken let us keep our weapons, which was really surprising. I'd seen Franks in action. If he wanted to kill every man here, he could probably do it without getting hurt too badly. I half expected to come out of the washroom to find a pile of dismembered bodies and Franks picking through them for replacement organs for any of his that had gotten shot in the process, but the garage was the same as before.

Thankfully, there was a cooler full of bottled waters that hopefully hadn't been filled out of the local tap, so I grabbed one. With the guards watching me carefully, I walked up to Franks so we could speak quietly. Nobody tried to stop me. "You're being awfully cooperative."

"I got reasons."

"You mean orders."

Franks just raised an eyebrow, but the way he did it told me that he hadn't misspoke.

"Wait. You're going along with Stricken's bullshit on your own accord? I figured Coslow had ordered you to."

"Priorities," he muttered.

So Franks was in the same boat I was: Deal with the pending supernatural mass casualty event first, revenge second. I could get with that plan. Knowing that Franks had unnaturally good hearing, I lowered my voice so our observers wouldn't hear. "You know Stricken will off us the second he doesn't need us anymore."

"Yep."

Great. We just needed to figure out exactly when that moment was that we didn't need Stricken anymore so we could kill him first. "Okay. Follow my lead."

Franks snorted at that. He wasn't much of a follower.

Sonya came out of the other bathroom, drying her hands on a rag. She came over to stand by me and Franks. "This sucks."

"I'm surprised you didn't knock out one of your shadows and try to sneak out wearing his face."

"My abilities only do so much for overall size. I wouldn't make a convincing man who is four inches taller and forty pounds heavier than me. Plus, I look terrible with a mustache." Sonya extended one hand toward Franks. "You must be Agent Franks. I'm Sonya."

Franks just stared at her until she awkwardly put her hand down. I knew those feels.

About half the soldiers kept an eye on us, while the other half got three SUVs ready. When the doors were open I could see that they were armored, with extra-thick bulletproof glass, and there were weapons stored in the back of each. I'm sure the local authorities frowned on trunks full of machine guns but Stricken had probably already paid off whoever needed bribing. One thing was troubling though. I didn't like how nervous the men looked, because their nerves weren't just because of us new arrivals. They were a lot more worried about whatever was outside the garage than what was inside with them, especially considering one of the things inside was Franks...

"So what do we do now?" Sonya asked.

"We play along and see where this goes. Do exactly what I say." She started to give me some smart-ass response, but I cut her off. "I'm not screwing around anymore. We're a long way from home. If you'd done what you were supposed to at the compound, we wouldn't be in this mess. When the time comes, we have to count on each other or we're not making it out of the jungle alive."

"I don't even want to go to any jungle! I just want this thing out of me before it kills me."

"Then you probably should have thought of that before you tried to escape and leave the rest of us hanging. And before you make any excuses about the succubus grabbing you out of the cell, I know about the map you stole from the archives." It was obvious my knowing about that surprised her. "You were going to make a run for it no matter what."

"I was just covering my bases."

"I'm not buying it. You want to survive, we have to trust each other. Speaking of which," I turned back to Franks. "You and the succubus..."

"It's complicated."

Complicated was a step up from *classified*. We were making progress. "I gathered that."

"That's who called me on the phone at the country store," Sonya said. "To make that offer tricking me to go see that lich."

"You sure?"

"Absolutely. You heard her. I've got an amazing vocal range and even I'm kinda jealous. She'd make a killing as a phone sex operator."

"Why'd your girlfriend send her to get killed by a lich, Franks?"

"Ex." Not that I'd expected Franks to expound on his relationship status further, but he nodded toward the door to warn me that Stricken had returned.

Stricken had ditched the combat gear and was back in a suit and tie. That outfit seemed more fitting because this was a man who preferred to delegate the trigger pulling to underlings. He was more of a schemer than a doer. The reason he'd been the one to confront us in Alabama probably had something to do with how complicated the portal magic was. If he'd been able to delegate it to someone else, he more than likely would have.

"Mount up." Stricken gestured toward the vehicles. The three of us started walking toward the SUV in the middle. "Nope. Each of our new recruits in a *different* ride. I hate to put too many eggs in one basket. Sonya, you're with me."

I didn't like being separated and isolated from the others, but I was committed now. There would have been a lot of easier ways for Stricken to get the Ward without loading us into a convoy as some elaborate ruse. Franks shrugged and went to the lead vehicle.

"Be careful," I told Sonya, because there had to be a reason that crafty bastard wanted a moment with her. "Don't tell him anything he can use against you later—or he will. Good luck."

Sonya nodded, wide-eyed and nervous.

Then I went to the last truck in line. "I've got shotgun."

"You ain't got shit." The Texan pointed toward the backseat. "Get in back." He got in the passenger seat.

I sat behind him. If he wanted to be a douche, then he could get the tall guy's knees in his back the whole ride. There was one man in the rear serving as trunk monkey, meaning he had a belt-fed in case our convoy got attacked from behind. One of the soldiers was driving. Another sat across from me. Except then the succubus showed up. "Scoot over."

"Don't you want to ride with Franks?"

"I don't think he's in the mood to talk to me right now."

"How's that different? He doesn't talk to anybody ever."

"True. He's not much of a communicator. Now make room."

I slid to the middle so Lana could get in. It took her a moment to fold her wings out of the way. The presence of the demon seemed to make everyone else really uncomfortable, especially since she made a big show of trying to fit the seat belt over her ample bosom. A few of the soldiers couldn't help but stare at her, which seemed to energize her. The driver touched the cross on his neck chain and kept his eyes straight ahead, which meant he was the smartest one here.

"Lana would be the funnest but final minutes of your life, boys. She ain't worth it," the Texan warned. I didn't know if the soldiers spoke much English, but they got the message. "Focus on the job."

"You're no fun, Jim."

"No, ma'am. I am not."

The garage door rolled up and our convoy headed out. I had to resist the urge to start whistling the *convoy* song. That was all Milo's fault. I'd have that stuck in my head for the rest of my life.

I didn't know what time zone we were in—it was still dark out—but it felt like that really tired time of the night, close to sunrise, so we had to be a few hours ahead of Alabama. There was a clock on the dash, and it confirmed my guess. It said 4:45 A.M.

"Jim, is it?"

"You can call me Mr. Curtis."

"What are daylight hours here?"

"About five-thirty to eighteen-thirty." I'd figured him for former military. Earl had told me Unicorn's human handlers were always recruited that way, sort of like my dad had been. "Why?"

"Nothing." I was just trying to figure out what the window was before I had to worry about the Drekavac again. There was no way he was going to give up. Assuming my friends hadn't removed him from the equation, he'd be back. I doubted he'd be able to get here and do anything before dawn. The window was too narrow and closing fast, but tomorrow night was a different story.

"He's worried about the Drekavac," Lana said. "Stricken didn't tell you that he's torn up his contract and he's coming after us now. He took it personal."

Curtis let out a frustrated sigh. "The boss doesn't tell us anything."

"That's because you work for an asshole," I said.

"Yeah, but unlike most of the assholes I've worked for over the years, Stricken actually does what needs doing." He looked back over his shoulder at me. "And you're here too. So I guess we're both suckers."

He had me there.

Stricken's hideout was in a really bad part of town. The streets were narrow and disintegrating into dirt and potholes. The regular buildings were mismatched and rotting, and in every available space between, and even on top of them, had been built shacks slapped together out of whatever was available.

"Great neighborhood," I said.

"We needed to set up at the nexus of some ley lines—those are like underground rivers of supernatural energy—in order to power the thing that brought you here. This *favela* was the only place in the region available that met our needs. The others were unavailable or had too many witnesses around."

"There was another nexus that was next door to a five-star

resort with a great dance club and some really nice restaurants," Lana said, "but Stricken said that wasn't *clandestine* enough. Oh, the sacrifices I make for you poor dumb humans."

"That nexus was inside a church that's still in use," Curtis said. "You would have caught on fire the second you came through the portal."

"Worth it. The resort has a very nice pool."

"I think you'd stick out there," I said.

"Of course I would. That's the point."

"I meant the wings and the fangs."

"Not into that?" Lana laughed. "This is my fighting body. Give me a few minutes to change into something more comfortable and I can look like whatever you want. We could have some fun."

My response was reflexive. "I'm married."

"You have no idea how many times I've been told that over the centuries." I felt her hand touch my thigh. "It never works."

She had some kind of magic aura or was secreting pheromones or something that made her extra hot, but I smacked her hand off my leg. Only it turned out not to be her hand, but rather the end of her tail. "Knock it off. I'm here to stop a massacre. That's the only reason I'm putting up with Stricken's bullshit. I don't have time for yours too. Keep your... appendages to yourself."

"Too bad." The succubus pouted, but she did swing her tail out of sight. "I was just trying to be friends. We're the same. I was coerced into this little adventure against my will too. I had a good thing going until Franks screwed it up and I got dragged back into this life."

"Tragic." I concentrated on looking out the opposite window.

Shacks climbed up the hillsides around us with thickly wooded hills beyond them. It was so early there weren't many people out, but there were some barefoot little kids and skinny stray dogs. It was nothing but graffiti and mud and razor-wire-topped chain-link fences as far as the eye could see. We were going surprisingly fast considering how curvy and narrow the road was, but if we hit a pedestrian, Stricken would probably just toss some cash out the window and the cops would call it good. I've visited a lot of places around the world, but this was the biggest slum I'd ever seen.

"Bingo." Curtis got on his radio. "I just saw a lookout on a roof watching us with binos. Could be the local drug lord's people, or it could be the cultists."

I couldn't hear Stricken's response, but it must have been to switch to an alternate route, because our lead SUV suddenly braked and turned. We followed it into an even narrower street.

"You expecting trouble?"

"Maybe. The Old Ones and Asag are fighting a shadow war here. I'd love to let them duke it out, but unfortunately, they're doing it on Earth, and people are just collateral damage. But their worshippers don't see it that way, and they'll do anything to stop us from meddling in their affairs."

Curtis had used his radio, which meant we were away from the jammer or they'd shut it off. I got out my phone to text my team. It was a good thing I'd kept my international plan because of all the travel I'd had to do in preparation for the siege, so it should work here.

I am in Rio with Sonya and Franks.

I hit send. Thought about it a second, because this next bit was complicated, so I just wrote, *Going with Stricken to stop big event in Amazon.*

A few seconds later, I got a message back from Julie. *Are you a prisoner?*

Kinda. Shrug emoji.

Tracking your position. We'll come help. It will take a while. Be careful. And then Julie sent me a heart.

"Awww. Cute," said the succubus who was watching over my shoulder.

"Buzz off," I told Lana while I typed, *Casualties?*

A few, Julie responded. *You can't worry about that right now though.*

I took a deep breath. She was right. There wasn't anything I could do for them anyway. There was some comfort in knowing that if it had been someone on our team, she would have told me. MHI were my people, but my team that I constantly risked my life with was closer than family. *Did you kill the last Drek?* I hit send.

The little bubbles popped up to show that Julie was typing something.

"Ambush!" Curtis shouted.

I looked up just in time to see something streaking toward our lead SUV. The engine block exploded. The shredded vehicle swerved hard to the side, crashing into a building made of scrap lumber and cinder blocks. It stopped with most of its back end blocking half the road. Smoke billowed into the street. The other drivers hit their brakes.

The visibility was bad. Our attackers had probably smashed most of the lights in prep, but I could see gun barrels being hung out of doorways and windows. There were a bunch of loud pops as bullets hit our car. The armored glass fractured into weird shapes but didn't break. There was a man running across a rooftop carrying a long tube with a bulbous end.

"RPG. Four o'clock high."

"Go. Drive!" Curtis ordered.

Except the second car had stopped and was totally blocking the way forward. Our driver threw it in reverse and stomped on the gas. A split second later our front window was washed in fire and dirt as the warhead hit where we'd just been.

Our trunk monkey was shouting something in Portuguese, but the warning was too late, as we slammed our rear end into the container truck that had just pulled out behind us. It was a sudden and violent stop. I think I might've gotten whiplash. I looked back to see that a big chunk of broken metal had punched through our back window and nailed the machine-gunner in the face. He was holding his eye and screaming. Everybody else was yelling at our driver in English and Portuguese. He put it in drive, but our tires spun uselessly. Our bumper was stuck.

Trucks had boxed us in on both sides. We were sitting ducks. They must have set up on more than one route to wait for us. Their bullets were bouncing off our armor for now but those rocket-propelled grenades would rip us apart. Our only hope was to hit back. I had a perfectly good precision rifle sitting between my knees and no way to use it. "We've got to fight!"

The merc to my left reacted too slow. But Lana opened her door and jumped out. Instead of running for cover she leapt straight up, and with two wing beats had launched herself into the sky. The wings weren't just for show.

I crawled out and hid behind the heavy door. If I'd had any doubt that the truck driver who had pulled out behind us was some innocent bystander in the wrong place at the wrong time, those doubts vanished as he stuck a subgun out his window and launched a hail of bullets into our roof. I shouldered Cazador and fired twice. Holes appeared in his door and he flopped from view.

There was a *lot* of gunfire. I picked out the muzzle flashes across the street and started shooting. I went as fast as I could. Put the reticle on one, fire, swing to the next, fire, swing to the next, fire. I didn't know if I was hitting anyone. We were sitting ducks, outnumbered, surrounded, and basically fucked.

Except suddenly fire arced across the sky above us. I thought it was a flamethrower at first, but it was the succubus' whip. She was spinning, slicing fire across the *favela* in a widening circle. When her whip hit flesh, it sliced smoking chunks of bodies. When it hit wood it set the surrounding structures on fire. She hadn't been exaggerating about getting some fighting upgrades!

Our ambushers turned their guns upward, forcing Lana to dive out of sight, but that momentary distraction had probably saved our ass. The men in Stricken's vehicle had bailed out and were shooting back too. They'd been trained to fight through an ambush.

Men rushed out of the burning buildings on both sides. Bright weapon-mounted flashlights illuminated our convoy. I concentrated on the ones who were on my side of the car, because there was nothing between me and their bullets besides the door I was crouching behind, and shot at the lights.

One of my targets spun around, illuminating his friends. They were all dressed the same. Not in wacky cultist garb, or even normal clothing so that they could blend in with the populace, but rather they were all in the same black uniform, like some kind of police or military unit.

Oh shit.

It didn't matter who they were as much as the fact they were trying to kill us. They weren't interested in taking prisoners. There was a terrible *snap* as a really big bullet zipped through our front window. Our driver popped like a blood-filled water balloon.

"They've got a fifty!" Curtis shouted.

Another huge bullet hit our grill and ripped through our engine block. Antifreeze sprayed out of the hole. The next shot obliterated our battery.

But I'd spotted that big flash from the sniper rifle's muzzle brake. It was on the roof of a building half a block away. I couldn't pick out the shooter with my naked eye, but my scope gathered enough light that I could make out the shape of his head. I aimed and brained that motherfucker.

The lead car had been shredded, wrecked, and had caught on fire. That rocket hit had probably killed everybody inside—everybody human at least—because then one of the doors was kicked violently open, and out came Franks, rifle up, and he went to town, dropping dudes left and right as he moved toward the truck that was blocking our way. It was frightening that somebody that big could be that fast.

Curtis had bailed out ahead of me and was using the engine for cover as he returned fire at our attackers. The other back seat merc should have bailed out my door because it was shielded from most of the gunfire, but instead he got out his side, and immediately got riddled with bullets. Our trunk monkey was smarter and crawled out behind me.

Franks reached the blocker truck. The driver stuck a pistol out the window to shoot at him, but Franks was too fast, and shot him in the head. He opened the door, flung the body out, climbed in, and started backing the truck up. Our path was about to be cleared, but our ride was dead in the water.

Curtis realized the same thing. "Move to the next. I'll cover you."

I got up and ran while Curtis fired over the hood.

Another RPG gunner rose on the rooftop across the street, but before I could shoot him, Lana fell out of the sky and collided with him, flinging the man screaming over the edge. Then she swiftly launched herself back into the air.

I reached the back of Stricken's truck and took a knee. One of the Brazilians was lying there, dead. There was movement in one of the *favela's* windows to my right, followed by a whole lot of machine-gun fire. Another of the men who had been riding with Stricken got nailed in the face. I flinched as I got hit with skull chunks, then dumped the rest of my mag through that window and the machine gun went quiet. I yanked a fresh mag and performed a fast reload. Ready to shoot again, I bellowed, "Move!"

Curtis and the trunk monkey ran toward us. The merc got hit in the back and fell. Rather than keep running to safety, Curtis turned back, grabbed him by the arm, hoisted him up, and dragged him along. I nailed the man who had shot him. Curtis shoved the wounded Brazilian through the door and climbed in after. That was it. I jumped on the running boards and banged my fist on the roof. "Drive! Drive!"

We took off.

Franks—being Franks—stubbornly shot people until the last possible instant, and then caught hold of our passing vehicle and hopped aboard. He was on one side, I was on the other, and even as projectiles were landing all around us, Franks kept on shooting his SCAR with one hand and effortlessly holding on with the other. I had to use both hands to keep from getting bounced off, because Stricken would certainly leave us to die in some trash-filled ditch.

I looked back. The light from our lead SUV's burning gas tank revealed a bunch of black-uniformed men running out into the street to take potshots after us. One of them caught my attention. He wasn't shooting. He was shouting orders. That was clearly the one in charge. I only caught a brief glimpse of him, an imposing man in a black beret with a beard, but there was something oddly familiar about him.

Then we were out of sight.

CHAPTER 26

It's really hard to hold onto the side of a vehicle racing over a shit road in a *favela*. We hit so many potholes I nearly bit my tongue off. I probably left finger-shaped dents in the roof rack and the bouncing was killing my calf muscles, but there was no time to slow down. If the bad guys had set up multiple ambush points, that meant there were reinforcements nearby who might be converging on our position.

The whole ambush had taken less than a minute. It had been terrifying, but I hadn't had time to process it. Now it was sinking in that it had been a miracle I hadn't gotten shot. I caught glimpses of a winged form shadowing us which had to be Lana. Or at least I hoped it was her, and not some other random flying monstrosity. Then we braked so suddenly that it almost yanked my arms out of my sockets, but I managed to not get tossed into the dirt.

The back door opened. "Get in." Curtis shoved our dead trunk monkey into the street. The poor guy had bled out, so no need for him to take up space. Extrajudicial Unicorn didn't give a shit about *leave no man behind*. It was pragmatic, but it definitely demonstrated that these guys didn't screw around. Franks and I got in the back and they floored it before we had even pulled the doors closed.

The driver turned out to be Stricken. From the amount of

blood all over the upholstery and the wind whistling through the huge bullet hole through the armored glass, their original driver had met the same fate as ours. Sonya had wound up in the passenger seat and was holding an old M16 which, from the amount of blood on it, the previous owner no longer needed.

After a few seconds of terror, we were all that was left of the convoy. *Holy shit, that had been close.* Humans could be scarier than monsters.

"Are you guys okay?" Sonya asked.

"Yeah," I said, even as I checked myself for holes.

Franks grunted as he inspected a wound in his shoulder. Then he grossed us all out by sticking his finger deep in the gash and probing around. A moment later he fished out a chunk of shrapnel. "I'm fine." He tossed the jagged chunk of metal on the floor. It was probably still hot. I'd have been screaming and bleeding. Franks just seemed annoyed.

"Who were those guys, Stricken? And don't lie and say cultists. They looked way too official."

"Well, yes and no." He laid on the horn to warn some street urchins to get out of our way. Thankfully, they did, because I had no doubt Stricken would have run them down. "Those were *Gatos Pretos*. The Black Cats. They're a death squad that sometimes works for the state, but in this case, they're taking orders from the cultists who've infiltrated their leadership, and they're going to use the *Gatos* to kill anyone who gets in their god's way. Which god they're working for, I've not nailed that down quite yet. But it's kind of irrelevant since both of them would love to see all of us dead."

I'd never heard of this death squad, but I had a nagging feeling that I knew their leader somehow. I'd not gotten that good of a look at him, but something was eating at the back of my mind. "Who is in charge of these Black Cats?"

"Don't know. It's not like they have a website. You'll have to forgive me for not having unrestricted access to the entire US intelligence apparatus anymore."

Whoever he was, that brief glimpse had set my teeth on edge. There was something familiar, but not... It was like my subconscious was trying to tell me something, but it hadn't clicked just yet.

"Sorry about your men," Sonya said.

Stricken waved one hand dismissively. "They were local hires. Temps. I didn't learn most of their names. Them's the breaks."

"Nance was in that lead car with Franks, sir," Curtis said.

"That the other American?" Franks asked.

"Yeah. We were on the task force together."

"He died quick," Franks said simply.

"Shit..." Curtis stared off into space, then he punched the seat.

"He was a good man," Stricken said, though I honestly couldn't tell if Stricken actually meant that or he was just trying to placate his remaining volunteer. After being thrown out of the government, he was probably running low on willing helpers. "We'll make sure his sacrifice wasn't in vain."

One second we were speeding through a *favela*, and the next it was like a switch had been flipped and we were in a different world. We went around one gentle turn, a patch of trees, and just like that, the road was paved and smooth and straight. The buildings were new, tall, and clean. There was no trash or graffiti anymore. It was a jarring jump between extreme poverty and respectable prosperity. It was almost as quick as falling through the portal from Alabama. I'd heard of bad side of the tracks, but Brazil took that concept to a whole new level.

Stricken was checking the mirrors as we got onto a wide, straight, two-lane road. He even wore his sunglasses at night. "I think we've shaken them. I don't see a tail."

Now that Stricken was deprived of his mercenary army, Franks must have recalculated his previous cooperation because he pulled his Glock and stuck it against the back of our host's head.

Curtis reached for his handgun, but Franks' other hand shot out and grabbed Curtis' wrist. The poor guy winced as Franks twisted. He was so damned strong that he could have snapped every bone if he felt like it, but he refrained. His attention was on the jackass in the driver's seat.

"I should've seen this horrible betrayal coming," Stricken said. "Oh, wait. I did. Relax, Franks. I needed the private army on hand until you cooled off enough to be rational. You've been briefed on what the MCB knows about this situation, so you know it's serious enough you can't risk me being wrong. I'm the key to stopping this, and you obviously get that, otherwise the contents of my head would already be all over the windshield."

Franks said, "You killed Strayhorn."

I didn't even know who that was, but the way Franks said it, Strayhorn had obviously been somebody important to him.

Stricken took a deep breath. "Indirectly. And I know you'll make me pay for that eventually." For being a former danger guy turned desk jockey, Stricken still had ice water in his veins, because I've had Franks point guns at me, and there's never any doubt that he's willing to pull the trigger. "But we both know what Dwayne Myers would tell you if he was here right now."

"I can't ask 'cause you killed him too."

Stricken suddenly shouted, "Bullshit, Franks. You know what he'd say. You know damned good and well Myers would tell you the mission has to come first. I know about how your status has changed. You can't just shrug off that many innocent lives being lost like it's no big deal anymore. This is the era of the more sensitive, kinder and gentler Agent Franks. You have to do the *right* thing now."

I had no idea what any of that meant either, but we were doing eighty and climbing. If Franks shot our driver, we were hosed.

Sonya was thinking the same thing. "Don't do it, Franks. You'll kill us all."

"Maybe you should have him pull over, *then* shoot him," I suggested as I buckled my seat belt.

"I'd be fine," Franks said, and that was probably true.

"No, you wouldn't," Stricken said, and it was obvious from the way he said it that he wasn't talking about a car accident. "If you're gonna do it, fucking do it. None of you have a second to waste. I die, you can try to stop this without me, but by the time you figure out what you need to do, it'll be too late, and all the bloodshed and carnage and suffering that result will be on *your* head. Yours alone, Franks. How's that going to go over with the big man upstairs, throwing away all those innocent lives just because you wouldn't master your pride just long enough to work with me? I wouldn't want that on my soul."

I doubted Stricken had a soul, because he'd probably already sold it to the highest bidder. I wasn't sure if Franks had come equipped from the factory with one either, but as Stricken said all that stuff, Franks just frowned even harder. His beady eyes got even squintier. For a second I thought for sure Stricken was going to die.

Except Franks slowly lowered the Glock. He let it linger on

Stricken's spine, as if still tempted to put him in a wheelchair for the rest of his life instead, but then Franks put the pistol back in the holster. He let go of Curtis, who snatched his battered arm away, wrist already covered in spreading bruises.

"I'm still gonna kill you."

"I'd expect nothing less! Alright, with that uncomfortable real talk out of the way, Franks is now officially on the team too. Fantastic. *Finally*." Even though he'd been a few ounces of trigger pull away from death, Stricken got right back on track. "Our destination is only a few miles away. The VIPs will be there promptly at sunrise. I know it's a terrible time for a big powwow, but the sun thing is symbolic with them. Be on your best behavior. They'll probably have some muffins and OJ or something but don't eat or drink anything they offer."

"What?" Sonya was shocked. She might have been hyper-ventilating. "We're still having a *meeting*? We just got blown up! Franks has a hole in him. We're all covered in blood! Like ten dudes just died right in front of us and you're talking about breakfast etiquette?"

"You want to end up beholden to them over some gift obligation, that's fine with me, but do it on your own time," Stricken said. "Of course we're still going. We're on the clock. And if you want that thing out of you before it kills you—and yes, there's a clock on that too—then you'd better shut up and pay attention."

I had to remember that Sonya was relatively new to all this and probably freaking out. "It's going to be fine." I used my calming voice. It was the same one I used on Ray when he got mad that I wouldn't let him put something disgusting he found on the ground in his mouth. "Just relax and breathe."

"Listen to him, kid. Collect yourself. I didn't have a chance to talk about this earlier, but we need to put on a united front during the briefing. If they don't get on board, this mission is scratched before it even starts."

"If that happens, there's no reason not to kill you." Franks almost sounded hopeful.

"True...and guilt-free too," Stricken said slowly. Apparently, he hadn't thought through *every* angle. "So let's not screw this up, team."

"We need details on the meet," I said. "Who with and why?"

"The why first. We need something, oh, the best way to think of it is an all-access visitor's pass but to another dimension. This altercation between the factions has spilled onto Earth, but it didn't start here. It's in a connected realm. There's an intersection between several worlds out in that jungle."

"Far beneath an ancient pyramid, where some horrible creature from the Old Ones lurks," I said, thinking of the ancient memories I'd been shown of where Lord Machado had been cursed.

"Sort of." Stricken didn't get surprised often. He clearly didn't like the feeling. "How—"

"On the clock, remember?" It felt good to not let the man who seemingly knew everything not know a secret, but I'm petty like that. "Keep talking."

"That's not the crossing, but it's near where an Old One has been slumbering. The war between the factions has gotten that thing stirred up. Its nasty behavior is what your Catholic buddies have been fighting. That intersection is getting mighty crowded and some weird shit is going down in that jungle. But stopping those things doesn't fix the underlying problem. It's just slapping a patch on a leaky tire. If the Vatican had gotten the Ward like they wanted, they'd only be able to use it on this side of the veil. It's the other side that's the real problem, and mere regular humans can't get in there without an invite. We can fight a holding pattern on this side, but that's it. Eventually one of the factions will win on the other, but when they do, it is going to rip a permanent festering sore in our world."

"Coslow told me a few million casualties, conservatively speaking."

"Is that all? Harold's getting optimistic in his old age. If we're going to stop that from happening, we have to be able to cross over into the other world where the battle's actively raging, and we can't do that without the landlord's permission. They're super picky about keeping out the riffraff and too proud to let any regular dirty humans help them. That's the why. The who is a Fey queen."

"You've got to be kidding me," Sonya said.

"Don't worry. Not the one your dad annoyed. Totally different branch of the species. This royal family is less about the fine-print legalese and more about the honor and glory . . . Come to think of it, probably a totally different dimension of origin. I don't know. Their family trees get really confusing. They used to be worshipped as gods up and down the Western Hemisphere; Incas, Xingu, Olmecs, Aztecs, all the way up to the Eskimos, and everything in between, this was their turf. Different creatures appeared in different forms to different tribes and they're remembered by a bunch of different names. Only they're not nearly as strong as they used to be. Amazing what a lack of worshippers and human sacrifices will do for your magic. But they still think of themselves as gods. They call themselves the Court of Feathers. Since these Fey look at mankind as their inferiors, only specific offices or bloodlines make the cut to get in. I'd be happy to let the stuck-up pricks get crushed by the Old Ones, but that leaves Earth with a vulnerable flank."

"What's that mean?" Sonya sked.

"It means that until we stop this, there's going to be a hole in the jungle endlessly barfing up terrible creatures and evil spirits into our world," I said, thinking of the City of Monsters.

"That's part of it," Stricken said. "Our contact with those dark realms is relatively limited right now. The spirit worlds inhabited by the Fey are between us and them. This would remove that layer of separation. The Fey, though dangerous and often malicious, are relatively harmless in comparison. Think of it as having the worst neighbors ever. The Fey are like having a meth lab next door, but they keep to themselves and don't blow up often. In comparison the Old Ones getting a toehold would be like living next to the Chernobyl radioactive toxic waste dump with a never-ending, giant, tire fire and them tossing used AIDS needles over the fence all day for our kids to play with. Having them would really lower the old property values."

This week kept getting worse. The last time I'd dealt with the Fey I'd gotten chased across the Nightmare Realm and ended up in a duel. "If these are the kind that want a musical challenge, you should've got my brother instead of me."

"We're already past that phase of the negotiations. I've got this all figured out. The groundwork is laid. Let me do the talking. In fact, as far as they're concerned, I'm humanity's sole official representative, and if I wasn't around, somebody else would have to start over from scratch. Years of work wasted." Stricken looked in the rearview at Franks. "This is a perfect example why Coslow was willing to cut me a deal. You need me."

Franks made a noncommittal angry noise.

"There was no way I could sign Coslow's deal, by the way. I'm no slave. I'm tired of putting in the work so that somebody squeamish can appear in my chain of command, hesitate, and ruin everything. I'm going to save mankind from itself whether it wants me to or not. Bunch of fucking ingrates."

"You talk a lot of smack for somebody who has to kidnap people to be his coworkers," Sonya said.

"The old friends' list has taken some hits." Stricken laughed. "Okay, our destination is just ahead. Not the tall buildings, the grove on the other side of them. That's the site of one of their old shrines. Hopefully, I'll have a minute to clean up first." He wiped one bloody hand on the seat distastefully. "The rest of you I pitched as warriors, so it's okay for you to be scruffy. These Fey aren't the snooty kind. They're more on the primal side. Blood-soaked and crazed actually works for them. Lana should catch up shortly, but she and Curtis aren't high enough status so they won't be allowed inside, which offends my egalitarian sensibilities, but it is what it is."

"I'm truly fine with that, sir," Curtis said, as he tried to rub the feeling back into his arm. "Y'all have fun with the crazy space monsters."

I had my own resources, so I'd ask Julie to have our people look into what we knew about this Court of Feathers, so I wouldn't have to count on Stricken's devious interpretations of events. I got my phone out. We'd gotten interrupted earlier so I'd not seen her response to my last question.

The Drek vanished. He's still alive.

That meant tomorrow night was going to suck. "Bad news, everybody."

"Silas Carver," Stricken muttered.

"Yeah." Except Stricken hadn't said that like he was guessing. I looked up from my phone to see the glowing figure standing in the middle of the road a few hundred yards ahead of us. "Oh, hell."

The Drekavac had found us.

Man-sized, he was back in the big black coat and hat, with cutlass in hand. The absence of fog meant that whatever evil energy he had left was all gathered in that final body.

And we had no idea how much power that was.

"We don't have time for this." Stricken looked to the east. The horizon was taking on some color. It was nearly sunrise. "If we're late, the queen will take offense. No invite to the other side."

"Run him down," Franks said.

Stricken didn't hesitate. He gunned it. "Hang on."

Hopefully fast traveling to a different hemisphere had used up some more of the Drekavac's remaining strength, but he was walking right down the center line toward us as other cars swerved to miss him, and he didn't seem to care about getting hit. He was a monster on a mission.

I watched our speedometer climb. Stricken's spindly hands were on the wheel, gleefully turning our armored vehicle into a guided missile. "Should have taken my job offer, Silas."

The monster stopped and lifted his sword. The stance was different, but the attitude was like a baseball player ready to swing at a fastball. The air crackled with malevolent energy. *He wanted us to hit him.*

"It's a trap!" I shouted, too late, as our grill rushed to meet him.

The Drekavac *threw* his sword as he sidestepped.

A lot of things happened really fast.

The sword sheared right through our windshield. I saw it spinning, burning blue and spitting sparks through the center of our ride. The air was filled with flying glass and then big blobs of blood.

Stricken still managed to clip the Drekavac with our front fender, and it must have massed far more than it looked, because it was like hitting a wall. The body crumpled. The frame bent. And we were spinning out of control on screaming, smoking tires.

We hit the edge of the road and *flipped*.

Up was down, then down was up, and back again, as my body got yanked against the belt and slammed against the door. Limbs were flailing. Mine and everybody else's. Franks hadn't been buckled it and he collided with me, and then got flung against the roof.

We stopped.

Metal was creaking. The engine was making a ticking noise. I was dangling upside down. Tasting blood. Didn't think it was mine.

Everything hurt. Head hurt. Body hurt. Thinking hurt. I couldn't stop blinking. My throat was constricted and there was a lot of pressure in my chest, but I could breathe.

The threat was still out there. Have to assess. Have to act.

The ghost sword had spun right through the center of the cab. Curtis had been sitting in the middle of the back seat. The bottom half of his torso was still buckled in. His top half had landed below me. Sonya was ahead of me, also buckled in and hanging limp, unconscious. Stricken was...gone? The driver's seat was empty. The headrest had been sheared clean off by the sword.

Franks had landed in back. My shaken brain processed this from the noise as Franks crawled out the broken rear window. Of course he was the first to move.

I tried to get my seat belt unbuckled, which was when I realized that I was bleeding. The blood was dripping toward the roof, not squirting. So, minor cuts, no severed arteries. File that in the to-deal-with-later pile. I didn't know where Cazador had ended up.

When I got the buckle released, I awkwardly dropped, but I used my other hand to brace myself and not break my neck. Curtis' remains were below me, a hot sticky mess. My bullet-resistant window had popped out during the roll, and though the door was deformed, there was still room for me to squeeze through. I started crawling outside.

Franks was already standing there, because of course he was. Franks was indestructible. Except then I realized that he was missing his right arm. *Okay. Almost indestructible.*

He'd been hit by the flying sword, so sharp and moving at such a combined velocity that it had cut right through his MCB armor, flesh, and bone. And from the angle, it hadn't just removed his arm near the armpit, but it had cut *deep* into his chest too.

Franks looked down at the giant laceration, and then at his stump, and frowned. "Hmmm..."

"You okay?" I gasped.

"Lung collapsing. Primary heart badly damaged. I'm three minutes from being combat ineffective."

Oh shit. It took a lot to render Franks *combat ineffective.* For him that meant he would pass out, unable to do much, until his MCB handlers could do major surgery, transplant some organs, graft on some new limbs, and then weld it all together through his mystical elixir of life. But better him than me because if the blade had been angled the other way, I'd have died instantly.

Wobbling to my feet, I looked around. No sign of the Drekavac.

No sign of Stricken either. Maybe he'd been tossed free when we rolled? I couldn't remember if he'd been buckled in or not. I went to Sonya's door.

"Sonya, can you hear me?" No answer. "Sonya!"

She coughed. "I'm alive."

"Are you okay?"

"I don't know."

"Are bones sticking out or you're squirting blood?"

"No. I don't think so."

"Then you'll be fine," I lied, because internal bleeding was a bitch. I squatted in so I could see her. Her door was more crushed than mine, and the front roof was caved in, but she was skinny and could probably wiggle out. "Can you move?"

"Working on it." There was a thump as she got her seat belt unbuckled. "I didn't sign up for this shit, Opie."

"You kinda did."

Then Stricken walked around the crumpled front of the truck, holding the shotgun he'd threatened Franks with in one hand and making a big show of dusting himself off with the other. Somehow, that son of a bitch was in one piece. I didn't think there was even a scratch on him. But the way the top of his seat had gotten sheared off by the Drekavac's sword, he should've been decapitated. *How'd he do that?*

"That didn't go the way I hoped," Stricken said as he took in the debris-strewn field we'd landed in. "Okay, we can still salvage this. Let's go."

I helped drag Sonya through the broken glass and into the dirt; then we lay there, breathing hard.

"Sorry, team. Clock's ticking. We're going to be late. Who's up for a jog? That's the path right there." I think he might have actually been trying to make himself sound chipper. "Let's go. Chop, chop. The sun's about to rise. We can't be late."

We were a sorry-looking bunch. I didn't know about running. Franks would probably just bleed out faster with exertion. Sonya actually didn't look too shaken, but that was probably because being half kodama was a real lifesaver. I was wrecked.

"Damn it," Stricken shouted. "I didn't spend all these resources and do all this planning and gather you mopes for this mission just to have you punk out now. I need at least one Chosen and a Ward Stone to present to the queen or this mission is aborted!"

You want to save lives, Pitt, get up. You want your ten million bucks, Sonya, you've got to earn it."

"Ten million?"

Sonya was still lying next to me. "Contract renegotiation."

So that's why Stricken had wanted Sonya to ride with him. *Bribery.* "That song sucked."

"Still gonna buy a whole lot of trees."

"Incoming," Franks warned.

Silas Carver had survived the collision and was stumbling across the field toward us, coat tattered, and leaking tears of flame from his torn-open face. It was clear that the impact had really damaged him. The Drekavac was nearly dead, but an even nearly dead hellish creature like him could still destroy us, especially with our biggest badass Franks running on fumes.

"Tenacious bastard. You can see why I wanted to recruit him," Stricken said. "We don't have time to fight. We run, he catches us, we're all late. I only need to present one Chosen to the queen. So which one of you two badasses is going to do the heroic gesture and slow him down while the rest of us save the world?"

"I will," Franks said without hesitation.

It wasn't like I went through any sort of complicated decision-making process trying to get myself killed, but I got up, said "Bullshit," and shoved Franks. He stumbled and nearly fell over. Considering what a beast he normally was, that was telling. Normally, Franks would've seen that coming, and then body-slammed me through the planet for making the attempt. The gesture was rude, but we didn't have time to argue about how he was missing an arm and had a big hole in his heart. Carver would probably kill Franks and then come after us anyway. "See?"

"That settles it," Stricken snapped. "Here." He tossed his shotgun over and I reflexively caught it. "Everybody else follow me."

Franks gave me an angry glare for the shove, but then his expression softened because he knew I was right. Currently, right this second, he was toast. Patch him up, and he'd be far more valuable out there than I would be. With him, it was always *mission first.* Franks gave me a *respectful* nod.

That was probably one of the biggest compliments Franks had probably ever paid to anybody. If I hadn't been concussed and scared to death, I probably would've gotten choked up.

Franks limped after Stricken. Sonya had reached into the

wreck and retrieved the sword that Milo had given her. She looked up at me, wide-eyed, afraid but trying not to show it, as she realized I was about to sacrifice myself to save them and a bunch of strangers. "What do I do?"

"Stick with Franks."

"No, I mean—"

"Just do what your dad would've done." I put one hand on her shoulder. "I'll catch up."

"Sure you will," Stricken shouted. "Move your ass, Sonya."

"Thanks." Then she ran after them.

The Drekavac was less than fifty yards away and coming over to murder my ass. Stricken's shotgun was a Beretta 1301 with the shiny marine finish. I chamber-checked. *Loaded.* It had a sidesaddle full of slugs too. I shouldered it and put the front sight on the monster. If this final body was operating at the levels Gutterres and I had faced on the first night, what I had here should be enough to kill him. If it was like any of the later levels we'd just seen at the compound...I was doomed.

Here goes nothing.

I fired. The first slug nailed him in the chest. Fire squirted out the hole. The Drekavac didn't even wobble.

He started to run. I tried to slow him down by aiming low and putting a slug into one of his legs. It took a chunk out of it. He tripped but sprang right back up. The neurotoxin designed to fry Franks did nothing to Silas Carver's alien anatomy. His cold-fire-pumping heart didn't care about poison. I went high and shot him in the head. It blew a fist-sized hole out the back of his metallic skull. The Drekavac kept coming. I kept shooting.

He could have materialized a gun and shot me back. The fact that he didn't gave me some hope. Silas Carver was running on empty. All he had left was this angry husk and a desire for revenge.

The shogun went dry. I reloaded a single round from the sidesaddle and nailed him again. I got another shot off like that before he was on me.

I saw the punch coming and just barely got out of the way. The next one I wasn't so lucky and he tagged me in the shoulder. Flailing back, Carver was on me in an instant. I hit him with the shotgun butt across the teeth. He lurched to the side and I used that moment to pluck the last shell from the sidesaddle and shove it into the open port. Driving the muzzle into his gut, I shoved him against the flipped truck, dropped the bolt, and fired. Fiery bits flew everywhere. The heavy slug ripped right through him, ricocheted off the armored plate, and back through his chest. The deformed projectile still had the energy to fly past my ear at lethal velocity.

Good thing it didn't hit me, because if that jellyfish toxin could put down Franks, it would probably make me shrivel up and die on contact.

Carver hoisted me up by the armor and then hurled me back. I hit the grass hard, but reflexively rolled so that I could draw my sidearm... which was still in Alabama. *Shit.*

The Drekavac kicked me in the stomach hard enough to lift me into the air. I came back down on my face.

"My quarrel was not with you, Hunter. You should have let me fulfill my duty." Carver grabbed me by the drag strap on the back of my armor, effortlessly lifted all three hundred pounds of me off the ground and tossed me through the air. I bounced off one of the tires and landed in the dirt. "It was a simple contract. Retrieve the item and punish the thief. The Hubertian shackled my gift and the Hunters wounded me, delivering me into the hands of that vile manipulator, Stricken. For this you will pay."

Drawing my kukri, I slashed at him. He dodged aside, and then backhanded me across the face. It knocked me to my knees. Then he kicked me in the chest and launched me back into the wreck.

Desperate, dizzy, and out of breath, I looked toward the horizon, but the sun wasn't up yet.

He knew what I was searching for. "You expect the day to save you? In moments, this form shall return to dust, sparing your allies for a time. Only I will vow that I will reverse the Hubertian's rite, regain all my lives, and come for them when they least expect it. Every last transgressor will pay with their lives. The thief, the Hubertians, the Hunters, the plotter—all of them will die. As for you, there is more than enough darkness left to end your wretched existence."

I'd bought them time. They'd make the meeting. Stricken would do his thing, persuade the Fey, and mankind would have a chance to strike a blow against the other factions. I'd accomplished my goal.

"Why do you laugh?" Silas Carver asked, confused. "Is this another trick?"

"Job satisfaction." Struggling back to my feet, I wiped the blood from my lips. "Let's do this."

I swung for his head. The monster blocked the blade with his forearm. If that had been a mortal human arm it would be lying in the grass, but all my heavy blade did was take a sparking chunk out of it. Backing up, I raised my kukri and delivered a downward strike with all my might. It hit so hard the impact vibrated through my bones. It only took a chip out of the side of his neck.

He was far tougher than when Gutterres had decapitated him, and that was *after* walking off being hit by an armored car.

His fist nailed me like a high-speed iceberg.

When I tried to slash him again, he caught my arm and flipped me onto my back. This last form was still crazy strong. He was regular Franks strong. Driving his knee against my throat to pin me, he twisted my arm, grinding it in the socket. I roared in pain. He was going to rip my arm off with his bare hands. He was going to pluck all my limbs off one by one like a malicious kid torturing a bug.

"Assei!"

Suddenly, the freezing grip released and the pressure on my joint was gone. The Drekavac lurched away, spraying fire from one ruined eye socket.

Sonya had come back.

With her father's sword in both hands, she waded into the monster, striking over and over. Flaming bits flew off the Drekavac with each hit.

I hurt so bad that moving seemed mentally impossible, but I told my brain to shut up and got back to my feet. Sonya was swinging that sword so fast and with such wild abandon that it was like a steel weed whacker. She'd probably slice me by accident, so I flanked around to hit the Drekavac from the other side.

The two of us hacked madly at the monster as he desperately tried to intercept most of our blows with his arms. I took some fingers off. Sonya sliced a chunk of his face. But then Carver drove his shoulder into me, trying to get away from her, and it was like getting trampled by a bull. I went down and caught a freezing boot to the head that left me stunned.

Silas Carver was being driven back as Sonya kept wildly hacking at him. She wasn't some mystical sword master. It was clear she didn't know what she was doing. There was nothing smooth about it, except she was just supernaturally fast, terrified, and she was *really motivated.*

Except ultimately, she was just a kid, and Silas Carver had been killing people for centuries. The instant Sonya overextended herself, the Drekavac surged, and clotheslined her so hard that it probably caused an earthquake back in her family's spirit realm.

"Damnable mortals," Carver spat. He didn't even breathe but it was almost like he was winded. He'd been torn to pieces, nothing but a tangle of broken wires, bleeding mass and spitting fire. He lurched toward Sonya, until he stood over her helpless form. He lifted one fist to crush her head. "Worst contract ever."

I tackled him.

We hit the ground with me on top. I struggled up just enough to get a good angle, and then slammed the kukri through his face, planting it deep into both eye sockets. The steel sank in about an inch. Not good enough.

I left my blade planted in him, stood up, and stomped on the spine of the kukri, and I kept on stomping as the monster twitched and jerked, head wires popping, until I'd driven the steel all the way through and cut the top of his head off.

Silas Carver twitched a few times, and then he was still...
Liquid fire poured out as the contents of his skull emptied, creating a puddle of ectoplasmic mud. The body slowly began to crumble into ash. I checked the east. It was getting bright, but no sliver of sun quite yet. Thirteen and done. We'd defeated him before dawn. He was done forever.

I spit on the disintegrating corpse.

CHAPTER 27

As the sun rose, Sonya and I helped each other up the path toward the grove. We were both in bad shape. I don't know which one of us was leaning on the other more. I was over twice her size, but that whole spirit-hybrid-strength thing provided one hell of a boost in the durability department.

Okay, I'll be honest, she was the one mostly keeping me upright, because I was *messed up*.

"The Ward is going to be late," I said, punch-drunk with words slurred through my swollen lips.

"I told Stricken to stall them. He wasn't happy but he'll deal with it."

"You shouldn't have come back for me."

"You said to do what my dad would do. What would my dad have done?"

"Slutty elves." Then I giggled.

"Shut up. I'm trying to be heroic."

"Thanks." I meant it. She'd saved my life. And to think she'd said she wouldn't make a habit out of it. She was all about looking out for herself, but when the chips were down, she'd risked her life to save another's. "That was a very Monster Hunter thing to do."

She didn't say anything to that.

The path Stricken had indicated was easy to follow. It looked like a regular old hiking trail winding between the very lush

313

undergrowth. Thankfully it wasn't too steep, because if it was, I'd have to stop and take a nap, but that was probably just the brain damage talking.

"We've got company," Sonya said.

We were about a quarter mile from where we'd crashed and a couple hundred yards down the path, when I looked back over my shoulder to see that a green deuce-and-a-half truck had pulled off the road and was driving across the field after us. The tarp was down, revealing that the back of the truck was filled with men in black uniforms. The *Gatos* had found us.

We hobbled faster down the path, except from the way the truck was heading directly for us, we had already been spotted. I'd retrieved Cazador from the wreck, but there were far too many of them for me to try and shoot it out.

There were two stone statues just ahead, one on each side of the path. They were so weathered that it was hard to tell, but they had to be the image of some ancient goddess. They were solid enough to stop bullets though, so we could at least hide behind them.

The truck reached the edge of the field but was far too wide to make it up the path. It stopped. A bunch of men immediately bailed out and started shooting at us. The supersonic rifle bullets made a terrifying *crack* as they sped past. The subsonic pistol rounds sounded like angry bees buzzing by. The only thing that kept us from getting killed was the range, but they were making up for that with volume.

Except the instant we were past the statues, the noise abruptly stopped. It was dead quiet.

We had crossed a border.

This was Fey land.

The creatures appeared all around us, lining the path. Short and tall, thick or thin, but all oddly crooked things. Hairy beasts that looked like ogres but without heads and instead with eyes in their chests and mouths on their bellies. Gnome-sized things that looked like monkeys, but with a tail that ended in an all-too-human hand. And too many other strange new things I'd never seen before, all at once, jabbering and hooting, assaulting my already battered senses.

Marching toward us was a cadre of what had to be their soldiers, because their bearing reminded me of the Fey knights

I'd fought in the Nightmare Realm. Only these were seven feet tall, bronze-skinned, wearing uniforms made of animal skins and decorated with bones, and carrying strange wooden weapons that appeared organically grown rather than built, studded with obsidian spikes—but these were clearly Fey knights, and thus scary as hell.

I looked back. There was a pile of bullets lying there on the path, like they'd instantly run out of energy and just fallen out of the sky, except they were still spinning from their rifling. I had no logical explanation for that. The Fey followed different laws of physics than we did.

In the distance, the death squad had stopped shooting, and that same too-familiar officer I'd seen earlier was madly gesturing for his men to cease fire. Apparently, his orders didn't include starting shit with the Fey. Smart. I'd seen what these things could do.

Despite the crowd of fascinating weirdness, I had to stop and check myself for bullet holes, but my luck had held. "Are you okay?"

Except Sonya was just staring at the Fey, dumbstruck, because even though half her ancestors came from a different bizarro world, she'd mostly grown up like a human, and this had just gotten *weird*. There was a reason Earl always preached that the most important trait a Hunter could have was a flexible mind.

"Sonya!"

"I'm fine. Fine!"

The lead Fey knight stopped right in front of us. I couldn't see his face because he was wearing a helmet made out of the bleached skull of some kind of predator I'd never seen before. There was no greeting. No elaborate introduction. He just pointed impatiently for us to continue down the path. *We were late.*

Except I had to check one thing first. I aimed Cazador at the death squad leader, and then cranked the magnification on the scope all the way up to twenty-five power so I could get a better look at the man.

Impossible.

I'd only ever seen him in human form once, and that had been in the brief instant before I'd shot him in the head. Except I was absolutely certain.

I'd seen through his eyes, lived his memories, felt what he'd felt, and knew just how insane he had been five hundred years ago, and that had been before he'd been cursed by the Old Ones and turned into a force of absolute evil. There was no way he could be here now, alive and seemingly human, but there he was. I had no doubt it was him.

It was Lord Machado!

It took me a second to get over the shock but *fuck that guy*. I estimated the range, adjusted for the holdover and wind, flipped the safety off, put my finger on the trigger and—

The Fey knight violently slapped Cazador's muzzle down.

"Dahk!" That had to mean *no*. The blank skull face looked down at me and made an angry, disapproving gesture. Killing was not allowed. Just as the death squad wasn't allowed to start a fight with the Fey here, neither were the Fey or their guests allowed to attack the servants of the Old Ones. This was *neutral ground*.

Too bad the Fey were fools. They didn't realize how dangerous Lord Machado was. If he was back, things were far worse than anyone realized. But I also had no doubt these Fey would kill me before I could get off a shot if I tried again. I put Cazador back on safe. "After you."

As the big truck with my somehow-returned-to-life enemy drove away, the band of monsters led me and Sonya to the meeting.

It was like walking into a living castle.

The grove was made out of the thickest, greenest plant life I'd ever seen. It was probably a pretty normal place most of the time, but with Fey royalty present the plants had taken on unnatural vitality, grown at mind-bending rate, and woven themselves into intricate designs to please their queen. The forest had grown into the form of a throne room. The canopy created a dome fifty feet tall, but with plenty of gaps to let in the perfect amount of light and shadow. All the blooming flowers probably smelled nice to everybody else, but they were hell on my allergies.

There were hundreds of odd beings assembled there. Fey come in all shapes and sizes, some familiar, others not, making it even harder to tell what they truly looked like. It was hard to tell which of the furs, feathers, bones, and plants on them were part of the creatures, and what was clothing. The visible skin was often painted in wild colors. It was hard to read their alien faces and body language, but some seemed curious, others haughty and dismissive of the humans who were petitioning them.

Stricken and Franks were standing before a throne made of flowering vines. Upon that throne sat what had to be the single-most beautiful woman I had ever seen. I couldn't even begin to describe her features because there weren't human equivalents. She was absolute perfection. A goddess of sunshine, fertility, and rainbows, so I knew right away it was a bullshit illusion to trick us. Fey royalty looked like whatever they wanted to look like for their audience. From what I'd read about various queens, her real form could be a cockroach and she'd still come across as angelic if that behooved her at the time.

Stricken was talking. We'd caught him mid-presentation, giving the massaged version of Franks' résumé. "After defeating the hosts of hell, who brazenly tricked me into giving them Earthly bodies, Franks has since continued to serve as a Chosen of the God of Light, as a champion of righteousness and dispenser of indiscriminate justice."

Well, that was certainly one way to put it. Stricken was stalling because it had to be hard for him to give Franks such a fluffy introduction. Meanwhile, Franks didn't look too good. He'd TQed his arm, packed a bunch of bandages into the gaping hole in his chest, and since he was still standing, had probably taken some of his Elixir of Life. Despite that, the assembled Fey still seemed nervous or impressed, because Franks' reputation preceded him. Human, demon, Fey, or other, nobody wanted to mess with Franks.

The queen spoke. "It appears the rest of the supplicants have arrived."

As expected, her voice was melody incarnate. She made Sonya's angelic singing sound like a toilet flushing. Her powers of seduction made Lana's look like a five-dollar crack whore in comparison. It was no wonder the ancients had worshipped these things across the globe. I forced myself to focus on the task at hand. I wasn't going to let some Fey get into my head.

Stricken turned, saw that we were both alive, and then immediately went on with his pitch. I bet he had different intros prepared if I, Sonya, both, or neither had died. "To further demonstrate the seriousness of our endeavor, I bring before you a weapon of unmatchable power, placed inside the body of a royal of the Yokai Realm for safekeeping."

I looked at Sonya. *Royal?*

"And a second Chosen capable of using such a device, the breaker of time, the god slayer, Owen Zastava Pitt."

There were actually gasps and murmuring from the audience. Apparently, Franks wasn't the only one around here with a rep.

"Hey." I waved at the crowd.

Sonya and I took our place next to Stricken and Franks.

The queen looked over our motley bunch, judging. Either she was speaking English for our benefit, or her words were being magically translated for our ears. "It's unfortunate that these two insulted me by missing the ritual of the sainted sun."

"Sorry," I said. "It was a terrible commute."

The queen raised one magnificent eyebrow, and I shut up before she ordered me smitten. Smote? Whatever. It's hard to be tactful when you've had a week like I had.

"You are from Monster Hunter International, yes?"

Apparently, she had heard of us. Hopefully it wasn't because we'd blown a bunch of her subjects on some case I didn't know about. "I am."

"Do you know the Hunter called Chloe Mendoza?"

I think I'd seen that name on some really old PUFF paperwork from our California team, but that had been *long* before my time. "It sounds familiar, but no."

The queen nodded but remained inscrutable.

"Forgive them, your majesty. The forces of the Old Ones and Asag conspired to stop us. The evil factions do not wish an interruption to their war which is currently being waged across your lands. We do, in order to ensure the safety of your kingdom, and ours."

"As I was warned is your way, Stricken, you speak only part of the truth. I have been watching. You were also delayed because one of the creatures you tried to bend to your will had a mind of his own. You were not able to control that one."

"Silas Carver was an obstinate sort. I'm afraid that arrangement didn't work out as I hoped."

"I shall forgive the late arrival of the Hunter and the yokai. He showed courage and she demonstrated loyalty. While the fallen, who doubtlessly would have preferred to battle, stood in their place out of a sense of duty. Courage, loyalty, and duty are traits appreciated in my court. Thus I forgive this slight." The queen waved one had dismissively. "However, as for Silas Carver, he is not here."

That was because I'd stomped a kukri through his face, but I refrained from saying that out loud.

The queen seemed disappointed. "Alas, you knew what I required."

"Indeed, your majesty. When I approached your sister about arranging this meeting, she told me that you would require a special gift for your collection."

Collection? I had no idea what this particular Fey queen collected. Apparently, neither did Franks because he got an even grimmer than usual look on his face. I was really hoping she was into Beanie Babies or Furbies or something other than Chosen.

"I prefer to think of it as my menagerie, though you humans would call it a zoo. I have accumulated the finest selection of terrible beasts from a multitude of realms. One of the thirteen Drekavacs would have been a splendid addition. Delivering such a creature into my hands would've demonstrated your conviction and worthiness to move freely through my realm."

Stricken was even more malicious than I'd thought. He had tried to force the Drekavac into service not to use him, but to *sacrifice* him.

"Ah, but I always have a backup plan, your majesty. Which is why I procured another worthy gift, just in case."

"If you speak of your succubus, I already have one. They are not particularly powerful. I find their insatiable nature predictable."

"Indeed. I would never bore you by offering a creature so one-dimensional. Which is why I brought you *this*." Stricken reached into one of the interior pockets of his suit and pulled out a chain. He held it up so the amber ball on the end of it could catch the light.

"A lich's phylactery?" The queen seemed intrigued. "Is it full?"

"Yes. It contains the soul of a mad wizard named Buford Phipps, guilty of many heinous crimes and sins against nature over hundreds of years. I discovered the secret location of his phylactery, and then arranged for his physical form to be destroyed. Take it and do with it as you will. It is my gift to you."

This son of a bitch was full of surprises. Sonya looked like she wanted to punch him. Stricken had used her as bait to get MHI to take out Phipps for him. If Boone hadn't gotten the word from one of his contacts, Stricken probably would've had Lana give us an anonymous tip anyway. No matter what happened, Stricken was always ready to capitalize on it.

The queen made a gesture, and a little froglike humanoid bounced over to Stricken to take the phylactery. Stricken handed the cursed item over to the creature, who bit it like a coin to see if it was real. The monster croaked, which must have meant it was legit and chock full of evil soul juice, because the queen gave us a radiant smile.

"It is no Drekavac, but truly a wonderous gift nonetheless."

The frog thing took the phylactery and scurried out of sight. That was probably the end of the Shackleford family tradition of each generation getting to kick the ass of that particular lich.

"And with that, your terms have been met," Stricken said. His tone suddenly shifted from unctuous suck-up to his regular self. "All that mandatory courtly fluff out of the way, can we get down to business now? Both of our worlds are suffering while Asag and the Old Ones duke it out in your kingdom. We require your permission to enter your realm so that we can destroy their armies. This is a win-win for both our species."

"You will have to battle your way through great evil in your own world to reach the heart of the disturbance. The enemy will try to stop you every step of the way. How do you intend to accomplish such a feat?"

"There is an ancient saying among my people, *knowing is half the battle.* I have that knowledge. The other half is extreme violence, which is what I've got these people for." Stricken gave her a charming smile and she seemed to approve of his answer. "Now that Franks and Pitt are committed, surely a bunch of warriors from MHI and the MCB are already on their way to help too. Whatever Secret Guard who are still alive out there, and whoever else we can scrounge up at short notice will assist us along the Earthly path. Once we break through the enemy lines, the select few you have granted access to your lands will engage your enemy directly. I'm asking on behalf of these champions—we'll probably add a couple of werewolves with that title too—along with the scions of great family lines, like the greatest family of monster hunters in human history, to be granted free passage into and through your realm."

That was an accurate thing to say about the Shacklefords, but

I'd only married into that family. Stricken probably assumed Julie would show up, which was a safe bet with me being in danger. He didn't need to add that family line thing to get her a pass though, because she bore the Guardian's mark, which made her Chosen too. So either Stricken didn't know about that, or maybe he thought her brother Nathan might come too.

The queen weighed his words carefully. All Fey, even the war-like ones, were known for being tricky with their words. "A family title earned through blood and effort rather than inheritance... Very well. Those terms are acceptable. And then?"

"That select group will then destroy the forces of your two enemies using the Newtonian weapon which I've procured. Asag and the Old Ones will be driven from your kingdom."

"Asag fled to our lands after mankind destroyed his fortress in the north. The Old Ones saw their opportunity and attacked him there. My kingdom has been their battlefield ever since." The queen leaned forward; the shift was subtle, just a change in attitude more than appearance, but suddenly the grove took on an aura of menace. This was also a goddess of war, and she liked the idea of slaughtering her enemies in one fell swoop. "You have the Ward?"

"Show her, Princess."

Sonya hesitantly stepped forward, then pulled down the neck of her shirt to reveal the stone still embedded in her chest. If the crowd had gotten a little interested when I'd been introduced, they got downright chattery when they saw the Ward Stone. I didn't think it could blow up Fey like it did undead, but the device still seemed to freak them out. Or maybe it had a setting for that too? Isaac Newton had been full of surprises.

"Princess?" I whispered to Stricken.

"You called her that earlier. I thought you knew," he whispered back, not taking his eyes off the queen.

"I was being insulting."

"I was being accurate." Then Stricken raised his voice again. "As you can see, the heir of the Kodama line has risked her health to keep the Ward safe from harm."

"My spies tell me that this was an unforeseen development."

"I wasn't expecting Sonya to rob me, but I liked her moxy. We adapted and rolled with it. Now we are allies."

"Best friends forever," Sonya said, and managed to not sound too sarcastic. "We should get a pic of this for my Instagram."

Except the queen seemed to enjoy Sonya's presence. I didn't know how all the various realms worked, but they were probably distant cousins. "So many children of fate being drawn together is a sign of great portent. Come. I wish to examine this weapon."

The queen didn't stand up and walk over to see. That would've been too undignified. Instead she willed us closer, and the grass beneath our feet picked us up and carried us over like riding an escalator. We stopped right in front of the throne. Now that we were close, I realized that despite her seemingly perfect proportions, the queen was even taller than her Fey knights.

Sonya flinched when the queen reached out to touch the stone with one perfect hand. "Do not be afraid, child. Removing it will not hurt." And then the queen plucked the stone right out.

Sonya stared in disbelief at her unmarred skin. It was like it had never even been there.

"A curious thing." The queen looked at the Ward for a long time, as if pondering its very existence. "Such great and terrible possibilities. Anathema to the Old Ones. Poison to the deconstructive nature of Disorder. Were I to try and use this, it would split the very world in two."

"They really should put a warning sticker on it," I said.

"Humans are such odd creatures. Simultaneously feeble yet mighty. With this device, you can drive the usurpers from my kingdom so that I may return."

Stricken had left out the part where she was a queen in exile.

With that revelation, I looked around the throne room again with fresh eyes. This wasn't her regular court in all its glory. These were the refugees. These were the survivors who'd escaped.

"That's the plan," Stricken said.

"Very well." The queen held the Ward out. Stricken reached for it, but she extended her hand toward me instead. "This one shall bear the weapon from here on."

"Why me?"

"It is not my decision. That choice was made for both of us long before you were born. You have already been bound to do this deed by others. The weight of destiny is heavy upon you, God Slayer. The question is, will you be strong enough to earn that title a second time?"

It had been prophesied that I would die saving the world. Was this next mission going to be it?

Even if it was, that didn't change what needed to be done.

I took the Ward from her. "I guess we'll see."

She leaned back on the throne. "Humans are normally beneath our notice, but those of sufficient calling or bloodline will be honored as our equals for now. Our enemy has done this as well, gathering to them humans living and dead to aid their cause. It pleases me to do the same."

That had to explain how Lord Machado had come back…but why? Those things laughed at the boundaries between life and death, so it was in their power to do so, but at the end he had discovered that they had used and betrayed him, so why would they bring him back to serve them now? Except I didn't dare interrupt and ask because the queen seemed ready to announce her decision.

"There are great and terrible events afoot in my kingdom, the repercussions of which can be felt in your world. Thus I shall allow this quest."

"Thank you, your majesty." Stricken bowed. Franks just grunted in acknowledgement. Sonya was still too relieved at getting a magical time bomb pulled out of her that I don't think the idea that we were about to embark on an insane mission into an interdimensional warzone had sunk in for her yet.

"I decree that any who bears the mantle of a factions' Chosen," the queen nodded toward me and Franks, "or who is of a sufficiently notable bloodline," she gestured at Sonya, "will be allowed free passage through my lands. The deal is struck."

"We shall abide by these terms," Stricken announced loud enough for the entire court to hear. Then he suddenly turned his back on the queen and started walking away. "Let's get to it then. I've got an expedition to put together."

The queen laughed at his hubris. The monsters of the court decided that if she was laughing it must be funny, so they all laughed too.

"You get ahead of yourself, Stricken. I granted permission to these because they are without guile. You are but a pathetic man, cursed for drawing the ire of mighty beings. No faction has chosen the likes of you to represent them. Did you really think that I would allow the likes of you into the sainted Hall of the Sun, to rifle through my treasures and secrets unobserved?"

Except rather than be insulted by the laughter of the Fey,

Stricken turned back and gave her a malicious, knowing grin. "You're right. I'm not chosen by anybody. I forge my own destiny. Yet by your own decree—which once given can't easily be taken back—I'll just have to get by off my notable bloodline."

The Fey were notoriously tricky, but the queen stopped laughing, knowing that she had been outmaneuvered somehow. "What notable bloodline is that?"

"I already declared it and you agreed it was sufficient… The greatest monster hunting family to ever live."

That title clearly belonged to the Shacklefords, and for just a second I was tempted to scoff at him like the Fey were, but this was Stricken we were talking about. Stricken, who never gave his real name, because in these circles, real names held power. I thought of the many family paintings hanging on the wall of the Shackleford estate, and how not even Julie knew them all, especially the branches who'd wandered away from the family business.

Oh, hell. Was I *related* to this asshole by marriage?

"I was born Alexander Shackleford, son of Leroy, a direct descendant of Bubba Shackleford himself. I guess that makes me royalty too." The grove fell dead silent as Stricken walked away. "See you on the other side."

The four of us made it out of the grove and back into the real world. When we passed the ancient statues, the Fey court in exile disappeared, once again hidden from the eyes of mankind. We were in an unfamiliar country, surrounded by enemies led by my nemesis who had somehow returned from the dead. We were all hurting. Franks was missing parts. Help was far away.

Stricken just looked toward the sunrise, smiled and said, "I've always wanted to go on a quest."